The Prisoner's Dilemma

The Prisoner's Dilemma

Sean Stuart O'Connor

Winchester, UK
Washington, USA

First published by Zero Books, 2013
Zero Books is an imprint of John Hunt Publishing Ltd., Laurel House, Station Approach,
Alresford, Hants, SO24 9JH, UK
office1@jhpbooks.net
www.johnhuntpublishing.com
www.zero-books.net

For distributor details and how to order please visit the 'Ordering' section on our website.

Text copyright: Sean Stuart O'Connor 2012

ISBN: 978 1 78099 741 4

A CIP catalogue record for this book is available from the British Library.

Design: Stuart Davies

Printed and bound by CPI Group (UK) Ltd, Croydon, CR0 4YY

This is a work of fiction. Names, characters, places and incidents are either the product of the
author's imagination or are used fictitiously. Any resemblance to actual historical persons, events
or locales are largely coincidental.

For my family

Two things fill my mind with ever increasing wonder and awe ... the starry heavens above me and the moral law within me.
Immanuel Kant, 1788

Chapter 1

For perhaps the twentieth time that morning the prince lunged forward in his chair, his angry face marbled with a livid red crazing as he glared out from under his long court wig.

'And *who* ...' he was shrieking now, his blancmange body rustling with the cascade of pale blue silk and satin sashes that broke over him whenever he moved. Slowly, he lifted a shaking arm and a hooked forefinger quivered over an open page like a hovering kestrel. Then it hurtled down to impale an elaborate drawing of a heraldic crest.

'... *this* people?'

General Mallender sighed noiselessly and twisted in his seat to see what the terrible Hanoverian nail had stabbed now. Good God, hadn't he given the old bull enough time today already?

It was clear that the prince was not going to risk taking his finger from the hated crest and the thick paper buckled slightly as Mallender gently edged round the enormous bulk of *The Origins and Armorial Bearings of the Highland Clans* until he could see enough of the illustration to read the inscription.

'If I might just...' he began, and then 'ah, the Urquhain. Yes, indeed. The premier clan of Caithness. And very interesting they are, too. I am not personally familiar with the family although I did once have the honour to be a guest at their great stronghold, the Castle of Beath, when I was travelling in the area many years ago. That was when the clan's old chief, the present earl's father, was alive.'

'What is area? Where this place? Caithness?'

'It's right up on the roof of Scotland, your highness. You can scarcely go any further north than the castle.'

'You say name again,' ordered the prince, and he now jabbed at the florid type at the head of the page.

'Their name, your highness? Well, you'll recall that we were discussing another clan earlier spelt Urquhart and I said we pronounce it as Urket. This one has possibly the same root and I believe they would refer to themselves as Urken.'

The prince gave a grunt of displeasure.

'And what lord? This chief?'

'He is the Earl of Dunbeath, your highness.'

'Urquhain. Dunbeath. Scotland names. So stupid.'

Mallender inclined his head slightly to one side as if in agreement but looked with inward distaste at the podgy face beside him with its drooping cheeks and bulbous, wine-veined nose.

Here's a pot slandering a kettle, he thought to himself. If there was a competition for idiotic names the Urquhain card would easily be covered by your own – Prince Friedrich Ernst August von Suderburg-Brunswick-Luneburg. A fancy string of words but we all know that you were born a bastard. And if it hadn't been for your half sister chancing to marry a man who was the closest living Protestant relation they could find when fat old Queen Anne died you'd still be back in your piss-poor principality. So small, they say, that a man could ride out of it on a good day's hunting.

The general came out of his musing and turned his attention back to the prince. He looked sideways at him and saw his bulging eyes as he continued to glower furiously at the Urquhain crest, obviously deeply embedded in his self-righteous resentment. But in spite of the irritation Mallender had been feeling all morning he was surprised to notice in himself a sudden twinge of pity as it flashed across his thoughts. He knew that behind the angry bluster there was something pathetic about the elderly fraud that sat wobbling with fury alongside him. It was common knowledge that the prince had left his homeland to accompany his 'half' brother-in-law when he had been crowned King of England. But that was in 1714. And yet here he was in 1745, over thirty years later, and still lodged between the two nations. The now ancient prince had made no effort to become

English, he'd never been accepted by its people and he hardly even spoke the language; but then again he was certainly no longer anything to do with the German empire. Instead, he had become marooned by his dogged service to the Hanoverian monarchy.

His old friend, the king, had died years ago and the prince was now serving his son, the second George. Mallender could only imagine that even someone as dull witted and self-absorbed as the prince had to be able to see how determined this monarch was to reduce the ties with his father's Germanic background.

The general gave a slight cough but the prince paid him no attention and remained locked in his rancorous trance. Mallender shrugged slightly and went back to his silent contemplation, thinking further about the arrogant man that grunted and wheezed next to him.

He knew that the Hanoverians considered blood to be blood, sullied though it may have been by the illicit passions of the bedroom, and the prince had been found a pension of sorts and a fine set of grace and favour apartments at Hampton Court Palace. There he had his own little kingdom where he strutted around with his many mistresses and an absurd private army of – to universal hilarity – just two soldiers. Known to everyone except themselves as Dumm and Kopf this convoy were a couple of overweight, loutish aristocrats from the eastern border of his principality, dressed at all times in the ridiculous uniforms of their native hussars' regiment. The prince liked to keep them busy and they amused the other tenants at the Palace by spending hours each day practicing their sabre thrusts and blocking moves like a pair of carefree puppies. Then they would stroll the grounds with their master, intriguing with each other in a mixture of their army slang and an impenetrable Celle dialect – chosen because it was impossible for even German speakers to understand – plotting to be invited to court. This was yet more blind arrogance on their part for their aloofness

3

prevented them seeing the scarcely concealed derision they met whenever they went.

The prince poked again at the offending heraldry.

'They fight us?'

Mallender shook himself out of his reverie.

'The Urquhain? I couldn't be sure, your highness. The situation is still very confused.'

'But they Scots from high lands. Who give them lord?'

'I believe they received the earldom when King James came south to take the English throne. Many of the king's Scottish supporters were rewarded at the time.'

'King James was Stuart! So they fight for this Stuart now! This Charles Edward who think he have claim for throne. They say him Bonnie Prince Charlie. More stupid name. But they think him right king. They say king over water.'

The arm rose again and the crest was once more decisively impaled.

'I say. They fight.'

The general stiffened in his chair.

'I wouldn't be too quick to make that assumption, your highness,' he murmured.

Now Mallender leant over to point to the scroll under the cat's cradle of intertwined supporters, shield and coronet that made up the crest.

'You'll see the wording of the clan motto here, your highness? *Nos Unus*. I think you'd agree that this tells its own story. There was never a family that lived so faithfully to its guiding principle. You'll have made the translation by now and surmised its meaning, I have no doubt – *Us Alone*. How appropriate that is. The Urquhain have never shown loyalty to anyone, only to themselves. Who would they fight for? Probably whoever would make them still richer than they already are. They believe only in power and wealth. They have only ever had one aim and that is to side with the winner.'

4

'We have same like. In Hanover. Think they...' and here the prince risked removing his finger from the page to tilt his nose upwards in mock superiority.

More pots and kettles, thought Mallender, although he nodded thoughtfully.

'Oh, I quite agree in most cases, your highness. But the Urquhain have made their bloodline into an art form. Their children have suspicion bred into them. The finest tutors are always engaged for them but the real lessons come from within the family. Add wealth, each new generation is told, add power. But never add obligation.'

The prince gave another grunt although there was the merest hint of respect in its tone.

'This son. This earl. Dunbeath. He soldier?'

'Why no, your highness. Anything but. And that is another reason to think he may not fight with the rebels. No, he is an astronomer. I hear he thinks of nothing but his stars and moons. I'm told he never sees anyone and lives only for looking at the planets. They say he's the first Urquhain chief for centuries to care about anything other than counting his money.'

'Why you no talk him?'

'We may indeed try to treaty with him at some point, your highness, but our first priority must be to strengthen our forces in Scotland. And, of course, these Scottish lairds are notoriously difficult to deal with. They all have hair trigger tempers but even on such a measure I'm informed that this latest Dunbeath stands apart. He is reputed to have only the two days: gloom and rage, gloom and rage. And one can follow the other in the blink of an eye. No, I'd suggest that we leave this clan for the time being and turn the page. Ah, the Macdonalds of Ranochlainie. I think we can be rather more sure of where they stand.'

The prince gave another cry of rage and, once again, a quaking hand was slowly raised to strike.

Chapter 2

It was mid-February and the vicious cut in the easterly wind showed no sign of easing after four months of the harshest winter in living memory. Standing immovable against it, the Castle of Beath rose from the landscape, massive and unlit, its vast black bulk silhouetted against the watery moonlight of the frozen Caithness night.

The castle was an ancient place, built in the fourteenth century on a spit of land set in the Ulbster coast, by Dromnell Urquhain, a renowned madman and the first of the clan lairds. A violent, volatile man, embittered from his constant fights and ambitious beyond reason, he had used the massive boulders he'd found there as the foundation stones for a fortress so great that its very presence was designed to chill any thought of opposition. He had taken much care in choosing its position. The wild sea was where he wanted it, at his back, and the treeless tract at the castle's front was so narrow that it formed a highly defensible land bridge.

Although it was by now over four hundred years old, the hardness of the castle's stone remained undulled by the ferocious storms that constantly beat against it and the outward appearance of the colossal stronghold was almost completely unchanged from the day it had been finished. But one alteration to the structure was evident. On the battlemented top of what was called the Grey Tower a curious building had been more recently erected – an observatory with glassed sides and a curved roof that slid back to allow for the enormous telescope that now pointed out into the night sky.

If one stood with one's back to the castle's entrance, out of the pitiless dirge of the onshore wind, the headland was piled up to the left, south of the castle. But to the north the land dropped down to a sandy bay and this arced out in a wide open sweep for hundreds of yards into the distance. Massive, deeply rutted dunes lay behind the beach and at the end of this long, natural crescent a tiny hamlet of cottages was just visible, clustered around a small harbour that clung to the shoreline like a man-made limpet. This was the fishing village of Dunbeaton.

Beyond the headland that lay to the north of Dunbeaton, a beacon had been set in a crude, stone built tower. On the orders of the Urquhain lairds, its fire was never allowed to die and it now shone, as it always did, far away into the blackness of the deep sea, sending out its warning to passing ships of the evil rocks that lay in the bay.

Suddenly, from out of the gloom, two thin, ragged-looking figures crept onto the boulders below the castle's great sea wall. They were stooped low as though to stay out of sight but even a glimpse of their wan faces in the half light would show such a similar cast to their features that they could only be brothers: the elder of the two was James and the other was Alistair - the sons of Mona and Andrew McLeish of Dunbeaton.

Anyone that happened to see their furtive manner and the anxious, pinched glances they threw to each other would have known in an instant that the pair were up to no good. Yet it would also have been clear from their uncertain movements that whatever they were at was unusual work for them. Like so many others on this coast they were fishermen and, although still more boys than men, the harsh life of fighting the unforgiving winter sea for their living had taken its toll and made them appear far older than their years.

Standing on a great sea boulder that seemed to form part of the castle's very foundations, the two of them now gazed down with dismay at a narrow gap between two large rocks and discussed their next steps in low, hesitant tones. The gap was no bigger than the width of a man and the surf gurgled and sucked like a maddened spirit as it endlessly crashed forwards and back through the tightness of the opening.

'Are you sure the tide's at its lowest?' whispered Alistair nervously, every line of his face showing his reluctance at being there.

'Aye,' replied James grimly, 'you know it is. I've been watching this place for half my life. These rocks are always under water unless the tide's completely out. Don't go soft on me now, Ally. I'll no be backing out and neither will you.'

James looked at Alistair's frozen face and knew he had to act quickly before his brother's gossamer-thin resolve left him for good.

'I'll go first,' James said firmly, his face set and tense. 'There's only room between that gap for one of us at a time. If that drunkard McColl is right, then there's a cave in there with a ledge at the back. He said he saw it when he was washed in that time and he thought it looked man-made. But if it's just more of the nonsense he spouts when he's in his cups ... well, you can take my hand for the last time, Ally. If it's true, I'll call you when I make it. Then you jump down between the waves and come yourself.'

Alistair nodded his understanding.

'Some of these old castles have escape routes under them,' James went on, 'to get out by the sea. If that's what this is then it's a way in for us too. If I'm wrong and it's just a cave then I'm a dead man.'

Alistair stared at his brother and wondered yet again if he should try and talk him out of going.

'God willing and we get in, then there's not to be a word,' continued James in the same firm manner. 'We'll see what there is to take as we go to the top of the castle, then pick things up as we come back down. Otherwise we'll be hauling everything up to the roof. The cave will be underwater by the time we're finished so we'll have to leave by the main entrance. But...' and he tried a brave smile as much for himself as for his brother, '...we'll be as rich as lords ourselves by then. Wish me luck, Ally!'

James checked that the sack he'd brought was securely tied around his waist and then looked closely at the incoming waves.

Timing a slack moment and clutching a tiny, dimmed lantern, he leapt down and squeezed through the gap. He raced into a small, wet cave and as he did so, he opened the shutter of his lamp. By its thin light he saw a ledge and with a silent prayer of relief he flung himself up onto its surface. By now the sea was rushing in to fill the cave but he was untouched, above its level. He turned around to shine the light onto the back wall and his heart leapt as he saw that rough steps had been cut out of the stone. Just as he'd hoped, this must have been an ancient exit from the castle, put there when the foundations were first laid.

Those mad Urquhain, James thought to himself, they wouldn't even trust to six foot of stone wall to keep themselves out of trouble. He turned back from the steps and cupped his hands to call out to his brother.

'Ally man,' he shouted above the roar of the surf, 'come now!'

To give him his due, his brother didn't hesitate. He jumped down into the gap between the surging waves and sprinted through the cave. As he reached the back he was hauled up onto the ledge by James's eager hand.

Together they began the climb upwards. There were probably no more than a dozen of the slimey steps before they came to a ceiling of flat stone and James braced himself as he pushed up at it with his shoulder.

The stone lifted with a soft sigh and James pushed it carefully away. The brothers climbed through the hole and found themselves in the corner of a flag-stoned room, evidently hardly used and only then as a store for discarded and broken furniture and fabrics. Once they'd taken their bearings they gently replaced the slab and James noticed with an approving glance how it had been cunningly set into two pieces so that the corner could be removed for a handgrip. Yet when it was put back, the pieces went together so closely that even the most suspicious of searches would never find more than a crack in the stone.

They padded softly out of the room and began to move

stealthily through the castle, climbing staircases and heading for the top of the tower, and the observatory.

As the boys passed through the series of great salons they devoured, wild eyed, the richness of the decoration. Every inch of the enormous rooms seemed to be covered with architectural detail and as they crept carefully onwards they were overwhelmed by the sight of a wealth they had never imagined existed – the rich tapestries and exquisite carpets, beautiful furniture and proud, glorious paintings.

But while the Castle of Beath was clearly a treasure house, assembled from the plunder of centuries, there were signs of decay and negligence in every room. Wall hangings were awry, rugs carelessly rolled back and fallen objects left where they lay. Much of the furniture was haphazardly covered by dustsheets.

And, everywhere the boys looked, there were books. On tables, on chairs and on the floor, like the troubled surface of the sea outside, an ocean of books spilled across the rooms. Many were bent open where they'd been dropped. Others showed a mess of paper stuffed into pages to mark passages, once important enough to be noted but now, later, the reasons for them long forgotten. It was plain that introverted and scholarly though these Urquhain lords may have been, whoever had been reading here recently was oblivious to his surroundings.

Silently the brothers moved from room to room.

But as they left one of the glorious salons Alistair's thoughts had strayed already to the new life he would lead when their night's work was realised. His mind wandered and as he lost concentration his foot dug deep into the side of a casually coiled glory from the great Shah's workshops at Isfahan. He stumbled at first as he caught the curved side of the carpet and then brought his trailing leg down hard. This only made things worse. His momentum was now increased and as he pitched forward in the darkness he raised an involuntary hand to stop his fall but, to his horror, he struck a heavy mahogany door with his palm. It shuddered with the impact and then swung back, hammering the wall behind it in an explosion of noise.

They froze. Then Alistair scrambled to his feet and looked up to see the mask of fury on his brother's face. James glared at him and swept his arm down in an angry gesture of command for him to stay where he was and to wait.

It was too late.

A floor away, in a study set in the corner of a tower, the great stronghold's lord lifted his head with a start from the long table at which he'd fallen asleep. He had dropped where he worked, his face flat amongst the chaos of the table's vast confusion – its surface covered by mathematical tables and drawings, a large orrery, books and celestial globes. On top of piles of scribbled workings, lonely plates of food lay untouched and uncollected like so many forgotten islands.

The Earl of Dunbeath was immediately wide-awake. His face was sharp and determined, full of the ruthless certainty of his ancient line and flooded with the particular wrath that had come down to him from his ancestors. He rose silently to his feet and the moonlight fell across his profile. He was in his thirties, dark and strong featured and it was clear that the centuries of carefully chosen marriages had made this, the last of the Urquhain, a man of striking appearance. He was of above middle height, heavy shouldered and with a powerful, wide frame. The firm cut of his mouth was now tight as he listened intently in the dark. Around him was a heavy coat he'd thrown over his shoulders before he'd fallen asleep, made for his grandfather and now much frayed. He wore no wig and his once cropped brown hair had been uncut for months and curled like Medusa's snakes away from his still, tense face.

But even the most cursory of glances showed that whatever the Earl of Dunbeath had been working at was taking its toll. It was evident that he'd taken no care of himself for some time.

Moving deftly to one side, he reached over to the top drawer of a cabinet and took out a heavy pistol. He then crept stealthily through the open door and stood in the corridor, waiting as quietly as a predatory animal for any further noise.

The brothers had not moved. James held his hand out, palm first, ordering Alistair to be still. For five minutes or more they stood, straining every nerve as they listened for any sign that they'd been heard.

But Dunbeath was rigidly still too, sensing their presence in spite of the deep silence to which the castle had returned. It was true that there were always cracks and groans coming from the ancient building as it settled with the centuries but the earl knew instinctively there was something about the sound he'd heard that made him certain that, for the first time in its long history, someone had managed to break in.

A floor below him, James eventually nodded. The acute silence had convinced him that either Alistair's fall hadn't been heard or that the castle was empty. The brothers let out long-held breaths and together they moved on, pointing out to each other with quick, nervous gestures the precious pieces they would collect later as they came back down the stairs. On they climbed, higher and higher, one cautious step after another, until they emerged at last into the observatory. There they held their lanterns high and looked around in the pale glow, their eyes flashing in greed as they took in what there was to steal.

Like Dunbeath's study and the rest of the castle, the observatory seemed to have been the object of a malicious attack and a colossal mess of handwritten notes, scientific instruments and books spilled from every surface and flowed carelessly across the stone floor.

James had just moved over to where an oval table was covered with ziggurats of astronomical books and parchment-covered ledgers of star movements when his eye was caught by a sudden glint that reflected back from his lantern's thin beam. He moved some papers and let out a silent gasp, then reached down and picked up an exquisitely made telescope that had been half buried under a pile of celestial maps. It was a thing of the utmost beauty and James began to pant with short, shallow breaths as he felt its weight in his hand, hypnotised by its exquisite exterior. Little that he would have cared, the masterpiece had been crafted a hundred years previously for the fabulous collector, Ferdinando de Medici, but as James looked at the thick gold of the instrument's barrel, etched with hunting scenes and densely set with precious jewels, he knew only that the gorgeous thing was beyond value. Furtively, he glanced round to see if Alistair had seen him pick it up but his brother was half bent over something else, and James slipped the telescope quietly into the poacher's pocket of his coat.

What the eye didn't see, he thought to himself and, anyway, why should he have to share every last thing with Ally? Hadn't he practically had to drag him to the castle in the first place?

Moonlight flooded the room and the two boys pulled at books and moved charts in their search for treasures. Greed had so invaded their minds by now that it had overcome their caution and neither heard a slight scuffing sound as Lord Dunbeath crept to the top of the tower's stone stairs and slid quietly through the open door.

The earl now stood in icy silence, pointing his pistol at the brothers' backs. Eventually, something must have caught Alistair's eye because he looked up and gasped in appalled shock as he saw Dunbeath's wide frame. And then the pistol in his hand. As he heard his brother's cry, James glanced up and followed Alistair's horrified gaze. In an instant the three men were standing, rigid, staring at each other, the two of them frozen in shock and the other hard coiled with the lust for revenge.

At last Dunbeath broke the silence.

'How did you get in here?' he asked in a terrifyingly quiet tone. 'Armies have tried to storm this castle for centuries and failed. How did you do it?'

The McLeish brothers remained where they were, too stunned to answer. They simply stared back in a horrified silence at the black threat of the pistol.

Then Alistair began to plead in a thin, reedy whine.

'Oh, we're sorry, your lordship. God knows it, we're so sorry. We're just two stupid, hungry boys. Don't bother with us, my lord. We won't ever do anything like this again.' His voice broke with fear. 'Oh, please God, let us go!'

Dunbeath said nothing. He seemed to be so completely absorbed in his thoughts that he showed no sign of having heard the boy. Instead he appeared to be weighing up what to do next with all the calm concentration of a cat staring at a sparrow. He stayed like this for some time, swaying slightly as he turned the situation over in his mind before a hint of amusement seemed to come over his face. He had clearly come to a decision.

With a wave of his arm he ordered the pair through a door to the gap between the outside wall of the observatory and the ancient fortifications of the turret. Then, in an oddly disconnected voice, he barked an order at James.

'Stand up there!'

He pointed with his free hand at the battlements.

'On that stone.'

James looked at the raised teeth of the parapet with alarm. Four hundred years before, the castle's builders had followed the defence strategy of their day and projected the turret out from the side of the tower. The battlements hung over the sea far below and James looked at them, appalled. The top of each of the stones was hardly wider than a man's feet and slippery with frozen sea mist.

'I can't,' he stammered, his chest tight with fear, 'I'll fall.'

There was a second's pause before Dunbeath took a step towards him and put his pistol to the boy's head. He ground it into James's temple as he hissed at him in a low, urgent whisper.

'Do it. Or die here now. You've broken into my home. Who would ever say I was wrong to shoot you?'

James realised he had no choice if he was to survive. He moved mechanically over to the wall and put his foot on the lower of the stones. Then, with heart-sinking desperation, he levered himself up onto the surface of the higher level, first on his knees and then, with manic concentration, onto his feet. As he did so he had to lean outwards and he saw with sick terror the horrible sight of the drop to the sea below. He slowly straightened upright, every part of him concentrating on stopping his legs from shaking. Blood pounded in his temples, his senses scattered, his head spun.

'Turn to face me,' Dunbeath ordered.

Even in his shattered state James knew that the slightest wrong move would send him over the edge. He shuffled to one side, his knees bent and his feet making tiny movements to bring himself round. Terror was quickly overtaking him and as his mind solidified, so his limbs softened. Eventually, he succeeded in turning round.

'Now you,' snapped out Dunbeath, swinging the pistol to point at Alistair.

The younger man could take no more. He'd seen James's terrible climb and there was nothing left in him that could make him follow his brother's lead. He began to whimper, now deaf to Dunbeath's voice.

'Wait here,' said Dunbeath sharply, and stepped backwards into the observatory with his pistol still raised. Without ever taking his eyes from them he felt for the back of a chair and then dragged it outside behind him.

'Here. Climb up on that. Get on this stone here.'

Like James, Alistair could see no way out. Shaking violently, he stood on the chair and, by holding its back rail, he edged a foot forward onto the battlement's surface. Then he closed his eyes and lifted his other leg. He was now facing out to sea and he gibbered to himself as he slowly inched round to face Dunbeath. The earl seemed to inspect his work and then barked out his next command.

'Now, each of you, take the other man's hand. Go on. Both of you do it. Get hold of his hand!'

James and Alistair lifted their arms towards each other and linked hands. As they did so, Dunbeath pulled the chair back and threw it to one side. A hundred feet below them the surf roared ever louder with the pull of the incoming tide but, in their terror, the brothers heard nothing – they knew only that the slightest movement from either of them and they would fall.

'I'm going to give you some choices' said Dunbeath dispassionately. He had suddenly become a man of science, explaining an experiment.

'Listen carefully. You know I have only one ball in my pistol. If you both jump at me I could only shoot one of you. I might even miss. No doubt if I did you'd overpower me and throw me over that wall you're standing on. But if you don't want to try that then you can simply ask to get down and I'll take you to the sheriff in the morning. I see from your empty sack that you've taken nothing so you'll probably only get a light sentence, just for breaking into my property. Possibly a short spell in jail.

'But, concentrate now…' Dunbeath's voice rose in emphasis, '…if one of you steps down and pulls the other one off the stone, and he falls, then you have my word, that man can go free.'

He took a step back from them and his lips tightened into a satisfied smile.

James and Alistair began to plead, first with Dunbeath and then with each other.

'Ask to get down Jamie… give ourselves up,' stammered Alistair, his body shaking in the wicked cold of the wind.

'No, you fool,' said James urgently, 'jump at him! Come on, let's jump at him. We can do it together.'

Dunbeath seemed completely oblivious to their argument and

continued to stand quite still, pointing his gun in silence. Long seconds passed as he waited patiently. For all the world, he seemed no more than a gentleman scientist, fascinated to see the result of a chemical reaction.

As the cold black of the pistol's muzzle pointed at first one and then the other of the brothers, their heads pulled back in horror. Too terrified to be aware of what he was doing, Alistair lost control of himself and leaked noisily onto the stone of the wall.

Possibly prompted by this, Dunbeath's manner changed in an instant. His features hardened and his temper flared.

'Choose!' he now shouted at them angrily, 'what will you have? Choose!'

The earl had passed from cool control to manic fury in just a few seconds and he now began to step rapidly from foot to foot as if scarcely able to contain himself.

'Come on! What's it to be, gentlemen? Life or death?' He was screaming now, the rage that had flashed up in him almost as mind shattering to the brothers as the prospect of the sea below.

James looked across at Alistair. He was about to urge him forward again when he noticed for the first time his brother's sodden clothing and the moonlight glinting on the puddle he'd made in front of him. It was then, at this sight, that something gave in his deranged terror. In a second his fear went out of him and, instead, an extraordinary calmness came over him.

James was quite cold now as he looked again at Alistair's desperate, twisted face. He saw his brother's stretched skin and starting eyes, wasting his time pleading for his life with this half-crazed man. As he looked at him, James felt as if he had left his body and was floating gently above where they stood, looking coolly down on the whole insane conflict. It all seemed so suddenly clear to him – how he had always led the way with Alistair, forever caring for him and fighting his battles. He felt as if he'd been carrying him all his life. Now he'd pissed himself.

What a pathetic weakling he was. Well, he'd give him one last chance to be a man. He would pull his arm to make him attack Dunbeath. And if he fell? Then he should have fought harder. Shown more spirit! How typical it would be of him if he fell over the edge.

If Ally jumped forward when he pulled him, James thought, then they might have a chance with Dunbeath. But if the boy went over the edge? So, he'd go free himself. It was absolutely obvious to him now. *Either outcome suited him, the best thing he could do was pull.*

James looked away and then jerked his arm, wrenching Alistair towards him. As he did so he leapt forward from the battlement.

But Lord Dunbeath was ready for this and stepped quickly backwards, the pistol still outstretched. Like James, his eyes were on Alistair. Both of them now watched, fascinated as, in a moment of sudden quiet, the boy's face crumpled in incomprehension and his fragile balance was lost forever on the slick stone of the battlement. There was a slight scrape as his legs went from under him and then he fell heavily, bringing down an arm on the block that James had just stepped off. The two men heard the hideous slap as Alistair's hand struck and then slid off the wet surface. There was no cry at first and the boy only gave a small grunt of surprise. But then, as he fell, twisting, down towards the sea far below, he let out a long and despairing scream.

There was a deep, black silence. Too stunned to react for a few seconds, James simply remained unmoved, frozen in mute shock. Then he flung himself at the battlements and stared down into the dark roar of the sea.

'Alistair! he screamed. 'Ally!'

He shouted again and again, his voice becoming weaker with each cry. At last, with an agonised sob, he fell to the tower's floor, his head in his hands, whimpering in his utter self-loathing.

Dunbeath waited, quite still, seeming to observe James's

anguish with the greatest interest. Then he moved towards him and pulled him upright. The mad anger of a few minutes before had by now completely dissolved and he led the broken boy, almost gently, down the stone stairs and towards the main gate.

'I wanted him to attack you,' James sobbed when they'd reached the entrance hall. He continued, distraught and jabbering, all fight long gone. 'Why didn't he know that? I was pulling him to jump at you. Why didn't he? That's what I meant. Why didn't he jump?'

'He didn't jump because you pulled him off the stone,' said Dunbeath. 'You don't know what to think, but I'm telling you, you pulled him to his death. You chose to live. You killed him so that you could go free. That's what happened.'

As Dunbeath opened the castle's great entrance door, an odd compulsion seemed to come over him to share his conclusion.

'You had no part in the decision back there,' he muttered. 'I wouldn't blame yourself. It was just man's wickedness that pulled him to his death, not you. You did it because of the evil nature that's in all of us, in every man alive. You're no different to anyone else, it's only self-interest that makes us who we are. We think we're civilised, but every one of us would do what you did. We'd all kill to survive. Even a worm will twist to escape, a fish will fight the hook. You, all of us, we're no better than they are.'

James stared at him in disbelief.

'Do you mean you knew I'd do it?'

'Well,' replied Dunbeath grimly, 'I'd have wagered much that one of you would.'

James's manner immediately hardened. He stared at Dunbeath.

'Then you might as well have pulled him yourself. You made me do it. You murdered Alistair!'

'No,' said Dunbeath firmly, and he now looked fiercely into James's face. 'You did! And it's you that will hang if you talk about this.'

He pulled the huge door open and turned back to the boy.

'But I wouldn't think too long on it if I were you,' he added tersely. 'Have you never seen a map? Don't you know where we are? We're the most obscure dot that's marked in all Scotland, of no interest to anyone. Who will ever know what occurred here tonight? Or care? Go home now. Forget about what happened. Be grateful for your freedom.'

And with that Dunbeath pushed James through the open door and closed it again with all the finality of the Urquhain's long tradition of shutting out the inferior beings of the world.

* * *

James never knew how he got back to Dunbeaton that night. Weeping and bent, he stumbled through the dunes. It had begun to rain and the frozen air cleared his head enough for him to realise that he had to think. He couldn't tell the truth. He needed a story. His first thought was that he would say that Alistair had simply fallen off a rock as they'd been gathering mussels. But what were they doing out in the middle of the night? And, anyway, that old drunk McColl knew they were exploring the cave. What if he should blabber the truth?

At last he reached the cottage and beat loudly on the door.

'Mother! Mother!' he shouted out as he went in. 'Father! Quickly!'

James fell to his knees and sobbed loudly as they ran towards him, panicked by his manner. Bit by bit he stammered out a version of the night's events. Of how Alistair had begged James to go with him to explore the cave under the castle, fascinated by McColl's story. Of how Alistair had insisted on going first into the cave but had not reappeared. Of how the waves had pounded and pounded as the tide rushed in.

'It was so fast, so fast!' he wailed, 'I waited and waited. I kept calling out for him. But he didn't answer, he didn't call back.'

James fell to the floor and curled up, gasping in his sobs. His mother sat with him, rocking backwards and forwards, still too stunned for grief. But although she was shocked there was disbelief in her thoughts too. She knew that Alistair was a gentle, easily led creature. James had always been the bolder, the more dominant of her two sons. And now this change in them both. How had that happened?

She rose to her feet and picked up her shawl.

'Come out with me, Andrew,' she said in a flat, distant voice to her husband 'we must go down there and look for ourselves.'

Chapter 3

Once he'd closed the castle's great door Dunbeath strolled easily back to his study.

For an hour or more he sat deep in thought, gazing out of the window at the growing light of the dawn. Eventually he appeared to reach a conclusion. Taking a clean sheet of paper from a drawer, he loaded a quill with ink and quickly wrote a few lines. He then folded the page inwards, scribbled a name and address on the front and sealed the ends with wax, stamped firmly with the crest of his ring.

Leaving the room he went up a spiral staircase and along a corridor to a small door at the far end. He hammered hard on the wood.

'Annie! Annie woman, come down. I have something for you.'

He returned to his study and continued to gaze out of the window, his face blank with concentration, as if turning over a puzzle in his mind.

Annie McKay, his housekeeper, knocked timidly at the open oak door as she came in. She was in her sixties but looked far older. Stooped and beaten by life, her blotched face and half shut eyes showed only too well why she would have slept through the noisy turmoil that had taken place only a couple of hours earlier.

'There you are, Annie,' said Dunbeath grimly, glancing up at her sodden face. 'I want you to find someone in the village to take this letter to Edinburgh. A reliable man now. What about that cousin of yours? Tell him to walk to Wick and take the coach down. He's to wait for an answer.' He dug in a drawer for some gold coins. 'Give him these and tell him I expect him back with all speed.'

Annie nodded and began to collect some of Dunbeath's discarded dinner plates, but he waved her away with an impatient waft of his hand.

Four days later, Gordon McKay hurried through the wet streets of Edinburgh in the late afternoon, peering up at the houses with the baffled alarm of a country visitor. Lost yet again, he stopped and asked an elderly man the way. At last he found the house he was looking for. He checked the address against the letter, picked up the brass ring set in the lion's head knocker and timidly brought it down.

A young maid answered and McKay handed the letter over to her.

'It's for Mr Hume,' he said, 'I'm to wait until he's read it and then take an answer back.'

The maid nodded and stepped aside to let him in.

Ten minutes later David Hume stood at a window in his study holding the letter at an angle to catch the last of the afternoon light. He was tall, but his height was reduced by stooping, and his smooth skin and the babyish colouring of his cheeks were in odd contrast to the corpulence of his frame. He wore a small white wig and he pushed this back now as he read the letter for a second time, his kindly features composed in concentration as he absorbed its contents. Then he folded the paper and put it in the inside pocket of his frock coat. The coat was new that day and as he touched the cloth he realised with delight that there was a sliver of heavy silk that he hadn't noticed before at the lip of the pocket. He ran his finger over it now with an appreciative smile.

Today was his thirty fourth birthday and it was one of his great pleasures each year to mark the passage of time with a gift to his wardrobe. This year's addition was a spectacular success. The tailor was an artist, of that there was no doubt, and all through the day Hume had found himself delighting in the beauty of the gorgeous red coat's golden embroidery and the warmth of its heavy wool. Yet again his hand moved to feel the craftsmanship of the decorative work at his wrist, his senses secretly comforted by the touch to his fingers.

He looked through the window into the small garden and picked up a lost train of thought again. The coat had reminded him of his birthday, and his birthday of the march of time. Had he gone forward, he wondered? He turned to look at the study that he loved so much and thought that he had. He was a man that set much store by comfort and order and he felt that the threat of penury, without doubt his greatest anxiety, had retreated further during the year. When he'd left Scotland as an impoverished young man many years before he had worked as a clerk for a sugar importer in Bristol and he liked to keep the memory of those days of repetitive and unimaginative stock-taking fresh in his mind. The work had left him with a fear of tedium and a horror of debt; but it had also given him the deter-mination to earn his living by the power of his intellect and not by meeting the demands of others.

Yes, there had indeed been progress he felt. The *Treatise on Human Nature* that he'd worked so hard on had been published eight years earlier and it was now no longer the failure that it had once seemed. He remembered the exhilaration of its first appearance and then the terrible depression that had descended on him when it had – as he now felt able to joke with his friends – fallen 'dead-born from the press'. But sales had increased steadily over the years since then, as had his fame, and with them had followed the health of his purse and the standing of his reputation.

It was true that he had no wife yet but he set little store by this shortcoming. He was used to looking after his own needs and he enjoyed the company of men. And, of course, he said to himself, he was yet to meet a woman that he could converse with on the subjects that interested him.

And while it was also true that his hopes of a professor's gown at the University were in ashes he had accepted long ago that if the price of a chair was the rejection of his atheism then this ambition would have to be forever closed to him. Besides, he could be comfortable without it. His friends understood his position, even if they disagreed with it, and the sales from his books, his tutoring and the small amount he received from his family's rents were more than enough for this friendly house and its good cellar. And the warmth of his new clothes.

Yet again he was returning to ponder on whether to bring out a revised edition of the *Treatise* when he heard his maid's knock on the door. She stood shyly in the doorway, framed by the early evening light.

'Mr Adam Smith is here to see you, sir.'

Hume smiled broadly.

'Good, good. Show him in, please.'

And here was a further pleasure to mark his birthday, he thought to himself. He had heard so much about this Mr Smith and was greatly looking forward to spending an evening with him. Smith was by all accounts a prodigy, some were even claiming him to be a genius, and although he was not yet twenty three he was already being spoken of by Hume's friends as the coming man.

But there were other stories about him too and Hume smiled to himself as he recalled some of the things he'd heard. Of Smith's great intellect and insights there was never anything but confirmation. But what a strange fish he was said to be, speaking rapidly to the empty air as if he was arguing with himself and beaming suddenly into the winds to his imaginary friends.

'Still, he has the most beautiful smile a man ever witnessed,' Hume's friend Bruce McLean had said. 'There isn't a bad bone in his body'.

It now seemed that half the people of Edinburgh were laughing as every day brought new stories of Smith's absent mindedness. Charles Townshend had told Hume that he'd been in mid-conversation with him when Smith had fallen backwards into a tanning pit. Another friend had regaled a group of them with the story of how the young man had been so deep in a daydream that he'd found himself in his undershirt, lost in the streets, and had to ask a drayman to bring him back to his lodgings. Hume beamed again at the memory.

There were footsteps in the corridor as the maid returned. She stood to one side of the door as Adam Smith followed her into the room, walking in a kind of sideways shuffle and with his eyes fixed firmly on the opposite wall to where Hume stood.

He was tall and slight with a strongly pronounced nose and he seemed so very young and so awkward and disjointed that Hume had the impression an outsized boy was in his room. He was dressed in a plain blue frock coat with a simple neckerchief at the throat and his own hair pulled back in a bow. He now stood motionless, frozen stiff, apparently studying a spot on the skirting board.

David Hume smiled and held out a hand towards the thin figure's hunched back.

'Ah, the famous Mr Smith. How very good of you to come.'

Smith gave a tiny sigh and turned round in a kind of high stepping dance. His eyes followed and at last they slowed their frantic jumping and settled on Hume - and he smiled in reply. Good Lord, what a smile, thought Hume, his atheism dropped in his surprise. So it was true, Adam Smith did indeed have the most benign appearance he'd ever seen, with the smile of a man so completely absorbed in his own intelligence that he had no fear of another's thoughts nor, Hume guessed, much use for their company.

'Mr Smith,' said Hume again, now more softly, 'I trust you will stay for dinner. There are lambs already on the hills. And one has kindly laid down its life for us.'

* * *

Three hundred miles further north a storm had raged for three days after the two boys had been in the castle and a proper search for Alistair's body had been impossible. But with a lull in the weather on the next day, James and his father had approached the sea wall at low tide and James showed him the gap in the rocks that formed the entrance to the cave.

The surf was still high after the storm, far higher than it had been on the night that the brothers had made their break-in, and the two men had great difficulty even standing on the boulder, let alone making an attempt on searching the cave.

'By God, but it's dangerous in there,' said his father grimly. 'Poor Ally. Poor, poor Ally. No wonder he was trapped. What was he thinking?'

He came to a sudden stop and James glanced anxiously over at him. His father continued to stare into what he believed was his son's death trap and James saw his chest heave with the effort of swallowing down his grief.

'What can we do but hope he'll be washed out soon?' Andrew McLeish managed to get out eventually in a voice strangled with suffering, 'I'd ask no man to go in there to fetch him.' Like his sons he had been a fisherman all his life and the work had taught him many reasons to fear the power of the sea. Above all, he'd learnt the value of patience.

James looked away and breathed deeply for the first time in days. He glanced down at the gap in the rocks for one final time and then set off with his father for the sad, silent walk back to Dunbeaton.

But, the following evening he returned again, this time on his own. He made his way down from the dunes towards the beach, his expression blank but his mind racing. He stood looking at the gigantic structure of the castle, its enormous bulk sharp against the twilight. His face tightened as he saw a light from the windows in the observatory and he turned round to find a better place from which he could look up at it.

* * *

With a wave of his arm Hume directed Adam Smith into a small, panelled dining room in which a round table had been set for two.

Smith was shown to his chair and quietly gazed about himself without any sign of being overawed by the older man. David Hume leant over him as he poured his guest a glass of wine and then straightened as he said how delighted he'd been when he was introduced to him at Lady Culdross's house the previous Wednesday – and how much he had hoped that he would agree to come to visit him this evening.

'Your reputation goes before you,' Hume went on. 'Why, Francis Hutcheson, your professor at Glasgow, told me he had nothing left to teach you. And William Scott spoke highly of the great impression you made at Oxford.'

Smith smiled his sweet smile as he stared down at his glass but showed no sign of replying. After a pause Hume shrugged slightly and continued.

'We are both interested, are we not, in the workings of our human kin. Of course we are indebted in this to the great Englishmen, John Locke and Mr Hobbes, and even those Frenchmen, Monsieur Descartes and that delightful fellow, Voltaire. But in our own Scottish way I hope that we might also bring in a harvest from the fields of moral philosophy. Who knows, we may yet take our place in revealing some of the secrets of our nature.'

Hume looked up to see Adam Smith's ingenuous face now apparently transfixed by the candlestick. Could he be listening, he wondered? Yes, he thought he was. But what a very strange person he seemed. David Hume gave a slight cough and then decided to press on.

'So, Mr Smith, perhaps you'd be so kind as to outline for me your recent work and thinking? I would be very interested to hear of it.'

A peculiar change seemed to come over Adam Smith. His eyes left the candlestick and set off on a hectic journey around the room before they came to settle at last, staring upwards at the edge of the cornice. Then the words that had seemed so reluctant to come before, now tumbled out unchecked.

'My thinking? I know not why you should take any interest in my poor efforts. I have scarcely left Balliol these ten weeks. But I'm much affected that you should even ask. What are my thoughts? Well, I have few compared to yourself. I have twice read your *Treatise on Human Nature*; in fact, I was punished at Oxford for reading such a heretical work. But, sir, I think of you as Giotto drawing his perfect circle – we are all of us at your feet – and indeed there was much in your *Treatise* that I found interesting. Yes, much.'

Hume gave a wry laugh and waved his hand in mock protest.

'Yes, yes, but I notice you say 'much' rather than 'all''. He laughed again and continued in an easy-going tone. 'It's not often that I'm weighed in such a way. On the contrary, I have been reproached many times for what I say in the *Treatise* and yet other readers have been kind enough to praise it. But rarely have I been so reproached with praise in the way you put it.'

Keeping his eyes on Adam Smith, Hume leant forward to pick up his wine. He had been expecting a response from the young man but Smith simply brought his gaze down from the ceiling to his plate and he now stared at it in silence.

Hume decided to press on.

'Tell me,' he said with a shrewd glance, 'I'm far more interested in hearing your views on those parts of the *Treatise* with which you disagree.'

Adam Smith's eyes took up their restless flitting for a few moments and then, to Hume's surprise, settled on the older man's head as if he was studying the structure of his wig. He peered at it intently and then seemed to gather himself for a second before he launched into an answer.

'Well sir,' he said in his unchecked way, 'like yourself I would insist on this fundamental observation of our human nature: that life is a pitiless struggle between creatures and that our first thought is always to look to our own needs. This is nothing but the struggle for existence and although we may strive to disguise it, at base, we care for nothing but our own survival.

'Yet I was greatly struck,' he continued, 'by the observation you make in the *Treatise* that we are motivated not only by self-interest but by benevolence – a love for mankind. In fact, you say that man is naturally benevolent. And it is from this benevolence that you believe that trust in society arises.'

Hume nodded.

'You don't agree?'

Adam Smith's eyes resumed their erratic roaming while he dunked a piece of bread and butter dreamily into his wineglass.

'Why should I?' he said eventually. 'Even the most fleeting glance at human behaviour shows that there is little reason for us to suspect that society's relationships are built on, or maintained by, natural benevolence. All around us in life, in government, in trade and, in fact, in anything we do, it is the opposite that is undeniable. The world is dominated by self-obsession and deceit. Scratch any human and beneath the surface you will find nothing but utter selfishness. Natural benevolence is quite irrelevant. We can explain all human interaction – both the conditions under which it works and the reasons why it sometimes breaks down – without resorting to concepts such as your 'benevolence' and 'trust'. I believe you have fallen into the common trap for moral philosophers of viewing the world through your own eyes only. You have a reputation for being benevolent. You are known to be kind and compassionate. You see good in others. It follows that you view the world's behaviour shaped in this light. But I have a greater chill to my blood. I turn a cooler eye on people. However pleased we might be to find that benevolence exists, there is little reason to assume that it does.'

David Hume sat back heavily in his chair. It was a long time since he had been so harshly spoken to and he felt his colour rise as he absorbed the weight of the attack. His hand moved slowly to the comfort of the embroidery at his cuff.

Smith said nothing. His gaze shifted back to the cornice. Suddenly his eyes darted back to look directly at Hume and he smiled his beautiful smile. In an instant Hume's heart warmed and he realised that Adam Smith was incapable of wounding. Instead he was obviously in a world of his own intellect, without the usual understanding of the effect his words might have. McLean was right about him: this was a man who so verged on innocence that he simply said what he perceived to be true, not what he deemed to be socially acceptable.

Hume decided to stay quiet and wait. He now nodded to the younger man, encouraging him to go on.

'Far from benevolence,' Smith continued after a pause, 'I start from a different point to explain our natures. My beginning is the observation that humans differ from animals because man alone specialises his labour. I grant you that some animals may divide tasks in a crude fashion for a common end and they may even group themselves into a pack to do so, but only man will actively decide to specialise what he does and then work towards an unseen future. And it is this aspect of his nature, above all else, that drives his behaviour. In every other species each individual is self-contained, complete, reliant only on itself. A cat or a fish, any animal, depends only on itself once it is grown. It is only man that continues to be dependent on the way that others in his company have specialised their labour too.'

David Hume felt quite recovered and increasingly fascinated as to where the young man's logic would lead.

'I know it,' he replied, 'and surely this is why man has to live in society. By himself he is vulnerable and weak. I say so in my *Treatise*.'

'Indeed,' said Smith, 'but specialisation is also the reason for his success, and it is the reason for the bonds that exist in society. I believe this has led to a *need* for each other and it is this, not benevolence, which holds us together.'

David Hume put his head on one side and frowned slightly in enquiry. Smith continued.

'Please, let me illustrate what I mean. If you and I were to attempt to make a pin tomorrow, the most simple of objects and amongst the cheapest to buy, we might flounder at it all day and conceivably produce one or two. And no doubt poor things they would be. Yet I have witnessed a collective of ten people in which they produced fifty thousand pins in a single day. To buy one hundred pins costs only one fiftieth of a man's day. These pin makers have specialised their labour to make a tiny yet vital part of our lives. The customer gets a cheaper pin and the pin maker gets money to exchange for the other goods he needs or wants. He is an expert in the pin trade – he has no need to know how to bake bread or meet his other needs. He buys these other skills from other specialists. But even within this process the pin makers have specialised still further. One man sharpens the points, another has perfected the skill of flattening the heads. And look at the result! By working in this way they have achieved a mighty increase in their collective effort. In fact I call it mass production. And with this effort and organisation has come a great increase in their output and, therefore, in their collective rewards as well.'

By now Smith was looking dreamily out of the window. Without taking his eyes from some far off point, and in a voice that was anything but dreamy, he continued.

'It is this specialisation that one sees constantly repeated in society. Men who are very capable at one thing but have little or no knowledge of others. And why should they be concerned at this? Their specialism has earned them far more than any direct labouring could ever do. But while this approach may give man his success yet it places him, unlike the animals, in almost constant need of exchange with his brethren. And he will look in vain to expect it from their kindness alone. On the contrary, he's only likely to succeed and get what he wants if he has something to offer in return, a specialism of his own. He needs to get others to trade with him to further his own interests.'

Adam Smith came to a halt and the two men sat in silence for a moment as the dining room door opened and the maid came through with a joint of lamb and bowls of vegetables arranged on a tray. Smith didn't bother to glance in her direction before he continued with his point.

'You see, take this meal. It is not from the benevolence of the butcher and the baker that we expect our dinner but rather from their regard for their own self-interest. By getting the food from them we've addressed ourselves not to their humanity but to their self-love – we don't talk to them of *our* needs but of the advantages to *them*. And it's exactly the kind of specialisms they offer, and the competition that goes with people having the same skills, that allows society to be greater than the sum of its parts.'

As he finished saying this, Smith fished in his pocket and brought out a small copy of Hume's *Treatise*.

'Indeed sir, you say something of this in your own work.'

He held the book towards the candle's light and read aloud.

'I learn to do service to another without bearing him any real kindness because I foresee that he will return my service in expectation of another of the same kind.'

Adam Smith looked up from the book and began to stare into the corner of the room.

'You see, sir, that while I agree with you in the sentiment you have written here, I depart also because my exchange is one of specialisation, with money or barter as the means. It is this that lies at the heart of efficient markets and I have come to the conclusion that such markets have their own unerring logic – it is almost as if an invisible hand were guiding them – in which, for example, too much of one thing leads its price to fall or one specialisation loses value against another. A correction must take place for equilibrium to return. And good markets are in a state of constant flux to achieve this – a flux driven by people acting to further their own self-interests. In many ways it is this movement that keeps them healthy.'

For the first time in some minutes, Adam Smith glanced quickly at Hume and saw that the older man was gazing intently back at him.

'I have seen that look many times from my tutors,' he said. 'I assume you do not agree. Or have I offended you in some way?'

'Not at all, Mr Smith,' replied Hume, 'but answer me this. I think I understand your view that society is based on self-interest. Or rather the transaction of self-interested specialisations. But why, in that case, is there ever virtue? Or altruism? Why do people ever behave without reward? Why do they sometimes show compassion? And, more importantly, why do they regard such actions and sentiments so highly?'

'I know,' said Smith, and for the first time since he'd arrived that evening a doubtful tone entered his voice. 'A very good question indeed. And I have but a tentative answer. It is my observation that human beings share a taboo against selfishness. Indeed, it is almost the definition of what we would call vice. I agree that finding an answer to your question is vital. The praise people give to virtuous things seems always to be concerned with the welfare of others. I know that there must always be a requirement for sympathy towards one's fellow beings in our dealings with them but I must confess that I cannot explain virtue in the way that I can explain self-interest.'

'Ah,' replied Hume quickly, 'you reject my belief in natural benevolence but you'll accept what you call 'sympathy' will you? But surely this sympathy of yours is incompatible with the specialisation and self-interest that you say glues society together. How do you reconcile the two?'

Smith looked away into the air and seemed to speak more to himself than to Hume.

'Yes, I agree, altruism and compassion don't fit with my picture of a world based on rational transaction, do they? I've often wondered about this; about why people are ever good.'

He glanced back towards Hume.

'I have given this much thought and I suspect that these actions and feelings spring out of shame for our selfish natures, but I have no evidence to support my view.'

At this Hume smiled broadly. Then he laughed and reached inside his coat pocket and brought out the paper he had put there earlier.

'By the most remarkable coincidence, Mr Smith, I have just received a letter on this precise subject,' he said. 'In fact, I was reading it when you arrived. It is from an old university friend of mine, the Earl of Dunbeath. Perhaps you will permit me to read you what he has to say?'

Adam Smith sat more upright in his chair and nodded in interest. Hume picked up the candle and, holding it to the letter, he read aloud.

'*Hume,*

I understand you are to be called 'The Father of the Enlightenment!''

'I do beg your pardon, Mr Smith,' Hume said quickly, putting the letter to one side with an embarrassed grimace. 'I should have omitted that ridiculous comment. I'm afraid one must expect such a slash of irony from Lord Dunbeath to open with. Pray ignore it and permit me to continue.'

But your cause is the same as mine – to be empirical. To find evidence! Mine is to unlock the secret perfection of the planets, just as yours is to understand the secrets of our human natures.

Stony as my path may be, I would rather have my burden than yours.

But I have recently witnessed an event here that I believe would interest you.

It has set me thinking and I believe I have created a game – yes, a game (but what is life if not a deadly game with all its competition, strategy, bluff and self-interest?) that will prove to you mathematically and empirically the interaction of good and ill, of co-operation and selfishness.

Come and play my game of life with me! I call it The Prisoner's Dilemma.

I see nobody here and have only paltry help. So expect little to feed your body, but much to feed your mind.

Beware, you may not like the conclusions!

I remain etc,

Dunbeath.'

As David Hume finished reading, Smith lifted his eyes from the table. Hume had been delighted to see how deeply his objection to Smith's reasoning was received by him and the total absorption that the young man had brought to listening to the letter. So many of Hume's friends seemed to feel obliged to defend their views with an exuberant and noisy passion that it was refreshing for him to see someone be so open to a counter argument.

But now Smith smiled openly as Hume set down the letter.

'What will you do?' he asked.

'Well, I am due to be back in Dumfries with the Marquis of Annandale tomorrow. I am supposed to be tutoring him but I might as well be speaking to a sheep.'

'I heard his lordship was judged to be a lunatic.'

'Indeed he is. But should I exchange one certain madman that pays me well for an uncertain madman that I can be quite sure will not?'

David Hume beamed at Smith as he finished, turning over the problem in his mind.

'Perhaps I can do both?' he said finally.

Then he rose and strode to the door. He opened it with a theatrical flourish and called out for his maid. As she appeared he spoke loudly to her, half turning in the doorway so that Adam Smith could hear his answer.

'Elizabeth. Please tell Lord Dunbeath's messenger that I am obliged to travel south to the Borders for a short time but that I shall come up to Caithness when I am free after that.'

He thought for a moment.

'Please have him pass on my compliments to the earl and let him know that I should be with him in a month or so to play his new game with him.'

* * *

James McLeish had walked to a high point in the dunes before he turned to look back at the lighted observatory. By moving away he had given himself a better angle from which he could see some of the room and he now watched as Dunbeath's head moved about it, bending forward occasionally as if searching a table top.

Was he looking for something, James thought bitterly to himself? A telescope, perhaps? His lips moved in a muttered vow as he looked again at Dunbeath.

'You bastard. I shall never forget you. Never. Not a day nor an hour will go by that I shall not be thinking of you. Believe me, the time will come when I shall pay you out in your own coin. Though I may have to wait fifty years, you will know me yet.'

Then he turned and walked back towards the village.

* * *

Elizabeth tripped briskly back to where Gordon McKay was finishing the supper she'd given him and passed on the reply that he should take back to the Castle of Beath the following morning. She then returned to the dining room with the port and fruit and removed the cloth.

David Hume and his new friend sat in a comfortable silence as they cracked walnuts and sipped their port. These were the moments that Hume treasured most. To sit with a questioning and intelligent companion and press each other on the workings of the human mind was the greatest of his many pleasures. He looked at Adam Smith's ingenuous face, apparently turning over some stray thought in his mind. He looked at the good fire in the grate as it flickered its frantic shadows over the daub green of the panelling. He saw the deep red of the port, the peel of the oranges where the long loops had fallen amongst the dark shells of the nuts. He saw the light catching his fine crystal and the candles the colour of aged beef fat, all set against the patina of the table's surface. He loved these scenes with their rich palette of soft tones. They reminded him of the paintings of the Flemish masters that he had studied so closely in France and he saw in them all the flashes of insight and dark mysteries that so fascinated him when he looked at the twists and turns of human nature.

Adam Smith broke the silence.

'This Earl of Dunbeath, Mr Hume, did you know him well at the university?'

Hume nodded.

'Neither of us was there for long but indeed there was a time when I would have said I knew him as well as any. He was a great trial to his professors. A very fine mind indeed, but a troubled one. No doubt you know he is the clan chief of the Urquhain? A strange tribe of men they are too. He was much affected by the curse he had inherited from his ancestors, a great weakness of character known as the Urquhain Rage, a mania that was much admired in battle but leads to trouble in peace. Many people view it as little more than arrogance and impatience, however, and I'm afraid it's true that my friend suffers greatly from both.

'You'll have heard of the family, of course, hugely rich but constantly at war with the world. And themselves. The earl hadn't inherited when I knew him. He was known as the Master of Somewhere-or-Other, some ancient title, and he was as wild as they come. There was much drinking and fighting, I'm afraid, and the authorities despaired of him. For a time he was brought to a calmer state by the daughter of one of his tutors but she rejected him and this seemed to bring on some kind of mental collapse. He went back to his family and never returned to the university. I left soon afterwards myself.

'A few years ago I heard that his father had died and that he'd inherited. And then no word but a series of sad rumours about his increasing bitterness and isolation. He retired to a gloomy castle he has in the far north of Caithness, the old family seat. Apparently he lives there alone and without servants. The richest man in Scotland and no servants! He is never seen at his other houses. God knows there are enough of them – many of them have come through the fabulous marriages the Urquhain have always made. Glenlochlan is his. And the great house at Nairn. That huge palace you'll no doubt know at the far end of the Royal Mile, near to Holyrood, that is an Urquhain house too. A great mansion in St James's in London, of course. All staffed, yet he never goes to any of them. His factors' letters go unanswered and the estates, some people say they run to two hundred thousand acres, are all in a sorry state.'

Adam Smith had listened to Hume's story with great interest.

'I have heard something of this earl. Is he not involved with astronomy?'

'Involved, Mr Smith?' replied Hume. 'He's obsessed. It is his ambition to unlock the clockwork of the universe. He intends to be the first person to accurately determine longitude at sea. In the process he is set on winning the greatest scientific prize of this and, I'd wager, any other generation, the secret of navigation.'

'And no doubt win the Government's Longitude Prize,' said Smith drily, 'and the £20,000 that goes with it.'

'Very true, Mr Smith, very true. But the Prize means much

more to him than the money. Dunbeath must be worth twenty times that already. No, the real prize for him is glory. Glory for himself, glory for the Urquhain clan and glory for Scotland. I never met a man with a greater dislike of the English. I know Dunbeath and I know he won't rest until he's won this prize. He can see a day when the start point for all navigation, the prime meridian, will run through the home city of the person that solves the problem. And for Dunbeath that has to be Edinburgh. It would be where East meets West, where half the world shakes hands with the other. Where else should that be but Edinburgh, the greatest centre of learning of our age? He would rather die than see the honour go to London.'

Smith laughed for the first time that evening.

'How very, very interesting. I look forward to hearing about your visit and Lord Dunbeath's game. Perhaps you'd be kind enough to write to me while you're there?'

'I most certainly shall,' replied David Hume, raising his glass to his new friend. 'You have my word on that.'

Chapter 4

If the winter was harsh at the Castle of Beath this February, the thermometer was yet lower still, fifteen hundred nautical miles away in the south eastern Baltic, and it was there that the port of Königsberg lay huddled under a heavy blanket of snow.

Snow, rain or fine, however, trade was the lifeblood of the great city and trade would flow through its veins whatever the heavens might bring. The port sat on the banks of the mighty River Pregel and this great waterway washed around the two islands that formed the centre of the city before it drained into the vastness of the Frisches Haff, the more westerly of the two lagoons that connected Königsberg to the coast. From this enormous lake, ships would pass through a narrow gap in the long sandy spits that enclosed the lagoon, and from there out into the Baltic. It was this extraordinary natural position that gave Königsberg the most blessed of its attributes for it ensured that the port was ice free all year round. Unsurprisingly the city fathers took full advantage of this, and as Prussia's merchant elite, they made certain that the great trading centre was open for business at all times. Now, in this fierce winter, teams of men could be seen labouring around the clock to clear snow from the roads and lanes that led to the quays.

The people of Königsberg were as proud of the city's past greatness as they were of its current prosperity. For centuries it had been the capital of the monastic state of the Teutonic order, and although successive port masters had repeatedly modernised the warehouses and wharves that lined the river-banks, the burghers themselves preferred to leave unchanged the extraordinary medieval heart of the city.

Three men now walked away from the forest of masts at the main quay and headed towards this ancient centre. They made their way across the first of the famous seven bridges that connected the islands to the mainland, and from there on towards the Great Square, their bodies hunched against the harsh north-easterly that blew down from the Gulf of Finland. Slowly they passed the baroque beauty of the Marienkirche, then crossed the square itself and turned with relief into the relative shelter of the warren of ancient streets beside the Rathaus, the magnificent City Hall.

Two men flanked a far larger man that walked between them, padding along with a strangely deliberate tread, deep in thought. The outer two had the air of an escort although they wore the sailors' standard clothing of a thick jacket and heavy sea boots. Like so many of their kind on the quayside, they rolled unevenly as they walked, clearly less certain of a street under their feet than a deck.

But it was the central character that took the eye. Alexis Zweig. A sea captain.

Not only was he taller than his companions but he was far more powerfully built. Unlike most men of such stature, however, he wore his scale with such a relaxed air that his physical presence seemed more latent than actual. If one had to guess at his age, he looked to be in his early thirties but he carried about him a far more timeless sense of authority. Now, in response to a tiny gesture of command from him, the little party tacked at a junction of two lanes and turned to have the bitter wind at their backs: running under full sail they would have said.

As Zweig and his men made their slow way under the oriels and jetties of the ancient city, the crowds and traffic seemed to part in front of them in a kind of unspoken homage. Some that passed them glanced at Zweig with undisguised respect and some others even raised a hesitant hand in greeting. He seemed not to notice. Or if he did, he made no reply.

As they went by, a few looked back and whispered to each other: 'That was Zweig! Did you see him?' Then they would walk on, their heads coming closer together in the universal gesture of gossip, retelling the news of whatever latest coup he was said to have conjured. Most of the rumours about him were nonsense, of course, but some were more accurate. It was certainly true that he had come from nothing and yet had risen like a meteor to be the youngest captain that anyone could recall in Königsberg. And it was common currency that he had rewarded his early investors tenfold. It was said of him that he would trade in anything and stories of the way he'd secured the lumber contract for the great Winter Palace at St Petersburg and then negotiated a supply deal with the local amber mines, were spoken of with awe. Another masterstroke had seen him somehow manage to buy the rights to an extraordinary new paint that he'd named 'Prussian Blue' – and had then cornered the European market for it.

His strength was that he was both a fleet owner as well as a natural merchant, charming to deal with, fluent in five languages and conversant in several others; subtle, shrewd and remarkably honest. But his greatest achievement had arisen from the way he'd overcome Königsberg's most notorious shortcoming. The existence of a large sand bar where the lagoon met the city meant that only ships drawing less than ten feet of water could come into its quays. Larger vessels had always been anchored near Pillau at the mouth of the lagoon and merchandise had then been carried out to them from the city in smaller vessels. But Zweig had commissioned the construction of a fleet of large, shallow-draft traders that could moor in town – a market-changing coup that had given him such an advantage that he'd attracted the envy as well as the grudging respect of Königsberg's merchant elite.

Now, as the three men walked through the city on this bone-chilling morning, Zweig's great natural presence was further increased by his striking appearance. Under a wide-brimmed hat, edged with pale ostrich feathers, he wore his hair long and braided as if he was more used to the fashions of southern ports. His features were dark and strangely wild, his eyes like bloodstones, widely spaced and generally half closed in his complete self absorption. His dress was richly exotic and glinted with eastern silks, heightened by the occasional flash of pearl buttons and silver buckles. Across his shoulders hung a sumptuous swathe of the fur of a rare Siberian bear, held in place at the shoulder by a heavy gold clasp.

This was all mere surface adornment. It was Zweig himself that was so striking and intriguing and although his gaze was fixed downwards on the street, in the manner of one sunk in deep thought, he strolled with an air of such unhurried confidence that he seemed to exude an absolute belief in himself as well as a complete clarity of purpose. Anyone who even glanced at him was left feeling that they were looking at a man whose will would prevail, and would have to prevail for him to continue to exist - however long that might take.

He now moved through the ancient streets with an easy certainty and such a slow, deliberate step that his two smaller assistants had to break stride every few yards to stay alongside him.

One of them now looked ahead and spoke rapidly to his captain. Zweig looked up and saw their destination - a grand townhouse with a metallic trade sign of a giant boot set high up on its brick side. Above it, spelt out in large brass letters, were the words 'Johann Kant. Leather Merchant'.

But the captain's passage up the crowded street had already been witnessed from inside the house. Kant's daughter, Sophie, had seen them as they'd rounded the corner, just as she'd come onto the small landing of the staircase's return, a half round that projected out over the front entrance. The glass sides of this mezzanine were designed to let light into the stairwell but they also allowed people on the stairs see up and down the street and as Sophie now stood watching through the windowpanes, she smiled with pleasure as she realised that the three men were helming over towards the house. She'd seen Zweig glance up at their trade sign and it was with a thrill that she realised that they were altering course to make for her father's door.

Sophie had met the extraordinary Captain Zweig only twice but she remembered both occasions well. Such was the strange and powerful attraction she'd felt – and the huge sense of excitement – that she'd lived in the hope of seeing him again. And as soon as possible. On the second of the two occasions, at a gathering of merchants at the Rathaus before Christmas, he had even remembered her name and had paid her some attention. As they'd spoken, she'd been conscious of the envious stares of strangers and the hesitant, half smiles of her friends as they clustered around the two of them, silently watching how she dealt with the famous Zweig, 'the great man of tomorrow' as they'd called him. As he'd towered over her he'd shown no sign of being aware that they were the centre of such attention and instead had been serious and grave and deeply courteous in the way he had talked. After he'd been called away she was only too conscious of how much she'd enjoyed the glances and compliments of her companions.

'Of course he's noticed you, Sophie!' said her friend Gretchen when she tried to make light of the meeting a little later. 'Didn't you see the way he looked at you? You might have been a treasure map, the way his eyes lit up! And why shouldn't he? We all know you're one of the two great beauties of Königsberg. You and the cathedral. But you're only twenty three – you have four hundred years on your side!'

Sophie was far too spirited to give in to such flattery but even she had been rendered speechless as her friends had laughed and gently prodded her sides in affection. She was, indeed, one of the great sights of Königsberg. Blessed with the beautifully curved brow of a Botticelli goddess, she had a perfect yet intriguing profile, a glorious, full mouth and expressive eyes of the softest green that told their story of her intelligence and independence. Framing her was a mass of rich, dark hair in which a thousand different colours fought for prominence as it curled and twisted to be released from whatever constraint her mother tried to bring to it. But Sophie Kant was more than simply beautiful. An impression of spirited self-reliance shone from every glance of her eyes and gesture of her body. And it was a secret known only to her family and a few others that an intelligence that matched her beauty was being fed by two of the leading mathematicians at the university who came to tutor her at home, hidden from the criticism of a society that held that women should barely be educated, let alone in the sciences.

Sophie had suffered after the evening at the Rathaus. She may have found Zweig captivating but she'd also been disturbed by the strength of the feelings that he'd unleashed in her. To her dismay she'd realised that she hadn't been able to dismiss him from her thoughts as easily as she'd have liked. She was concerned by this. Was this love, she wondered? Was it the need for possession? The great power of her mind could make sense of most things but these feelings had made her confused.

More alarmingly she'd even found that the fascination of the mathematical texts she so enjoyed immersing herself in no longer had the power to captivate her in the way that they once had. These had always taken her away from the trivial realities of daily life yet she was finding that Captain Zweig was showing a still greater power to distract her thoughts. The previous day her mind had even wandered as she'd tried yet again to tackle Leonhard Euler's famous challenge. The great Swiss mathematician had thrown down the intellectual gauntlet to find a walk through Königsberg that crossed its seven bridges once, and once only. It intrigued her that half of Europe was considering the problem and she'd been determined that it should be an inhabitant of the great city itself that found the theory to answer it.

Now here was Zweig to distract her in person. And she was delighted! Perhaps he really had noticed her.

The little party in the street approached Kant's front door and

Sophie heard a heavy knock as it echoed through the house. She turned to look down to the hall and saw that her mother and father had emerged onto its ocean of black and white stone tiles and were now standing, waiting for the maid to appear and open the door.

Both of them were dressed as always in the sober black of Königsberg's merchant nobility, but although they were still as they waited for the servant to come, she saw that they were unusually ill at ease, and that their features were stressed with anxiety. Sophie was startled by the sight. She'd noticed that they had both seemed distant for some days but she'd pushed the thought away. Now she saw them whisper to each other in urgent tones and her mother unconsciously ground her hands together before reaching up to brush her husband's shoulders.

At last the maid appeared and pulled at the door. Captain Zweig nodded to her in greeting and then left his companions in the lane and stepped into the hall. He removed his hat and bowed to Frau Kant with a show of the greatest sincerity and then gave a brisk salute to Sophie's father. Together the two men walked towards a side door that led to Kant's study and Sophie was still smiling at Zweig's exaggerated politeness when she suddenly saw her mother lift her chin in a fierce, determined gesture towards the closed door. This small, unseen act of defiance seemed to exhaust her because, with a sudden sob, she buckled at the waist and buried her head in her hands.

Sophie gave a small gasp of alarm and hurried down the stairs to take her mother in her arms.

'Oh, Sophie, Sophie,' her mother wept when she was buried in the soothing embrace, all restraint gone, 'I'm so sorry. I'm so, so sorry.'

'But what is it, Mama? Why are you sorry?'

'It's the end of us. That man is set on seeing us finished.'

'What man? Captain Zweig? Surely not, Mama. Whatever can you mean?'

There was no answer as sobs overwhelmed her thin, tense body. Sophie knew that her mother was a proud woman – she and her husband had worked hard to take their place among the elite of Königsberg's merchants. But now all was falling around them. Bit by bit Sophie heard the worst.

'Zweig was commissioned by your father to bring a large cargo of leather from Spain. The whole ship was his order alone. Papa was advised to wait until the weather eased in the spring but, you know your father, he wouldn't listen. Business is good, he kept saying, the army needs more bridles and harnesses – King Frederick is set on seeing through his fight with the Austrians. We must have more hides now. Zweig was the only captain that would take the journey on. Everyone else said the weather made it too dangerous. But Zweig had Papa sign contracts to underwrite the voyage and ...' she faltered at this point as tears overtook her again, '...the ship has foundered. Everything is lost. We are due for the money now and we can't possibly find the full amount, even if we sell everything we have. Your father has ruined us, Sophie, ruined.'

Sophie stood in silence, absorbing the impact of what she'd just been told. There was little she could say and the two of them stayed quietly entwined for a few more minutes as her mother regained some composure and with it a measure of her lost strength. Sophie let go of her and gently wiped her face.

'We'll be all right, Mama. We shall see.'

Shortly afterwards the door opened and her father emerged, followed by Zweig. Again the captain bowed deeply to the two women but if he'd noticed any change in them he gave no sign of it. He picked up his hat from the table and walked in his strange, deliberate manner towards the door. As he did so, Sophie glanced towards her father and was shocked to see how he quickly looked away from her.

The door closed and silence returned to the house. Johann Kant stood still, waiting for the maid to go about her business.

Once she'd left, he lifted his eyes from the high polish of the floor and quietly muttered to his wife in a laboured, broken voice.

'Mother, we must speak. Sophie, will you find Immanuel please and join us in my study in five minutes.'

Sophie was about to object when she saw her mother give a quick nod of agreement. She turned and hurried up the stairs, heading towards where she knew her brother would be, as he always was, with his nose in a book. As she reached his room and rushed into the cramped library he'd made for himself in a far corner he barely raised his eyes. But one glance at her tense, shocked face was enough for him to urgently put his reading down.

'Why Sophie, you look terrible. Whatever's the matter?'

Sophie suddenly realised that she hadn't given any thought to how she would break the news of her father's downfall and now, as she looked down on her brother's anxious face, her heart began to fail her.

Immanuel was twenty-one, only two years less than herself, but he had always seemed so childlike and so very much younger than she was that the difference in their ages seemed far greater. His bookishness was already legendary and from an early age he'd been removed from the demands of normal life. He had enrolled at the university when only sixteen and, to nobody's surprise, he'd already decided that he would make his life there. He was quite different to his sister and in place of her spirited personality and fierce, quick intelligence he was already settling into a life of withdrawn eccentricity into which a strict routine and an unbreakable timetable ruled his days.

She braced herself to tell him the news but even as she did so her mind raced forward with a sinking depression. Who, she now began to panic, would look after this introverted and unworldly soul when their fortunes fell?

There was nothing to be done but repeat what she'd just heard. Immanuel listened hard and then turned to look at the wall.

'Poor Papa,' he muttered more to himself than to Sophie, 'he will take this very hard. How cruel the world is. Perhaps we shall all go hungry now?'

Sophie gave a brave smile. She leant over towards him and they embraced.

'We must go down,' she said softly, and Immanuel closed his book and together they descended the staircase. Sophie looked at him as he went ahead of her – so young and so naïve, she thought to herself, really, he's just a child. What would become of him?

They came to the hall and Sophie knocked on the door of the study. There was no answer and she gently pushed it open and peered around its edge to see if they could enter. As she did so, her mother caught sight of her and rushed across the room, her arms outstretched.

'Oh, Sophie, Sophie. Only you can save us.'

Sophie took a step into the room in alarm.

'What do you mean, Mama? Save you? Papa, what is this? What does she mean?'

Sophie looked towards where Herr Kant was standing by his desk but instead of meeting her eye he glanced quickly away and gazed down at his hands. He drew a deep breath. Then, slowly and in the grip of much wretched stuttering, he explained the story of his ruinous agreement with Zweig, of his insane gamble and of its terrible outcome. As he finished he turned away and spoke in a bitter, despairing gasp.

'In short, I am due for the cost of the hides, the ship and the loss of income that Zweig has suffered. I have only one week to find the money. You saw that he came here earlier to press me for payment.'

He looked away and his chest rose and fell in heavy, anguished panting. Sophie continued to wait for an answer to her question. Her father came out of his thoughts and squared his shoulders.

'But he came also to give me an alternative. He has put a proposition to me that ...' Kant stopped speaking for a moment and put his hand on the surface of the desk. He seemed to stare at it now as if he had never noticed it before, but then looked up, frantic and tense, and blurted out his news.

'Oh, Sophie, it is like a dagger in the heart, my dearest. He has proposed a way out that only you can fulfill. It ... it seems he has fallen in love with you. He says he knew it from the first moment he ever set eyes on you. And he has ... he has asked for your hand in marriage ... and in place of a dowry he will forgive the debt. There, it is out. I have said it.'

He looked up at Sophie with his head half lowered and he smiled at her in a way she had never seen before. It was part embarrassment, part shame and, she noticed with a sick realisation, part pleading.

Never had the words of the great Prussian poet, Dieter Goehren, been more apt.

'How narrow is the path of the human mind,' he had famously written, 'the smallest step and we cross from one side to the other.'

Sophie now took just such a step. In an instant she saw how deeply foolish she had been in her regard for Zweig and how utterly misled she had been by the blind delusion of her heart. What she had taken for careful thoughtfulness in him she now saw was simply the worst kind of low cunning. Now, too, she saw that his great and seemingly sincere courtesy was little more than an elegant arrangement of bait for the unwary. And his natural authority, that sense of command that had so intrigued and attracted her, well, it was nothing other than the need to bully and oppress. She saw him clearly now; she saw him stripped to the baseness of his motives, the fine clothes he had cloaked them in removed and discarded. Why, he was no different from any other money-grabbing trickster. Worse in fact, he was a tyrant, a monster!

'How disgusting, Papa. What a disgusting proposal!' she cried. But, even as she did so, she saw a twisted, pleading look come into her father's face. She persisted, hoping against everything she was seeing that her father would not abandon her.

'How could he hold you to ransom like that? I don't even know him. How can he suggest such a thing – it's despicable!'

Her parents glanced at each other and her mother took a step forward.

'But, Sophie, my dearest, you are wrong. He is a good man. Everyone says so. A powerful man, it's true, but good. Dearest, we are on the street if you refuse him. We shall starve. You alone can rescue us.'

Sophie took a step backwards and her hand went to her mouth, horrified to see how quickly Zweig had travelled in her mother's opinion from someone who wished to have them finished to being a good man.

Worse to see was the way her father nodded his agreement with his wife's views. His earlier reluctance and stammered embarrassment seemed to have evaporated.

'Please say you will accept him, Sophie. Or at least say that you will consider his proposal.'

'I can't believe you are asking this of me,' said Sophie, frantically. 'How can you?'

Her father spoke quietly and firmly.

'Sophie, with Zweig we can rise again. Without him we fall. He leaves in three days on a journey that he says will make him a greater fortune than all his others. When he returns in a few weeks, he will be one of the richest men in Königsberg. Please let me take your answer back to him. Please let it be your agreement.'

Sophie was silent as she struggled to take in what she was hearing. Then, from nowhere, she was struck by a thought.

'But if your ship was lost in these awful storms, why is he taking the same risk in the same weather? What if this voyage should see this ship founder as well?'

Kant returned in an instant to his business-like self.

'I asked him that myself and together we have reached an agreement. The journey should take no more than two months. We added more days to account for a setback. But, if the captain does not return within a hundred days then the debt will be cancelled.'

'A hundred days!' Sophie repeated. 'Then we must pray that he fails. And count the days.'

Her father looked down at his desk again, his negotiating position appearing to stall before his eyes.

'I fear there is another condition, my dearest. I am so sorry. He is insisting that you go with him on the voyage. He says that he would not want you to marry him without seeing him as he is. He wishes you to get to know him better. I'm sorry. He was unmovable on this point.'

Anger rose in Sophie again.

'So, I am to be sent off into this awful winter weather, which has already claimed one ship and with it our livelihood. To be with that loathsome man?'

She looked at her parents' exhausted, yearning expressions and could take no more. She fled from the room and ran, weeping, up the long staircase to her room. There she stayed, refusing all food or company, despite the protestations and pleading of her mother that came from beyond the locked door. But two days later she softened, exhausted, thinking of her poor little brother and his strange unworldliness, and of her mother's terrible anguish. She unlocked the door and sat back down on her bed. Frau Kant turned the handle and came into the room, tense and red eyed.

'There is no way out,' said Sophie flatly, her gaze fixed on the wall. 'I shall have to go. Oh, Mama. What can I do but go? Who would ever care for you or Immanuel if we were to lose every-thing? How can I ever have anything but contempt for Zweig after this but ...' and she looked away with such fear on her face that her mother instinctively gasped '... if, ...if I survive, I shall be able to say I now know him, know everything about him, and still feel nothing but disgust.'

Her voice rose as her spirit returned.

'Let him want to marry me then! If he dare. And who knows, he may be so rich by the time he comes back that he'll have lost interest in having a viper like me at his throat. Come, Mama, we must find clothes for a sea voyage.'

Chapter 5

Later that night Zweig stood at the stern of his ship and watched as the cargo was loaded. There were few people about the quay other than a scattering of dockside idlers and some of these muttered to each other as they observed the air of secrecy that seemed to be surrounding the operation. A couple of them, huddled together, speculated in hushed tones about what kind of commercial rabbit the captain would be pulling from his hat this time. The crew worked steadily on and orders were given yet again that time was of the essence.

Suddenly from out of the gloom came a low voice.

'Captain Zweig?'

'Yes, who's that?'

'My name is Schwerin, sir. I come with information about a lady.'

'Up here. Brunner, let him through.'

Schwerin nodded to the quartermaster as he came aboard.

'I thought you might be interested, sir,' he said as he reached Zweig, 'I am on friendly terms with the Kant household, well, with one young lady's maid in particular.' Zweig waited in silence for the man to continue. 'I understand there has been some hesitation. But the lady in question has now decided to see foreign lands. I thought you would wish to know.'

Zweig looked at the man's smirking face with dislike and then moved to gaze over his shoulder to where half a dozen of the crew were moving the arm of a derrick, hoisting on board some particularly large barrels.

'Take great care with those barrels!' he called out in a fierce whisper. 'Brunner, tell the men to be more careful. They are not to be dropped at any cost. Not if you wish for a share of the voyage. And you ...' he dropped his voice as he turned back to Schwerin and passed him a coin, '... on your way now. And not a word of this ladies' gossip to anyone.'

* * *

By the next morning the work was complete. The ship stood ready to depart as a bitter wind hurtled across the dockside, shrieking in the rigging of a hundred or more vessels that fretted and leapt at their moorings like so many head of cattle before the slaughterhouse gate. Sleet slashed down from the north, and the mouth of the river was shrouded in a mist so dank that it chilled the blood. The misery in the weather, however, was as nothing compared to the blackness that had descended on the little party that approached the quayside. At its centre was Sophie Kant, holding her father's arm as she leant on him for support.

To her horror she saw the ship's crew lined up on the deck, dressed in their best uniforms and with flowers in their hats as if for a wedding. Their honest sailors' faces seemed to beam at the prospect of their captain's happiness. From his position aft, Zweig had seen the party arrive and he now came towards them in delight.

'Welcome. Welcome to the Schwarzsturmvogel,' he called down. 'Sophie, how wonderful it is to see you, you have made me very, very happy. And you have never looked more fine than you do today. I thank you from the bottom of my heart for agreeing to come on our voyage. Herr Kant, Frau Kant, you will be worried for her, of that I do not doubt. But you have my word that I shall bring her home safe and happy. I shall protect her with my life, you may rely on that, with my life I say.'

Sophie looked again at the sailors and their flowers.

So, they know, she thought, and if they know then the whole world will know. Now, more than ever before, she realised that she should never have come – how could she have relented? Even if she returned and somehow managed to reject Zweig she would always be the woman that had sailed away with him, unmarried and unaccompanied. Her shoulders sagged at the thought and she gave a deep groan. Bitterly, she saw the future: if she returned then she would have no reputation left to her - or rather, she would have the very worst of reputations. And if she did not? Then she would have died, and died alone.

As the full enormity of the step she was taking fell on her, her courage finally failed. She sank again onto her father's arm and the tears that she'd been holding back for so long now poured out unchecked. The little family gathered around and it was only when Immanuel stroked her arm and murmured that he would see her again in as little as two months that her resolve stiffened. She gave a small nod of her head to a waiting sailor. He picked up her cases and, without a backward glance, she walked up the gangplank towards the Schwarzsturmvogel's deck.

* * *

Three days later Sophie had still not left her cabin.

At around eleven o'clock on the third of these, there was a soft knock on her door. The handle turned and Zweig's great frame filled the tiny doorway.

'Sophie. Good morning. I trust you are well,' he said brightly. 'I had feared that you were seasick but I'm told you are a natural sailor.' There was no answer but he continued to smile down at her as she sat by her berth. 'I was looking forward to showing you the ship, he continued, I know of your scientific interests and I thought you would like to see how we navigate our position and work the sails.'

Sophie continued to stare bitterly down towards the slatted flooring of the cabin, refusing to answer or even acknowledge his presence.

'Please don't stay shut away in here,' Zweig said, now more quietly, 'the men are worried for you. And, you must know, I wish for nothing but your happiness.'

Whilst he said this Sophie had not taken her eyes from the decking. Now she lifted her head and rose from the chair to look

Zweig full in the face.

'If you do not know why I am here then you must be a madman.' She whispered this quickly in a low, hoarse voice but her tone rose as the anger mounted in her. 'Yes, a madman. You think I'm here for my happiness? You think I want to be with you? You come to my father's house with your disgusting blackmail; you do not so much as look at me, never even a word. Then you take me as a hostage for your debt, a debt so deceitfully arrived at that you should be in prison for it. And now you think I can make all this disappear in the name of your one sided love! Be clear Zweig. I see through you. I see through your schemes. How dare you presume that I should ever feel anything for you but contempt. Happy? Leave me alone.'

Zweig listened to this torrent in silence, his look downcast. There was an air of immovable dignity in his manner as he heard Sophie out. Of understanding, but not without sadness. Now he replied in a soft and measured tone.

'Sophie. You must know this. I have loved you from the first second I saw you. For weeks afterwards I thought of nothing but you. I had no rest, I moved about as if in a dream. Then I saw you again at that bear garden in the Rathaus. We spoke and I knew then that my soul would never be complete as long as we were apart. I had no idea how to proceed. But fate intervened. Your father fell into debt with me and I knew he would be ruined if I insisted on repayment. Then I saw that some good could come of it. There was no blackmail, it was just my destiny that I saw before me. The money means nothing to me. My life will be unchanged without it. But my life would be destroyed without you.' He paused for a moment to look at her. 'I see how you feel about me now but I hope and pray that you will come to view me in a different light in time. Sophie, you know it all now.'

There was a silence. Sophie continued to stare coldly back at him in reply and he knew there was nothing more to be said. He gave a quick nod of quiet respect and took a step back, gently closing the door as he did so.

* * *

For two days more Sophie endured the suffocation of her tiny cabin. The weather had been kind to them in the Baltic as they'd travelled west towards Kiel but now as Zweig altered course north towards the Kattegat the vessel beat into the vicious headwinds that hurtled down the length of the Storebælt. Progress had been painfully slow for thirty hours or more and the troubled seas had exhausted the crew as they'd fought for every inch of headway. At last they'd reached calmer waters as they rounded the top of Sjælland and, as the wind veered round, Sophie decided that facing Zweig again was preferable to the insanity that threatened her if she spent another day in her cot.

As she emerged from below deck two sailors passed her and knuckled their foreheads. She ignored them and walked aft towards where Zweig stood looking out from the stern rail with his sailing master. The two men were deep in discussion as they prepared to let out a thin line with a log attached at the head and knots at regular intervals. She saw them work and watched in absorbed fascination as Zweig threw the log to trail behind the ship and the Master turned over a measuring glass. As the sands ran through, Zweig marked the distance by counting the knots in the line. The two of them then conferred, their heads close together, huddled over a compass and frequently turning to consult the wind and current conversion tables they had with them.

Sophie had not moved, astonished that this was the way they must be navigating. She'd had no idea that their methods would be so crude and she saw at once why so many ships could be lost at sea.

A sailor moved towards the two men and coughed. Zweig glanced up and, seeing the sailor's pointed nod, looked beyond him to where Sophie stood watching them. With a delighted smile he immediately passed his calculations to the Master.

'Sophie!' he called out. 'How good it is to see you on deck.'

He began to walk towards her but before he had taken a dozen steps disaster struck. High above them, a tar called Burkhardt was shaking out a furl in the topmast staysail when he glanced down towards the deck and saw his captain striding up to Miss Kant – the Miss Kant they had all been discussing. So, she'd decided to face him again, he thought, more than interested to see what happened next. In spite of the strong blow that was keeping the topmast crew glued to the arm he whistled excitedly and called to the next man outboard on the ratline, a high spirited, freckled boy who was known, inevitably, as Schnapps.

'Schnapps! Look below. The captain's beauty is out!'

Schnapps was little more than a child and barely two weeks into his topmast time. Anxious and eager to please, he grinned at Burkhardt and his attention shifted as he looked quickly downwards to where the man was pointing towards the deck. Many were the times that Burkhardt had told him the priorities of safety but in his excitement the rules were forgotten. A wicked yaw threw the vessel sideways and as the masts came over the boy, his concentration lost, slipped his handhold. Too late he tried to save himself, grasping desperately at nothing and then clawing the air as he tumbled towards the sea, shouting for help as he fell.

Zweig heard Schnapps scream out and immediately ran to the rail as the boy hit the water. He saw his hand come up and as the boat righted and surged forwards again, he grabbed a wooden raft and threw it out as far as he could in the boy's direction. He then turned and shouted an order to the sailor that was standing next to him, staring down into the water.

'Mark him with your arm! Point now.'

Zweig wrenched his jacket off. He stood on one leg as he pulled at first one and then the other of his boots. He glared at where Sophie was standing, looking anxiously into the sea.

'Point at me in the water. Never let your arm drop!'

With a fierce last look at her he turned and bellowed at the Master.

'Figure eight!'

Zweig then sprang up on the rail and hurled himself into the blackness of the cold waves. Sophie saw him surface and strike out powerfully towards where the boy had last been seen. She had no idea why she'd been told to point but she knew that if the boy's life depended on it then she must do as she'd been told. As the ship pitched and rolled in the swell she'd see and then lose Zweig in the waves and she now saw why she and the sailor had been ordered to point – if they had not the two men would very quickly have been lost against the darkness of the background.

'About!' yelled the Master as he helped the helmsman push the wheel hard over to bring the ship's head through the wind and back to the men in the water. Sophie, unused to the maneuver, suddenly found that she had to run to the other side of the ship, her arm still outstretched. For long seconds it seemed as if she'd lose Zweig's head in the blackness of the sea and a terrible temptation surged through her to drop her arm or point away. She was quite sure that if she did, she could be rid of him in an instant. But then she saw his head break surface and she knew that she had to see the boy saved.

Zweig looked towards the ship, seeing where the two arms pointed and quickly estimating where Schnapps was. He struck out strongly once more and soon came alongside him. He swam behind the boy and cupped his head in his hands, just as his wild thrashing was coming to an exhausted end. Zweig then waved with his free hand to the watching helmsman.

The ship passed them on its return and the Master swung the wheel again to bring its head into wind. Slowly it turned and came to a stop alongside the men as the sails flapped hectically, all sheets loose. The crew flung rope ladders over the side and sailors jumped down to manhandle the exhausted pair up on deck.

Poor Schnapps couldn't stand and his eyes rolled back as strong hands helped him below. But Zweig climbed over the rail and waved away the offer of a cloak, his clothes clinging to his colossal frame and his chest heaving as he struggled to recover his breath. In spite of her anger Sophie had to fight to hide the admiration that arose in her.

Zweig stood panting for a few moments before he moved towards where he'd left his boots. As he passed he stopped by Sophie and turned to look into her face.

'Thank you,' he said simply.

'For what? she spat back. 'I did nothing.'

Zweig smiled.

'But you did. You chose to save me. You decided I shouldn't die.'

Sophie felt her colour flare.

'No, I didn't. I saved the boy,' she replied flatly, and turned to return to her cabin.

* * *

Mona McLeish sat on a large stone outside her cottage as she washed clothes in a tin basin. James stood near her, looking out to sea. Since Alistair had died he didn't like to leave his mother on her own and he frequently found excuses now not to go out with the Dunbeaton fishing fleet when it sailed.

Three men rounded the cottage, two of them carrying a long and obviously heavy object, bound tightly in sailcloth. Mona looked up and with a mother's instinct, knew that Alistair had come back to her. She ran towards them and flung herself at the wrapping, tearing it apart.

'Oh, Ally, Ally,' she sobbed to the bloated grey face, over and over again as the small group looked on, wringing their caps in their hands. James ran to join his mother. He seemed to be on the verge of collapse as he stroked his brother's hair.

'Ally, man, why did you go in there?' was all he could cry. Any sign of guilt was buried too deep within his wailing for anyone to see.

Chapter 6

After a further three days the weather changed. For some time the Schwarzsturmvogel had beaten along with a strong northerly on its beam, taking them through the Skagerrak, beyond Kristiansand and past the southern tip of Norway. Then Zweig had altered course, set due west and began to fly across the open sea and towards the Scottish coast.

But after a day of this the good wind they'd been enjoying had suddenly dropped completely and the Schwarzsturmvogel found itself in such still air that it could have been the equatorial doldrums. Now, in the late afternoon, Zweig and his sailing master stood on the aft deck looking out at the sea's glassy calm and a surface so oily that the low winter sun reflected a cloudless sky. The sails hung limp from the yards and an uneasy lassitude descended on the men as they went about their duties. The more superstitious among them could be heard muttering their usual panicked predictions but even the stronger minded glanced frequently astern of their position, oppressed by the heavy atmosphere and only too well aware of their captain's anxious manner.

'There's a bad blow coming, Hartmann,' Zweig said in a low voice to his sailing master, 'short and fierce, I have no doubt. Perhaps you would spare me the time to speak together in my cabin.' The Master nodded and Zweig called out to a passing sailor.

'You there, send word to the first mate that the Master and I shall take a glass below. And the rest of you,' he shouted more loudly, 'cease your whistling for a wind. You may have your wish before too long!'

The two men clattered expertly down the stairwell to Zweig's quarters. They removed their sea jackets and sat down, spreading charts out on the table. Not for the first time that day they reworked their position and then reworked it again. Of the latitude, there was little doubt: they had taken a good noon reading and the compass had held firm. But the longitude was still too uncertain. Zweig pointed at the line of the north Scottish coast as it weaved its ragged way on the chart, and he drew with his finger the path he believed the ship had taken.

'We shall see our landfall soon if we pick up our wind again before too long,' he said, almost to himself.

He tapped the chart.

'You know this port here, Hartmann? Wick? I believe we shall see its lights later this evening. No doubt you've been there yourself and you'd agree with me that we shall feel happier when we can pick up its sighting lines and come down the coast.'

As he said this, his finger finished its meandering. It now stopped on a small inlet marked on the map about twenty miles south of Wick.

'This is our landing place, Hartmann. I can tell you that now. You may have thought me strange for not giving you our journey's end before but I've had my reasons for acting as I have. But we are close to it now and there will be a strong tide running soon and when this storm hits us we'll be fighting a following sea. If the weather gods will it, we shall reach this inlet by the early hours of tomorrow.'

There was a silence as Hartmann carefully studied the chart.

'But there is nothing marked there, sir,' he replied at last, 'just the mouth of the river. There's no village on the chart there or anywhere near it. Nothing. How are we to land our cargo?'

'Have no worries on that, Master. It is a sheltered spot and I've been assured that we'll be roped into a wharf that our clients will have made. I've no doubt there will be men enough to unload us.'

Hartmann took a step backwards and gave Zweig a look that managed to combine a respectful concern with his natural obedience.

'We have sailed together these ten years or more, sir,' he said quietly, 'and with much success. But will you not tell me why we are coming here?' Hartmann hesitated for a moment and then added more nervously, 'and what we carry?'

'All in good time, Master. Know enough for the present. But have the men check those barrels again. I've heard you say yourself that the greater the calm the greater the storm. I've seen these signs before and that's no ordinary storm that approaches. We shall be shaken like a mouse in a catspaw before long and if those barrels aren't secure we won't be going home. Yes, double the bindings if we still have the time. But tell the men to employ no naked flames down there, just lanterns.'

They returned on deck to where the hands were lashing down spars and checking the boats. Although a feather would still have dropped like a stone in the static air, Zweig shortened yet more sail and sent a further man aft to the wheel.

As the daylight fell, Sophie came on deck. She had heard the shouted orders and sensed the tension above her, increasingly certain of the sense of latent crisis. She now stood by the stairwell canopy as the temperature plunged and darkness swallowed the ship. Around her she saw men glance up and nod to each other towards where a swirling, evil-looking black mass was growing ever larger behind them.

Before it had dropped the wind had come from the north but the slight breeze that came to them now was from the east. It had begun to freshen when Kittzinger, one of the topmen that had been sent up to bring in yet more sail, threw an arm urgently off the starboard beam and yelled to the deck below.

'Land! Land! A light there!'

In an instant Zweig had a telescope up to his eye and had found the faint flicker.

'This is bad, Hartmann,' he said urgently, 'that must be the Urquhain beacon at Dunbeaton Head. We are far closer in than we thought. This cursed tide and the swell have been pushing us all the time. We've been making no way – we've missed our course for Wick and drifted further south. How long do we have before that black hell is on us? We must bring our head up before it hits. There's not a man amongst us that can't see the danger here – if we're blown down onto that lee shore we'll find nothing but a graveyard of rocks.'

Even as he said this the wind was increasing by the second and as the sails now filled the ship sprang forward in the churning sea like a crazed bull released from its pen. Two short minutes later, the full force of the gale was on them, shaking the ship with a terrifying savagery. Zweig had turned and was running aft to where two men struggled to hold the wheel when he saw Sophie standing at the rail. As he approached her, the ship gave a huge lurch and Zweig snatched at a handhold and spoke to her in a tone that left no room for discussion.

'You must go below, Sophie. We are in for some bad weather here.'

'Bad weather? I have seen the faces of your crew. They tell a different story. Bad weather is the least of what they expect. I am here to see the end of your mad adventures, Zweig. God may yet have a hand in your plans.'

Zweig smiled and leant towards her, suddenly calmer and yet still utterly forceful.

'There will be no end here, Sophie. You will wait in vain. Now go below, please. There will be much to occupy us. The men have enough to do without worrying about you.'

Sophie began to bridle but the weight of Zweig's personality brooked no argument. She turned and carefully retreated back down the bucking stairwell.

* * *

Lord Dunbeath sat at a round table in the window of the great dining salon. He was reading a small leather-covered book as Annie ladled soup into his bowl, seemingly oblivious to the storm that now screamed outside.

'It's a terrible night, my lord,' Annie said, glancing up as lightning ripped across the sky, 'did you not see it earlier? Not a breath of wind. Now this. By Saint Columba, I hope there are no fishing boats still out.'

'I have the roof closed in the observatory,' said Dunbeath flatly, turning over a page. 'I shall open it later. There will be enough moonlight for me to take my readings and I'll be working late. That's enough now, Annie. You may go to your bed.'

* * *

The Schwarzsturmvogel shook like a cornered rat. Zweig had set and reset his sails three times in under an hour and yet the ship still refused to slow its sideways slew towards the cliffs and gullies of the Caithness coast. Deep in the pit of his stomach Zweig saw the signs only too clearly and he knew well that he would be taken to account for the shallow draft of his boat – much as this was an advantage in the approaches to Königsberg so it would send them skidding into the lee shore in this raging sea.

The wind had been rising with each passing minute and it now screamed in the rigging with all the mad vengeance of a spiteful phantom. Around them, the sea was being whipped to a foam-flecked horror and an unremitting swirl of spindrift lashed the deck and weighed still further the sodden sails. Exhausted and half drowned, the men glanced frequently at the ever-closing distance between themselves and the terrifying rock-lined coast.

Zweig called his sailing master over.

'We'll play another card, Hartmann,' he yelled against the howl of the storm, dashing spray from his face. 'We shall beat this inferno yet. Take in all the sails but then prepare to bend on every scrap of foresail we possess. Just foresail. When you have that ready, drop a canvas sea anchor from the bow on my order. That should bring the head round. Then spread everything you have for'ard. The staysail, the topmast staysail, the jib. Even the skyscraper and the stargazer if you can set them. Yes, I know, much of it will be carried away but we should be pointing up by then. Be ready to cut them away and bend on the for'ard storm-sails when her head's up. Then let the anchor go. If we can just round that headland we may escape this yet.'

The Master nodded and ran forward, bellowing orders as he went.

'Schnapps,' shouted Zweig, waving at the boy to come over to him, 'go below and tell the cook to dowse his fire. Cold fare until this is over. And Schnapps ...' he looked down at the boy's frightful colour and smiled as he shouted in his ear '... have no fear, youngster, we've been in worse spots than this.' The child grinned and scampered to the stairwell. He slid down the handrails and ran into the galley to where the cook was lashing down his pots and plates with all the urgency of an octopus hiding its young.

'Captain's orders, Mr Cook. Dowse the galley fire, please.'

Above them the topmast crew clung desperately to the yardarms as they fought to furl the sails. A few minutes later, all was away but with the sails now completely reefed the ship was picking up ever greater speed. It was now hurtling sideways towards a wide bay when a shout went up from the helmsman.

'She's not responding, sir! She won't answer!'

Zweig ignored the man's cries and held up an arm. The foredeck crew waited for the signal, grimly holding on, lashed by the torrential waves that fell over them. Their anxious faces turned towards their captain.

'Now!' shouted Zweig, bringing his arm down. Hartmann and his crew reacted as one and with the sea anchor flung into the turmoil, the sails were spread, the flapping canvas howling as the sheets tightened. The ship shuddered, shaken by the sudden change of direction, and the stern swung round as the foresails filled. The Schwarzsturmvogel's head now pointed up and the ship momentarily seemed to be making way. A great cheer went up from the crew above the scream of the wind, and the men looked back to where Zweig stood, his eyes squinting into the slashing gale, each of them certain that their fabled captain had found a way to safety.

It was at that precise moment that the ship struck the first of the underwater rocks.

The stern hit first and came to a standstill. Then the rest of the ship swung round, swept forward by the mountainous waves. Sideways on now, the whole vessel struck and rode high on the reef, up and up until, for long seconds, it seemed to rest there as if uncertain what to do. Then, with a terrible grinding shriek, it collapsed onto a further row of the evil black mass. As suddenly as it had hit, the ship came to a complete halt, now fallen towards the land yet still high out of the water.

There was chaos on board. The impact had flung men to the deck and many slid towards the rail, snatching desperately at anything that came to hand. Some were swept clean through by the weight of the waves that pounded the static ship. The more fortunate clutched at ropes or posts. But, even in the midst of the mayhem, time seemed to stop and every man now looked up to where the masts shook forwards and then back again with a violence that had only one end. They gave a great quiver once more, cracked, then wrenched and groaned as they sheared away under the impossible force of the ship's sudden end. First one and then the other gave and in seconds both were in the foaming sea like so much loose lumber.

Zweig was the first to recover. In an instant he was on his feet, his legs bent on the sloping deck. He took in their position with a sideways glance and began to run aft.

Below deck was yet further catastrophe. The ship's cook had a scuttlebutt of water lifted to drown the galley fire when the ship had struck. His balance completely lost, he'd been hurled off his feet into a crossbeam and he now he lay unconscious, red hot charcoal from the fire scattered around him. In seconds a smashed lantern flared up from its spilt oil and in another blink there were leaping flames, fanned by the screaming wind that made its way below decks. Before a minute was out, even the galley furniture was ablaze.

* * *

Dunbeath leant down to make a note and then returned to the eyepiece of the enormous telescope. He looked through it as clouds flew wildly across the image. He focused again to take a further reading. From behind him came a loud banging on the observatory door.

'Come quickly! You must come, my lord.' Annie was yelling frantically. 'There's a ship on the rocks. They're coming down from Dunbeaton now with ropes. Will you no come and help?'

'Go away woman,' replied Dunbeath with a growl, 'what's it to me if they live or die?'

'Sir, sir!' Annie was shouting in her panic. 'Please, you must come. There may be a chance for them yet.' Desperate for him to take notice she threw caution to the wind. 'What's your work for, my lord, if it isn't to save poor sailors' lives?'

'Go away,' Dunbeath called back again, more quietly this time as he coolly put his eye to the brass lenspiece. Then he muttered to himself. 'Save lives? That's good. They have God to worry about that. I'm about winning the Longitude Prize.'

* * *

The Schwarzsturmvogel lay some three hundred yards from the shore at the Dunbeaton end of the bay's wide sweep. It was now in its death throes, locked in the open jaw of two massive lines of rocks whose black teeth would appear above the waves and then

71

be lost from sight again as the sea poured in to cover them up once more. The ship was broken now, listing badly, and as they stood, huddled together on the shore, the villagers could see the crew on its sloping deck, fighting to free the boats. They watched as a man raised and then brought down an axe on the bindings of a tender – but no sooner had he severed the last of the ropes than a gigantic breaker smashed into the ship's side and snatched up the boat, hurling it far out towards the shore with no more drama than a child tossing a ball.

The Master had called two sailors over to him and together they'd worked their way to the aft rail. They were now attempting to launch a rescue rocket with a line attached, a novelty that Zweig had been sold by an engineer in Königsberg after Kant's ship had sunk. They had never tried it before and the crew now devoured Hartmann with their agonized looks, praying that he had taken the launching instructions seriously.

'Where do we point it, Master?' screamed one of the assistants above the deranged roar of the gale.

'Point it high,' bellowed Hartmann, lifting his arm at a sharp angle, 'high – let the wind take it to the shore.'

Hartmann made a final adjustment and staggered to the wheel. He held it to steady himself and then wrapped the lighting cord around his wrist. He braced himself and gave a firm heave. The friction plate sparked and to his amazement and relief the rocket shot manically upwards, high into the night sky, a wild trail of sparks and flames gushing behind it. There were many hearts that soared along with it but these same hearts were broken almost immediately as it became clear that the rocket's very speed had taken it too high through the wind. It now burnt out in a blazing flash, well before it reached the waiting rescuers on the shore.

* * *

Dunbeath jerked his head away from the brass eyepiece, blinded by the sudden glare that had pierced the storm's blackness. In an instant the ever-burning embers of the Urquhain Rage flared up in him unchecked. Who were these damned people that had stopped him taking a reading? He rubbed his eye and stepped back to the telescope. He had moved to adjust the setting when a vast sheet of lightning drenched the bay and he looked coldly down at the ship in the sudden glare, a couple of furlongs or more off the village, and saw it held fast in the murderous grip of two lines of hidden rock. He looked again, expressionless and without a trace of concern for the people that must be so terrified on board. Instead, a righteous anger surged through him once more and with it came a poisonous, vengeful wish came to see for himself the stupid vandals that had interrupted his vital research.

He lowered the great telescope until it pointed downwards, now towards the ship. He swiveled the eyepiece around for the shortness of the new focus and put his eye to it again. In the moonlight he could see blurred images of panicked sailors, running on the listing deck and he stepped back and brought the minor adjustment bar down.

Now he had it in focus. He swung the image right and slowly ranged over the mayhem the terrible storm had wreaked. He moved right again and came to a sudden stop. Filling the image was a tall, striking figure, standing with his arms crossed in front of him, deep in thought. The man's air of authority was extraordinary. Instead of sharing in the crew's blind confusion there was something almost supernaturally calm about him and Dunbeath watched in amazement as he remained, almost rooted to the spot, completely still amongst the chaos.

Dunbeath focused again. He now saw the man look up as two sailors had clearly answered an order and were bringing a woman to stand in front of him, their hands under her arms. She was covered only in a long white dress and as she came into the foreshortened image Dunbeath could see that she was a young, slim girl. And, extraordinarily beautiful.

At an order from the man the sailors began to strap lifesavers around the girl's waist and chest and a small wooden spar across the shoulders at the back of her neck. They fastened them expertly and finished by tightening light ropes under her arms.

Dunbeath then saw the man lean forward to say something in her ear. He spoke for some seconds. She seemed rigid as she heard him out and made no sign of responding. Dunbeath could only imagine that she was frozen in terror.

The tall man hesitated for a second. Then he moved his head forward once more. Again he leant down as if to say something in her ear; but now he turned his head slowly towards her - and kissed her cheek.

The girl's manner changed in an instant. She lifted her head with a sudden, furious movement and took a step backwards. Then she angrily wrenched her arm from the sailor's grip and Dunbeath saw as she brought it high above her shoulder. She seemed to twist to stare upwards, full into the man's eyes and then brought the flat of her hand down hard on the side of his face. The giant seemed to falter for a second but immediately recovered himself and smiled at her in reply.

Dunbeath pressed closer to the eyepiece, astonished that he could be seeing a fight at a time like this. Surely this was no time to be settling scores, they would all be dead before the hour was out? To his amazement he then saw the man nod at the girl with the deepest show of respect. He watched him as he bent down and picked her up with no more effort than a mother would use to lift a baby. He then walked to the side of the ship and gently held her over the rail, still struggling wildly. Dunbeath focused again and saw that the man was now standing still, steadying himself, evidently waiting for the right moment. The girl continued to buck and twist in his arms but she might have been a small dog for all the trouble she gave him. A monstrous wave swept over the ship and Dunbeath saw the man bend down and carefully drop the figure over the side and into its path.

Dunbeath refocused the telescope for a broader view. It was obvious that the ship couldn't last much longer, stuck fast on the rocks and with the full force of the storm shrieking into its side. Enormous waves were now pounding the stricken vessel like a blacksmith's hammer and as Dunbeath watched he knew that the rocks beneath it would be grinding the planks out of the ship's hull with all the swift certainty of a Dunbeaton fisherman gutting a good catch.

Dunbeath had seen enough. He stepped away from the telescope and picked up his notes, quite sure that the end must be near. The ship would break up before dawn rose and he saw little point in it interrupting his work any longer.

* * *

Onboard Zweig was like a man reborn. There was no calmness about him now as he called his men towards him, shouting orders as he did so.

'Bring up a long cable from below. Enough to reach the shore,' he bellowed.

Before long the thick rope was being passed up and two men were then ordered to attach the lightest cord they could find to its end. Zweig inspected their work, pulling hard at where the two lines met. He satisfied himself that the join would hold and then ripped off his heavy weather jacket and sea boots. The crew looked at him with disbelief and yet with a hope born of despair. He tied the light line around his waist.

'Hartmann,' he yelled in the Master's ear above the howl of the gale, 'I shall swim for it. When I'm on the shore I'll get those people there to pull the cable down. When we have it secure at that end, tighten it around the capstan. Lift it clear of the waves and then send the men down.'

Zweig took no notice of Hartmann's feeble attempt to restrain him and simply checked again that the light line was tight around his waist and trailing behind him. Then, without a backward glance, he jumped up on the rail and flung himself into the boiling sea.

At first he swam strongly towards the beach. He made a hundred yards and every man on board urged him forward. With pounding hearts they would see his head break surface and then a collective prayer would be muttered when it disappeared once again. With each stroke he made, the line fed out and Zweig's men could only guess at the drag he must have been fighting. At intervals they would see him stop and then desperately tread water as he leant backwards to manhandle the thin rope towards him. With it pooled beneath him he would strike out for the shore once more.

Another hundred yards was gained. As each inch played out the sailors cheered more wildly. Any other man would have been spent by now but his crew knew that their captain's huge strength, and his unbreakable determination, were driving him on to success or death. Nearer to the beach the breakers grew ever larger and Zweig would be frequently lost to the men's view for half a minute or more. Then he'd reappear and they'd see an arm come over for yet another stroke. Yard by yard he closed on the beach. There could only be thirty or forty left.

Just as the onlookers began to dare that Zweig might succeed, the crazy turmoil of the disturbed surf sucked him onto a line of hidden rocks close to the shore. Even the captain's great strength was no match for the weight of water that forced him below the surface and in an instant he was pummeled and tossed before being spat out, blood streaming from a great gash to his head, lifeless, face down in the foam.

The villagers knew the reef and had seen the disaster. Those closest to the water's edge pointed urgently to the prone body and Mona McLeish snatched up a line and tied it round her son's chest.

'Go, James, you may save him yet,' she shouted and, with a push that left no argument, the boy plunged in to swim the short distance to where Zweig's body was floating. Yet even though it was so close to the beach James was nearly spent as he reached Zweig and he shot out a desperate arm to grab at his half sunk frame. The villagers saw his hand close about Zweig's shirt and with a huge roar they ran backwards with the rope, pulling the two men to the shore.

They now lay on the beach, James shattered by the effort and quite still as his mother, proud of him beyond measure, rubbed his back. Bit by bit his breathing steadied.

Zweig was unconscious and blood streamed unchecked from a long wound over his right eye. He had been left on his side, higher on the beach, as the villagers took the line from around him and started the long operation of pulling it in. The light rope was little trouble but once the weight of the heavy cable followed their real work began. But they gained, manhandling it yard by yard through the turbulent water, the rope bucking and jumping as if a wild animal was at its end. At last the cable reached the shore and once they had enough of it looped on the beach, a boy was sent up the side of a large boulder with it.

'Take it twice around the top,' shouted Andrew McLeish. 'Now loop it round the rest of the line!'

Strong hands pulled at it until the villagers were sure they had it securely anchored. Once done, the little group turned and waved frantically to the ship.

On board a great cheer went up from the crew and the Master gave out brisk orders. Their end of the cable was quickly wrapped around the capstan and the villagers could see the men run to snatch up the winch's poles. A dozen turns later and the slack in the line had been drawn smartly into the capstan's rotating barrel.

Hartmann looked on as the cable started to tighten and his

mind began to turn to the future – and the chances of salvage and insurance. He left the men to their long task at the ratchet and raced below to retrieve the ship's logbook and other papers, vital if there was ever to be a claim for the lost ship. He ran down the companionway towards Zweig's cabin but twenty steps were enough for him to become aware of the other disaster that was engulfing the ship. He pushed open a cabin door, only to be immediately forced backwards by the huge sheet of flame that leapt out to meet him.

Yet more of the same, he thought to himself, resigned to seeing all their troubles coming at once - there was little he could do about the blaze, and anyway the poor old barky could have little time left. If there was ever to be a tomorrow, then such things as claims would have to take care of themselves.

He went back the way he had come, climbing the lurching stairwell and making a slow progress along the angled deck. He saw that the men were finding it difficult to circle the capstan because of the list but they pressed on and yard by yard the line drew gradually tighter. As he approached them Hartmann even allowed himself a second of hope as he saw the cable begin to stretch clear of the surface of the water. Each turn of the barrel was lifting the hearts of the crew and a few of them now started to cluster at the rail, desperate to be climbing down the rope.

On the beach the villagers were shouting that the line was tight at their end. They now waved wildly to the ship, screaming that the crew should start to make their escape. They were all standing, looking towards the wreck, so distracted by their yelling that not one of them had noticed that a few yards behind them Zweig had given a strangled cough and then retched seawater. Slowly his gasping settled and his mind began the long ordeal of clearing its confusion. He pushed himself up onto an elbow, his senses fighting to understand how sand could be beneath him, bewildered at not being in the sea. Gradually he took in the cluster of villagers in front of him. He heard them as they shouted to the ship and he rose unsteadily to his feet and stumbled towards them. The mists began to dissolve. He saw the cable he had brought to the shore, now clear of the water's surface. Then he saw his doomed ship. He looked towards it, squinting to bring it into focus.

In an instant he recoiled in horror. Through the slashing rain that drove into his face he'd seen the tongues of fire as they shot through the deck gratings. Then he saw the angry redness of the lower decks, showing through an open port lid. In spite of his injury the danger was obvious and he raced wildly towards the water's edge, waving frantically to the tiny figures on the angled deck and screaming into the fury of the gale.

'Fire! Fire! No! Jump for God's sake. Get in the water. Get clear of it!'

The villagers had parted to let him through. Now they watched him as he repeatedly flung an arm out in a series of frantic orders that his men should jump.

A second later they turned back to look out to sea as an enormous rumble came to them above the shriek of the storm. This was followed immediately by a flash of intense light and then a colossal explosion lit up the night sky. The ship had exploded. No, it had virtually vapourised. And the crew with it. Three hundred yards away on the shore, Zweig was knocked to the ground by the blast and slipped gratefully into a deep unconsciousness.

The Schwarzsturmvogel's cargo was no longer a mystery.

* * *

There was little the villagers could do but carry Zweig back to Dunbeaton. Flesh from a great gash hung down over his face and Mona McLeish took off her shawl and bound it gently around his head.

Together, four men put their arms under his great frame and

linked hands. They lifted him and set off, half sideways and half shuffling, for the short distance back to the village.

Once they were there Zweig was taken to the McLeish's cottage and the villagers laid him out on a simple bed of rushes in front of the peat fire.

Mona now sat beside him, weeping, praying, bandaging his head, rubbing his hands, substituting her grief for her dead son into a crazed determination that Alexis Zweig might live.

* * *

When Annie had left Dunbeath in the Grey Tower she'd hurried down to fetch her shawl and then set out for where she'd seen the villagers shouting on the shoreline. She'd taken the path through the dunes and as she'd looked over at the little group she thought she saw a rope rising above the maddened surface of the waves. She struggled forward against the ferocious wind and cursed Dunbeath's callousness again and again, bitter that her own poor people were doing their best to help the crew, but that he, with so much, should care so little. Once more she had looked out to the wrecked ship with its tiny, frenzied figures and imagined what horrors those poor men must be suffering.

As Annie lifted her head from the howling wind and looked at the sea's crazed confusion she suddenly stopped. She held her hand over her eyes for protection and looked again. What was that being hurled among the waves, close in to the shore? She squinted again through the driving rain, wondering frantically if she'd seen something moving there. Again, she thought she saw a long white form. Did something rise there?. Was that an arm? Could it be possible that a person was struggling in the water?

She left the dunes and ran down towards the beach. The object was being driven away from the ship by the incoming breakers and as she came onto the sand she saw again that there was a movement from it. Yes, it was definitely an arm. It could only be someone making a despairing attempt at a stroke.

Without a thought for her own safety Annie raced into the sea. Soon the whirling surf was up to her chest. Now she was alongside the figure. Her outstretched hand caught hold of some white cloth – yes, it was a person. And still alive, a young woman! At last she had the figure under the arms and she began the long task of dragging the body backwards through the waves. She stumbled twice, falling back under the water, terrifying herself. But she clung on and, step by step, she made progress. Just as her strength began to leave her, she felt the suck of the backsurge weaken and with a final effort Annie pulled the poor creature up onto the sand. The old woman had completely exhausted herself and she lay now on the beach, her chest heaving as she desperately tried to get her wind back. She breathed deeply, once, twice.

And then the night sky lit up and a huge roar echoed around the bay.

Annie gasped and sat up quickly to look out to sea. The ship had gone, utterly destroyed. She turned back towards the girl she'd saved and saw that she was a beautiful young thing – and a garbled prayer of thanks poured from the old housekeeper that the poor child had been spared.

Annie got to her feet and stared out to where a few timbers sparked and smouldered in the water. Then she looked back to the pathetic figure in the white dress that lay at her feet on the sand. The old woman had had very little to love in her childless existence and an unshakable determination now rose in her that this lovely girl shouldn't die. She opened the clasp knife that hung from her waist and sliced through the livesaver's ropes. She managed to get her arm about the girl and, half carrying and half dragging her, she moved the limp figure along the beach and up the steps to the castle entrance. At last she had her inside and by the big fire in her kitchen.

She gently lay Sophie on the floor as close to the warmth as she dared and tore off her soaked dress. Carefully she rubbed her with a towel. At some point Annie remembered that she'd heard that drowning people should be on their side and as she moved Sophie a great shake went through the girl and she began to cough and choke. Then she was still though, and lay exhausted on the floor, panting whilst the housekeeper put dry clothes on her.

As her strength returned Sophie pushed herself up onto an elbow. She looked at Annie's smiling face but seemed to be so shocked and bewildered that she stared uncomprehendingly at the kindly old woman. Nothing made sense to her and she broke down in tears, utterly distressed and beaten, crying out in hysterical and sob-ridden bursts of German. Annie hugged and gently rocked her, urging her to be calm.

The door opened and Dunbeath came in. He glanced down at the two women and walked casually past them to where a barrel of whisky stood. He drew off a glass.

'What's she saying, Master? I cannae understand the poor wee thing.'

'She's crying for her mother,' he said flatly.

Without another word he turned and strode back towards the Grey Tower.

Chapter 7

As the first pink rays of dawn spread over the ancient castle the storm began to blow itself out. Just as the violence of the previous day had seemed to rise from nothing so the wind now dropped again to the merest breeze and thin winter sunshine broke through the heavy cloud and washed gently over Dunbeaton Bay. The sea had calmed and its surface now sparkled in the brightness. Even the castle's grim granite seemed to come alive as the soft light bounced off the tiny specks of quartz on the face of the stone, and the horrors of the previous night, just a few short hours before, now seemed impossible.

In the kitchen Annie sat at her table, smiling yet again as she watched Sophie asleep in front of the fire. The old housekeeper had woken often during the night, panicked that her exquisite flotsam was suffering and she had frequently jumped up to adjust a blanket or build up the flames in the grate.

Sophie's eyes flickered and then opened. She lay still for a moment, gazing at the red embers in the fire before she jerked feverishly upright, blinking wildly as she looked about her.

Annie came quickly over.

'Oh, hush, hush, my heart. Lie down. You're safe here.'

Sophie blinked again, and then replied in heavily accented English.

'Who are you? Where is this?'

'Why, you're in the Castle of Beath, my lovely one. In Scotland. Do you not remember?'

'Scotland?' Sophie turned away and then lapsed into German. 'So that was where the lunatic was taking us.'

'Let me make you some porridge. You will need to eat to get your strength back.'

As Annie began to prepare the oats Dunbeath strode into the room, an open letter in his hand. He glanced down at Sophie but then turned away to speak to Annie.

'Your cousin, McKay, returned from Edinburgh this morning. I saw him as he was walking to the castle. We shall be having company soon. I wrote to a friend of mine, Mr David Hume, inviting him to visit and he's written back to say that he will be with us in a month's time. He has commitments, he says, and could not come any earlier. Give him the Blue Room when he arrives. You will have to make it ready.'

'Company you say? A friend? Well, I am very glad for you, my lord. Aye, I shall make his room most welcome. But will you no say something to this poor child? I found her in the water last night, more dead than alive.'

Dunbeath looked coolly down at the girl.

'Where are you from?'

'Königsberg. It is in Prussia. Do you speak our language?'

'Yes, of course,' Dunbeath replied in German. 'I am a man of science. The literature is often in your tongue.'

'I speak English,' she replied, also in German. 'My grandfather was from Scotland. How strange I should find myself here. My father taught us English and we spoke it at home. We have a Scottish name but my father changed the spelling.'

Dunbeath had already wearied of this trivial exchange and had turned to leave. Sophie quickly continued.

'Can you tell me how I came to be here, sir? There was a terrible storm. We were on the rocks. I remember I was thrown into the sea.'

'Annie McKay here found you. She says you had nearly drowned. You owe her your life.'

Sophie looked quickly towards the housekeeper.

'Yes, yes, I do.'

She paused and then turned back to Dunbeath.

'And the ship? Did it sink?'

'Sink? Yes, of course. It blew up. Exploded.'

'Exploded? Why would it explode?'

Dunbeath looked down at her, his indifference now replaced

by a sardonic gaze.

'You don't know? How strange. You sailed in her but you weren't aware of the cargo.' His head tilted slightly and he sniffed. 'I presume it went up because it was full of gunpowder. Now, why would that be?'

Sophie answered quietly.

'I don't know.' She looked away, silent in thought. Then her gaze moved back to Dunbeath.

'Do you know what became of the crew, sir? Was anyone killed?'

Dunbeath started as if hesitant to break the news. Then his studied disdain for the human race returned.

'Yes. They all were.'

'All? All?'

Sophie sat up straight, suddenly completely revitalised by this news. She threw back the blanket and jumped to her feet. Annie had been unable to follow their German conversation and she now looked up in amazement at the sight of Sophie so apparently recovered. Not half a minute ago she had seemed closer to death than to life but now the girl held her arms in the air and began to dance around the room, waving wildly. As she did so she laughed and sang, repeating the same phrase again and again.

'Alle gestorben! Alle gestorben! Zweig ist tot! Zweig ist tot!'

Dunbeath stood as if contemplating her performance for a moment before he glanced blankly at Annie and walked briskly out of the room for his observatory. As he left the room Sophie came to a sudden stop and her smile faded. She stared into space.

'But, poor Schnapps. Poor Schnapps.'

* * *

Although it wasn't yet noon the people of Dunbeaton and the surrounding villages had been at their work since the wind had dropped in the early hours. Taking advantage of the change in the storm's ferocity they had launched their boats and had been scouring the surface of the water for anything to be found of salvage value. Occasionally they'd come across a half submerged body amongst the wreckage and would put a rope around it and drag the poor dead thing to the shore. A line of burnt and mutilated sailors now lay on the beach, their pockets carefully emptied.

In Dunbeaton itself Mona continued to watch over Zweig's unconscious figure. His breathing continued to be dangerously shallow and yet he would half rise every so often and mutter orders as if he was still fighting for his ship. Then he would fall back with Mona's hand behind his damaged head and escape again into a deep black sleep.

Outside the cottage a pile of recovered items grew by the hour as Andrew McLeish brought in blocks and shackles, cordage and even lengths of ragged sailcloth from the bay. After a particularly fruitful journey he left his work and came into the cottage to sit watching Mona as she bathed Zweig's head.

'How does he do?' he asked in a low voice.

'I have sat with him all night and I fear for …' Mona stopped her reply and looked up in alarm. From outside the cottage there had come a sudden clatter of horses' hooves and then loud voices and shouted orders, given out in angry, arrogant tones. And unmistakably English accents.

'Oh God, no! Redcoats! Quick Andrew, help me drag the poor man over there.'

They both jumped to their feet and with little thought for Zweig's comfort they pulled him quickly to the darkness of a corner.

Mona threw nets and bedding over him and then glared up at her husband with a face of fierce defiance.

'Why are the soldiers here?' she whispered urgently.

'They'll have heard about the explosion. They probably think we had something to do with the ship coming here. What shall I tell them?'

'Just tell them that they all died,' Mona hissed with a show of savage maternal spirit. She looked down at Zweig's livid red pallor as she covered his head and vehemently whispered at him.

'They won't have you. You hear me? Nor will you die. I'll not have another death!' She looked up again at her husband. 'Don't tell them about him. Don't tell anyone. Nobody, you hear! Nobody.'

The English cavalry had come down from the softness of the dunes onto the hard cobbles of the old hamlet and as they wheeled to a halt the stamp of the horses was mixed with the loud, grating orders that their officer was now bellowing out. Raised voices seemed to come naturally to these soldiers. Many of the most feared of English regiments had been rushed to Scotland when the Jacobite uprising had begun to take root but though Harrington's 17th Dragoons had been stationed in Caithness for only five months they'd already established a particular reputation for intolerance and suppression. Nobody looking at them now could be in doubt about the meaning of their presumptuous manner. It was that of an occupying army.

At the head of the troop was Major Enoch Sharrocks, a square, bullnecked man who pulled at his reins as he looked down at Dunbeaton's huddle of cottages, a sneer of distaste on his face. His reputation for harshness was well earned and had gone before him to even such isolated villages as this one. It took only one glance at his mean and furious face to see the loathing a brutalised bully had for his victims. Since he'd arrived it had become plain to anyone that had tried to deal with him that there burned within him a deep suspicion of all Scots.

Looking down now he saw a small boy trying to scuttle away.

'Hey, you,' he barked, 'come here! Get me someone who saw the explosion last night.'

'I'll get my uncle,' stammered the frightened boy as he backed away towards the McLeish's cottage. The child turned and ran the short distance to their door. He thrust it open and blurted out the officer's demand into the gloom. When she heard this, Mona looked up and nodded grimly at her husband to go out and face the redcoats.

Andrew McLeish emerged blinking from the dark interior of the cottage. As he approached Sharrocks's horse the major bawled down at him.

'Did you see what happened last night?'

'Aye. That I did.'

'You saw the explosion?'

'Aye.'

'What were you doing having that vessel come here?'

'It was no coming here. Can you no see the rocks out there? They're death to anyone that doesn't know them as we do. And anyway we havena way to land a ship of that size. Coming here? Why they were fighting to get her out of the bay. We were just trying to save the poor boys' lives, that's all.'

Sharrocks stared angrily down at him in silence. Then he looked out to sea again.

'How many of them got ashore?'

'None,' said McLeish, 'unless you count those there,' and he waved an arm towards the long line of corpses on the sand. 'Why don't you take a look at what's left of them. There's hardly one that all of a piece. Blown apart they were. Come ashore? You cannae have a brain if you think that.'

Sharrocks immediately brought his attention back to McLeish and in an instant fury his fingers closed tightly about his riding crop. He was about to lift it to deal with McLeish's insolence when a dismounted trooper called over to him from the pile of salvage he'd been sorting through. He now held up a smashed section of wood from the stern of a rowing boat.

'Sir. This could be the vessel's name. Looks like that stupid

German writing to me.'

'Schwarzsturmvogel.' Sharrocks slowly read the gothic script, his brow furrowed with the effort. 'Bring that with you, man.'

He shot an ominous last glance at Andrew McLeish and wheeled his horse's head. The sergeant gave out a final shouted order and the troop rode back up towards the dunes.

* * *

Dunbeath had been in the observatory for some hours. Yet again he swung the great telescope as he measured a planetary distance. He made a detailed note of his finding.

The door opened quietly and Sophie came hesitantly into the room. She gazed in fascination as she looked about herself and then walked lightly over to where a small table stood against a wall, buckling under the weight of a carelessly piled stack of books. Dunbeath seemed not to have noticed her. If he had, he made no comment. There was silence. Then Sophie picked up a book written in German that covered the size and nature of Saturn's five moons. She turned the pages for a time, seemingly absorbed in what she was reading, and then looked towards where Dunbeath squinted through his eyepiece.

'What are you doing, my lord?' she asked shyly. 'What is your work?'

Without taking his eye from the telescope Dunbeath immediately replied in a low, commanding tone.

'You are not to speak. Not now. Not ever.'

* * *

By late that afternoon, Zweig was dying. He had appeared to rally for a short period earlier in the day but now, as the sparse sunshine faded at the single window and darkness fell in the tiny cottage, his breathing became more laboured and with each passing minute his fever rose. Mona had not left his side all day and as she gently wiped his face, slick with sweat, she constantly urged him not to slip away.

The last of the daylight fell across Zweig's fretting body as her husband opened the door of the cottage and looked across at the prostrate figure as he came into the room.

'No better?'

'Oh, Andrew. Worse,' she whispered. 'There doesn't seem to be any fight left in him. It's almost as if he's willing himself to die.' She bathed Zweig's face again and looked down at his sick grey pallor.

'You poor man. You've lost everything haven't you? Your ship, your crew, your cargo. Everybody you knew is dead. Perhaps you're right to let go.'

'We have the sailors laid out on the beach,' Andrew McLeish said after a pause. 'What injuries they have, Mona! I've never seen anything like it. Thank God, they must have all died together in an instant. The minister is coming tomorrow from Lochanairlie and we shall bury them in the forenoon. But you say that everyone on board was killed – I'm not so sure that's right, Mona. Annie McKay was down here earlier getting his lordship's supper and she told me they had one of them alive up at the castle. A girl she found in the water. Not a scratch on her.'

As he said this Zweig's breathing came to a sudden stop. His neck seemed to stiffen and his head rose fractionally from the rushes.

Then his eyes snapped open.

* * *

Seven miles to the south west of the Castle of Beath the exquisite baroque beauty of Craigleven sat on a slight rise in the landscape. The long straight drive to the great house began at the Lybster to Wick turnpike and passed between a pair of classical lodges before cutting through the treeless Caithness countryside and widening as it reached the mansion's formal gardens.

Built in the 1690s by Sir Donald Grant, a gentleman architect who had spent many years in Holland – and indeed had acted as a go-between at the time of the Restoration – the great house's wide frontage showed how deeply he had understood the design vocabulary that was then in vogue on the Continent. With the passing of the years, its fame had grown and its delicate symmetry and modern comforts had now become the model for a new generation of Scottish dream houses that were the envy of the lairds that still occupied their ancient castles and towers.

After Grant's death Craigleven had descended through marriage to the Duncansby family. The present Viscount Duncansby was an ambitious man who spent his time in London looking for preferment and he had been only too willing to co-operate when approached with the request for a company of Harrington's regiment of horse to be garrisoned there.

Now Major Sharrocks strode fiercely through its beautiful series of enfiladed staterooms. As he reached the last of these a redcoat soldier guarded the final door. Sharrocks stopped as he reached it and knocked hard on its polished walnut surface.

A voice inside called out for him to enter and Sharrocks walked briskly across the high shine of the intricate woodblock floor and came to attention in front of a rococo desk where his commanding officer, Colonel the Honourable George Annesley L'Arquen, rifled listlessly through some papers, the very picture of elegance. Sharrocks stood silently at the desk as L'Arquen continued to flick idly over the pages of a closely written document with a look of utter boredom on his face, occasionally glancing across to check on the fall of his beautiful linen cuff as it extended from the perfectly pressed tailoring of his gorgeous frockcoat.

Although he was his superior, L'Arquen was much younger than Sharrocks. He'd been bought a commission only fifteen years before by his father and since then much family pressure had led to a fast advancement within the regiment, in spite of his limited field experience. Compared to this exquisite figure, Sharrocks was one of the most battle-hardened professionals in the army, a veteran of Dettingen and a man that had literally and figuratively fought his way to promotion. He patiently waited for a minute and then cleared his throat.

L'Arquen looked up as if he had forgotten the knock at the door.

'Ah, Sharrocks. There you are, dusty as ever. Out and about I'll be bound, up to your neck in action. How I envy you, you would not believe how tiresome these endless updates are. I have had to read over as many as twenty pages today already.'

L'Arquen shook his head in exaggerated exhaustion as he looked down at the evidence of the cares of office and then continued in the same languid voice.

'Now, what have you to report? I do not believe you were here earlier when I sent for you.'

'No, sir. Well, you will recall that I was making investigations into the ship that we heard had exploded.'

'Indeed. No, I had not forgotten. Well, what did you find?'

'We established that the ship was driven onto rocks near a fishing village to the north of here called Dunbeaton during last night's great storm. I interviewed some of the villagers and they were all certain that the ship was not making for their bay. It has no deep water, no landing quay and the rocks there are well known to be dangerous. It's more likely that the ship was blown in there by the gale. It was wrecked before it exploded. There were no survivors.'

L'Arquen gazed in silence at Sharrocks with one eyebrow lazily lifted.

'I see. No more?'

'We found the name of the vessel, sir. On the stern of one of its boats.'

'Send a man down to Dundee and tell them to have it traced. It would be useful to find out where the ship came from.'

L'Arquen rose from his desk and went over to where a large map of the area hung on a wall.

'And where was it going?' he said quietly, tracing the coastline with his finger and then moving inland. He tapped a spot a few inches from Craigleven.

'There was a report yesterday that some of the rebel highlanders have been seen not twenty miles from here. The ship was obviously bringing gunpowder for the rebellion – but where was it going to be met?'

L'Arquen's finger wandered up the coast again before returning to tap a large illustration of a castle.

'Now,' he continued, 'who owns this great thing here?'

'The Earl of Dunbeath, sir. He is the largest landowner in the area.'

'Dunbeath?' murmured L'Arquen. 'One of that name was in the Lords with my father some years ago. They are the clan chiefs of the Urquhain – an ancient Scottish line.'

This was enough for Sharrocks.

'Another Scottish bastard allowed to be in London, sir? In the House of Lords! If you'll permit me, sir, but why do we allow it? They are nothing but disloyal bastards, the enemy within. Most of them are nothing more than traitors that want to see us kicked out of here. So they can have their Bonnie Prince damned Charlie on the throne.'

'Yes', said L'Arquen, half to himself, 'an Italian instead of the German that we have now.'

But Sharrocks had reddened with anger, inwardly raging at L'Arquen's high handed treatment of him and his questioning reaction to the report – but submerging his fury under an exaggerated show of duty. He stepped forward in emphasis.

'You are quite right, sir. Where was that damned ship going? Find that and I believe we find the Jacobites. I'd like to take some men and put that village under surveillance. I'm quite sure they know more than they're saying.'

L'Arquen looked coolly away. There was a pause as he considered the request.

'Very well, Sharrocks. But you are to be covert. That means I don't want you or your men to be seen. We're unpopular enough here as it is. You are not to stir up trouble unnecessarily – it just makes these people side with the rebels. We're not at war you know, Sharrocks. Not yet anyway. You may investigate and report back. I'll give you a few weeks to find something. But do not be seen, d'you hear me? And certainly not by that Dunbeath fellow.'

* * *

Much as Annie had prayed, her instinctive love for Sophie was being returned with interest and it was not many days after her rescue that they were sitting on a windowseat, with the old housekeeper laughing away at Sophie's strangled English. She now tossed her head back in a gentle mockery of Sophie's youthful manner and mimicked her strong German accent. But Annie could see that in spite of her playful teasing, Sophie was fast polishing the English that she'd learnt as a child. It was now her greatest hope that the girl would stay at the castle and provide the companionship that she so much longed for.

As they rattled on, they sewed, making clothes for Sophie. Annie looked up and her laugh rang out again as she repeated something that Sophie had just said. In her delight she mentioned this to Dunbeath as he happened to walk past, deep in thought. But the earl didn't even break stride and Annie's face fell, plainly dismayed at his silence.

'His lordship is not one for games,' Sophie said quietly, looking down at her work.

'No, he is not,' replied Annie. 'You will learn, he is not one for others at all. He prefers his own company.'

There was a pause while Sophie completed a line of stitching. She took a deep breath and then embarked on a subject that she knew would be painful for the old woman.

'Annie, would you do something for me? Do you feel you could ask Lord Dunbeath if he would make me a loan of the money I need for a passage back to my home? My poor mother will be desperate to see me again and I fear that it is only a matter of time before rumours of our shipwreck will work their way back to her ears.'

Annie was even more shocked than Sophie imagined she would be. The old housekeeper hadn't given any thought to her beautiful friend having a family or even a past. And now this blow had fallen. Her spirits fell and there was a sad edge to her voce as she replied.

'Oh, I could not do that, my love. I've never known anyone ask such a thing of him. You don't know his lordship – he cares nothing for others' problems. Can you not rest for a while and gather your strength here? Perhaps he will get used to seeing you in time? You might even make yourself useful – and then you can ask him yourself.'

* * *

Time passed and once Zweig had decided to live, there was little that would slow his huge strength and iron determination from completing an almost incredible transformation. It was not yet a month since the fatal wreck that had brought him here, but even in that short time he had progressed from being a hopeless near corpse to the helpful, outwardly cheerful and charming guest that now stood outside the cottage, joking with Mona as he helped her to hang stones to hold down the turf roof. The captain spoke good English from his long experience of trading and just as Mona had restored him, so he was restoring her. Nursing him had been the best of therapies and simply being in the company of his colossal personality was gently easing her grief.

The weather has been kind for some days too and, as she laughed at an idle comment of his, a long-forgotten warmth began to seep through her. She now looked over at him.

'You know I told you that the girl that survived the shipwreck is at the castle down there,' she said, indicating the far end of the bay with a nod of her head. 'Would you like me to get a message to her? I could send word through Lord Dunbeath's housekeeper the next time she comes down here. We've told nobody about you being here for fear it would get back to the English but perhaps you'd like me to speak to Annie now that you're better?'

'No, please don't,' Zweig replied with a cool shrug, fully aware that he was in no position yet to deal with Sophie. 'The girl was just a passenger on my ship and we'd hardly exchanged two words. We were only taking her as far as Dundee so I'm sure she'll complete her journey by land when she's ready. No, I'd rather she didn't know I was alive – she'd probably blame me for her troubles! But thank you for asking me all the same.'

He smiled at Mona with obvious fondness and then looked up at the roof.

'Now, I think you'll find that the turf is secure. Give me something else to do. I have to repay your kindness somehow and I don't think Andrew will ever allow me near a boat!'

Mona laughed and coloured with delight as she thought for a second.

'Well there is a job that needs doing. It'll be very dirty though. I've been asking James to do it for days but he keeps putting it off.'

'Anything. Lead me to it.'

'Well it's over there,' she said, pointing towards the pigsty. 'Poor pigs. They need their bedding replaced. Do you think you could do it?'

'Do it? Why I'm almost a pig myself. Just give me a shovel.'

A few minutes later Zweig was bent double inside the sty and cleaning away the ground mess with a will. He had the old straw outside and he now moved towards the back wall to dig out the soiled earth.

He hummed as he worked, thinking to himself that he'd do the messy job properly for once and 'give the old hull a good scrubbing'. He dug deeper, swinging the spade as best he could in the tiny space. But with his third stroke the blade hit a long thin stone and he pushed it to one side and lifted the shovel again. But an unconscious instinct made him hesitate. He wasn't quite sure why, but something had bothered him. Then he realised that there'd been an odd noise when the metal blade had struck. He tapped the stone again. There was definitely a muffled sound rather than a metallic ring and, curious now, he reached down and pulled the strange shape out of the earth. It was definitely not a stone – it was long and cylindrical and soft to the touch. He picked it up and carried it out into the light. He now saw that whatever it was had been covered by an oiled cloth and then tied up with twine. Intrigued, he looked more closely at it and pulled the string away. He glanced quickly around to see if he was being overlooked and then unrolled the covering. His head dropped in amazement. Lying in his hand was a sight so incredible that he muffled the urge to shout out. It was a beautiful, jewel-encrusted telescope of extraordinary quality. Once glance had been enough to tell him what it was and he looked quickly around once again to check that he hadn't been seen.

Zweig hid the beautiful instrument in the folds of his clothes and walked up behind the cottage and onto the dunes. He climbed for some time until he came to a vantage point from where he could see the castle. He checked once more that he couldn't be seen and then took the telescope out and examined it more closely, running his finger in amazement over the embedded jewels, each one the size of a large ring. He then lifted the gorgeous thing to his eye and focused it on the stones of the castle's roofline. Even to someone as experienced of nautical telescopes as he was, its power amazed him and he slowly moved the enlarged image, first looking through the glass walls into the observatory, then swinging it away to examine minutely the great fortress's layout.

A movement at the castle's land side made him sweep it down and he now saw the greatly magnified image of a carriage coming up to the entrance. A portly man in a deep red coat stepped down by the front door and dug around in his pocket for coins to pay off the driver.

Zweig put the telescope into the inside pocket of his coat and walked back to the cottage, deep in thought, puzzling over where such an unbelievable object could have come from. He wrapped it again in its oilcloth and retied it up with the string. He then hid it under a stone, well away from the cottage and went back to his work, smiling broadly and quietly singing a snatch of folk song:

'Wie bist du doch so schon, O du weite, weite Welt.'

'How jolly is life. And how wide is the world'

Chapter 8

David Hume gave an exhausted last look at the departing carriage and put the remaining coins back in the pocket of his coat. Glancing down to the ground he checked yet again that the driver had set down all his many pieces of baggage.

He took a step backwards and gazed with fascinated distaste at the huge blocks of joyless granite that made up the castle's intimidating entrance and then at the forbidding front door, set uninvitingly deep within the sharply cut masonry. But in spite of the grimness of the vast frontage that towered over him, he breathed deeply – at last, his hideous trial by coach was over. He had returned from his duty to the mad Marquis after a painful few weeks of effort and had then left Edinburgh twelve days ago for a journey that should have taken no more than four or five. He had found the country so alive with rumours of an imminent rebellion and so fearful of imagined conspiracies that every garrison of English redcoats he'd met had set up roadblocks.

At every twist and turn he had been stopped and questioned, sometimes so absurdly frequently that more than once he had begun to doubt his decision to leave the comfort of his Edinburgh home and take the long trip north.

One particularly difficult officer near Inverness had held him for four days while a copy of the *Treatise* that Hume had with him was pored over for signs of sedition. Eventually a local nobleman had been found with whom Hume had a passing acquaintance and who had rather reluctantly vouched for him. Without this, God forbid, he felt he would have been held there still.

Now he looked up at the carved heraldry over the great entrance and saw with a drooping heart the Urquhain motto, incised deeply into a vast stone crest.

Nos Unus, eh? he thought grimly. He sincerely hoped not – if he'd come all this way just to have Dunbeath serve his own ends then he'd feel it was time doubly wasted.

To his surprise the door swung suddenly open and to his even greater astonishment it was Dunbeath himself who stood there, wigless and dressed in the oddest of working clothes.

'Hume! I thought it might be you. I heard a carriage on the drive. Well, you're most welcome – although I was expecting you many days ago. A terrible journey I've no doubt, with the English army seeing spies everywhere. Well, come in out of this terrible cold. Annie, help Mr Hume with his cases.'

Dunbeath looked about him and saw Sophie standing in the hall.

'And you, girl,' he shouted sharply, 'take these bags of Mr Hume's and escort our guest up to his room.'

Hume stared at Dunbeath with amazement. To find an earl answering his own door was extraordinary enough. But, far more than that, he was struck forcibly by his old friend's appearance. He was shocked to see the signs of such an obvious lack of attention to himself and the tension and strain in him that must be the reason for his drawn skin. More than this, he saw his feverishly high colour.

'Why, Dunbeath!' he stammered, 'it's good to see you again after so many years. But you are changed somewhat. Are you not in the best of health?'

'I do quite well, thank you,' Dunbeath said over his shoulder as he carried a bag up the great staircase. 'I sleep poorly of course, but which of us does not? But I see your old powers of observation have not left you, Hume. You are quite right. I have a chill from this damned cold winter, nothing more. It is attempting to floor me but I believe I shall have the better of it soon. Now, here is your room. Perhaps you wish to rest for an hour or so? But then please join me in the drawing room and we shall take a glass of whisky by the fire to simmer our blood.'

* * *

Two hours later Hume sat with a large glass of fine whisky in his hand and warmed himself in front of the salon's colossal fireplace. But the atmosphere in the great chamber was somewhat cooler and he glanced anxiously across to where Dunbeath sprawled in silence on a low, gilded sofa, gazing with a blank, distracted air into the fire's flames. Hume looked about himself at the sensational piece of theatre that made up the room, and studied more closely the ornate play of Italian plasterwork on the ceiling and the way that it cascaded down to the swags, columns and caryatids of the enormous chimneypiece. Vast tapestries lined each wall, no doubt made for the room, he thought, beautifully proportioned for the space and set between fluted pilasters of peerless oak. The salon was an enormous rectangle with large windows at each end, one looking down to the beach that stretched in a great crescent northwards towards Dunbeaton and beyond, and the other to the south and the headland there. In the centre, opposite the fireplace, the outside wall of the room's double cube was interrupted, and instead bowed out into a fabulous curved window of stone mullions and polished plate glass that gave out onto the breathtaking canvas of the open sea.

On a hard chair in this alcove Sophie sat quietly by a small table, her eyes respectfully downcast but her attention evidently focused on the two men by the fire. Hume's eye now rested on her and a doubtful crease flashed across his brow.

The Earl of Dunbeath came out of his reverie.

'And Mr Black? Does he still progress at the University?'

'Indeed he does,' replied Hume with his usual good humour. 'He is the power in the land now. I dare say we shall be calling him Rector soon.'

They lapsed into an uncomfortable silence again and Dunbeath resumed his staring. Hume groaned inwardly: if the earl had brought him all this way just to keep up such gloomy small talk then he might as well start the tiresome journey back to Edinburgh. At least then he could sleep in his own bed rather than the colossal, curtained affair that he had been shown to by that odd girl over there. He decided to take the lead in the conversation.

'So you live here alone, I see. Just a housekeeper for company. I salute you for it is much the better to be undistracted by domestic matters if one is engaged in fierce study. But, tell me, you seem to have another with you as well.' And he looked away from Dunbeath and turned his eyes towards Sophie.

Dunbeath followed his gaze towards the window.

'You refer to the girl I suppose, Mr Hume. Take no notice of her – she's just the castle cat. A plaything for my housekeeper that the wind blew in a few weeks ago. I hardly notice her anymore. I'm told her name is Kant and she likes to sit with me when I take my readings, but thank God she never says a word. Still, I'd swear that she understands everything I'm at; she even seems to know when I require things. Why, the other day she handed me an instrument before I realised I had need of it.'

He paused as if considering something for a second.

'As it happens you may find the circumstances of her coming somewhat interesting.'

Dunbeath sat up and put his legs on the floor, suddenly energised by the meaning of what he was about to relate. Briefly he told David Hume of how the German ship had arrived some weeks before, driven into Dunbeaton Bay, and of the dangerous reef of rocks that had wrecked it. He finished by describing how the fire on board had led it to explode.

'There is only one explanation, Hume. It must have been carrying arms and powder for the clans that have committed for Prince Charles Edward. I understand that more clans are joining by the day. There's war coming for sure if so much ammunition was being bought. I haven't been approached myself yet but I should not be surprised if my own people do not come to me soon. But, tell me, what are you are hearing in Edinburgh about this uprising?'

'How odd your story of the ship is,' replied Hume. 'I was talking with some friends only the other day and we were speculating as to how the rebellion was to be equipped. How ironic it would be if the Hanoverians are overthrown by German powder. But you ask me about the opinions on the Jacobites that I've been hearing.'

David Hume then began to speak about how the authorities were reacting to the expected landing of the man everyone was calling Bonnie Prince Charlie but he came to an abrupt stop when he realised that his voice could be carrying to the alcove, and to Sophie. He looked over towards where she sat, anxious that their conversation was being overheard. Dunbeath understood his thoughts and got to his feet. He spoke sharply to Sophie in German and she immediately rose from her chair and left the room.

'You are quite right to have been concerned, Hume. She speaks English so take care. If I have to speak to her I do so in her own tongue – I don't want her becoming familiar.'

* * *

The two men spoke further into the afternoon but by seven o'clock that evening Dunbeath had taken his leave and was in his observatory taking readings. It was now early April and the spring light that came through the glass walls was casting a soft glow over the great telescope and throwing dancing shadows around the room. As ever, Sophie stood to one side of the earl, carefully arranging a table of measurements.

The sound of shallow, laboured breathing could be heard and David Hume eventually came panting to the top of the tower stairs and emerged through the door into the glass-sided observatory. He smiled genially as he looked about himself, a recently refreshed glass of whisky in his hand. He came to a stop as he saw Dunbeath's bowed back, bent over the eyepiece of the main telescope.

'So this is where you have buried yourself these long years, my lord. Longitude, longitude, longitude! How often have I heard that spoken of in Edinburgh as if it were the Holy Grail. So, my old friend, do you think you're close to an answer?'

Dunbeath stood up slowly and turned to face Hume.

'Yes,' he said with great emphasis. 'Yes, I am.'

He left the telescope and came over to where David Hume stood. He looked at him intently, his flushed face etched with a passionate determination.

'Yes. I am close. It's twelve years now that I've laboured over these ephemerides, sometimes making new measurements, sometimes building on the work of other dedicated scientists. Yes, twelve years of my life, mapping every lunar distance. You see these tables? Just a tiny fraction of the whole. But here in these calculations is the secret. And my grasp is closing on it.'

He pointed towards the twilight sky and glared at Hume as if he was daring him to deny his achievements.

'When we know where we are up there, we shall know where we are down here – wherever we may be in the world. You have my word, Hume, the problems of longitude are nearly over. In a few days time I shall have the final data I need to solve this great quest. There is to be the second of the Transits of Venus and when I've recorded that the evidence it'll give me will slip the noose over this enigma forever.'

As he said this he snapped his open hand into a fist as if catching a passing fly.

'And then the Prize will be mine!'

Hume glanced with concern at Dunbeath's feverish passion.

'I give you joy for your discoveries, my lord, but you must humour me. What is a Transit of Venus?'

'Of course, you would know nothing of these things, Mr Hume. You must forgive me. It is when the planet Venus passes precisely between the Earth and the Sun. This alignment of the three planets is extremely rare. Transits come in pairs, eight years apart but only one pair every century. I measured the last Transit when it occurred and this new observation will give me the precise distance of the Earth to the Sun and, with it, the validation I need for these findings.'

His excited features began to relax for a second and Hume thought he even saw the beginnings of a smile of triumph form on his lips. Then Dunbeath straightened again.

'The next meeting of the Board of Longitude cannot be far off and I intend to present my findings and my conclusions to it. The meeting is usually held in the spring and I'm waiting to hear the date for this year. Then, Mr Hume, the Prize shall be mine and all Scotland will recognise the achievement. And, God willing, I shall dedicate it to our new king.'

'Have a care, my lord,' said Hume looking towards Sophie in alarm at Dunbeath's sudden indiscretion. It had become plain that Dunbeath was very overstrung. Hume glanced anxiously at his flushed face and asked again if he was unwell.

'Many regrets, Mr Hume,' Dunbeath replied, clearly taking hold of himself to control his thoughts, 'I run ahead of myself. This damned chill of mine, it tries to take me in its maw. I may be gaining the upper hand but the effort causes me to be quick tempered. I have to take care of my health,' he continued grimly, 'you'll remember that I'm cursed with that strange madness of ours, the Urquhain Rage.'

Hume smiled encouragingly, anxious that Dunbeath should distract himself by telling him more of the science behind his researches.

'You have my heartfelt congratulations on your findings, Dunbeath. And my profoundest respects. I know little of the subject, of course, but I was talking to Professor Bruce a couple of months ago at the University and he was telling me that there is another method of discerning longitude being spoken of. Not by celestial navigation at all. But by using a clock. It seemed an absurd claim to me but can this be true?'

Hume's heart sank as he saw Dunbeath's temper start to rise again.

'What? You have heard of this nonsense. I presume you are referring to Mr Harrison and his plaguey watch. His so called chronometer!'

Hume bowed, aching to reduce the sense of conflict that had flared up again.

'As I say, I know very little of such matters. Least of all I cannot imagine how a clock can tell you where you are in the world.'

Dunbeath gave Hume a withering look but then seemed to make an effort to restore a semblance of his good manners.

'There is a theory that a timepiece can calculate longitude, Mr Hume, by knowing the difference in time between that on the ship and that in its home port. It takes the earth exactly twenty four hours to rotate on its orbit so finding the elapse in time between the two should give the distance the ship has travelled – once a navigator has calculated for the latitude. That is the theory. But it could never work in reality.'

'Why not?' said Hume, breathing more easily now that a degree of calmness had returned to Dunbeath's voice.

'Because there is no clock in the world, now or ever will be, that could remain precise enough. God knows it strains the clock-maker's art to be accurate on land but the crashing of a ship's movement, the wet atmosphere and particularly the changes to metal that take place from the tropics to the cold regions – all these things make it impossible at sea. There are also variations in gravity at different latitudes – to say nothing of rust and the changes to the viscosity of oil in a watch over time.'

Dunbeath turned away and walked back to the telescope.

'No,' he said with renewed fierceness, more to himself than to Hume, 'it's impossible.'

Hume looked at him as he bent over the instrument once

more, wondering at the anger that he'd seen erupt in the man. It betrayed his inner thoughts. He had no idea whether the clock idea was possible – how could he – but it was quite obvious that the earl was deeply concerned by the threat.

Dunbeath seemed to have recovered a little of his self-possession after the outburst and with it had come the recognition that Hume was in the castle on other business. He now rose again and tried to remember that he was there at his own invitation.

'Yes, I am close, Mr Hume,' he said with greater courtesy in his manner now, 'very close. But I'm afraid you must bear with me for a few more days while I complete my readings and observe the Transit. Then, I promise you, I shall show you the Prisoner's Dilemma.'

* * *

High on the dunes, overlooking the beach, Zweig scrutinised Dunbeath and Hume through the beautiful telescope. He turned the eyepiece as he focused again and saw Sophie behind them, evidently listening intently to the two men's conversation. He stood for a minute or two as if thinking through what he'd seen and then closed the instrument and wrapped it in its oilcloth. His mouth tightened as he turned and set off for the walk back to Dunbeaton.

* * *

The following day Zweig huddled alongside the McLeish family around the table in their tiny cottage, a simple supper laid out in front of them. But all was not well. For some weeks now it had become increasingly plain to everyone that James was withdrawing further and further into a sullen darkness, apparently grieving for his dead brother. Little could anyone have guessed, however, that it was not grief that was working its corrosive mischief in him but, instead, the overpowering sense of guilt he felt about that terrible night at the castle. With each passing day the weight of his unshared secret had grown within him, and with it had come an unrealised, but longed-for need for release.

The small group ate in silence, the tension in the air obvious to each of them. Now, with a sudden spasm, James leant forward and aggressively forked another potato onto his small wooden plate. His other arm was draped on the table's surface, meaningfully wrapped around his place and the set of his hunched shoulders showed only too clearly the smouldering ill temper and hostility that radiated from him. But although the confusion in his mind was increasingly driving him to confront the group's attention, Zweig ignored the boy's anger and smiled placidly as he gently pushed dishes closer to him.

He now looked over towards Mona.

'I must thank you for yet another delicious supper, madam. I am even more in your debt,' he said, in a tone that only added to the obvious difference in manner between himself and James. Mona smiled in acceptance as she rose to clear the table.

'I thank you, Captain Zweig. It is good to cook for someone who shows a little gratitude for my poor efforts.'

This was the final straw for James. As his mother finished speaking he flung his chair violently backwards and leapt to his feet. Turning to face Zweig he seemed to have found the focus of his unhappiness. Rigid with anger and reddened with frustration, he now lost control and leant threateningly over Zweig, balling his hands into fists. Then he jammed his face into the captain's contented smile.

'Damn you, Zweig and damn your smooth tongue. How dare you speak to my mother like that? You have more oil in you than a whaler's hold. You may sit in Alistair's place. You may even think to wear his clothes. But don't you ever, ever dare to grease your way into my mother affections in that way! How I wish I had never gone into the sea for you that night; how I wish you had drowned along with your ship.'

Zweig said nothing but continued to look up at James, nodding quietly as if in agreement. Andrew McLeish raised an arm in a half-hearted attempt to calm the boy, although he continued to chew stolidly on his stew. Mona was less indulgent. She ran around the table and grabbed James by the shoulder, then pushed him round towards the door.

'Go out! Go out, now. I'll not have this, do you hear? Alexis is our guest and he is welcome to rest here as long as he wishes. Go out of here I say.'

James needed no second bidding and the cottage door slammed behind him. There was a deep silence for a few seconds but then Zweig lifted a conciliatory hand.

'Let me speak with him, Mona. I understand his anger. He has much to be angry about with the world. Let me make my peace with him at least.'

Zweig left the cottage and looked around for the boy in the evening twilight. He saw him sitting higher up on the dunes, hunched over and staring out to sea with a glazed expression of loathing on his face. The captain strolled easily over and found a flat spot to sit on a short distance away and silently waited for James's furious tension to subside. After some minutes he saw his rigid shoulders slacken and he called out softly to him.

'I understand, James. I understand. You have taken the death of your brother very hard. But that is as it should be.'

The dam that was James's fury broke. It had found an outlet.

'Understand?' he spat at Zweig. 'How could you understand? What do you know of it?'

Zweig realised that James had unknowingly invited a conversation and he quietly rose and walked over to sit next to him.

'You may be right that I do not understand your mind, James,' he said gently, 'but I do know something of your distress. I have my grief too. I saw my crew die. They were my friends, my family. I have lost everyone and everything.'

Zweig dropped his voice, allowing the conversation to lapse. The two men sat in silence, each apparently distracted by his thoughts. But, like a great musician, Zweig was timing his moment. Now he entered exactly on the beat.

'You know, I have found the telescope, James. I discovered it when I was cleaning out the sty yesterday.'

In spite of the gathering darkness he could see the boy recoil in shock.

'Have no fear,' Zweig continued quickly, 'I have moved it to a safe place. No-one would ever find it now.'

He turned to glance at James and was pleased to see how off balance he was. It was time to press his advantage.

'There's only one place you could have come upon a telescope like that, James. So you did go into the castle that night. You said you hadn't.'

James tried pathetically to fight back.

'No, no. I ... I found the telescope on the dunes. Someone must have dropped it,' he stammered.

'No, you didn't,' said Zweig emphatically, 'I know the truth, James. It is Lord Dunbeath's telescope.'

Zweig paused in his recital but didn't put his instrument down. James's silence told him that he had won.

'Then when did Alistair die, James?' Zweig continued, conscious that it was now the time to raise the tempo. 'On the way in? You told your mother that he went ahead of you into the cave and that he never came out. But we both know that if he'd drowned in there you would never have gone on into the castle. You wouldn't have passed his dead body and continued on with your mischief. So, you must have gone first, he must have come after you.'

By now Zweig was scanning James's stunned face, seeing where his blows were landing, sucking the truth out of him. He moved closer to the boy, his palpable determination and huge physical presence increasing the suffocating pressure. James shrank back into the darkness, overwhelmed by the attack and the weight of Zweig's intense personality.

'So, why did you tell your mother and father that Alistair had died on the way in, James? Why did you lie?'

Zweig had gone as far as he could with his logic. Now he would need to take more risks. He'd push and see the story as it arose on the boy's face.

'Something happened in there, didn't it James? Something that made you want to say that you'd never been in. What was it? You must have been discovered – otherwise you'd have taken more than just the telescope.'

The boy twitched and Zweig knew he'd scored a hit. Once more he raised his tone.

'Of course, you were discovered. Who found you, James? There are only two people that live in the castle. The old house-keeper would have been no trouble to a pair of strong young men. So, it was Lord Dunbeath wasn't it? What happened then, James? Did Lord Dunbeath kill Alistair? No, how could he have? No, your mother told me that there were no wounds on his body. Certainly nothing to show a pistol shot. And there were two of you - two against his one. And, why would you have lied if he had killed Alistair? Quite the opposite, in fact. But if Dunbeath didn't use a pistol then the two of you would have overpowered him.'

Zweig saw the signs – there was something in James's haunted, crumpling face that told him that the truth was about to emerge. He extended an arm and waited two bars, then pulled James towards him in a gentle embrace. The release of tension and the weight of guilt were too much for the boy to bear. James started to sob.

'I'll hang,' he wept, 'I'll hang.'

* * *

At the very back of the dunes, where they met the flat of the unrewarding Caithness farmland, Major Sharrocks focused his telescope yet again. At last, there seemed to be something interesting. And not before time – the colonel was asking for results and he'd had precious little to report. Worse then that, the men's morale was suffering, watching for days on end in this unending cold with nothing to excite them.

The boy was crying now, he saw that, the big man was comforting him. And they had seemed to be such enemies not three minutes ago.

'What's going on here?' he muttered to the trooper he had with him. 'I don't think they're talking about the price of fish.'

* * *

Zweig knew well when to substitute battering with sympathy. He had spent a lifetime handling boys like this, hearing of their drunken sailors' foolishness, the broken hearts, the broken promises and, always, their stupid, threadbare excuses. It usually wasn't hard to get to the truth from this stage. 'Let them run like hooked fish,' he'd often said to Hartmann in the past, 'give them lots of line but always keep the tension on. They just want to unburden themselves.'

He now brought the weight of his huge personality to bear and added to it his most unnerving weapon – the ability to suggest that he already knew what was going to be said. He smiled gently, nodding in encouragement as the story of the night unfolded. At last, James reached the end.

'I understand,' Zweig murmured. 'You were pulling Alistair's arm to get him to attack Lord Dunbeath.'

'Yes, that's right. He wouldn't do anything, you see. He just stood there as if he was frozen. I had to get him to move.'

'Of course you did James,' encouraged Zweig. 'And Lord Dunbeath was laying a trap for you, wasn't he? Offering you your freedom if Alistair fell.'

James felt a surge of gratitude. Zweig understood. He was a man of the world, a ship's captain, yet he understood. Yes, that was right, it was a trap, he had done nothing wrong. He suddenly felt better, stronger than he had for weeks. Now he saw that he had been forced to kill his brother by that monster Dunbeath, making him take such a risk as to pull his arm. It wasn't his fault that Alistair had fallen, it was Dunbeath's. He looked up and saw Zweig's smiling encouragement.

But it was a step too far. In an instant, fear gripped his heart as never before.

Panic broke over him as he realised that Zweig knew his secret now. He couldn't believe that he had told him so much. How he had been led on by his show of friendship. And yet how could Zweig truly be his friend when he must know how much he hated him?

At the realisation of the fresh damage he had brought on himself James gave into despair and broke down once more. His thin body shook.

'You may say you understand,' he stammered between sobs, 'but you will talk about this to others that will not. How could my mother ever see things as you do?'

Zweig turned to face James. He put his hands on his shoulders and dropped his head slightly to look up at him. He spoke softly, but with a fierce intensity to his tone.

'James, your secret is safe with me. I would never do anything to hurt your mother. You must know that. She brought me back from the dead. And you saved my life when I was on the rocks that awful night; I could never betray you.'

He looked towards the sea as if reliving his ordeal.

'But, more than that,' he continued in a whisper, 'you know my secret too. You know that I was bringing gunpowder for the uprising. If you report me I would also hang. You see, we both have to be silent. We have to co-operate. We have to trust each other.'

James began to breath a little easier and Zweig looked back out to sea – but only for the theatrical effect of swinging his gaze back again to wrong foot the boy.

'But, James,' he continued, as if the thought had only just occurred to him, 'you'll understand that I must keep the telescope for the present. Without it you have more evidence than I do. You may deny that you ever went into the castle – and it would be difficult to ever prove you did – Lord Dunbeath would deny it of course. But I can't deny that I came from Königsberg. So I'm sure you understand, I must keep it for the present time at any rate - to even up our bargain of silence.'

James was too exhausted from the pounding he'd had in the last few minutes to argue. The loss of the telescope was a terrible blow to him and he began to cry again. Zweig pulled him gently upwards by the arm and set him on his feet and the two slowly turned and began the short walk back towards the cottage.

* * *

'I wonder what all that was about,' murmured Sharrocks as he snapped his telescope closed. 'The boy was all at sea about something. But it may not be anything that would interest us. Perhaps I'm wrong about this place after all.'

He turned to the trooper he had with him as they walked back to their horses.

'I think we'll give the village a rest for a bit and take a closer look at the castle tomorrow.'

They mounted and set off back to Craigleven.

Chapter 9

The following day Dunbeath was too ill to leave his room. Annie took him soup in the afternoon and he sent his apologies back with her.

'His lordship says he will join you later,' she said to David Hume when she saw him on the stairs. She moved as if to pass him but then turned back with a worried sigh. 'Oh, sir, you know him well. Have you ever seen him like this before? We had the same some two years ago and it frightened me so much. Shouting for days. Such a fever I thought he was for his grave. But he came through it then – perhaps this time will not be so bad.'

David Hume reassured her as best he could; nonetheless he stood, gazing after her with concern as she carried the uneaten soup back to the kitchen.

That evening Hume was reading alone by the fire when Annie came in with whisky for him. He saw immediately that her mood had lifted from the anxiety she'd been showing earlier and was delighted when she told him that Dunbeath was in the observatory.

'His lordship is much recovered, sir, and sends his compliments – he is asking if you would care to take your dram there while he works.'

It was plain to David Hume, however, when he reached the top of the tower and came into the glassed room, that Lord Dunbeath was far from recovered. The earl's face was a disturbed mixture of chalk white and red flushes and it was evident that he was unsteady on his feet. As Hume had entered he'd seen him wince as he bent down to take a reading. Sophie was sitting quietly besides him with an open notebook and she glanced quickly up at Hume as he came across the observatory floor towards them.

'Mr Hume. A thousand regrets,' Dunbeath said, looking up

from the eyepiece, 'I know I have been poor company for you but I am very much the better now. However, I fear you must oblige me if we delay our discussion on my game yet a little longer. The Transit is tomorrow and you will find me more attentive when that is over, I promise you. You were clearly intrigued by my letter to you and I greatly look forward to our discourse.'

'Well, I too look forward to it, Dunbeath. I admit I have rarely been so interested. If I followed your letter correctly I understand you to be proposing a method of investigating – indeed you said mathematically – the very mechanics of human behaviour.'

Dunbeath stood away from his observations although his shaking hand continued to clasp on to the big telescope for support.

'Yes,' he replied, slurring slightly as he spoke, 'that is so. You have discerned exactly the conclushion I have come to.'

David Hume inwardly grimaced at hearing Dunbeath's verbal near miss.

'I fear you are still sickening, my friend,' he said gently, his soft features creased into a concerned smile.

'Not at all,' replied Dunbeath distantly, but his eyelids began to close and he rocked slightly on his heels. 'I do well, but I have need of a little air.'

He gave up his grasp on the telescope and went to a window, straightening up as he did so in his resolve to feel better. He stood for a few seconds looking down at the crashing waves and then glanced over at the dunes behind the beach as he turned to come back. He seemed to tense as if he'd seen something and then immediately peered out more closely – his eye attracted by a sudden flash as a piece of glass reflected back from high up on the dunes.

'One moment, if you please,' he mumbled to Hume as he picked up a small telescope. He went back to the open window and focused the instrument. He twisted the focus again and his whole body stiffened. As he looked out he had seen Zweig, sideways on, surveying one of the castle's windows through a telescope. *His* telescope. Now he saw him slowly scan the battlements as if working something out. The next moment he watched as he swung the instrument down to the windows – and then up to the observatory. He was now pointing directly back at Dunbeath. The two men stared at each other for a second, transfixed, each focused on the glass of the other.

'Good God!' Dunbeath cried with a wild look, pointing frantically towards the dunes as he turned back to Hume. 'My Domenico Salva!'

'What's that you say?' replied Hume, looking across the room towards him in alarm. But Dunbeath simply stood as if he'd been struck, an arm still outstretched towards the dunes and his lips moving soundlessly. He madly pointed again, as if insisting that Hume should also look, but the light in his eyes was dying. Now they rolled back in his head and a great shudder went through his body. It was the end and he fell backwards, striking his head with a sickening impact on a window ledge as he collapsed.

Sophie jumped to her feet with an anguished cry and she and Hume ran to where the earl lay. She felt the heat of his forehead with her hand and then quickly rose to look out of the window to see what could have shocked him so much - but Zweig had ducked out of sight, well aware that he'd been seen.

* * *

Eventually they succeeded in manhandling Dunbeath to his bed. It had not been easy and the Grey Tower's spiral staircase had been the worst of it. But, to Hume's intense surprise, Sophie had completely taken charge of the operation, directing Annie and himself with the calm and confident authority of a battle-hardened general – and with all her instructions given out in a clear and astonishingly perfect English.

More than once Hume caught himself amazed and yet

profoundly grateful. He wondered what had become of the mouse that had been sitting so quietly in the drawing room, hardly able to believe this change in her. Dunbeath had told him she was just a survivor from the shipwreck, a plaything for his housekeeper he'd called her. What did it matter though, Hume thought yet again, and he once more gave silent thanks that she was so capable.

There was a greater surprise to come. He watched as the girl cleared some of the chaos in Dunbeath's bedroom and then sent Annie to light a fire in the grate and warm water to bathe his fever. She now asked Hume to sit by the bed and told him to bring her word if Dunbeath should appear to be failing.

'Why, Miss Kant, where are you going?'

'I shall be in the observatory,' she replied briskly. 'I must complete the night's readings. And then I have to study Lord Dunbeath's books on the Transit of Venus. I do not believe he will be well enough to observe it for himself tomorrow.'

David Hume opened his mouth to reply but before he could gather his scattered wits she had swept from of the room.

* * *

It was past midnight when Hume made his exhausted way to the top of the tower and came puffing into the observatory. Sophie was transferring her records of the evening's measurements into Dunbeath's notebooks and she looked up with a smile of satisfaction as she saw his anxious face appear around the door.

'Ah, Mr Hume. How pleased I am to see you. You must be tired. How is his lordship?'

'I don't know how to answer, I fear, Miss Kant. I have no knowledge of such things, but he seems very ill. Such a fever – I could feel the heat of it from where I sat. And he is much disturbed, mumbling all the while about something or other.'

Hume looked down at the planetary recordings she'd made

and at her confident writing.

'How do you do here? Did you manage to complete the measurements?'

Sophie shrugged.

'Oh yes, it wasn't difficult. I've seen Lord Dunbeath take such readings many times. The pattern is clear. But tomorrow may be a different story and I shall need the night to read my way through to the Transit. Luckily many of these books of his are in my own language and I have some hours to study the techniques and procedures I shall need. May I suggest that you go to your bed now, Mr Hume? I shall be with Lord Dunbeath throughout the night while I read but I would be grateful if you could relieve me in the morning.'

* * *

The great clock in the hall had struck eight the following day, however, before David Hume came sheepishly into Dunbeath's bedroom and saw Sophie sitting by the vast four-poster bed, sponging his head as he twisted and grimaced in his fever. As Hume looked on, the earl threw back the covers and flung out a leg, groaning in his pain, but Sophie gently pushed his shoulders back to the mattress and a few seconds later he lapsed, muttering, into a shallow slumber.

'I must apologise, Miss Kant. I meant to take over from you far earlier but I'm afraid I slept too deeply. I fear this episode has fatigued me more than I could have imagined. Is he no better? Did you have a bad night of it?'

Sophie continued to gently bathe Dunbeath's face as she replied.

'Do not concern yourself, Mr Hume. You could have done no more if you had come earlier, I would have stayed anyway. I have some experience of this work. We had an outbreak of the sweating sickness two years ago in Königsberg, what I believe you call influenza here in Scotland, and I learnt something of its treatment. But I never saw a fever like this one. He has scarcely slept all night, raving and raving away. I confess I have wondered at times if there is more to this than just the illness. He seems to be ravaged by something more profound, almost as if he is having an attack to his senses as well as a physical collapse.'

She looked down at Dunbeath as he gibbered and twitched on his bed.

'He must sleep more deeply if we are to get this fever down. I decided that Annie should go for the doctor and she set out an hour ago to walk to the town of Wick. She will ask him to bring sleeping drafts and other medicines.'

'But, Miss Kant,' Hume replied with a start, 'I did not know this was your need. Why, I have just such a draft with me already if you think it will serve. My friend John Brown prepared a compound for me before I came here. I believe the world may yet hear of his great powers – he is a considerable physician in Edinburgh. He has a new preparation that he calls laudanum and I can assure you it has a powerful effect on all who use it.'

Sophie agreed immediately that they should give some to Dunbeath and Hume hurried to fetch the tincture that Brown had given him some weeks earlier. She heard him coming back, shuffling along in his haste, breathing heavily from the effort. Together they propped Dunbeath upright and forced a deep dose of the liquid between his quivering lips. They did not have long to wait before they saw his body relax and his breathing become easier and more regular.

'Praise God for that, Mr Hume,' Sophie sighed as she arranged the bedclothes around Dunbeath's body. 'If your Doctor Brown is correct he may sleep for some time now. Would you sit with him, please, and come to me if you think he deteriorates? It is the day of the Transit and I shall be starting the observations in three hours.'

She picked up some volumes from where they had fallen next

to her chair.

'I think I may make a passable attempt with the reckoning – these books are fairly clear about how I must proceed.'

* * *

It was some hours later that Hume rose from his seat and decided as he looked down at Dunbeath that he could leave him for a few minutes. He had a horror of illness of any sort and it had been an ordeal for him to sit watching the earl's flickering features and to feel his burning fever. He had wondered more than once as he'd sat there what Sophie had wanted him to do but he stayed nonetheless, watching Dunbeath as he twisted and jabbered, shouting out in bursts of passionate nonsense.

He climbed the stairs of the Grey Tower and came through to the observatory just as Sophie was measuring the room's temperature. She'd seen him come in through the door but had said nothing as she concentrated on recording her findings. She now glanced up briefly but went back to the telescope's eyepiece.

'No change?' she said as she focused the instrument.

'None that I can see, I'm afraid, Miss Kant. But he keeps yelling out the words he used when he first collapsed up here. You probably heard him yourself. He shouts out 'Domenico Salva' again and again. Sometimes it's even 'my Domenico Salva!' Who do you think that can be? Is there someone here with that name, do you think?'

Sophie continued to look through the lens. She murmured to Hume as she did so.

'Domenico Salva was the Michaelangelo of telescopes, Mr Hume. He was working in Florence early in the last century and was as much a genius as any of the great artists of the renaissance ever were. Ferdinando de Medici was his patron, of course, obsessed as he was with all such instruments. I recall that Salva's finest work was carried out with a jeweller called Giacomo

Palametti. Apparently the best of them were exquisite things, much sought after by astronomers of the time. But what do you think Lord Dunbeath meant? Do you imagine that in his fever he thought he saw a telescope out there?'

'A telescope?' Hume's pained expression showed his incredulity. 'You don't think the poor man has lost his senses, do you?'

Sophie made no answer and Hume let her continue with her work uninterrupted. He strolled over to the door that led out to the gap between the observatory wall and the battlements. He went outside and looked over the parapet at the long drop to the sea. He recoiled at the sight and stepped back, shuddering slightly as he did so.

* * *

Major Sharrocks arrived just as the trooper he'd stationed the previous day was gazing intently through the long-range spyglass.

'You may want to see this, sir. People arriving.'

Sharrocks lay down and lifted the instrument on its tripod, focusing it on the castle's entrance. He saw a pony cart draw up and a plump man jump down holding a small case. The man hurried inside the castle with Annie following closely behind.

'Hello,' said Sharrocks. 'Who's that? The old woman's the housekeeper but who's the man? Something's going on here. Dunbeath never sees anyone and now he's got a damned house full.'

* * *

The doctor came briskly into Dunbeath's bedroom and walked over to the bed.

'How long has he been in this fever?' he asked, taking his

pulse and then drawing back Dunbeath's lids to stare intently into his eyes.

Hume tried to separate night from day.

'I'd say this was the third day he's been dead to the world, although the sickness has been in him for longer.'

'Well, he must have more air. And I'll need cold linen to wrap him in – drench it in seawater, would you?' the doctor continued, looking at Annie. He reached into his bag and brought out a cloth roll of scalpels. He withdrew one. 'And I shall bleed him of course. We have to get this pressure down. But I fear it may be too late for him. Or, perhaps worse, too late for his brain, should he survive.'

* * *

Zweig lay hidden in the dunes, intently studying the observatory through the Domenico Salva. He was still appalled that he'd been discovered when Dunbeath had spotted him a few days earlier. Nonetheless, he still couldn't understood why no-one had come out to confront him, particularly as he'd guessed that the earl must have seen that he was using his telescope. This concerned him and he had constantly moved his position ever since, redoubling his watch on the castle's drive.

He'd seen Sophie often in the observatory since then but there'd been no further sign of Lord Dunbeath. All of this baffled him. Sophie was evidently using the big telescope, that much was clear, but why? Why had she suddenly been entrusted with it? And why wasn't she trying to spot him in the dunes? Was Dunbeath watching out from another angle? Zweig had thought this likely and had circled the castle many times, looking for signs, movements in windows or a sudden darkness in one of the many arrow slits in the stone. He'd seen none. Perhaps Dunbeath had left during one of the past three nights? Again, unlikely. And who was the man that had arrived with the housekeeper? Zweig frowned and brought the telescope up to his eye again.

* * *

Sophie put her quill down and rubbed her forehead. Between taking readings of the Transit and nursing Dunbeath she had worked virtually without sleep for three days and she stretched as she looked out of the observatory's open window. It was now dawn and another beautiful day was breaking. She gazed out to sea and thought yet again that the light was so beautiful on this coast that she could sit in its glow forever. Then she gave a slight shake of her head and walked to the stone staircase to find if there was any change in the earl.

She reached the bottom of the Grey Tower and walked to Dunbeath's bedroom. As she came in she saw Hume and the doctor asleep in chairs. They woke at the sound of her footsteps and the doctor quickly left his seat and walked briskly over to Dunbeath's side and felt for a pulse. He looked elatedly back at Hume, smiling broadly when he saw that the earl was sleeping soundly for the first time in days.

'Mr Hume, I think the fever must have broken. I believe he will live yet.'

As he said this Dunbeath opened his eyes and saw the little group standing by him. He seemed quite different – calmer and milder – and he gave an exhausted, almost childlike smile and closed his eyes again.

But an instant later his manner changed and he jerked himself upright into a sitting position. Now in a blind panic he demanded to know what he was doing in bed and then asked in an angry shout how long he'd been sleeping. With a deranged effort he leapt out of bed when he was told by the doctor that he'd been ill for four days.

The sudden attempt to stand was too much for his weakened frame and he was quickly pulled back to the bed by anxious hands. But he thrashed back at them and grimaced with rage.

'How could you let me rest?' he screamed. 'You all knew full well I had to record the Transit! Four days! I have missed it. Missed the Transit! And with it goes everything I've worked towards.'

Hume leant forward over the bed.

'My dear Dunbeath. You must calm yourself. All is not lost. Miss Kant has taken the observations. She has been a worthy pupil to you.'

But Dunbeath was too distraught to understand what he meant and pushed back at him, his weakened arms making little progress against Hume's weight.

'What? What are you saying Hume? What impertinence is this? Who is Miss Kant? What, this girl? Let go of me, I say.'

Hume's fabled good humour and tolerance were at stretching point.

'Lord Dunbeath,' he said sternly, 'I take exception to this. We have nursed you these past days and nights and you will hear Miss Kant out. My dear, please come here and speak to his lordship.'

Sophie quietly walked past Hume and sat on a chair by the bed. Dunbeath stared at her in fury but as she started to speak he gradually began to focus on the lifeline she was offering. She explained the readings she'd taken of the Transit and as she did so he embarked on a rapid technical cross-examination – had she compared the findings with the projections from the lunar tables? Had she compensated for nutation? Had she weighted the results for the temperature at different observation periods?

Sophie calmly nodded and smiled in answer to each of his questions.

She then summarised the findings, the precise distance to the Sun and the conclusions she'd drawn from comparing these latest recordings with the Transit of eight years before and the records of other observations that she'd read about.

By now Dunbeath was listening spellbound, only stopping Sophie with further questions of detail – but even these were now being asked in an increasingly respectful and admiring tone. Bit by bit he relaxed. Eventually he leant back on his pillows.

'But how have you managed this? Where can you have learnt so much, Miss Kant?'

'Well, my brother and I were active in Königsberg, my lord. We worked together – he even introduced me to Professor von Schleimann at the university there, you may have heard of him?' Dunbeath undoubtedly had. 'I was planning a short monograph on the eclipses of Jupiter's moons before I left on my unhappy voyage. Also I have learnt a great deal from watching you at work these past few weeks. Your instruments are far more powerful than anything I have ever used before but fortunately their actions were fairly simple to follow.'

Dunbeath was staring at her intently and from his amazed features a never-seen smile now broke out.

'I am greatly in your debt, Miss Kant. You have saved my life's work. I confess I am much moved. Changed even. The sickness has cleared. I feel strange. It is as if I have come to the top of a hill and everything is arrayed before me. I can see so far, it is all sharp, I can see so much now.'

Sophie was sitting with an arm resting on the bed looking at him as he said this, smiling gently and leaning towards him. As he looked at her Dunbeath wondered how he had not noticed the line of her neck as it stretched upwards. He had never seen anything so beautiful.

'All is bright,' he murmured, 'all is in its place. I feel alive. At last.'

Chapter 10

The doctor stayed for a further day to check on his patient's progress but once he'd satisfied himself that Dunbeath's furious impatience was the best medicine for him he decided to return to Wick. Sophie came with him to the front entrance and saw him into his trap.

'I must thank you most sincerely, doctor. I don't believe we could have seen this through without you. You were very good to come so promptly.'

She hesitated for a moment, concerned that he should think her too inquisitive, but then decided to press on.

'But please tell me, do you believe that his lordship will make a complete recovery?'

'I don't see why he shouldn't, Miss Kant. I feared for signs that the fever had attacked his brain, it's not unusual you know, but I've seen no sign of it so far. However it is essential that he should rest. I know he is refusing to keep to his bed but he has had a major assault on his life and at least you should insist that he eats well to build himself back. Plenty of beef broth and the like. Well, goodbye, Miss Kant, and again, my congratulations on recording the Transit.'

Sophie waved him down the drive and then walked back to the kitchen where she found the old housekeeper at her fire. She told her about the doctor's instructions.

'Someone must walk over to Dunbeaton for fresh vegetables and strong meat, Annie. Perhaps we could go together? I would be delighted of a stroll on a day like this and I'd very much like to see the village. I am no longer tired now that so much has been achieved and I believe a walk in this fresh wind would shake the tension of the past few days out of both of us.'

Annie agreed and they fetched their shawls and gathered at the front door. They were about to set off when a raised voice came down to Sophie from the top of the staircase. It was Lord

Dunbeath, still very pale, and shaking slightly as he began to descend, holding hard to the handrail.

'Where are you going, Miss Kant? Do you have to leave? What is that needs your attention so much that Annie cannot do it alone?'

Sophie walked to the bottom of the stairs and gently called back to him.

'You should still be in your bed, sir. I have my instructions from the physician.' She gave a light laugh. 'He has placed me in charge of your recovery and he will return to scold me if I do not do as I'm bidden. You have been dangerously unwell, my lord, and you must rest. Annie and I shall be back soon but we must provision for the sake of your health, nothing but the very best.'

Dunbeath's perpetually distant manner appeared to have evaporated.

'I have recovered already Miss Kant,' he said as he walked down to her. 'It is a new man that you see before you, and rest is the last thing I want.'

He had reached Sophie by now and stood gazing intently at her, searching her face, almost as if he was seeing her for the first time.

'Please, don't go,' he murmured in a low voice, designed not to carry to the housekeeper, 'don't leave me so soon. I have no doubt that Annie will be most capable of following your instructions.'

Sophie paused to cover her astonishment. The earl had clearly found an interest other than longitude. She thought for a little longer but decided that continued opposition was her only option.

'There will be too much for one person to carry,' she smiled in reply. 'But we shall come back very soon and ...' she looked at him in a mock impersonation of a parent chiding a child and laughed gently, '... I shall want to find you in bed. If I do, we can discuss the Transit further. If not ... well.'

She turned and gave him further hope with a little inclination of her head and then walked through the great door to where Annie was waiting for her on the drive. An impulse made her turn back and she saw that Dunbeath had remained in the hall, continuing to stare after her, charmed, baffled and yet seemingly compliant at being so crossed.

* * *

Sophie and Annie walked with their arms linked, their spirits high to be outdoors on such a beautiful spring day, laughing and gaily talking over each other as they strolled along the beaten path through the dunes from the castle to the village. Sandy hummocks rose high on either side of them and clumps of marram grass waved gently in the onshore breeze.

Much as Sophie seemed to be listening to the old woman as she prattled on, however, she was also thinking hard. So, she now had Dunbeath's full attention, she felt – and gratitude. Or the nearest he had to such a feeling. Could she now begin to hope that he might be approached for a loan to see her back to Königsberg? She decided to choose her moment to raise it with him if the way he looked at her was still so warm when they returned from Dunbeaton.

Meanwhile, Zweig had been busy thinking too. He had seen the two women through the telescope as they'd set off from the castle and he'd tracked round to a high point on the dunes where a sharp corner in the track had eroded the sandy banks into a steep and narrow passage. He now watched them from above, waiting until they passed below him, relaxed in their laughter and casual in their stride. And then he dropped down on the path behind them, cutting them off.

They turned, startled by the sudden noise. Sophie was the first to react. She shrieked in alarm and her head flew backwards with the shock of seeing him. Then her hand went to her mouth.

The two women clung to each other, rigid with fear. But as Zweig raised his hat and bowed to them with a deep show of courtesy, Annie began to thaw. Sophie was still badly shaken but as she gathered herself, she became gradually more animated. She now forced Annie behind her as if protecting the old housekeeper from a wild beast and faced Zweig, baring her teeth and panting heavily in short, determined breaths.

The captain behaved as if he'd just chanced on them during a Sunday stroll. He smiled gently and held his head on one side, encouraging a conversation.

'Madam, I am in your debt forever,' he said, bowing again towards Annie and murmuring to her in a voice as soft as gentle music. 'You saved Sophie's life and in doing so you brought me back from the dead, too. I shall never forget that.'

Sophie still stared at Zweig, but her fighting spirit was fast returning. He now looked at her and spoke quietly in German.

'Sophie. It is so good to see you. You seem well, thank God. As you can see, I too was miraculously spared.'

Sophie's wild eyes told him that she did not share in his opinion of divine intervention. Zweig seemed not to notice and he continued in his low and easy style.

'We have been away from home for some six or seven weeks now, Sophie. Your family will be concerned for you and we should attempt to make our way back soon. I suggest that we can walk to Wick and make our way from there by coach to Edinburgh. I have contacts in the city and will be able to raise funds to pay for our journey. From Edinburgh we can pick up a ship to Königsberg. We could be home within a month or so, perhaps even less.'

By now Sophie had so gathered her wits that she immediately gave her answer – she would not be going anywhere with him.

'Don't pretend to me that you do not know how long we have been away!' she hissed, bending forward from the waist in emphasis. 'Six or seven weeks, you say. You know as precisely as

I do that forty-six days have passed since we left Königsberg and there are a further fifty-four yet to go before my father's debt to you will be cancelled – and I shall be free. Yes, free from you, you madman. Back to Prussia? You can go alone if you wish. But I know you well enough by now, Alexis Zweig, and I know you will not leave without me.'

She stepped forward, her face still inflamed from the shock of their meeting.

'So, while I stay here the debt is secure. Without me returned there would be no repayment. The hundred days will pass. So, if you want me to come, you'll have to force me!' Her eyes flashed with defiance and she seemed to be goading him to lose his temper.

Zweig smiled his sweet and confident smile. A lifetime's experience of trading and the patience needed to succeed was not about to be squandered.

'I see that we have taken up again where we left off on that terrible night, Sophie,' he replied wistfully, 'I greatly regret it. You must know my true feelings for you. And you are right – I shall stay with you now as I shall stay with you forever. There is no life for me without you. As to the debt, we have spoken of this before. It is already forgotten. I have no fear about such matters. I shall make good this amount ten times over.

'So, please reconsider, Sophie,' he continued and took a step towards her, his hand held out as if to take hers, 'we must thank these good people for their kindness, but we have no business here.'

Sophie stared fiercely back at him, her resistance clear. There was a frozen moment of silence. Then they all heard the unmistakable sound of a firearm being cocked. It came from behind, high above them, and Zweig looked quickly over his shoulder. A pistol was pointing at his head.

'Now sir,' said Dunbeath, jumping down from the dune with the gun in his outstretched hand. While he had clearly witnessed some of the encounter he had not been close enough to have heard what Zweig was saying. 'Step back and return your arms to your sides. What mischief is this that you should threaten two defenceless women in this way?'

Zweig had turned completely and now faced Dunbeath. He smiled pleasantly, almost as if he had been expecting him. He bowed and began to introduce himself but Dunbeath dismissed him with a wave of his free hand. Instead, he kept the pistol pointing at Zweig's head, his arm shaking slightly with the effort.

'Ah, my Lord Dunbeath,' said Zweig evenly. 'A pleasure to meet you. But I have heard something already of your determination when you hold a pistol and another does not. What can I do for you?'

Dunbeath narrowed his eyes and continued to study him as if considering the weight of what Zweig has just said.

There was a long pause as they eyed each other and then Zweig murmured in a cool tone.

'I see how it lies, my lord. I believe Miss Kant has made an impression on you. You would not involve yourself in the lives of two poor foreigners if that were not so.'

Dunbeath's head tilted back slightly in his disdain. There was a further silence while Zweig continued to smile encouragingly. Then Dunbeath stretched out his arm and spoke in a low, grating voice.

'My business with you is just this. You have something of mine. A telescope.'

Zweig bowed again and immediately took the Domenico Salva from his inside pocket and passed it over with a courteous tilt of his head. Dunbeath leant forward and grabbed it from his outstretched hand and then brusquely told the two women to get in front of him. Together they started to return to the castle.

Zweig simply continued to smile placidly as he stood in a dignified silence. But once the three had taken a few paces he called out in a knowing tone.

'And how do you think I came by it, my lord?'

Dunbeath chose not to answer; indeed, he showed no sign of having heard Zweig at all, and the little group walked on for a few more yards. Then Sophie turned round to look again at the captain. Now that her wits were gathered she seemed almost exhilarated by the experience. But Zweig simply continued to stand quite still, apparently peacefully accepting the situation. He gave a last graceful inclination of his head as a farewell to Sophie and slowly turned and began the walk back to Dunbeaton.

* * *

Major Sharrocks put his telescope down. He paused for a moment, considering what he'd just witnessed. Then he gave a jerk of his head to the two troopers with him, and together they mounted and rode off.

Chapter 11

Sophie forced herself to be calm. She slowed her step to even the rhythm of her pace – that would clear her head, she felt. So the madman was still alive! Of course he was. It would take more than a shipwreck to kill him. He was a force of nature, even if the livid scar on his head showed he could bleed like a human. She had forgotten what a colossal man he was, towering over them like that. But how much better he had appeared without his tassels and fur – just simple fisherman's clothes and an old tweed coat.

Thank heaven we spoke in German, she thought to herself. Annie would have followed what we were saying otherwise and understood what all this was about. Luckily Lord Dunbeath had been too far away to hear. She walked on, thinking through what she would say to them about Zweig. They would want to know who he was and what he wanted. She knew she couldn't avoid telling them he was on the ship – Annie would have guessed that anyway – if not, she'd be bound to gossip in Dunbeaton and no doubt the villagers there knew who he was. Yes, it was bound to come out that he was the ship's captain. But why should she hide it anyway? Did it really matter?

She walked a little way further, still deep in her thoughts.

Dunbeath would question her. That look he'd given her when she'd sat by his bed, and then how he'd stared at her before she left for the village. Yes, of course, he would probe. And she'd seen how the two men had looked at each other back on the dunes. Like a pair of rutting stags, sizing each other up. And Zweig had said that thing about making an impression. Yes, Dunbeath would want to know.

She gazed out to sea and felt the freshness of the breeze on her face.

But if they were going to know about Zweig being the captain, why shouldn't she explain about the debt agreement too? There was no need to speak about the marriage contract. Her being the security on the debt was the explanation – that's why he needed her to go with him. She was sure this was the right approach.

To her astonishment, Dunbeath mentioned not a word when they eventually climbed the long steps to the drive and entered the castle. Was he too lofty to have seen what was going on, she wondered? Too removed in his aristocratic superiority? Or perhaps too locked in the workings of his mind and his ambition to ever acknowledge the squabbles of lesser beings?

Whatever the reason, Dunbeath merely turned and muttered to Annie as they came into the hall.

'Put the horse in the trap, Annie. Take the road to Wick and provision there. Or buy from the men that bring things to the castle. There's no reason for you ever to be in Dunbeaton. I don't want you going there again.'

He walked up the stairs to the drawing rooms but had only climbed a half dozen steps before he turned back.

'Before you go, Annie, send my compliments to Mr Hume and ask him if he will meet with me in the great salon at noon. Miss Kant, perhaps you would care to join us there? And, Sophie,' he added, now more quietly and with no little concern in his voice, 'you may wish to let me know in future if you are leaving the castle.'

Sophie's downcast look showed him her agreement. She turned to walk away, glad of the opportunity to cover her astonishment. Sophie! How would he have known that was her name? He would have heard Hume call her Miss Kant, but how could he have learnt of Sophie? He could only have been speaking to Annie about her. How he would have suffered to have stooped to that. Yes, Zweig was right, she had made an impression. But perhaps God was at work here? After all, the longer that Dunbeath was interested in her, the longer she would be able to stay in the castle, under his protection. That would make certain that Zweig couldn't somehow force her back to Königsberg. This had to be the only thing that mattered for the next few weeks – as long as she was safe in Scotland the debt couldn't be called.

Her face tightened in determination once she'd reached her conclusion – she had to stay in the castle for the sake of the debt: that much was clear, yes, that was the only thing that mattered.

* * *

It wasn't long before Annie had found David Hume and an hour later he and Dunbeath were standing in front of the open fire, glasses of whisky in their hands and an evident sense of promise in the air. Sophie was continuing where she had left off before Dunbeath's collapse, clearing up the years of neglect, restoring the great rooms, rehanging curtains and sorting through the mass of discarded books.

Eventually, Dunbeath's tense features showed that he was about to embark on the most loathsome of obligations for him – an apology.

'I must plead forgiveness for taking up so much of your time with that damned illness of mine, Mr Hume. I owe you a great debt for your concern for my wellbeing and for being so attentive. You have been most patient. But now, at last, if you are still willing I shall explain the Prisoner's Dilemma to you. And then perhaps we might even play a few hands.'

David Hume's usual good humour was in full blossom as he smiled and waved a dismissive hand.

'Not at all, Dunbeath. It is behind us and I am glad for your recovery. And at last I am to hear about the mysterious Dilemma! I've been greatly looking forward to this; but I must confess I'm still completely perplexed as to how you can claim that a game can ever give an insight into our natures.'

'But all life is a game, Hume. What are we doing if we are not constantly dealing with each other, playing a great game, forming alliances, weighing up our options, misleading, trusting, not trusting, saying what we mean, what we don't mean, shifting our ground, working out our stratagems? Above everything, all of us, all the time, are playing to beat our fellow man.'

Well, I would agree with much of what you say,' replied Hume, 'but you seem to place great emphasis on winning. Where is fraternity and harmony in your games of life?'

'Harmony? In humans? Really, Mr Hume, you are too naïve – and I intend to show you why. As to my game, I'm not talking about pastimes like chess where there must be a solution, a right procedure for any position. Real life is not like that. Real life consists of bluffing, of little deceits, of feints, of asking yourself what is the other man going to think I mean to do. That is what games are about in my theory. My interest is in understanding the things we are doing instinctively, a hundred times a day, unknowingly most of the time and always supposing that we are in the right. It is about seeing how we look to gain an advantage and how we solve problems.'

'Well, again, I shall concede to you on that description of life. But a game?'

'Yes, because games show us the ways we are trying to win in life. Let me give you an example. A very simple game. You have two squabbling small boys – they will agree on nothing. Now, how do you cut up a cake between them without a fight? When neither would ever agree that it would be divided fairly?'

'A desperate situation, I grant you,' replied Hume with a light laugh. 'Small boys would be second only to university professors in their sense of grievance that somebody, somewhere, might have something that they do not. But let me try to give you an answer.'

There was a pause while Hume thought further about the question.

'I believe I would try to get them to see the shortcomings of ever expecting perfection. I would tell them that there can never be perfection in life. I'd explain that a careful eye and a steady hand should ensure a clean cut to the cake and that any thought of the crumbs of difference between the two pieces should be ignored. Perhaps a trusted intermediary could be asked to make the cut and then choose who gets which slice? Or perhaps they could toss a coin to see which of them would have first choice? I suppose that would be my message, given in as peace-loving a way as I could deliver.'

'I disagree with you,' said Dunbeath, with more than a slight air of triumph. 'I would see the boys as willing competitors in a game. Cunning and potentially deceitful opponents. I would tell them that one can cut the cake and the other can then choose which piece he wants. Each is now responsible for the outcome. Neither can complain. It may be a simple story but it shows you how a contract of greed, a low impulse you would no doubt say, can lead to harmony in a way that persuasion never could. Far from your idealistic ambition for them to be peace loving, one would rely instead on their passionate hostility to each other to find a solution.'

Dunbeath thought for a second and then continued, stretching out a finger for emphasis.

'One of the boys has to make a choice knowing that the other one would also be making a choice. Each child anticipates what the other child will do. In a similar way, the Prisoner's Dilemma also shows the way we constantly use strategies for dealing with each other.'

Hume chuckled happily.

'I enjoyed your story. A very elegant solution. So please explain the so-called Dilemma to me. I hope it is as intriguing.'

'Very well,' Dunbeath nodded. He took a sip of his whisky and considered for a few moments before he began.

'I want you to imagine that there are two prisoners. They are being held in two separate cells, some distance apart. They certainly can't see or hear each other. They have been picked up together, near a house that has been burgled, and they are suspected of the robbery. The authorities are quite sure of their guilt but there's no sign of any of the stolen property and they don't have the hard proof they need for a conviction.

'The captain of the guard visits the prisoners in turn and tells each of them exactly the same thing.

'He says to them: 'Listen carefully. We know that you were near the scene of the crime. We also know that you and your companion are thieves. But the fact is that we don't have the watertight evidence to convict you. So, I need you to tell me that you did rob the house. Yes, I want you to admit to the crime.

'Now, if each of you confesses and pleads guilty then I shall see that the court hears about your honesty and you'll be given lesser sentences.

'However, if you both remain silent and don't admit to anything then I shall still send you for trial. But, without the evidence I need, you will probably only be convicted of trespass. And for that you would get far less time in jail than you would if you came clean about the theft.

'But, and pay very careful attention to me here, if you confess to the robbery – and your friend stays silent – then I shall see that he hangs alone for the crime. And you'll be rewarded by being set free.

'I'll come tomorrow morning at seven o'clock to hear your answer.'

David Hume was very still as he absorbed the drama.

'Now,' continued Dunbeath, 'the thieves sit in their cells and think about this. Each of them concludes that the best outcome would be for both of them to stay silent. That way they can only be tried on the minor charge of trespass. But the more they think about it the more each of them has a horror … what if *I* stay silent and *he* doesn't? He'll give evidence against me. I'll hang and he'll go free. What if he doesn't care about me but only thinks about himself? Can I trust him to keep quiet?

'All night long the prisoners think about this. The terror of the three o'clock chimes and the blackness of their cells eat at their confidence. And, of course, it's not long before they both come to the same conclusion – the risk is too great. I'll confess. That way I'll go free if my partner stays silent. He would hang but I'd be free. But if he thinks the same way and confesses as well – then we'll both get a lesser sentence anyway. The captain promised that.

'The captain comes at seven but he's been playing this game for a long time. He already knows what he'll find. Both of them confess.'

'How interesting,' said Hume softly, 'how very pretty. Although it would be obvious to each that staying silent would lead to the best result for the two of them – they dare not trust the other to think in the same way. I can see what you're saying. That it would appear rational to confess even though there would be a better result if both were irrational – and had trust in each other. Yes, very pretty indeed. I congratulate you, Lord Dunbeath, you have very neatly summarised the leap of faith that is behind the nature of trust.'

Hume raised his glass and sipped it as he turned the story over in his head.

'But I fear I must disagree with your conclusion,' he said at last. 'You would have me believe from this illustration of yours that a lack of faith in a colleague leads to a desirable outcome. I cannot accept this. I'll grant you that you may be right about the defective morals of a pair of thieves, snatching at an advantage to save their miserable skins, terrified in their cells, the darkest hours breaking their human instinct to be honourable – they would behave in this way. But not a thinking, reasonable person. Not someone in this enlightened age'.

Dunbeath said nothing. Hume pondered further.

'But, I was quite forgetting,' he said after a pause, 'you said you had invented a game. Presumably you have based it on this tale. How could this questionable parable of yours possibly become a game?'

'Oh, but I believe it can,' replied Dunbeath, 'and more than that I believe it will show you how wrong you are in what you've just said. In fact I believe I shall illustrate that to you in only a few minutes. Let me first suggest that we give each of the possible outcomes a score. Then we can play against each other for an hour or two. That should see us have a considerable collection of games, choices if you like, and we'll see who can assemble the most points.

'Let me begin by proposing a way of scoring that would reflect you confessing but the other person staying silent. You get five points for going free but he gets none, no points, as he is the only one that's convicted. In fact he's been hanged, he's dead, so no points at all. The average of these scores is two and a half, so let's make the reward for *both* staying silent more than this. Say it's three.

'And then let's agree that both confessing and getting a lesser sentence is lower than this but obviously better than being the only culprit. Make that one point. Is that clear?'

'I think so,' said Hume brightly. 'The four outcomes are worth five, three, one and no points. Yes, I think that's the right reflection of the possibilities. So, if two people take the obvious route of co-operating then they'd get six points between them – two threes – rather than someone getting the maximum score of five for betraying a colleague. I like that. Trust is rewarded over selfishness. But I'm still not sure how we proceed.'

Dunbeath pointed to the table in the alcove.

'Good. I'm glad you agree to the principle. Then come over here and we'll play a few hands.'

Saying this, Dunbeath walked Hume to the table and showed him how he had piled up books to make a high dividing wall in the middle of its surface. He gestured to Hume to sit on one side of the books and he went to the other. He showed him that each side had some sheaves of plain paper and a quill and ink alongside them. They then sat down and made sure that they couldn't see each other, nor what they were writing.

'So, game one,' called out Dunbeath. 'Write down if you would stay silent – in other words co-operate, trust the other person – or whether you would confess. I call a confession Defect because you would be defecting from trusting your colleague. If you want to co-operate write 'C' and if you wish to defect, write 'D'. We can't see or hear each other so it's just as if we are in separate cells. In fact, to make things absolutely safe, don't do the down stroke on the 'D', just make a reverse 'C'. That way neither of us will ever be able to guess from the scratch of the quill what the other is doing. Very well, the first play, make your decision.'

They both wrote a letter.

'I've written 'C' said Hume, looking around the book wall. 'I chose to co-operate. No doubt you did the same.'

'No, I have written a 'D'. I defected,' replied Dunbeath. 'Five points to me and none to you.

'Now, game two.'

They began to write.

Chapter 12

Zweig slowly padded in his strange, deliberate way along the foreshore, his head down, deep in thought. He had now lost everything. For a time he had felt he'd held a card by having the telescope, but Dunbeath had seen to it that even that had been lost – and with it, much worse, the hold he had over James. There was now the great danger of being exposed to the English by that weak-minded, murderous boy. There was no longer anything in his hand.

He stopped by the water's edge and looked out to where the surf broke over the rocks that had seen the end of his ship. But there was no sign of self-pity or defeat in his face, only a trance of concentration. For ten minutes or more he barely moved, his thoughts progressing with all the discipline of a regiment of guards as he carefully relived recent events in his mind, seeing the people involved, weighing them up, listing their strengths and weaknesses. Imperceptibly, he seemed to swell as if he was absorbing the power of the sea, reaching deeper and deeper into himself, marshalling his resources and planning his next steps, seeing his options, plotting his moves.

Eventually he lifted his head and gave a minute nod as if to confirm his conclusions to himself. His mind was plainly made and there was a renewed determination in his face as he turned and began the walk back to Dunbeaton, now with a quite different substance to his tread.

* * *

It was early evening and the candles were throwing their mad, twitching light about the plasterwork of the great salon.

'And I defect again,' said Dunbeath with more than a slight note of provocation in his voice.

Hume's fabled equanimity was wearing thin. His hand

strayed yet again to the embroidery at his coat cuff.

'I estimate from my notes, Dunbeath,' he said with a terse edge to his voice, 'that we must have played this game of yours a further five blocks of ten times this hour. And all you have done is repeat your choice. On every occasion you have chosen to defect. I cannot see the point you are making.'

Dunbeath's face had returned to the look of blank disdain he wore before his illness.

'My point? Surely you can see that I am making my point every time we examine the outcomes we have chosen? I defect. You too could have done so and yet you almost invariably choose instead to co-operate, no doubt in the hope that I can see some kind of benefit from it.'

'Of course I do,' replied Hume, his voice rising in emphasis, 'we would both get three points if you would only do the same. When I defect as well you only get one. As do I. Do you not see that co-operation leads to more points? We would get six points between us rather than one each or even the five to you.'

'And do you not see that I have over two hundred points and you have but five,' said Dunbeath looking down at the score he had been keeping. 'That is the real point. I am *beating* you. Is this not enough for you? Do you not see the truth about life here – that it is simply a struggle between self-interested creatures? It is about winning and losing. And this game is the proof of it. Humans may sometimes be tamed by their cultures, or laws or force, but by nothing else – and certainly not by the prospect of your wish for co-operation, by some vague hope of yours that it leads to what you call trust.'

An unpleasant edge had come into Dunbeath's tone, a kind of triumphant bitterness.

'You've had your chance to defect as well, Mr Hume, indeed many chances, but you've chosen instead to act irrationally, imagining that your benevolence can get an opponent to co-operate. Have you not concluded from the game that when you choose 'co-operation' and I choose 'defect' then you get nothing? Really, are you such a fool as not to see that whilst the prisoner may perceive a dilemma a rational man would not. Can you not see that?'

As Hume listened to Dunbeath's hectoring tone and the harsh words he was spitting out, a horrible, cold realisation began to sweep over him – a realisation that the earl hadn't brought him to Caithness to play this game with him at all. That he'd foreseen all this. That he'd got him to come so he could crush him with this unpleasant little drama. Hume began to think of why he'd done this. He imagined Dunbeath becoming aware of his own small amount of success in Edinburgh, and of how a man like the earl couldn't bear to think of an old acquaintance outstripping him, or for him to allow even a modicum of fame in someone he'd consider well below him, below an Urquhain. In an instant Hume could see the years Dunbeath had spent at the castle, miles from anywhere, buried under the weight of his research, getting no recognition at all – and knowing with an utter conviction, even if he'd be the only one that did, that he was superior to such a trivial person as a mere thinker. How that must have eaten at him! How much he would have felt the need to put him in his place.

As David Hume came to the end of his frantic musing he saw that the light in Dunbeath's eye was rapidly becoming a fire.

'Yes,' Dunbeath repeated for the second time, 'can you not see that? I've read your work, Hume, that *Treatise* of yours. I've read that nonsense you spout about benevolence and trust. But I have proved beyond argument, have I not, that this is a strategy for failure. In this world it is the strong that realise this. That is what the Prisoner's Dilemma shows.'

His face was now quite twisted in his anger.

'How do you think the Urquhain rose from this piece of useless wasteland, from just a patch of rock and sea, to where we are now? How have we climbed? Believe me, because I know it to be true, we are the richest family in Scotland. And, how do you think we've done that? It's because we've been playing this game for centuries. We know how to win. Put that in your next book, Hume, accept that the world is for the powerful and have done with it!'

Hume's face was puce with the unfairness of the attack. In friendship and interest he had made the trek to Caithness and now this madness was breaking out about his head. His hand crept yet again to stroke his cuff but even this no longer had the power to calm him. By now the two men were on their feet.

Over by the fire, Sophie had been quietly listening as the games had been played. She now looked over with alarm as their angry voices filled the room.

'I cannot remember ever being so ill treated, Dunbeath,' said Hume, struggling to keep his tone even. Like all men of a naturally even temperament he was bewildered and hurt in the face of injustice. 'I will not endure this. That you have brought me all the way from Edinburgh just to waste my time with your theories and then to rub my nose in this selfishness – this 'proof' that selfishness wins. Really, Dunbeath, are you so angry with the world that you would trick me into coming here, just so you could make your point?'

By now Hume was fighting to keep his temper and he made to take a step towards the door.

'I bid you goodbye, Dunbeath. I'd thank you if your house-keeper would arrange for a trap to take me to Wick.'

Dunbeath didn't answer and the two of them remained facing each other, both rigid with fury. Neither had noticed that Sophie had walked across from the fireplace. She was now between them.

'Surely, *that* is the point?' she said calmly.

Both men looked at her intently, their concentration broken for the first time by her presence.

'Surely,' she repeated, 'the point is that Mr Hume has decided not to continue the game. He has decided that you, my lord, will always defect and he sees no future in continuing to play with you. He is, in other words, behaving in exactly the way that a reasonable, co-operative person does when faced with such intransigent selfishness – he has decided to avoid you.'

There was a stunned pause and Dunbeath's face began to work with instinctive anger at being so criticised, so crossed. But, as he looked at her in his rage, his features softened just as quickly as they had set. And, to Sophie and Hume's amazement, he gave a quick laugh. Then he appeared to smile at his own change of mood and he turned to her, almost affectionately.

'Only you, Sophie, could have said that to me. And only since my illness.'

He strode over to the curved window and brought back a decanter of whisky.

'A peace offering, Mr Hume. A dram with me for our friendship. It is only when one has known someone as long as we have that we do not take offence. Is that not so? A glass with you, Hume. I trust you will reconsider your wish to leave. We still have much to explore with this game.'

He raised his large crystal rummer in a sign of regard and drained the whisky. Hume raised his own in return but saw that Dunbeath's mood had changed again now that he'd considered that the discussion had come to an end.

'I must away to my study,' he said briskly. 'Sophie, perhaps you would join me there? As you know I am much troubled by these lunar distance errors that I can find no cause for. Do you really believe they are time dependent? Your knowledge of the orbits of Jupiter's moons may help to explain them – they are the universal timekeeper. Perhaps you could share von Schleimann's formula with me?'

'Yes, indeed,' she replied, still astonished by the extraordinary journey of his mood, 'there is much still to cover. I shall come in a few minutes – just as soon as I have finished here.'

* * *

Zweig had walked around the headland and was now working his way down a low cliff to the foreshore, where the surf met a line of jagged rocks. He looked intently into the pools the retreating sea had left, apparently searching for something.

After half an hour he seemed to find what he was hoping for and he leant down to pick it up. It was a strong, straight piece of broken tree branch, sodden and heavy with seawater. He felt its weight in his hand and then went to sit on a nearby boulder.

Reaching inside his jacket he took a sharp gutting knife from his pocket and began to whittle the sides of the stick, shaping it into an even cylinder.

* * *

'Are you not joining Lord Dunbeath, Miss Kant?' said Hume once they were alone.

'I shall do so in a short while, Mr Hume, but I would appreciate it if I might ask you a question first.'

She looked at Hume's gentle features with concern.

'I fear I do not understand his lordship at all. Why does he think there is a need for such anger? You know him well yet you feel able to forgive his attack.'

'Dunbeath? Oh, he is not a bad soul, Miss Kant. No, not at all. I think we both know that. You have to look beyond the man you see standing before you. You have to see four hundred years of a family's relentless need to succeed. An unbroken chain of duty that stretches over the generations – win, win and never leave off winning is all they ever think of. Enough is never enough, others must fail. And all this fire and ambition ends in him. The Urquhain are not alone in this mania, Miss Kant, I have seen it in other clans and families as well. Far from being dismayed by Dunbeath, I pity him. He has only ever known the separation from other people that comes with superiority, endless duty, competition, and the constant need to keep his inferiors down. He's never felt any affection or ever been allowed it. And yet I believe he yearns for it more than any man I know.'

'You may be right, Mr Hume,' said Sophie, turning to look at the flames in the great fireplace, 'I had not seen him with the clarity you have. I admire you for your forbearance though. He is not an easy friend.'

* * *

Later that evening Hume and Dunbeath made further amends to their old relationship as they sat opposite one another at the long dining room table. Sophie came in holding a plate loaded with yet more dividends from Annie's expedition to Wick and David Hume glanced up at her over his wineglass, now far happier with the world – and with Dunbeath.

'Ah, Miss Kant. More food eh? You and Annie are too kind, too kind'

He paused, uncertain of how he would best express a sincere regret.

'But while you are here,' he continued, 'I would like to apologise for becoming so exercised with Lord Dunbeath this afternoon. I have said as much to him myself. I am indeed glad that I did not set off back to Edinburgh. I would have missed this fine dinner. But since we parted then I have also given the Dilemma a deal of thought. And I have concluded that my old friend was correct in his views.'

Sophie set the dish down in surprise as Hume pressed on.

'Yes, I have reflected and now see that there is only one possible conclusion. I have come to realise that when two completely rational, mutually competitive, cold hearted people have a 'one time' game like the Prisoner's Dilemma – *and are set only on winning at that time* – that indeed there can be only one outcome. Lord Dunbeath must be right. The only rational way to proceed in such a game is to defect.

'In fact,' continued Hume, 'when you have two clear thinking players who have set any notion of friendship or trust to one side and whose interests are completely opposed, I can see no alternative but that a state of equilibrium arises very quickly from which neither player would *ever* be able to change their choices – however much it might improve their positions if they did so. And no doubt their lives.'

'I believe you are describing many a marriage,' laughed Dunbeath, his own anger now completely dissipated by Hume engaging with his concept and allowing him his victory.

Hume laughed in reply, but then held up a forefinger. He was now completely serious.

'However. Life is more complicated than that. The way we played the game this afternoon is unrealistic. In the Prisoner's Dilemma there was no communication – you'll remember that the prisoners were in separate cells and you tried to replicate that with your book barrier – whereas in life there is. In fact, this is very much the point because in reality we *do* communicate with each other, we give off clues about ourselves all the time and project a thousand and one seen and unseen signals about what we're thinking. You said as much yourself, Dunbeath, when you explained your game. All that bluffing and feints and deceits you spoke about then.

'But, more importantly than that,' Hume's voice now rose in emphasis, 'we have our histories, we have our backgrounds, we have our *reputations*. We become known for how we've behaved in the past. People already know what to expect from us. They know already whether we've shown ourselves to be co-operators or defectors. And whether we're likely to be so again.

'You see, the Dilemma resides in the prisoner having only two options in his choices. To co-operate or to defect. But this is where the game departs from reality – because in truth a person cannot make a good decision until he knows the choice of the other player. Rather like your little boys and their cake, Dunbeath.

'So, having given the Dilemma a certain amount of further thought, I believe that the key to making this game an insight into our real lives must be to repeat it. But, *openly*. To keep meeting the same person and to have the potential to reward or punish him for his actions. In other words, to deal with him. There can be no dealing in a one-time game where the risk of error is death. But in reality, in daily life, the stakes are seldom so high, nor is the decision so final. So, instead of having a metaphorical book barrier the *opposite* is actually true in life – we actively show people what we're like. If you keep playing the Dilemma in an open way then the game changes and you realise that it pays to co-operate and rational to trust – because you can expect a reasonable opponent to co-operate in return.'

Sophie had been listening carefully to Hume and she now pulled up a chair to sit by the two men.

'Of course,' she said excitedly, 'you must be right, Mr Hume. The interests of the prisoners in the game were completely opposed. But in fact, even then, they would have known each other, and on that basis they might have made a different choice.'

'No, you're not thinking deeply enough, Miss Kant' interrupted Dunbeath sharply, 'because however much you think you may know your opponent, if there's the possibility of the other person defecting, then you're better off defecting too. That way you'll always get one point rather than potentially getting none. And of course you stop the other man from ever getting five. But if your opponent co-operates you are still better off defecting because you'll get five points instead of three. Whatever the other person does, you are better off defecting.'

Sophie thought for a moment while she considered this.

'Yes, but perhaps we should not use the word 'opponent'. It immediately implies conflict and defection. You see, if each person argued in the way you just have, you'll never achieve anything but one point each – when you could have had three each if you'd only co-operated.'

As she said this David Hume began laughing, his normal easy humour completely restored.

'Well,' he said quickly, 'if you imagine two people playing a hundred times and think forward to the outcomes, the range of possibilities must be from one player getting 500 points for always defecting while the other would end up with none for constantly choosing to co-operate. But the other person is bound to defect once he sees that there's no point in co-operating. Neither extreme is feasible. Both people co-operating, on the other hand, would lead to 600 points for the pair and a very easy relationship that would be.

'But one can see very quickly how tempting it would be if the other person was always co-operating to slip in the occasional defection just when the other player is lulled into thinking that there would never be any change. Five additional points while the other gets none. Yes, very tempting indeed. Imagine, for example, one of our thieves hiding from the captain of the guard. He's been given sanctuary in a monastery where the monks treat him with trust and kindness. How long would it take for him to rob them? To grab five points for defecting while the poor monks would get none for their troubles?'

Dunbeath smiled.

'Exactly,' he said.

'But what seems to be clear to me,' Hume continued, ignoring Dunbeath's pointed comment, 'is that when we find people we like and want to deal with, the game changes. It stops being a dilemma. What begins as irrational behaviour in trusting the other person – to think of the outcome for both people rather than just for themselves – becomes a rational decision in the long run, as long as there is a long run, as both players ought to co-operate.

'In any case, perfect rationality must be a fiction. To expect it is, if I may say so, to despise your fellow man so much that you withdraw from his company.'

'I presume you are referring to me?' said Dunbeath. But he didn't seem displeased by Hume's remark.

'But it's interesting, is it not,' continued Hume without being drawn to answer Dunbeath, 'that in the animal world the most robust of the species also seem to be the ones that are the most co-operative. And, shouldn't man, with what my friend Adam Smith calls his 'specialisations', be even *more* open to the benefits of co-operation.

'So, is selfishness an animal instinct, and trust – for surely that is what co-operation must be – a civilised one? Are the most successful animal species the ones that are continually attacking each other or those that show the greatest mutual support? I think you'd agree that most observations would point to the latter. Indeed, their world is so often a lesson to us. Everywhere one looks one sees co-operation even to the point of sacrifice. Does not a bird call out to its flock when it sees a cat – even though it gives its own position away? And look at so many of them when they are together. Particularly the more dangerous species. See in what a ritualised way they behave – twisting and retreating, sudden rushes and snapping. But mainly glowers and feints and noise. How interesting, though, that they very rarely do each other real harm.

'So what might this mean? Well, I think the start point has to be that if we're alive at all then we have to be examples of some kind of successful strategy. The only certainty in life is that our ancestors didn't die celibate. Perhaps the behaviour they employed to enhance our survival was thriving at the expense of the behaviour that failed for other people? This sole fact alone points to us being the living proof of some kind of winning approach. We humans may think that we are subtly individual but really we are just machines bent on survival. What is it that's making us behave instinctively in the way that we do?'

Hume leant back in his chair and picked up his wine again.

Dunbeath was so pleased with Hume's observations that he was now smiling.

'I am in your debt, Mr Hume,' he said, 'you nursed me back to life and now you are making me think. I believe I profoundly disagree with your conclusions but I very much look forward to continuing our game.'

Hume set his glass down.

'Well, I'm delighted to hear that, my lord. I shall greatly enjoy doing so. By the way,' he continued, 'what was it that you witnessed that made you think of the game in the first place?'

'What's that, what do you mean, Hume? Dunbeath said with an abruptly renewed sharpness, 'I've no idea what you can be referring to.'

Hume persisted with his question.

'When you wrote to me in Edinburgh you said that you had recently witnessed an event that had made you invent the Prisoner's Dilemma. I wondered what it was.'

Dunbeath's stickiness immediately started to return.

'What? Did I say as much? Well, there was nothing. I can't imagine why I would have said that.' There was a tense silence and Hume exchanged a quick glance with Sophie. Then she rose quietly from the table and started to pick up the used dishes to take back to the kitchen.

* * *

Early the following morning Zweig returned to the shoreline to finish shaping the branch with his knife. He'd shaved it to be quite straight, stepping down the width of the cylinder towards the end and then bringing out the final section in a bulge. Now he cut slits in the upper part and began to force small stones into them, making certain that they would be held in place as the sodden wood shrank. Eventually he held the finished piece up to the light and then bounced it in the palm of his hand to check its weight.

It will pass, he thought to himself – as long as it isn't looked at too closely.

He took the oilskin cloth from his pocket that had covered the Domenico Salva. He carefully wrapped it around the wooden cylinder and then ran his hand over the cloth. Bundled up in this way it looked and felt like the lost telescope. He quickly tied it with the original string and then set off to walk back to Dunbeaton.

Chapter 13

It was two weeks later and Dunbeath and Sophie were alongside one another at the great table in the tower study. Dunbeath glanced up from their papers and picked up a book of ecliptic tables, now thankfully found under the huge mass of written calculations that Sophie had carefully classified, organised and arranged. He could scarcely believe the changes she'd wrought. For the first time in years he was no longer drowning in paper and he still found it strange to be able to find things instead of having to wade through the quagmire he'd allowed to build up. His hand moved to stroke his chin, pleased too that he'd finally found the time to be clean shaven and the will to attend to his appearance.

A warm breeze came through the open window, gently ruffling Sophie's curls and pulling at the piles of written work, so neatly laid out on the table's surface. Dunbeath moved his head closer to Sophie's as they pored over a mass of celestial charts and interplanetary readings.

She now tapped with her finger at a table covering the measurement of parallax angles.

'I have thought about our problem overnight,' she said, 'and I think this is where the error has been stemming from. You see, these lunar distances are changing over time at a rate of half a degree, or thirty arc minutes every hour ...' she continued to take Dunbeath through her detailed reasoning and a few minutes later approached her conclusion, '... thus I think this could be inducing an error of as much as one quarter degree in longitude or about fifteen nautical miles at the equator. The core issue is one of timekeeping and I'm sure that by always using the periods of the Jovian moons rather than working with a clock we can be sure to resolve this.'

Dunbeath sat back. Sophie continued to study her workings but out of the corner of her eye she was conscious that Dunbeath was looking longingly at her from the side.

'I knew I had gone astray somewhere, Sophie,' he said at last. 'I knew the perfection of the heavens couldn't be at fault. It had to be my error and thanks to you it's now exposed – and furthermore you have a solution. I can scarcely credit this, indeed, I can scarcely credit everything that has happened recently. At last all my years of work and research have come together. That it has is much due to your help. And, of course, to your observation of the Transit.'

Sophie began to bridle gently at his thanks but Dunbeath wouldn't be deflected.

'I'd worked for twelve years without missing a single reading,' he went on, now looking closely at her, 'and yet you saved me when I could not continue. And then you've exposed these great errors of mine. Now, at last, the answer is here. You must know how much I am in your debt, Sophie, and I believe these findings are now in a position to be presented at the next meeting of the Board of Longitude. It should be held soon – there's usually one sometime in the spring. They've often been in May in the past and, in fact, I'm surprised I haven't been told of a date yet. I'm convinced these findings will put me so far ahead in the race to satisfy the criteria for the measurement of longitude that the Board will be hard pressed not to award me the Prize immediately.'

He looked again at Sophie and his tone changed. He began to speak to her in a voice of quiet intensity.

'Sophie, I couldn't have achieved this without you. You may have saved my life when you nursed me through my illness but you saved my life's work too. Will you agree to come to London with me when I go to the Board? I want them all to know of your contribution.'

Then he took a deep breath as if preparing himself to say something vital.

'Sweet Sophie, I want you to be with me then – and I want you to be with me when we return. Nothing must come between us. You've brought this old castle back to life. More than that, you've breathed a new life into me – you have changed me. I want you to stay here. Will you consider this?'

Sophie reeled in panic. What was this? Was it a prelude to an offer of marriage? Or did Dunbeath just see her as a collaborator in his research? She had thought she understood him for the impatient, distant man he was ... and yet here he was calling her 'sweet Sophie'. That was singing love songs from the hills for a man like him. She may only recently have washed up in Scotland but she knew enough about these aristocrats to know that they saw marriage more as an opportunity to add wealth and power than anything to do with the heart. And Hume had told her that gain was all that motivated the Urquhain. She hadn't anything to offer. So what could he mean? She thought further and then firmly decided not to press him – she might not wish to hear the answer. She just had to buy time. There were still thirty nine days before her father's debt fell away – and she had to have Dunbeath's protection until then. Whatever it was that he meant, she had to play for time.

Sophie gazed at Dunbeath, looking deeply into his eyes. Then she blinked and looked away.

'Well, my lord, I'm flattered by what you say. Indeed I am greatly affected. I owe you so much too. You forget that. You, too, have saved me.'

As she spoke she listened to her heart. There was undoubtedly a great affection there for the man, in spite of his anger and restless arrogance. But perhaps what had begun as a fascination in her had not yet turned to love? Perhaps it would? And did it matter anyway? If he should mean to press for marriage then the security and status that he could give her were far more than she could ever have hoped for. In any event, marriage or not, if she stayed with Dunbeath she would be able to do so much – she would greatly prize working with him to continue their research together – and there was little doubt that his great wealth could help her poor father as well.

In an instant she had weighed up her position: her heart might not be full but that could change in time, particularly if his was truly full for her. And her head told her not to show any sign of rejection. She had few options anyway, and anything that protected her from Zweig and the debt had to be agreed to.

'Yes, I would be very happy to go to London with you,' she said warmly, carefully ignoring any deeper message he may have meant. 'Thank you. I greatly look forward to hearing of the date.'

She looked down as she tried to steer the conversation away from any further discussion about their future. Her eyes were now on the table and she stretched out a hand to pick up the Domenico Salva from where it lay on a sheet of planetary movements.

'This really is the most beautiful piece of work,' she said, looking at the chasing of the gold case. She ran her finger over the jewelled exterior and then lifted the telescope to her eye and focused it on a boulder set in the beach at the far end of Dunbeaton Bay. 'And what superb lenses it has. I've never seen another like it.'

She set it down again and continued to speak quietly and with no small trepidation. She knew the time had come – she had to find out what Dunbeath knew of Zweig.

'But, why do you think that ship's captain had it? Did he steal it from you? Do you remember he said - 'how do you think I came by it?' - when he jumped out at us on the dunes? What do you think he meant by that?'

'I don't know,' replied Dunbeath, suddenly his old sharp self again, 'I'd never seen him before.'

'Yes,' Sophie carried on, a slight trace of incomprehension entering her tone, 'but what do you think he meant?'

'How could I know what he meant?' Dunbeath was beginning to bridle. 'I told you, I'd never seen him before. I had no idea who he was.'

* * *

Once Zweig had returned the wooden fake to the original's hiding place he'd turned his thoughts towards how he could steer James away from his growing obsession with having the telescope returned to him. The boy had been becoming more querulous by the day and he was now insisting on seeing it again. The previous afternoon, he had even spoken of exposing Zweig to the English army if he didn't get his way. At least with the fake to draw on, the captain felt, he had something that he could wave in front of him if the need arose. In spite of this, he knew that James could only be held off for so long and Zweig now decided that he had to bring forward the second part of his strategy.

The boy was a factor to be considered, that was true, but he was just an irritation compared to the larger plan to win Sophie round. Zweig knew her mind, though, and he was quite sure that the debt schedule was the leverage he needed for his next steps. Sophie had already shown him how aware she was of the dates – and she would know only too well that time was running out for them to return to Königsberg and so trigger the repayment. He could be certain that she would see this as the ticking clock. A further two weeks had passed since he'd seen her on the dunes and he could be sure she would be aware that there were now just thirty nine days left. Many fewer and she would think that Zweig wouldn't be able to make the journey to be back within the hundred days that Kant had set. He couldn't leave things any longer – now was the time to bring matters to a head.

He took a deep breath. He knew there would be much pain in the next part of his strategy and he set his shoulders as he steeled himself for the ordeal ahead. After a few moments he shook himself slightly and began the short walk to the castle. It wasn't long before he came to the top of a large dune and he stopped there to look down at the granite slab that made up the side of the great Urquhain stronghold.

About a hundred yards from the vast fortress the constant working of the tides had so eroded the front of the dunes that a small raised peninsular of grass and sand stretched out onto the beach. The end of this was in full view of every window on the castle's north face and it was here, he had decided, that would be his battleground.

Having satisfied himself again on his choice, Zweig walked towards the hummock. By now there was such evident purpose in his stride and such great determination in his features that it was plain that his mind was quite set.

He reached the end of the spit and turned towards the castle, checking the sight lines from the windows. Apparently satisfied that nothing would obstruct a view of his position he sat down and carefully folded his legs under him in the way he'd seen practiced by the monks of the east.

Then he closed his eyes.

Above him the sky darkened as rain clouds blew in from the sea. Now, facing towards the largest windows, his eyes still shut, his body stiffened as if he was summoning up his inner strength.

Then he opened them again and his face was composed in a trance of concentration. He stared fixedly at the castle and he tensed again as if distilling every particle of energy to serve his colossal will. Then he leant forward from the waist with such an intense show of force that some strange power seemed almost to shimmer off his huge frame.

This will take much time, he thought to himself. He had to be patient, he had to stay alert.

* * *

Hume and Dunbeath had moved their game playing from the salon to the dining room. For much of the last two weeks

Dunbeath had been taking part only intermittently, his mind more occupied by the navigation problems that Sophie had recently resolved. Hume had not concerned himself too greatly with this delay and had instead attacked the great Urquhain library, devouring whole sections of the Greek thinkers that he'd found on its shelves.

But, with the solving of the celestial problems, the Dilemma was drawing the two men together again and they now sat opposite each other at one end of the long table, the record of their recent turns spread out between them. Flames from half a dozen enormous logs in the great fireplace threw their shadows about the room and the ornate plasterwork and fierce staring caryatids seemed almost alive in the glow. Above the pair's hunched backs, a vast barrel shaped ceiling of raised strapwork and long, pendulous roof bosses loomed over them, a master-piece that dated from the time of King James.

Sophie sat next to Dunbeath, glancing occasionally at a large sheet of paper on which she'd been keeping the score.

Hume sighed and sat back in his chair.

'We do not seem to be progressing at all, Dunbeath. Yet again you have chosen to defect. Whilst I know your logic in doing this I can only repeat that I can see no encouragement to deal with someone who never shows any sign of reciprocating my evident wish to co-operate.'

'But Hume,' replied Dunbeath crisply, although in a far less provocative tone than he'd used during their earlier games, 'even though you know how I shall always play I still don't understand why you can't see that I am beating you. And that must surely be the mathematical lesson of the game.'

'No,' said Hume firmly. 'Sophie and I were discussing this yesterday and we've both concluded that it is exactly this belief that exposes the Dilemma's fundamental principle. And it is this. We believe it is a mistake to talk of 'beating me' or to see the game as one of winners and losers.

'If this is so, then nothing is ever *added*, nothing is ever built. Sophie has called this a 'nil sum game' because if one man's gain is exactly matched by the other man's loss then there is no gain, nothing is created, the sum total is, indeed, nil. But even the small boys with their cake showed that co-operation – although it was based on greed and the fear of losing – *can* add something. In their case the gain may simply have been an outcome of unusual tranquillity but if one thinks of it as peace between warring factions then that is indeed a giant step forward.

'The trouble with these nil sum games is that if one man is winning only at the expense of the other person losing then there will never be a lasting relationship. How can you ever trust someone who you know is always trying to beat you? Indeed, did we not come near to losing our friendship over your own strategy? And was it not your insistence that you were beating me and that this was all that mattered that led me to give up on you? On the other hand any merchant will tell you that while he would wish to profit from you, he wishes you to profit also. In that way you can both be satisfied. And the likelihood is that the two of you will then continue to trade.'

Hume stopped for a moment and looked into the fire. He had given the Dilemma a deal of thought these past two weeks and he now wished to bring the sterility of their repetitive contests to an end.

'Let me give you another example,' he continued looking back to Dunbeath, 'you'll recall that in our grandfathers' day the English and the Dutch spent ruinous sums on great navies to protect their commercial interests as if the gain of one would be the loss of the other. But we learnt, did we not, that it was actually due to the competition between them that world trade grew. It became evident that it was not the *share* of the trade that one country achieved that mattered so much as the *growth* in the custom itself. Both countries could be winners – in fact, the evidence was that they were.'

'You may be right in both your examples,' Dunbeath replied thoughtfully, 'but nonetheless it is the rational player in these games – as in life itself – who will do better when he plays an irrational one. These leaps of logic you describe may be obvious to the distinguished moral philosopher I am addressing here at my table but they will escape the normal man. They are therefore not present in everyday exchanges. Far from it, it is the calculating fellow who will always beat the naïve.'

Hume sighed heavily and his shoulders sagged.

'Sophie, can you help me here? I really don't think this is a conclusion that I alone have reached. I think we only have to look at how people go about their daily lives to see that.'

Sophie looked down at the scores.

'Perhaps it's easier for me to give an opinion as I haven't been caught up in the competition of the game,' she replied, 'but it must be plain that the answer about how to play depends on what one's aim is. If one wants to gain from society by building the order and reliability of that society, and therefore to profit from it, then co-operation must be the correct strategy. Essentially the way I see it is that, over time, one is not escaping the hangman's noose of a one-time Prisoner's Dilemma but instead looking for people to play high scoring games with – to live to fight another day rather than to be beaten. To win wars not battles. And to do this one has to recognise that it's the *collective* score that matters more than the individual's, just as keeping silent would have helped both prisoners if they could but have trusted each other.'

Hume nodded at this and smiled encouragingly at her as she continued.

'Unlike the prisoners and your attempt to replicate the two cells with your book barrier – in real life we *do* communicate. In reality we remember how people have behaved in the past and how they are likely to behave in the future. And therefore we can decide who we want to deal with. On the other hand, the key to dealing with constant defectors is to decide not to play with them. To avoid them and find other partners instead. Once one's found co-operative people then stable relationships and stable societies can be formed that will bring real benefits to the individual. That is how a man wins, not by constantly trying to beat someone in every single exchange. This much seems evident to me. However, it also seems that the real problem then arises with people who take advantage of a society in which *others* are co-operating.'

Hume and Dunbeath both looked at her with interest.

'What do you mean by that Miss Kant?'

'Well, let me give you an example,' she continued, becoming more confident that the two men were genuine in their wish to hear her views. 'Take, for instance, a ferry. It crosses a piece of open water. The price of the passage is low, say it's a penny. The ferryman depends on this income to provide the service, to keep the boat seaworthy, feed his family and so on. The people in this little community, of course, equally depend on a reliable and efficient way of making the crossing. It's late one evening and the ferry is full. It's about to leave when a man silently jumps on without paying and without the ferryman noticing. Now, will the ferryman be impoverished by this? No – don't forget, he was leaving anyway. But this defector – let's call him a 'free rider' because he's travelling for nothing – has gained an advantage from the co-operation of others, from people who *have* paid.

'This free rider is simply doing something that we might all be tempted to do in the same circumstances – but if *everyone* actually behaved like this then it would be disastrous for society. In fact, I'd go so far as to say that any situation in which one would be tempted to do something, but one also knows that it would be catastrophic if everyone did the same thing, is likely to be a form of Prisoner's Dilemma.'

David Hume was listening closely, clearly very intrigued by the story. He scratched his head and then lifted a hand.

'I hope you don't mind me adding to your argument, Sophie,' he said, 'but I can see an important insight into society's ways here. You see, if the free rider was seen by the other passengers when he jumped onto the ferry then he's known to be the thief that he is. He's given up his right to be trusted. For the sake of a penny!

'But you're not alone in drawing a conclusion from this kind of tale, Sophie,' he continued, straightening his beautiful coat with the pleasure of the conversation, 'I was hearing the other day about something one of the French thinkers had written. He was describing a stag hunt in which the men of a village had formed a circle and were closing in on a fine specimen they'd surrounded. Suddenly one of the men saw a rabbit and left the circle to catch it. The man's logic was understandable at that moment because the rabbit would feed his family. But the stag rushed through the gap he'd left and was lost to the village. Would the rabbit feed the group? No. But the stag would have done. And no individual would have been able to kill the stag on his own.

'Even though one can see why the lure of the short term reward of catching the rabbit was so attractive to him, this defector would have eaten his full if the stag had been caught. And he wouldn't have earned the disgust of his neighbours. The logic of his defection is now seen to be very different from the impact of the price he was made to pay for his actions later.'

Hume took a deep pull from the whisky he had in front of him.

'Surely both stories are making the same point,' he continued as he put the glass down. 'Where one has a society based on co-operation like the paying ferry customers or the stag hunters then the selfish man will defect easily – but at a considerable price. Society may be the loser but society will respond by seeing him for what he is. And people won't trust him in future. The Frenchman's interpretation was that because the man would have made the right decision for himself but the wrong one for the group, the story showed that ever expecting social co-operation is absurd. But surely that's wrong? Surely the right view is that it simply shows how important it is for society to exclude free riders and rabbit grabbers?'

Dunbeath grimaced.

'Exclude them? Perhaps shooting them would be more telling.'

Hume smiled but decided to avoid rising to Dunbeath's provocation. Instead he nodded and went quickly on.

'Very well, then, let me give you another parable which amused me when I thought of it. You have a group of people. A rich man has gathered them together in a room and he says to them … 'I shall give each of you £50 if you can all stay quiet for just sixty minutes. But if someone breaks the silence and shouts out during that time then he alone will get £20 and the rest of you will get nothing!' The rich man turns over an hourglass and the group stands, watching the sands as they run through, all of them tense, willing the flow to come to an end. Time passes. Now, what would you do if you were one of those people? Obviously you'd think to yourself that you'd be better off if everyone kept their mouths shut. But then you'd think again … what if one of these people gets it into his head that he wants to be superior to the rest of us? What if he thinks it's more important to get something and for the rest of us to get nothing? In fact, he'll think he's been clever. Got an advantage over us. And then you think – well, if that's what other people will be thinking, why don't I be the clever one instead? You may want the £50, you may want to be a good member of the group. But can you risk someone else not thinking that he'll outsmart you all? And the £20 is certain, the £50 is at risk. What do you do? My friends, if you're thinking intelligently, you'd shout.'

Hume laughed, pleased to see the way that Dunbeath was evidently thinking about how he would have behaved.

'This little tale,' he continued, 'the free rider story and the Prisoner's Dilemma, all seem to me to be revealing a great insight. They are surely all versions of what happens when collective and individual interests are in conflict. But what the Dilemma and these other little stories show is that the winning strategy is the one based on *seeing the future*. It is the ability to have this vision, to be able to use one's imagination and to weigh things up, that separates man from the animals. Man can imagine the future. He can see the consequences of his actions and the likely actions of others and can shape his behaviour accordingly. It is why he lives in hope – and frequently in tears. But if you take the mechanism of the Dilemma, he's able to see that rewards come to those who co-operate. In other words he wishes to appear to be unselfish, to be co-operative, but only because he selfishly wants the rewards that doing so will bring!'

Hume came to a sudden, abrupt stop. He appeared to retreat inside himself, stunned, apparently silenced by the realisation of what he'd just said. Then he looked upwards towards the ceiling, deep in thought. A moment later he still seemed so struck by his own conclusion that he got to his feet and stood, fidgeting by his chair. Once again he said, murmuring slowly, more to himself than to the others, *'one wishes to appear to be unselfish but only because one selfishly wants the rewards that doing so will bring.'*

He gently shook his head and smiled in astonishment at what he'd heard himself say. There was a silence from Dunbeath and Sophie as they looked over at him and Hume shook his head again and smiled. They both watched as he then walked to the window, absorbed in his thinking, to where a long sideboard stood with a decanter of whisky on it. He refilled his glass and then looked out of the window at the darkening sky.

'I think a big storm is brewing,' he said abstractedly, still astonished and excited by his insight. He gazed over at the clouds massing to the east and was about to turn back to the room when he glanced down at the beach. It was then that he saw

Zweig staring intently up at him.

'Hello,' he called out over his shoulder, 'what's going on here? You have a strange watcher down here on the beach, Dunbeath. What do you imagine his game is?'

Sophie and Dunbeath came to the window to see what Hume was talking about.

Sophie shrank back when she saw that it was Zweig but Dunbeath became immediately aggressive.

'It's that fool of a ship's captain,' he said angrily.

'Which ship?' asked Hume.

'The one that blew up.'

'But I thought everybody but Sophie had perished. How on earth did he escape from the blast? Was he blown here?'

'No, he must have swum ashore,' muttered Dunbeath without thinking. 'I saw him through my big telescope when he was on deck.'

Sophie looked closely at Dunbeath.

'Oh, you had seen him before then. You told me you didn't know who he was when you took the Domenico Salva from him on the dunes.'

Dunbeath said nothing and Hume spoke quickly to save the tension from developing.

'Have you ever seen such an intensity in someone? The man seems to be on fire. What do you think he wants?'

But Dunbeath simply wheeled away from the window. The anger that had so obviously flared up in him came as much from having Sophie cross-question him as from having Zweig make such a provocative and public invasion of his territory.

'Come away from the window,' he said tersely, 'we don't need to concern ourselves with him. I dare say the next tide will wash him away.

Chapter 14

Once Zweig had seen first Hume and then the others come to the window he'd allowed himself the minutest of satisfied smiles, only too aware that the game was now afoot.

It was over four hours since he had taken up his position but not once had he wavered in his concentration. He knew that he never could. Again and again he summoned up the meditation techniques he'd learned in the East, shown to him when he'd been trading between the Baltic and the Straits of Malacca, bringing back shiploads of the fashionable blue and white china that the Russian market so admired. The monks he'd spent time with there had taught him their secret ways to a mental process so intense in its focus that it never allowed the mind to drift. So far he had succeeded but the ordeal was just a few hours old and he knew that he was still in the foothills of the mountain he had to climb.

Night was falling and a fresh wind had sprung up and with it the portent of heavy rain. He was pleased – the weather would stiffen his resolve and a rainstorm would keep him fresh for the task.

* * *

In the castle Sophie woke with a start, a chill at her heart and the sick memory of the sight of Zweig on the dunes clouding her dreams. She turned over yet again. A further five minutes passed before she admitted to herself that sleep would never return while she lay fretting over whether he was still there.

She lit her candle and threw back the heavy covers, then pulled a shawl over her shoulders and walked to the window. Even before she reached it she knew from the shriek of the wind and the mad pattering of the rain that a wild storm had broken.

She pulled back the curtain to see the windows being lashed

by the violent squall. She put the candle to one side and then cupped her hands to the pane to look out through the glass. As she did so her eyes gradually adjusted to the dark and she took in Zweig in the distance, drenched, his clothes clinging to his iron physique, impervious to the slashing deluge. Then with a sick shock she realised that he was staring directly back at her, quite still, focusing solely on her window.

She shuddered and drew the curtains again.

Zweig had indeed seen her – first the flash of her candle and then the whiteness of her face. He was also pleased to see the speed with which she'd retreated, so obviously shocked at the sight.

'Three. Five,' he murmured to himself, counting the floors and then the position of her window from the castle's end.

* * *

The next morning opened fair with a drying wind and a warm high sun that promised much for the day.

Major Sharrocks arrived, coming up quietly behind his sentry.

'A wet night, trooper,' he said without much sympathy, 'what's happening? Is he still there then?'

'Yes, sir,' replied the redcoat putting down his telescope, 'never moved a muscle. Been there all night, just staring like.'

'What the hell's going on?' said Sharrocks, testily. 'Something's happening here – and I mean to find out what.'

* * *

Sophie had slept little. In the early hours she'd tossed and turned before deciding eventually that there was nothing she could do about Zweig and came to the conclusion instead that she should immerse herself in the Dilemma as a distraction. She'd risen and gone to the dining room and five hours later she was there still, surrounded by pages of mathematical workings and wrapped in her extraordinary concentration. So deep was she in her calculations that she didn't notice as David Hume wandered into the room in the hope of breakfast, but she looked up as he peered over her shoulder in amused bafflement at the mass of figures on the table in front of her, and then shrugged and strolled over to the window. He looked down at the beach.

'That man is still there, Sophie. Did you see him when you came in? What on earth do you think he wants? He's looking at me now. He's a fierce one, isn't he? I can almost feel the energy coming off him. It's quite astonishing.'

'Is he?' replied Sophie with little apparent interest, not looking up as her quill hurtled across yet another page of calculations.

Hume's shrewd features showed that he was now in little doubt that there was more to the man's presence than Sophie would care to have him know.

'You look as if you have been worrying over our little puzzle for some time, Sophie. What are you at?'

Sophie put the quill down at last, and a tiny flicker of self-satisfaction flashed across her face.

'I'm looking for the strategy for a successful life,' she said with a laugh, 'and I can tell you that it's no small matter!'

'How interesting that sounds, Sophie. What do you mean?'

Sophie yawned, suddenly tired.

'I've been exploring different approaches to playing the Prisoner's Dilemma,' she said, rubbing her eyes. 'I've been looking at the many possible outcomes that arise from playing both sides of the game and I'm trying to find the optimal strategy for getting the most points by playing it repeatedly. You don't actually need two players to explore the theory, it can be done mathematically. In other words I'm doing what Lord Dunbeath suggested you should do originally when he first wrote to you in Edinburgh. I'm looking for a mathematical solution. You see, those stories we were amusing ourselves with yesterday set me thinking. If a good society is one in which people lead trusting, productive lives – in other words high scoring games with a large number of partners – then there must be a strategy or an approach that achieves this.

'But the Prisoner's Dilemma can only be a start point in this process. It's like a stone in this castle. A building block. Of course it tells us what the castle's made of and other things like its colour and hardness – but it doesn't tell us what the castle itself is actually going to look like.

'So while it's fairly easy to agree that good societies are like games in which people are constantly getting three points, it's also easy to see that others can take advantage of this situation by defecting, by behaving like a free rider and grabbing five at the society's expense. The questions I put to myself were these: how do you deal with these people, these defectors? Is there a strategy to discourage them from acting in this way and instead encourage them to co-operate? And how do you find it?'

She waved her hand over the mass of mathematical workings on the table.

'The alternative is obvious – an unproductive society in which nobody trusts his neighbour. In which everyone is defecting and only ever getting one point. I think of this as being a bit like a forest. All the energy of the trees is spent in growing higher than the others in the search for light and air. If they'd only stop competing in this way and agree to all be shorter then they could expand their branches and live longer, easier lives. You will never see a tree in a forest that grows as large or as strong as a tree on its own in a field. A society made up of defectors follows the analogy – it's an exhausting, short-lived place where there's no trust and no long term thinking.

'But what I've been trying to find is whether a co-operator could ever induce a defector to co-operate? For him to become educated in trust in other words. Could a defector, for example, be punished and given another chance? '

She smiled at last as she looked at Hume's kindly expression. He raised a questioning eyebrow.

'And, yes, I think they can, Mr Hume. I suddenly saw that where the Dilemma departs from the reality of life was that it's very rare that we deal with each other simultaneously. In fact we try and avoid it. We generally react *sequentially*, one after another. The way we communicate when we talk to one another, or write letters, or even when we look at each other, is almost invariably sequential. What we're almost always trying to do, even though we may not be aware of it, is see what the other person is doing and saying before we respond. Or commit ourselves. Unknown to us, we are doing actively what the small boys were made to do passively with their cake. What was it Lord Dunbeath said about that? Didn't he say that each child was making a choice knowing that the other child would be making a choice too?

'And then I saw that the key to success was based on this observation and I applied the simple principle that *the right thing to do depends upon what the other person does.*'

She stopped and laughed at herself.

'It suddenly occurred to me that if there's no finite end to the game – in other words it's *not* like Lord Dunbeath's one-time Prisoner's Dilemma – then one should do unto others as they have done unto you. Yes, I know, Mr Hume, it's not quite what Aristotle, Plato and all the ancient religions have instructed us. They all tell us to do unto others as you would have them do unto you. And, of course, that should be the approach when one meets a new player. Nonetheless, I rather suspect that the survival instinct in us would prefer to know what the other person is doing first!'

She laughed again, encouraged by Hume's obvious fascination.

'In other words, it's the very opposite of the lack of communication that the prisoners had in their cells or you had to contend with when you were made to sit behind the book barrier.'

'So, what do you think the implications of this thinking are for the Dilemma, Sophie?' asked Hume, now intrigued to see if her conclusions fitted with his earlier insight. 'Did you actually arrive at a strategy that would do this?'

Sophie waved her hand over the reams of workings.

'Well, I've tried many different approaches but it's only when you've played enough hands over a long period of time that the strengths and weaknesses of different strategies begin to show up. I've been playing against myself for hours, trying everything from ironclad discipline to a mixture of the prescribed and the random. But, yes, I do believe that I'm making progress. I wondered early on if the simple choice of always co-operating would not bring the most points – in the way that the saintly hope they will bring round the wrongdoer. But I came to the view that once selfish people see that they can defect with these committed co-operators without any loss to their own points then the temptation to take advantage of their good natures would be too great for opportunists to resist. Then, for a time I had great hopes for the tactic of simply repeating the same choice if one won but changing it if one lost. It produced promising results for a time but then began to disappoint. However, I persisted with the underlying aim of following one's opponent's choice, and yes, there is indeed one strategy that keeps winning.'

'How very interesting Sophie,' said Hume, now completely captivated, 'what is it?'

' Well, I think of it as Tit for Tat,' she replied, 'and it works by simply repeating the choice of the other person. So, when the other person defects I play 'defect' next. When he co-operates I do the same. It seems to me that it wouldn't take long for him to realise what's happening. In fact the whole point of the Tit for Tat strategy is that it shouldn't be a secret. You actually want the other person to know what you're doing.

'And it turns out to be a very powerful way of playing, just because it's so transparent – it's so easy for your opponent to understand. Its strength comes from an irresistible combination of trust, retaliation, forgiveness and clarity. By 'trust' I mean that the other person can trust you to play co-operate if he does. If he doesn't – and instead plays defect – then he knows that you will immediately retaliate. And this discourages him from persisting whenever defection is tried. The reason is obvious – why would he want to get just one point when he can see that three are available?

'Once he stops playing defect and goes back to co-operate you restore co-operate as well, so it's a kind of immediate forgiveness. And the strategy's clarity makes it intelligible to the other player, because what you're doing is so evident – and it therefore achieves long term co-operation.'

'But Sophie,' said Hume, excitedly, 'did no other strategy achieve the same end?'

'No.' Sophie shook her head. 'At first, of course, the nasty, defector strategies kept winning at the expense of the naïve, co-operative players. Only retaliator strategies like Tit for Tat where you have a co-operator who will immediately switch to defect if the other person defects, were able to resist them. But gradually the nasty approaches ran out of the easy pickings of killing co-operators and then defectors kept meeting each other – and obviously their numbers began to decline. This is really the key point. If the defectors kill the co-operators then they're left having to deal with each other! They then dwindle because they kill each other. This was when one sees the success of the Tit for Tat strategy because its retaliation mechanism eventually takes command of the game. Do you see now why I say that there must be a way of playing that educates defectors and rewards co-operators?

'The way it works shows itself over time – it may lose or draw each battle, but it wins the war. It ensures that most of its games are high scoring encounters and so it constantly brings home the most points. The crucial insight about the Tit for Tat strategy is that it isn't trying to 'beat' its opponent – success need not be at the price of someone's failure. A nil sum game is the last thing you want. Tit for Tat is an agreement not a contest.'

* * *

It was now mid morning and Zweig was in agony, his muscles screaming at their continued contraction. For a bad few minutes he hadn't even known whether he could continue. Then he summoned up a vision of Sophie and yet again he demanded a further effort from his tortured body. He knew there was no going back now, that this was a fight to the end and that his whole being would never allow himself to fail. He leant forward once more, forcing himself to focus his pain on the image of Dunbeath's sneering face that day on the dunes. Slowly his mind conquered the shrieking muscles and again he settled down for the battle with himself that he knew would have to be won.

* * *

'Of course,' Sophie continued as Hume listened, increasingly intrigued by her unfolding logic, 'the principal requirement for Tit for Tat to work is for two people to have a stable, repetitive relationship. In fact, the longer a pair of individuals interact, the greater the chances of co-operation. On the other hand, the more casual and opportunistic an encounter, the less likely it is that Tit for Tat will succeed in building co-operation. New players are wary. They don't know if they are in a one-time contest like the desperate choice in Lord Dunbeath's original Prisoner's Dilemma or whether they are embarking on a longer-term relationship. And, if they are, are they dealing with a serial defector or with someone who would wish to share in a co-operative relationship?'

David Hume sat quite still for a few seconds, turning this over in his mind.

'I can only repeat that I find this most revealing, Sophie,' he said eventually, before giving a slight grimace as his thoughts alighted on an objection. 'But, of course, there is much more subtlety in this problem than the Dilemma allows. There must be a great difference, for example, between a 'bad' defector who ruthlessly defects as a matter of policy and personality and a 'good' defector who's defecting only to protect himself. I'm afraid that Lord Dunbeath, for example, has shown himself to be unable to break free of the Urquhain obsession of never trusting anyone. But there are many other people who would defect out of a natural sense of self-preservation and who would actually prefer to co-operate. Still, I think your Tit for Tat strategy is an extraordinary insight. It's exactly the kind of empirical solution that could show us how our behaviour towards each other has evolved.

'If the Prisoner's Dilemma is, as you say, just a building block in showing how a society can function then I'd suggest we have to imagine how it works in situations closer to reality – with lots of players rather than just two. And each of them playing with all of the others. The possibilities of all these multiple Dilemmas make the head spin. I've no doubt that as my friend, Adam Smith, would say about markets, some invisible grinding force would come into play eventually to restore equilibrium.'

He rose to his feet and walked around the room, deep in thought. Sophie followed him with her eyes, quite certain that he was about to bring a further twist to what she had outlined.

'But if you're right about Tit for Tat – and I think you are – then everything makes sense,' he said at last.

'In what way, Mr Hume?'

'Well,' Hume replied, eager now to take Sophie's conclusions further, 'if you think of defectors as hawks and co-operators as doves then the hawks would easily keep defeating the doves – as

Dunbeath did to me – until they were killed, or went back to Edinburgh, or there were so few of them left that the hawks kept meeting others like themselves. They then kill or negate the other hawks because they know no other way. This is very much as you've just said.

'However, say there are what you called retaliators - doves that fight back and behave like hawks – then the hawks would decline to them because the retaliators would work in teams to succeed. They know how to share. We see this in societies that become threatened, don't we? Where good, peace loving people reach a point where they say they are 'standing up for what they believe in' and suddenly become surprisingly warlike. But, going back to my parable, when the hawks have been defeated or change their ways and the retaliators turn back into co-operative doves then the process would end with the evolution of a stable, co-operative, three point gaining society. I'm not saying that there need be a rapid progress in this but I do believe that it is one that would have an inevitable outcome.

'In other words although the possibility of retaliation remains as a strategy, after a bit the players in a co-operative relationship begin to look as if they are no longer playing Tit for Tat but instead have chosen what we might term Always Co-operate – and are always receiving three points. But a defector would find that this is untrue if he tried to free ride, to grab an advantage at their expense.'

Sophie was about to reply to this when the door burst open and Dunbeath flew angrily into the room. He glared at them as if they were somehow at fault and then went over to the window, shouting loudly as he did so.

'That stupid ship's captain is still sitting out there, Hume! He is beginning to irk me with his constant staring. What is he looking at? What does he want? Much more of this and I shall shoot him! I wouldn't be surprised if I found he was within range from this very window.'

Sophie immediately tried to deflect their attention from Zweig and to defuse the situation.

'Will you not join us in our discussion, my lord? Mr Hume and I are making great progress in finding a mathematical approach to the Dilemma. Would you like to hear about an interesting strategy we've arrived at?

Dunbeath managed to drag himself away from the window but just glowered at her.

'What's that you say, Sophie?' he said testily, clearly struggling to control his anger. 'The Dilemma? No, no I have no time for that. There is still much to do to prepare for the Board of Longitude. It must be soon. It must be. Damn it! Why haven't I been informed of a date yet?'

* * *

Major Sharrocks walked slowly through Craigleven's great state-rooms towards L'Arquen's office. His progress was little more than a crawl and he shot an exasperated glance at the soldier alongside him. The trooper was aware of the major's irritation and he gave another shove to the bent figure that shuffled so slowly ahead of him. The man could barely walk, bound at the ankles and with his hands tied behind his back. Sharrocks looked with disgust at the torn tweed of his kilt and his mud caked face. By God, these people were repulsive, he thought and wondered yet again why on earth he was here, trying to control such barbarians. For the life of him he couldn't see why anyone would want to have these filthy Scots as part of the kingdom.

Eventually they reached L'Arquen's beautiful walnut door. At first there was no answer to Sharrocks' knock and he banged on the door for a second time. He turned to the guard.

'You're quite sure he's in there?'

'Yes, sir. Without a doubt sir,' said the man with a flush of embarrassment.

Sharrocks turned to the trooper he had with him.

'You wait here with this revolting specimen,' he said, nodding towards the highlander. 'I'll call for you in a minute.'

Sharrocks knocked a third time, more loudly than before, and pushed the door gradually open. Peering around it he saw L'Arquen lounging with his feet on the desk, his eyes closed, a mass of papers carelessly thrown in front of him.

'Our noon meeting sir?' said Sharrocks, refusing to be drawn into L'Arquen's absurd power game.

The colonel opened his eyes at last.

'Mmm? Ah Sharrocks, there you are. Is it midday already? So soon? Well, come in, come in, what have you to report?'

'You will recall that there was a man on the dunes in Dunbeaton Bay yesterday, sir, staring at the Castle of Beath. He is still there. We observed him all night and he did not give up his position for so much as a second.'

'How very curious, Sharrocks,' replied L'Arquen, now moving to sit upright in his chair, 'but it may be nothing. Keep him under surveillance – but covertly. I have told you many times, I do not want it known that we're keeping watch. As I say, it may be nothing.

'Speaking of Dunbeaton, I have something for you, major. Our people have reported back that the ship that blew up, the Schwarzsturmvogel, had sailed from Königsberg. It is in Prussia, Sharrocks. Apparently it was bound for the quarrying trade in France. I have the captain's name somewhere.' L'Arquen leant forward and rummaged about his papers. He drew out a military signal. 'Yes, here it is. His name was Alexis Zweig. No doubt he was among the corpses you saw. Still, I have sent word back that they are to make further investigations. So, what else do you have?'

'We have a suspect sir. Found near Lanochburn. You'll remember that we had reports of rebels in the area and we've been keeping an eye on the place for some days. He was hiding in a hay barn. Refuses to say anything, even to give his name. We have him outside your door.'

'Very good, Sharrocks. Bring in him. We shall have a quiet word with him.'

The major opened the door and beckoned to the trooper. He came into the room, pushing the prisoner before him and then set the man in front of the colonel's desk. L'Arquen stood up, his face wreathed in smiles.

'My dear sir. How very good of you to give us your time. I must apologise if you've been brought here against your will but you'll know that we live in uncertain times. Now, I'd be very grateful if you would tell me where your friends are. We must find these rebels of yours and stop their nonsense before they can do any more harm. Would you be kind enough, please, to tell me where they have hidden themselves?'

The man lifted his eyes from the floor and glared at L'Arquen, hatred scored in every line of his face. He said nothing. After a few seconds the colonel broke the silence.

'No answer? I fear that does not speak well of you, sir. If you have no part in all this then I would simply like you to tell me that.'

There was a further tense, black pause.

'Harken,' said L'Arquen softly, his voice barely more than a whisper. The room froze, the soldiers only too aware that a terrible abyss had been reached. Not for nothing was the colonel known to his men as 'Harken L'Arquen'.

'Harken,' he said for a second time, again very quietly, 'I would greatly appreciate it if you would tell me what you know.'

The highlander stood quite still, his mouth a tight line. L'Arquen gave a low sigh.

'Very well. I quite understand. You have nothing to say. Well now, my dear sir, this gentleman here is called Trooper Williams and he will take you away again,' the colonel waved his arm towards the soldier, 'and if you should change your mind and want to come back to see me later then you will always be most welcome.'

The trooper manhandled the prisoner out of the office and L'Arquen rose and went over to the map. He looked at it closely, trying to find Lanochburn, and then stood for a time with his finger on it as if considering the implications of the rebels' position. In the distance, possibly in a room behind the office, someone began to scream. At first there was a note of surprise in its tone but that quickly gave way to a kind of indignation, then anger, pleading and finally to an animal shriek of such pure pain, so wild and so all consuming that there was no human thinking left in it.

Sharrocks winced at the sound. He might loathe the Scots but this was not his way. He looked at L'Arquen with misgiving.

But the colonel continued as if he hadn't heard anything.

'Your little play on the dunes intrigues me, Sharrocks. There is plainly some heat in all this and I rather suspect the drama may come to the boil soon. Report back to me if the play has not moved on by tomorrow.'

* * *

That night David Hume sat at the desk in his bedroom writing a letter by candlelight. A slight smile played over his lips as he wrote. He knew he had to be brief as Annie would be up at dawn to take the trap to Wick and he wanted the letter to be with her to deliver to the mail coach for Edinburgh. He smiled again as he thought of his new friend Adam Smith and what he would make of their discussions at the castle. Briefly he described the progress they were making with the game:

...I have written to tell you before of Miss Kant. She is the most remarkable woman I believe I have ever met. What a mind! She is a mathematician and she has set herself to play game after game of the

Prisoner's Dilemma looking for the best way of accumulating points by encouraging long term co-operation. She has arrived at a solution that is so elegant that I have no doubt it has the inevitability of truth about it.

I have so much to tell you when we next meet but, briefly, the results are leading me to a conclusion on the reasons for trust and the nature of benevolence that's far beyond anything I described in the Treatise.

It is nothing less than the realisation that the reason we are ever virtuous with each other is because we instinctively know that it is a winning strategy. If you want to win in life you have to be selfish yet disguise your hand in the pretence that you are not. And add to this the key ingredient of irrationality – trust.

In other words, Mr Smith, the mathematical conclusion the Dilemma leads us to is something that I have written about in part but never so completely. It is that the origin of all virtue is selfishness. Yes – all!

It is because we are calculating, selfish beings whose base instinct is to survive and prosper that we are ever virtuous. Is this not then the linkage we sought between my belief in man's natural benevolence, the altruism and compassion we see in people that we admire so much and of which we spoke – and your mechanism of self-interested specialisation? Is this not the solution to the problem I put to you when we first met? That ties our base drives to our inexplicably sympathetic natures?

Hume reread the letter, thinking hard about what Smith could find wrong in his conclusions. Yet again he allowed himself to imagine how much his young friend would have enjoyed being at the castle with them. And how much they would have enjoyed hearing his thoughts.

* * *

Zweig was unchanged. He seemed impervious to the wind that picked at him, plucking his clothes and flicking hair in his face.

His eyes burned as he once more focused on the salon, very aware that he was embarking on a second night.

He cast his mind back to a desperate fight for survival he'd had when sailing in the southern ocean. For four days and three nights the crew had pumped and changed sail, scavenging for every inch of way while a screaming typhoon tore into them. This ordeal here was as nothing when compared to that or to so many of the other terrible dangers he'd been in. Two or three days without sleep was not new. Yet again he muttered to himself to be steady and that the battle was yet to come.

Chapter 15

The following morning Sophie rose early and went immediately to her bedroom window. She'd blown out the candle the previous evening and waited a minute before creeping over to arrange the curtains so she could see Zweig through a slight separation in the folds. But, as she looked out now, her heart sank as she saw that he was still there. And still staring at her. She was beginning to panic, astonished that he could know that she was at the window. Then she rallied, telling herself that he couldn't, that the glass must be completely black from the outside, that she must just carry on. She resolved once again to say nothing of this to Dunbeath. The madman was bound to give up soon.

She dressed and went down to the earl's study. She had woken in the night, anxious that an error might have crept into the nutation values of the ecliptic in her calculations and she now unravelled the presentation papers they'd prepared for the Board and set to work on yet a further check. After about half an hour she concluded that all was well but as she got to her feet she felt herself being pulled, once again, to the window. She stood well back from it so that she couldn't be seen. How did he do it, she brooded, watching Zweig as he carefully studied the castle for any sign of motion? He seemed as alert now as when he'd started.

As she stared down at him she was only too aware of the mass of conflicting feelings that were rising up in her. Distrust and disdain certainly; and yet unquestionably, admiration and concern as well. Above all, she was nagged by a great uncertainty – was the man motivated only by his greed to recover her father's debt? Or was he really driven by the love that he'd told her of when they were on the ship? He'd said that day, and then again on the dunes, that he would never leave her. Would he really put himself through this extraordinary ordeal simply for money? Or was he trying to show her his true feelings?

She looked at him more closely and saw the simple

fisherman's clothes he now wore. He looked somehow more sincere in them. There was less ostentation, less pretence.

She was so deep in her thoughts that she didn't hear Dunbeath as he came into the room behind her. He began to speak and she jumped at the sound of his voice.

'What do you think he wants, Sophie?' the earl said quietly, walking over to the window and then gazing down at where Zweig sat. 'What compulsion do you think is driving him? This is the third day your captain has been here, lined up in full view of the castle like a besieging army, calling us out to battle. You speak of co-operation but see for yourself what a man will put himself through for his own ends. I dare say he would like to tell us what game he's playing but I think we hold the better hand, because we do not wish to play with him at all.'

He turned away from the window and looked at the papers that Sophie had laid out neatly on his desk.

'Ah, Sophie, I see that you have been testing the logic of the presentation yet again. I have done so myself so often that I have to believe it now rings true. As far as I can tell the charts are all in order for when we shall see the Board of Longitude. Everything appears to be ready for them - but you will still come with me when I go to London, won't you?'

'Yes, of course. I look forward to going. It will give me a rest from the Prisoner's Dilemma.'

Dunbeath turned to gaze at her, his expression struck by a mixture of regard for her mind and an almost childlike adoration for her personality.

'That odd child of mine, the Dilemma. Yes, I'm so sorry I wasn't there when you were explaining your findings yesterday. Hume has told me about the success of your Tit for Tat stratagem. It's very clever. It seems so simple – and yet you say that it constantly beats other ways of getting the most points.'

'Yes,' said Sophie eagerly, only too happy to move away from the window and distract Dunbeath from looking at Zweig – and also from the thoughts that were clouding her own mind, 'if by that you mean over a long period of time and in willing and repetitive relationships, then yes. In other words it apes the reality of life. The irony of its success is that a player that would have been described as irrational in your original one-time Prisoner's Dilemma, by trusting his partner to stay silent, is now seen to be rational. He is the calculating one, choosing partners to build high scoring relationships with and punishing those who abuse his trust.'

'But Sophie,' said Dunbeath, becoming suddenly testy at yet another assault on his own conclusions to the Dilemma, 'haven't you now introduced the idea of personality into the game? When we first played it we were at pains to agree that the players had no moral code. Rather they were utterly competitive, with no room for sentiment.'

Sophie looked at him with the gentle care of someone calming an invalid.

'I have to agree that the process began in that way – that only logic should prevail in looking at our instinct for survival. But if one accepts that the true insight from the game comes from seeing it played repeatedly and sequentially, then it's obvious that judging who one can trust is the key skill in telling whether other people are defectors or co-operators. After all, the only way of finding out if you can trust someone – is to trust them!'

'And this skill of yours, Sophie, how do we develop that?' Dunbeath was drawling his words now with more than an echo of the arrogant and cynical tone he had first used with her.

'I don't know that we do,' she replied, 'I think instead that the need for trust, just like the need for exchange or barter in society, has become woven into our natures. It's an instinct. But why should we think this is so odd? Why do we think that instincts are only animal impulses? Most animals know instinctively from birth how to walk, to eat, to fly even. We, on the other hand, spend years being unable to survive without the constant attention of others; we spend months as just tiny babies, and then years as children, capable of nothing without being cared for. This vulnerability must have left us with other gifts. I would suggest that one of them is that we can sum each other up in the blink of an eye.

'I believe we know instinctively who we think we can trust. Who might help us. We don't need to stumble along until we come to the conclusion that 'one good turn deserves another'. Nor do we need to be taught this. We are not shown it any more than an animal might be shown how to stand or to walk. It is an instinct, and this instinctive knowledge must come somehow from our ancestors – and our continued existence is evidence of their success.'

'Oh really, Sophie,' said Dunbeath, clearly becoming irritated, 'this talk of trust bewilders me. My experience is that hoping for trust in others is nothing but a fool's idea of paradise. On the contrary, my maxim is not unlike the Urquhain motto. Trust nobody - and you won't be disappointed. I mean to say, how does your Tit for Tat idea deal with people who would break your trust in them? When your instincts prove to be wrong.'

'But that is its strength,' replied Sophie. 'The mechanism works even if one makes an error in trusting someone. Tit for Tat shows that we can turn our back on a defector. Most people learn quickly that even the occasional mistake can't obscure the lesson that the gains they can make are worth the risk of trusting people in the search to find co-operative partners. That must be why, when one plays these repeated versions of the Dilemma, it is the 'shadow of the future' that's deciding the outcome.

'In my view these games of ours show up the key principle that the right thing to do depends on what other people do. It's a simplified insight into how the world works. You see, while the only thing to do in your original version of the Prisoner's Dilemma is not to trust the other person, because you don't know what he will do, Tit for Tat shows us that an approach that tries to co-operate with people can succeed *when the Dilemma is openly repeated.* The strength of Tit for Tat is that it doesn't envy or want to beat its opponent. It wants a fair share of a growing whole, not to be fighting over a smaller pot. The image comes to me of a primitive man killing someone for an old bone when he should have been working together with him to hunt for more game.

'I really am convinced now that humans have evolved an understanding that trust wins because it leads to co-operation. And that an ability to judge who you can trust is a crucial skill in life. Where did this come from? Perhaps a great change came over the way we viewed each other about the time that hunters gave way to farmers? People must have realised that co-operation meant bigger harvests. Life was more secure. After all, your neighbour couldn't steal a field of wheat in the way that he could take a deer or a rabbit you'd just hunted for the pot.'

As she spoke Dunbeath had begun moving from foot to foot, irritated by her conviction on the mechanism for co-operation, yet determined not to lose his self-control.

'And what are your conclusions to all this, Sophie?' he now managed to say in a fairly even tone.

'Well, I think that at base this instinct has made us very clever, cleverer than we know. You see, unlike these games we are not simply playing in response to what the other person actually does. We're going further than that. We're *interpreting* our opponents' thoughts and actions as well, and each of us is behaving on the basis of what they think the other will do – imagining and concluding on how the 'shadow of the future' would affect other people's next steps.'

But this had finally gone too far for Dunbeath and he began to show signs of his old arrogance as he listened to Sophie's insistence on the natural place of goodness. He was far too cynical and wedded to his sense of superiority to understand such a counsel of sharing.

'Now, let me understand you, Sophie,' he said slowly, and

with more than a trace of harshness in his voice. 'You say that if you found a partner, a co-operator, someone you felt you could completely trust, you would never cheat on them. That you would never tire of getting three points. You say you'd never take advantage of your partner's trustworthiness and be tempted to slip a defection in. Is that right? After all, you'd be rejecting the opportunity to get five points and seeing to it that they got none. You'd win the game easily over the long run if you did that, wouldn't you?'

'No, I would never do that,' Sophie replied slowly. She'd heard his tone and wondered what trap he was setting for her now.

'Then let me ask you this,' continued Dunbeath, 'if I gave you £100 and told you to split it with Annie, what would you do?'

'I'd give her half.'

'And why would you do that? After all, if you gave her £10 she would still be delighted. It would be £10 she didn't have before – a great deal of money to her. And you would have £90. No doubt £90 would be welcome, should you want to return home to Königsberg.'

Sophie was shocked when he said this. She had never asked the earl for money and yet he had guessed her mind. She now drew herself up to give greater emphasis to her answer.

'No, I couldn't do that. It wouldn't be fair. It wouldn't be right.'

'I see, so the reason you wouldn't do it is because of your wish to be seen by her to be dealing fairly. But if you could see that she got some of the money and I could *guarantee* that she would never find out where it came from. It would be a complete secret. How much would you give her then?'

Sophie went quiet. Dunbeath smiled and gently leant towards her in a little show of triumph.

'Exactly. Your hesitation shows you are human after all. You will agree with me then that the issue is one of reputation and not one of integrity. Of not wanting the other person to know that you haven't shared equally. If it were a secret from her how the money was divided then you would think differently. In other words the way you'd behave reflects your view of the future – your concern to be seen as fair in Annie's eyes – rather than your instinct for survival. And a passage to Prussia.'

There was a silence as Sophie considered Dunbeath's questioning. She felt annoyed with herself that he had led her so easily into admitting such a very human weakness, such a secret instinct for gain - even such a longing to go home - but her nature was too honest for her to have pretended otherwise.

Dunbeath looked down at the floor and then quietly continued. He had been waiting for just such an opportunity to press his advantage.

'Now Sophie, I must ask you about that ship's captain of yours. He is still sitting on the dunes. It's been two nights already and now we have a further day, and he still shows no sign of weakening. A remarkable performance I grant you. But what is driving him? Nobody would last this long without a madness to prevail, to win even. I feel you owe it to me to say what this is about. What is it that he's after?'

With a sigh Sophie realised that she could remain silent no longer. And so she took Dunbeath back to Königsberg and told him of her life there. She described Zweig's great rise amongst the merchants and the shipping powers and then she recounted the story of her father's disastrous loss and the debt this had led to with Zweig. Dunbeath listened intently, occasionally putting questions to her and then asking how, sad though her father's miscalculation had been, this situation could have ever involved her. She sighed again and painfully told him of how she had come on the voyage as a hostage for the money her father had to find. She finished by saying that the debt would be annulled if the two of them did not return within a hundred days of their departure.

But, crucially, she omitted to tell Dunbeath about Zweig's wish to marry her. And her suspicion that his love for her was making him risk everything as he sat outside, demanding to be dealt with. Instead, she finished by saying that she lived with her heart in her mouth, counting the days until her father's position was safe.

'And how many are left?' asked Dunbeath intently.

'Thirty four.'

'My God, Sophie,' Dunbeath said bitterly at last, nearly choking on his anger, 'I am so sorry to hear this. Why didn't you tell me earlier? I shall have the greedy fool shot for this. There's many an Urquhain that would consider himself privileged to do it for you!'

He went across to the window and stood looking down at Zweig.

'There is your defector writ large, is it not, Sophie? What a base compulsion greed is, but see how powerful it can be. Here he is in full view of the world with a rebellion about to come down around our ears and spies everywhere. And all he thinks about is the filthy money that's owed to him. Why, I need only tell the English army that he's here to have him arrested. I dare say they would be extremely interested to speak to him about the arms and explosives that he was bringing for the uprising.'

Sophie had anticipated this. She was happy to have Zweig gone but she needed to stay under Dunbeath's protection.

'Oh, please don't say that, my lord, it frightens me so. If the English army should hear about this they would take him and then who knows what he would be made to say. If he tells them about me I should be imprisoned as well.'

Dunbeath's face darkened as he considered this. Inevitably, his temper began to rise.

'You are right, Sophie,' he said fiercely, 'but I shall bring an end to this nonsense. I shall go out and tell him to be gone.'

* * *

Seven miles to the south of the castle, a mounted messenger slowed his horse to a trot as he approached the checkpoint that straddled the turnpike outside Craigleven's twin lodges. The rider now wearily waited for the redcoat guard to come over to him, his horse steaming.

'Where are you from, friend? And where are you going?'

'From Edinburgh. I've ridden up these past two weeks. I have an urgent letter for Lord Dunbeath at the Castle of Beath but I've been sorely delayed by your army roadblocks. A three day journey has taken me all this time. I don't believe I shall be welcome when I get there.'

'Well, you are about to be sorely delayed again, mister messenger. My orders are to report anything and anybody that's travelling to Dunbeaton or the castle. Now, now, calm yourself,' he added as the man groaned with frustration, 'this trooper here will escort you up to the big house and the major will want a word with you before you can go on.'

The messenger set off with his escort, his shoulders sagging, but ten minutes later Major Sharrocks was preparing him for even worse news.

'I see you have a letter for the Earl of Dunbeath. Who's it from? What is its message?'

'How could I know its contents?' the messenger demanded indignantly. 'It's sealed, isn't it? All I know is that I was engaged by the office of the Earl of Morton at the Philosophical Society of Edinburgh to bring it to Lord Dunbeath with all haste. My orders are to put it in his hand and none other. Please let me go on, major, I've been so delayed by your checkpoints. Take pity on an old soldier, sir. I was with the cavalry myself, the 7th Horse, fighting in Bavaria with the Earl of Stair. Wounded, I was'

'Not possible, for you to go on,' said Sharrocks, but more sympathetically now. 'I need my commanding officer to know about this. Come on now, you're to settle down,' he continued as the messenger began to howl in dismay, 'I'm sure you're very exercised by a further delay but we have our orders to look into what's passing between the clan leaders. We won't be long but you will have to calm yourself. Don't worry, the letter won't be opened or interfered with, but as long as I have it I know you won't think of doing anything foolish like running away. Now, cheer yourself, friend, my trooper will take you to the kitchen for something to eat and he'll even find a corner for you to spend the rest of the day in comfort. I've no doubt you can continue your journey tomorrow. Be at your ease, what can a further day matter to these nobs?'

Sharrocks turned to walk away but before he had taken half a dozen steps he stopped and called back to the man with a further thought.

'Here's something to lighten the mood of an old comrade from the Dettingen days. I was at the affair myself and I shall ask my colonel to give you a letter of passage that you can show when you're stopped on your journey back to Edinburgh. It will save you days of interrogation at our checkpoints. There you are now, what could be fairer than that? No more long faces now.'

* * *

Although Zweig's eyes had never left the castle's windows he was only too aware of the fury in the figure that now stamped with such aggression across the beach towards him. The wind had moved around from the south and it began to blow from the sea, pulling at Zweig's clothes and lifting a fine sand into his face. In the distance, the raised surface of the water shone brilliantly as the afternoon sun flashed between high clouds.

When Dunbeath reached Zweig's dune his insane energy seemed to carry him up its side without any apparent effort. He now strode towards the summit, reddened with threat. But in contrast to the turbulence that seemed to be coming from Dunbeath, Zweig rose easily to his feet with a great air of contentment and greeted the earl as if he were an old friend, joining him at a picnic.

'My Lord Dunbeath,' Zweig murmured, smiling broadly, 'it is a pleasure to see you again.'

But Dunbeath was all business and had no time for such niceties.

'Now, you listen to me,' he growled through clenched teeth, 'I have had enough of your impertinence. I have had enough of you sitting here, staring at my castle with those insolent intentions so clear on your face. You are to leave and leave immediately.'

Zweig sighed sweetly and shrugged as he shifted as if to sit down again.

'I think not, my lord. This is God's strand. I think I may put myself where I please.'

'In which case you can sit here for another month if you must,' hissed Dunbeath with barely restrained violence, 'but your filthy debt will come to an end soon and this wind will turn you to dust. Miss Kant is under my protection and you can go to the devil.'

Zweig smiled and inclined his head slightly to one side.

'Debt? Is that what you have been told. No more?'

Dunbeath's rage was in danger of exploding but as he turned to go he allowed himself to grind out a reply.

'No more? What more do I need? You have my warning. You will be gone in an hour or I shall send a messenger to the English. They will be interested to meet the man who was bringing guns and powder to their enemy.'

Zweig beamed pleasantly again.

'Very well, if you wish it. But, if that were to happen I would have every opportunity to tell them of how you forced the murder of a young man. Of how you compelled a man in cold blood to kill his own brother. Yes, you may put a hemp rope around my neck, my lord, but I would see to it that you should have the silken.'

Dunbeath was knocked silent. For half a minute or more the two men stood staring at each other, the one smiling and relaxed and the other puce and rigid with anger.

'But, I have the telescope. You have no proof,' Dunbeath said at last.

'Ah, the telescope,' Zweig replied slowly, twisting slightly as if he was about to aim a blow. 'Yes, but I have the witness. He has told me everything. You see, my lord, we both have cards in our hand. It seems we may have to deal each other. We may have to co-operate.'

Dunbeath didn't alter his fierce staring into Zweig's face. Then he blinked and murmured bitterly to himself.

'More damned co-operation. Another damned Prisoner's Dilemma.'

'I beg your pardon?' said Zweig encouragingly.

Dunbeath didn't answer and there was another long silence.

'Just what do you want?' he muttered eventually.

'I simply want Miss Kant, my lord, so that we might leave and return to our homeland.'

'So you can trade her for your disgusting debt?' snorted Dunbeath. 'And now you're trying to bargain with me over a fisherman's fairy tale. You are nothing but the lowest kind of blackmailer. You can rot in hell for all I care.'

At this Zweig smiled respectfully at Dunbeath and bowed as if he was congratulating him on a fine speech after a fine dinner. Then he gave him a quick last nod and sat down again on the same spot. He stiffened as he resumed his fixed staring at the castle.

Dunbeath turned on his heel with a deep growl and strode back the way he had come. A few minutes later he flung open the door of his study and passed Sophie without a word, his face livid as he went to a table in the window and snatched up a decanter of whisky. He poured himself a glass and put it to his lips with a shaking hand.

'I have seen your captain, Sophie. He will be gone soon. You have my word on that.'

* * *

The trooper snapped closed his telescope.

Much more of this spying nonsense and he would go mad, he thought to himself, wondering yet again what that bully Sharrocks wanted. It all just looked like a family spat to him. He weighed up now whether he'd seen enough to warrant going back to Craigleven with an update or whether he'd be stripped down for giving up his post. His aching back gave him the answer and he walked stiffly to his horse, determined though to add a little spice to his report.

* * *

The long early May evening now stretched ahead of Zweig and even his iron determination began to soften under the hammer blows of fatigue and the disappointing emptiness of his exchange with Dunbeath. But he rallied yet again and, as the sea continued to thunder, his eyes still burnt with the light of determination and the spark of his extraordinary will.

He was aware that this was the third night. A fourth day would be dawning tomorrow. Something had to give. Zweig knew that the earl wouldn't rest easy. He knew his kind well and he was quite sure that the easy manner he'd adopted and the delicate way he'd spoken to him would eat away at him until the pain forced the man to act. Yes, he knew these superior types, he thought once more. They could stand anything but the courtesy and politeness of other people. He would wait. Something would give.

Chapter 16

It was at around three in the morning, and the night was at its darkest, when the Indian servant tripped lightly up the dune and made a deep bow in front of Zweig. He was a magnificent looking man with a wide sash around the waist and a glorious turban of many soft shades of madder, the ends of which fell in two long loops of cloth behind his back. Under one arm he held a small wooden tray, inlaid with mother of pearl, and as he smiled respectfully and asked what he could bring him, Zweig faltered as he considered which of many delicacies he should order first.

They remained like this for a couple of minutes, Zweig's mind staggering in indecision while the servant swayed before him. Then the wind picked up and, as sand blew into his cheek, Zweig's hold on himself began to return.

He shook his head, for once giving up his rigid determination never to move his position. Slowly, the Indian melted and the harsh outline of the castle sprang back into focus.

A chill went down him at the realisation that the demons were visiting him already. This was the third night, he thought, and the dabbawallah would be just the beginning; no doubt there would be musical processions and wild cats before long. He shook himself again. Something must give soon, something had to give, for better or worse.

* * *

At Craigleven, L'Arquen, too, sat pondering a breakfast some hours later. He was quite alone in the centre of a long mahogany dining table, its beautiful surface intended to see thirty or more entertained for dinner. Ahead and around him was the loot of the land, much sent of it up to Scotland by his adoring mother and much other plundered from the surrounding villages and made delicate by his personal chef. Compotes of summer fruits, sugared sweetmeats, half a dozen cuts of fowl and game, freshly baked breads and plates of salted seafoods and fish, all fought for his attention. Behind him a uniformed footman, long abandoned by Lord Duncansby, stood in watchful attention.

'Bring me a cup of chocolate,' L'Arquen drawled to the man with a waft of his hand over the crowded table, 'and put this food out will you?'

The footman was about to step forward when there was a sharp knock at the door. Major Sharrocks strode into the room and crossed the floor to come to attention on the other side of the table from the colonel, his respectful gaze aimed high over L'Arquen's head and boring into the panelling.

'Why, Sharrocks. Back from your rounds, already, eh? Well, you're most welcome. Why don't you take your ease and try some of this fish? Mackerel, I should imagine from the look of it.'

'No, thank you, sir. I've already breakfasted.'

'Have you indeed. Well you seem alive with news. What progresses?'

'More on the Dunbeath situation, sir. We stopped a messenger coming from Edinburgh to the castle yesterday with a letter to the earl. I had the seal lifted – never fear sir, my man's an artist, the most suspicious of chancery lawyers would never spot his work. We've opened it and here it is, sir. When I read it I thought it best to keep the messenger here overnight. There didn't seem to be any merit in Lord Dunbeath receiving it before we say so.'

He handed the letter to L'Arquen whose face tightened as he read it in two quick glances.

'So, Lord Dunbeath is required by the Board of Longitude in London to present his findings to them on May 9. Why, I believe that's in seven days time. He'd have been hard pressed to get there if he'd left two weeks ago. Yes, you made the correct decision, Sharrocks. There is no hurry to our delivering this. God knows it's taken long enough to get here already. Did you notice when it was sent? Over a month ago. You're quite right though, the less time he has, the less likely he is to attempt the journey.'

L'Arquen looked away for a few seconds as he weighed up the situation.

'Have that criminal of yours reseal the letter but keep the messenger here until I say he can go. I'd far rather have Dunbeath where I can keep my eye on him than run the risk of him causing trouble in London. Good, that's decided. What else have your men to report from there?'

'A strange development, sir. Lord Dunbeath came out and spoke to the man on the dunes, the one he pointed his pistol at a few days ago. There was some kind of exchange and then Dunbeath roared off back to the castle. High dudgeon wouldn't describe it. A rage more like.'

'Spoke with the man, eh? What d'you think's going on, Sharrocks? Something's not right. Why would an earl consort with a madman?'

L'Arquen rose to his feet, his face flushed with irritation.

'What do you imagine all this nonsense is about? All I know is that we're spending far too long on this snooping of yours, looking through telescopes and creeping about the countryside. Tittle tattle about who's speaking to whom. You'll be looking through keyholes next, Sharrocks. I want your men to be out looking for rebels not lying around in the grass enjoying themselves.' As L'Arquen spoke he seemed to be feeding his own ill temper. 'I'm bored with all this and bored with your inactivity, Sharrocks. Bored, do you hear? Much more of this and I might as well call on Dunbeath and ask him what he's up to myself?'

He stopped as he said this, considering his own thoughts. Then he turned to snap at Sharrocks again.

'Yes, yes, that's exactly what I shall do. I shall go and ask him what he's doing. And why not? I wonder I didn't think of it before. Rouse out the troop and have them ready to leave in ten minutes.'

* * *

David Hume reread his letter to Adam Smith. He made a minor
change to a paragraph and then folded it for sealing.

His young friend would certainly be intrigued by Sophie's
exploration of the Dilemma, he mused, wondering yet again
whether Smith would ever receive the information he'd been
sending him. He knew it would be a miracle if they were ever to
arrive with the amount of confusion there was on the roads. More
than that, it would be an even bigger miracle if Smith were ever
to write back.

* * *

Once Sharrocks had given out his orders for the escort to
assemble, the troop had made good time from Craigleven and the
colonel and his men were soon crossing the land bridge that led
to the Castle of Beath. They arrived at the front entrance, their
horses snorting and steaming and L'Arquen dismounted and
glared up at the massive stone masonry. He grimaced as he read
the clan motto and then hammered at the gigantic door, stamping
in irritation for half a minute until the diminutive figure of Annie
appeared to pull it open.

L'Arquen had decided on a policy of gratuitous good humour
and he murmured pleasantly to the old housekeeper in spite of
his annoyance at being kept waiting for so long.

'And what is your name, my dear?' he cooed.

Annie answered and began to ask him to stay where he was
while she found her master. But L'Arquen quickly rode over her.

'No, no, don't leave me here in the hall. I shall come with you
and introduce myself to Lord Dunbeath. No, I insist on it, now
lead on.' He clapped his hands behind her in mock encouragement, as if he were seeing a child into bed.

'On, on.'

Reluctantly, Annie led the colonel up the stairs and towards the great salon. She put her head round the door to announce him but L'Arquen pushed roughly past her and came briskly into the room, smiling broadly as he saw Lord Dunbeath and David Hume standing by the fire.

'Ah, gentlemen, good day to you, good day to you, indeed. Please excuse my intrusion,' he said as he advanced over to where the pair stood. 'My name is Colonel George L'Arquen of Lord Harrington's regiment of dragoons. You're no doubt aware that we are stationed at Craigleven. How d'you do? How d'you do?'

Dunbeath eyed L'Arquen coldly, clearly quite unamused by his entrance.

'L'Arquen, you say? A strange name. How do you come by that?'

'It is Norman, sir. We came with the Conqueror. But less of me, am I to believe that I address the Earl of Dunbeath?' Dunbeath nodded curtly. 'Then again, I must apologise for taking up your time, sir. But perhaps you know something of my family already? Do you recall my father, Gracehill, from your days in London?'

'Viscount Gracehill? Yes, I knew him in Parliament. When I could be bothered to attend the place.'

L'Arquen continued to smile placidly.

'A great shame you do not, sir, my father esteemed your presence. Indeed I had heard it said that you were no longer able to take your place in the House. There was a rumour put about – I've no doubt it was untrue – that you were given no choice in the matter. It was said that you had refused to take the Oath of Allegiance.'

There was a profound silence for some seconds. Dunbeath felt quite sure that the redcoat fop had intended to land a blow and he began to colour and bridle. But L'Arquen appeared not to notice the tension and instead looked about the room as he chatted amiably on.

'I must congratulate you, Lord Dunbeath, what a room this is! It must be one of the finest in all Scotland. I've rarely seen such tapestries; no doubt they came direct from the Gobelins Manufactory in Paris itself. Made for the room, I'll be bound. And what stories they show, eh? How they loved their allegories then. No doubt about this one,' he said, waving to a picture of a young girl in medieval dress about to bring her sword down on an armoured soldier, 'Charity Overcoming Envy', I'd wager. And there, to the right of the window, Judith with the head of Holofernes.' L'Arquen gave a short laugh. 'How fond the ancients were of women chopping off men's heads, eh.'

He turned to Dunbeath, still beaming, and then looked beyond him to focus on a large piece to one side of the fireplace.

'And, if I'm not mistaken, here are our old friends, Gyges and Candaules. What a story that is. So often the tale, eh? Two men at odds because of a woman. It rarely fails to amuse.'

Dunbeath's colour continued to rise but he somehow managed to control himself enough to change the subject. He waved an arm at Hume.

'Mr David Hume, newly arrived from Edinburgh.'

L'Arquen's appearance changed in an instant. Gone immediately was the insincere beam and, in its place, a look that bordered on violent interest came over him.

'Am I to understand, sir, that I am in the presence of the author of the *Treatise on Human Nature*?'

Hume bowed in reply.

'Well sir, I would live in hopes that I might have the pleasure of discoursing with you on this at a later date. How extraordinary it is to find you here.'

There was a slight pause as L'Arquen gazed fixedly at Hume. Then he seemed to shake himself out of whatever was preoccupying him.

'Unfortunately,' he continued, 'I am much occupied at present with more unpleasant business. I exclude the two of you from my comments, of course, but I refer to the troublesome Scots.'

He had turned his gaze back to Dunbeath and he now looked hard at him, his voice pitched at its most provocative.

'Who would ever believe that there are still fools in this country who would try to put Charles Edward Stuart on the throne, eh? Bonnie Prince Charlie, indeed! The English throne. The English throne whose king is the Head of the Church of England.'

L'Arquen ground on, his head inclined menacingly to one side.

'Yes, Head of the Church of England. Hardly a role for a Scottish papist I shouldn't have thought. Less still a half Polish, Italian speaking papist.'

Dunbeath returned L'Arquen's stare, glowering at him with a scarcely concealed loathing.

But L'Arquen clearly still wished to provoke, and he started once more in a tone that dripped with irony.

'You would both be astonished to learn that there are people in Scotland who are still not reconciled to the Act of Union. We have been one United Kingdom of Great Britain now for near on forty years and yet there remain enough stupid people who object to this simple fact for me to have to spend my days in this windswept emptiness.'

The two men stood by the fire in silence and L'Arquen clearly felt that he had softened Dunbeath enough to get down to business.

'However, I must put the pleasure of this charming conversation to one side and tell you that I fear I am here on an army matter. You will know that a ship ran onto the rocks in this bay about three months ago and then exploded. We have looked into this and it seems that the vessel was coming from Königsberg in Eastern Prussia, loaded with powder for a quarry in France. I'd say it was badly lost, wouldn't you? In fact, we rather think it wasn't lost at all. The idiot rebels are known to be but twenty miles from here and I've no doubt that this explosive would have been useful to them in their stupid endeavours.

'We do not believe the ship could have landed here. More likely it was going down the coast to a less dangerous harbour. Now, I am quite sure you knew nothing of this, Lord Dunbeath, and yet...'

He came to an abrupt halt at the unmistakable sound of a door handle turning. There was a slight groan as the heavy wood swung slowly open and Sophie came through into the room, reams of mathematical workings in her arms and her gaze down, so deep in thought that she had taken three or four steps towards the men before an instinct made her glance up. She immediately saw L'Arquen in his red uniform and her eyes widened in involuntary alarm. She stopped dead and looked at him and then at Dunbeath who was standing behind him. Dunbeath instantly gave a fierce shake of his head and motioned her to leave with a swivel of his eyes. As soon as she saw this, Sophie spun and urgently retreated the way she had come.

She had never looked more beautiful.

L'Arquen spoke first.

'And who was that, Lord Dunbeath?' he said, his attention very plainly aroused.

'That? That was nobody. A maid, the housekeeper's niece, recently come to us from Inverness.'

'She did not appear like a maid to my mind. Rather, if I might say so, like someone on more intimate terms with you both. Perhaps you would be good enough to ask her to step back into the room so that I might speak to her?'

'No, I would rather that she wasn't interrupted in her duties. She is painfully shy and should not be troubled.'

L'Arquen looked at Dunbeath doubtfully.

'Nonetheless, I would like to talk to her.'

This was the last straw. Dunbeath's temper gave out.

'Am I not master in my own house, L'Arquen?' The earl had begun to speak in an irritated tone but this had quickly progressed to shouting. Now he was yelling, all restraint gone.

'I have told you not to trouble her. You have come here unannounced, uninvited, abusing my country and now you demand to speak to my servants. It is intolerable, L'Arquen, intolerable do you hear!'

There was a silence while L'Arquen coolly gazed back at Dunbeath, one eyebrow lazily cocked. Then he spoke in a quiet and level voice.

'I must apologise, my lord. I was quite forgetting my manners and assuming I was among friends. Of course, I shall leave you all in peace. A peace I sincerely hope will not be broken.'

He bowed to Dunbeath, said 'Mr Hume' in a respectful tone and turned to leave.

He had taken a pace or two towards the door when he suddenly swung back. He touched his forehead as a tutor might to the slowest of his charges.

'I almost forgot. One last thing. There's a man sitting on the dunes outside the castle. He's been there for three days. I wondered if you knew who he was? My major tells me that you spoke with him yesterday.'

'What?' snapped Dunbeath, testily. 'That man? He is just a nothing, a ruffian. He followed the maid you saw here from Inverness and is obsessed with her. She's refusing to return his attentions. I told him to go away but you know what notions get into the heads of these lovers.'

'Indeed I do,' laughed Larken archly, 'but my men also told me you held a pistol to his head two weeks ago. I'm impressed you should be so solicitous of your servants that you've become involved in a lovers' tiff.'

At this Dunbeath took a step towards L'Arquen and looked at him very darkly.

'What is this? You mean you've been spying on me? How

dare you, L'Arquen. I take this information very ill.'

'Of course, of course,' said L'Arquen with a complete lack of concern. 'I quite understand. I shall go now. But I hope that if you should hear any more about the rebels, you'll keep me informed.'

L'Arquen left and hurried down the great staircase. He pulled on his gloves as he went, his face clouded with anger. He emerged into the morning sunshine and strode fiercely over to where a trooper held his horse, waiting to help him mount. He settled in the saddle but, as he turned the animal's head, he looked down the beach to where Zweig sat motionless on the peninsular of the nearest dune, apparently unaware of the troop's presence.

They set off towards the turnpike, Sharrocks riding alongside him. L'Arquen glanced over.

'There is much amiss here, Sharrocks. I have been lied to. Keep your surveillance up, I rather think something will be happening soon.' He shook the reins, then added, '...and let the messenger bring his letter now. That will shake things up.'

* * *

As soon as the troop had ridden off, Dunbeath, Hume and Sophie gathered together in the salon to discuss L'Arquen's visit. Hume was very agitated that Dunbeath had lied so openly.

'But Mr Hume,' said Dunbeath sharply, 'if that man had spoken to Sophie he'd have heard her German accent immediately. He seemed less of a fool than his father and he clearly knew that the ship had come from Königsberg. If he'd put two and two together and taken her into Craigleven for questioning, she'd be on a gallows somewhere before the month is out. She has not asked to be caught up in our wars. Now, that is an end to it.'

'You may be right about that Dunbeath, but why on earth did you say that the man on the dunes was from Inverness?'

Dunbeath gave a slight shudder. God knows how the German

208

captain had found out about his little experiment with the two boys. Still, he had, and Dunbeath knew he couldn't take the risk of him talking to L'Arquen about it. He thought he'd never met a pair of viler men. Nothing would give them greater pleasure than to invent trouble for him.

Dunbeath darkened as he thought of how to steer Hume away from the dangerous subject.

'Mr Hume, the colonel's manner convinced me more than ever that war is inevitable. Even if Prince Charles Edward chooses not to land that man would invent a reason to kill as many of us as he could find. What was your view, Sophie? Was he what you would call a co-operator? I think not. So, our ship's captain may be of more use to us alive than dead. There is an old saying that my enemy's enemy is my friend and I believe this might possibly be the case here. The captain is of no use to us in the hands of the English and he would certainly place Sophie's life in much danger if he was.'

'Nonetheless,' said Sophie, 'it was an opportunity to be rid of him. Perhaps this might have been the one time not to have remained silent.'

There was an awkward pause and Dunbeath quickly filled it with a false show of enforced humour, laughing off their anxieties.

'You are not to be concerned about the intelligence of English army officers. And anyway, if by any chance Colonel L'Arquen cares to think of us again, I shall simply say there was a misunderstanding. What crime is there in being wrong? You have changed me, Sophie,' he continued lightly, 'I would be happy to say I was wrong. Now, we still have work to do, we must make some final changes to the presentation for the Board.'

He gave a final, forced smile and swept from the room. As he did so, Hume and Sophie exchanged a dark glance, each as worried as the other at the new turn of events.

* * *

Zweig's head had cleared entirely. He was now thinking more sharply than ever. Although his fixed gaze had not wavered when he'd seen the soldiers arrive, the officer's manner when he had emerged from the castle had told its own story.

Hold fast, he thought to himself yet again. Something was about to unfold. He had never been more certain of anything in his life.

Chapter 17

Less than an hour after L'Arquen had allowed him to leave Craigleven, the messenger had secured his horse at the castle's entrance and was explaining his business to Annie. She'd heard him out and then immediately led him up the great staircase to where Dunbeath was sitting with Hume and Sophie in the long dining room, a sparse luncheon on the table in front of them. As soon as Dunbeath saw the letter in the man's hand he jumped to his feet.

'Ah, at last! That must be Morton writing to me.'

He broke open the seal and glanced at the signature at the bottom of the page.

'Yes, it's Morton. He writes to say that the Board of Longitude is sitting on ...' he stopped and stared at the page in disbelief '... what! It can't be. May 9 – but that's just seven days away!'

Sophie rose quickly and went over to look at the open sheet in Dunbeath's shaking hands.

'Oh my God, Sophie, look!' he shrieked. 'The letter was sent over a month ago. Why has it taken so long to get here?'

He turned in a fury towards the messenger.

'How long have you had this? Where have you been all this time?'

'The letter only came to us two weeks ago, my lord. No doubt the rest of the time was spent getting it to Edinburgh from London. As for me, I left immediately I could and have been struggling for every foot of the way with the English army stopping me ever since. The roads are in uproar, sir, the army has checkpoints everywhere. My papers have been taken from me and studied two dozen times or more.'

'I'm not surprised to hear this,' Hume called over from the table, 'I had the same treatment when I came up from Edinburgh myself.'

'But how am I to get to London in time for the meeting?' cried

Dunbeath as he heard this. 'Sophie, Sophie, what am I to do?'

Sophie turned her anguished face towards Dunbeath. She was at a loss to know how to reply but the silence was broken by the messenger giving a meaningful cough.

'My lord, perhaps I could be so bold as to suggest a way through? The last place I was detained was at the garrison just a few miles south of here, Craigleven. The officers there took pity on me and wrote me a pass I can show when I'm stopped on the way back. They said it would see me through roadblocks without hinder.'

Dunbeath turned to Sophie with a cry of sudden hope.

'Then, that's what I must get as well! I must see L'Arquen at once. I shall need safe passage papers or I'll never get to London in time. As it is I shall be riding day and night with the devil behind me. Come and help me saddle the horse.'

He went to the door and shouted for his housekeeper.

'Annie, Annie! Help us here!'

Dunbeath gave a final grunt of frustrated rage and ran towards the stairs, Sophie following behind. Hume stayed in his place. He pulled his napkin from the collar of his red coat and looked up towards the messenger with a plaintive smile.

'I wonder if you would be good enough to deliver a letter for me when you return to Edinburgh?'

* * *

Half an hour later, Dunbeath was hurtling through Craigleven's great staterooms, a trooper padding unhappily along beside him. He reached the final door and dismissed the guard there with an imperious wave of his hand, then swept into L'Arquen's study without a knock, the heavy red of his complexion showing the speed of his journey as well as the obvious agitation that was always so near the surface in him. He careered across the floor towards L'Arquen's desk as the colonel looked up at the explosive sound of his entrance. L'Arquen rose to his feet and waved away the complaining trooper that had tried to stop Dunbeath, a contented smile playing on his lips.

'Why, Lord Dunbeath. We meet again. Twice in so many hours, you honour me. But what can I do for you? You seemed distressed by something.'

'Now see here, L'Arquen, an urgent letter has just come telling me I have to be in London. But your army interrogations have held it up abominably and I now have only a week to get there. It's a matter of the greatest importance to me, the annual meeting of the Board of Longitude. If I miss it my life's work is at stake.'

'Indeed, my lord,' said L'Arquen in the gravest tone of mock concern, 'that is indeed unfortunate. The antics of your countrymen seem to have conspired against you. The confusion on the roads is slowing everything. Indeed, we are all suffering at present, my laundry is taking weeks to come back from Buckinghamshire. You have my deepest sympathies.'

'L'Arquen, you must listen! I can still be there in time if you would only give me a letter of passage. The Board sits on the ninth. That's in seven days time. I can ride every hour that's available if I have to. The messenger told me you had written such a letter for him. I have to get to London! There isn't a moment to lose. Can you not write me one now?'

L'Arquen's eyes travelled to his desk, where papers spilled over the surface. He spread his arms sideways as if to show the sheer volume of the problem.

'I fear not, my lord,' he said in a low, sad tone. 'How I would like to help you. I gave a pass to the messenger because he's just a nobody that will get his backside warmed by his master if he's any later than he already is. But my orders are to restrict the movements of all clan leaders until we can clear up the problems of these ridiculous highlanders and their muddle-headed ideas. Our intelligence is that Prince Charles Edward is calling for the clans to join him and obviously we have to put a stop to any movement by their chiefs.'

'But you must help me, L'Arquen, you must,' Dunbeath ground out, still at pains to keep his temper, 'I know nothing about this uprising. I appeal to you to help – I can win the Longitude Prize at this meeting.'

'If only I could,' murmured L'Arquen with a sad shake of his head. 'I know, I know, you find it odd that I could give safe passage to a mere messenger and not to you. What a strange game life is sometimes, eh? You'd think a man as distinguished as yourself would be freer to come and go than the lower orders. But with great position comes great duty, I'm afraid. We like to think we're free but it always seems that others are controlling us. But who are these 'others', I wonder? Are they any freer than us? Or do they have 'others' that control them also? Perhaps you'd like to ask your friend Hume about that?'

Dunbeath continued to rail at him but L'Arquen came smoothly around his desk and took the earl firmly by the arm. He steered him towards the door.

'I am sorry, Lord Dunbeath, but I'm afraid I must return to my duties. We are all of us trapped by this Bonnie Prince Charlie fellow of yours, aren't we? I, as much as you. Well, goodbye for now, and please give my regards to Mr Hume. And, of course,' he added with a sickly smile, 'your maid from Inverness.'

He stood at the door watching as Dunbeath strode furiously back down the series of great staterooms. A satisfied smile tugged at his mouth, but, once he'd seen Dunbeath turn the far corner, his expression faded and he spun round to scowl at his guard.

'Harken,' he whispered. 'If you ever let anyone into my room again without my permission you will find yourself in the interview room with Trooper Williams. You know how he enjoys his work, don't you? That was the Earl of Dunbeath and if you see him try to gain entry in that manner again you are to shoot him.

Do you understand? Now, find Major Sharrocks and tell him I want him here immediately.'

* * *

Sophie stood looking down at Zweig from the side window of the great salon. She knew better than to be seen by getting too close to the glass and she held well back in the shadows, studying him as he sat so alertly on the beach.

Yet again she wondered how he could keep going, her anxiety mingled with a grudging admiration. She thought he seemed fresher than she was. He'd never moved and yet he'd got them all jumping around in the castle, talking and thinking about nothing else but him. How would all this end? She looked again at the firmness of his expression. Great heavens, what a will this man had.

* * *

As Major Sharrocks came into the room L'Arquen waved to him to stand by the desk.

'I have just seen Lord Dunbeath. He came here a few minutes ago, barking and pawing like a wild dog about getting to London. I refused him safe passage, of course.'

Sharrocks nodded.

'Very good, sir.'

'Now, I have received reports of rebels gathering near the place where you picked that one up the other day. Lanochburn, I believe. You need to step up your patrols there. How many men have you still got at Dunbeaton?'

'Just two, sir, one watching the village and one the castle.'

'Well get them back. I have Dunbeath bottled up now, he cannot move. In which case you're spending too much time on your amusement at the Castle of Beath - the troopers are wasted there. They've been lying about in the grass for far too long and you've had enough time on this snooping idea of yours, Sharrocks. Now I want them – and you – out picking up more of these damned highlanders. Eventually we shall find one who's helpful.'

* * *

Sophie and Hume were sitting next to each other on a gilt sofa, their heads huddled over Sophie's workings on the Dilemma. Hume was about to murmur an interpretation to one of her findings when Dunbeath came running up the stairs and hurtled into the great salon.

'L'Arquen refused me!' he shouted. 'Said no movement was allowed by the clan chiefs. God, what a liar. He was never more pleased; smirking away at me that he wished he could help. What am I to do, Hume, what am I to do? If I rode without ever stopping across country and somehow avoided every road and every checkpoint, I still wouldn't get half way to London by the ninth.'

Dunbeath stopped his furious rant and instead began to frantically pace the room. Hume quietly stroked the braid decoration at his wrist.

'Forgive me if this is an absurd notion, Dunbeath, but would it not be possible for you to sail down to London by sea? Could that not be done in the time?'

Dunbeath stopped and looked at him.

'I had the same thought myself. But who could ever take me? My father's old helmsman is long gone. I don't know how to sail. None of the fishermen around here would know the way – there's hardly one of them that's ever gone beyond the headland. And anyway, they wouldn't know the Thames from the Styx.'

Hume paused and then quietly took a deep breath.

'Perhaps our captain there could be persuaded? He must have

sailed to London a hundred times – he would know the approaches.'

Dunbeath came to an abrupt standstill. He looked steadily at Hume, amazed at the suggestion. Nevertheless, it was clear that he was weighing up the idea. He rejected it. Then a picture of L'Arquen's grinning insincerity came into his mind.

'By God, Hume,' he said decisively, 'you may just be right. I dare say there will be a terrible price to pay but what other chance do I have? You are right, I shall see the man at once.'

* * *

Dunbeath ran down the stone steps by the side of the castle and out onto the beach. He tried to slow his pace, knowing that a difficult negotiation was ahead of him, but in spite of this, he could do little to disguise the urgency that showed in his every movement. Zweig saw him as he hurtled over the sands and rose easily to his feet. He could see immediately that Dunbeath's manner was quite different. That he was about to ask for something.

'My lord?' said Zweig with interest. 'Good afternoon to you.'

Dunbeath had reached the captain and now stood facing him, suddenly unable to speak, choking on his pride, finding it impossible to choose the right words. Zweig waited patiently and smiled back in encouragement.

Eventually, Dunbeath appeared to sit on his discomfort for long enough to talk.

'Captain Zweig. I have a proposition for you.'

'Indeed. I should be pleased to hear it.'

'I have great need to be in London with all speed. There is not a moment to be lost. I must be there in six days at the latest – I have a vital meeting to attend. Is that possible? Can you sail me there in time? I presume you know the approaches – can you navigate the Thames?'

'Of course, my lord,' said Zweig pleasantly. 'As to the journey, that would depend on the craft. But what is your proposal to me?'

Dunbeath gazed steadily at him, swallowing hard as he summoned up the will to be a supplicant.

'I have a boat moored at Dunbeaton. What the Dutch call a jacht. I imagine it is still there. My father would use it to see our lands on the Dark Isles and he always said it was a speedy thing. Now, Zweig, if you would sail me to London so that I can attend the meeting of the Board of Longitude and then bring me back safely, then I shall...' Dunbeath paused, hardly able to lower himself to bargain in this way.

'Yes, my lord, you will what?'

'I shall give you the boat. To return to Königsberg.'

Zweig looked at Dunbeath for a few seconds before he gave a courteous bow.

'I am most grateful for your kind offer, but I regret I must refuse. As you know, my lord ...' he smiled as he spoke, slowly laying out his trump card, '... my aim is to return Miss Kant to our homeland ...' In an instant he had weighed up Dunbeath's personality well enough to add the one thing that he knew would be understood the best, and would sting Dunbeath the most.

'... to clear the debt owed to me by her father.'

Dunbeath struggled to suppress his rage as he heard Zweig say this.

'Sophie will not be returning with you,' he ground out in reply, 'she will be staying here. She has agreed to that. You will not have her.'

Zweig put his head slightly to one side but continued to nod gently, as if in agreement.

Sophie? Now it's Sophie rather than Miss Kant, he thought to himself. Here was a place to stand. He bowed again.

'Then, my lord, without Miss Kant, and without the debt repaid, I'm afraid I have no option but to refuse your kind offer.'

He moved as if to seat himself again on the dune. But Dunbeath was too desperate by now to give up. Once more, the sight of L'Arquen's smirking face came into his mind.

'Very well,' he said bitterly through clenched teeth, 'I shall clear the debt myself. Whatever her father is due for, I shall give it to you. But you'll only get the money if you can carry me to London in time for my meeting.'

Zweig looked steadily Lord Dunbeath for a few seconds.

'Well then,' he replied, with a curt nod of his head, 'we have an agreement. If the vessel is sound we shall certainly be in London within the six days you have given me. You have my word on that. As to the money I am owed, do I have your word, as a gentleman, that you will pay it to me when we return here from London?'

'A gentleman? You have my word as a Scottish earl,' said Dunbeath with some heat.

'In that case we understand each other. We can sail on the next tide. I believe it will turn at about three tomorrow morning and I shall be anchored off the beach here with the boat then. Be ready when you hear me knock at the castle door – we shall need to leave immediately.'

* * *

Dunbeath ran up the great staircase as soon as he'd returned from seeing Zweig. He called out loudly as he stamped past the salon door.

'Sophie! If you'd be so kind. I shall be in my study.'

He continued to run along the corridor until he reached the small room in the tower. Sophie found him at his desk as she came round the door a minute later, and immediately saw that he was immersed in the presentation charts that they had ready for the Board. He looked up quickly as she came in.

'Yes, Zweig will take me! I prevailed with him. But Sophie,

I'm afraid that this means I must change my mind about you coming. I wish it were otherwise, but I dare not have you so close to that man. Who knows what he might attempt? I may be supping with the devil with him but I shall take that risk alone. You are safer here with Hume. It won't be for long, I shall be back in three weeks, a month at the latest.'

'But how on earth did you get him to take you?'

Dunbeath looked away and a bitter, tight set came into his face.

'I've agreed with your captain' he said tensely, 'that when we return from London he can keep my boat to sail back to Germany.'

'Oh, that is good news indeed, my lord. It gives me such joy to hear that. I can begin to breathe again, just knowing that he'll be leaving.'

'There is more, Sophie. He refused any offer at first. His only thought was for his filthy hold on your father's debt and of getting you to return to Königsberg with him. And so I told him I would pay off the amount that is owed as well.'

Sophie took a step backwards, stunned at what she was hearing.

'Yes, I know, it is a full price for the journey,' said Dunbeath, glancing at her shocked expression, 'but what other choice did I have? If I don't show my work at this meeting then that mountebank Harrison will undoubtedly be bending people's minds to his infernal clock idea. No, no. No dismay now on that pretty face, Sophie, be of good cheer. You will be free, think on that! I shall use Zweig for his seamanship and when I get back he will leave for Königsberg. He will be gone. Your anxieties are at an end.'

Sophie remained frozen as she heard Dunbeath out, her mouth still open in astonishment. But the earl now looked intently at her, gazing deeply into her eyes. He spoke again, with more tenderness than she had ever thought possible from him.

'You are not to worry, my dear one. I shall return with the Prize and Zweig will be back in Prussia forever. The money for winning the Prize will be far more than the amount your father owed him. If I don't get to London I cannot succeed, though. So using the captain is a good investment - just the kind of thing my men of business are always urging me to think about. So enough of this, we are not to discuss it again.'

As he said this Dunbeath reached down and gently took Sophie's hand in his.

'Sophie, my dearest, dearest Sophie,' he continued softly, 'I am happy to do this if you will but agree to stay here with me. I am quite decided now. I want to spend the rest of my days with you, sweetheart. I know that now. When I return, will you agree to be my wife?'

He showed no sign of noticing her stunned appearance but instead bowed his head towards her.

'Will you consent to marry me?'

Sophie was aghast. This was more than she had ever wished for. But she knew immediately that there was no turning back now. The slightest delay, the slightest sign of doubt, and the debt could return. She knew that she was substituting one man's hold over her for another's. But she had to accept. Was it also not true, she felt, that she had seen another side to this wild man? Hadn't Dunbeath shown real affection when he'd recovered from his illness? And hadn't she just witnessed the nearest thing to passion that he was capable of? And, yes again, would she not have huge riches and a powerful position to look after her family and pursue the kind of research that so fascinated her? No, there was not love for the man yet; but that could grow.

She looked him full in the face and smiled. One of her father's maxims sprang into her head: 'if there is something you dare not refuse,' he would say, 'then you must do it with a good grace.'

'Yes. My answer is yes,' she replied now, her face glowing. 'Yes, I shall marry you. And with all my heart. You are to hurry to London and hurry back. We shall be married when you return.'

Dunbeath put her hands to his lips and kissed them. There was a slight pause and then he returned to his brisk self.

'Good, I am so glad that is settled. Now, let's us check again that we have everything ready for the Board.'

Chapter 18

Zweig walked slowly back to Dunbeaton, utterly spent and deep in thought. He looked upwards into the clearest of spring skies and gave thanks to heaven that his ordeal had come to an end. He knew he couldn't have lasted much longer. As he walked he turned over the events of the past few days in his mind, smiling grimly to himself at how strange life was. In a million years he could never have guessed that this would have been the outcome. He'd known only that a man like Dunbeath could never have tolerated him sitting in his view for long. And now a boat and the money to start again! This was more than he could ever have hoped for. All he had to do was get the man to London and then sail him back. He could even drop him off in a dinghy near the shore when he returned – he wouldn't be surprised if he'd have to stand clear of the English by then. If they'd worked out who he was they would have his head in a noose before he could blink.

But this could only be the first stage. If he managed all this he had still to arrive at a strategy for Sophie. He suddenly felt bone weary and knew he would have to put these thoughts to one side for the present. A few hours of blessed sleep would have to come first. Then he would be able to think more clearly about his next steps.

He eventually arrived at the cottage door. As he pushed it open he saw Mona McLeish tending the peat fire and she looked up quickly as he came in and jumped to her feet, beaming in relief at seeing him.

'Alexis! At last. We've been so worried for you.' She turned and spoke to her son as he sat hunched over a bowl of fish stew at the table, 'James, move along there. Make a space for Alexis.'

She smiled again at Zweig with obvious affection.

'You'll need something to eat. Then we can talk.'

She ladled a bowl from the pot over the fire and came over to sit with him as he ate at the table. He'd said nothing since he'd come in, but as the thick broth warmed him he looked over his porringer to where she sat smiling with affection.

'Thank you, madam. Yet again you have restored me. Well, no doubt you know where I've been. It took me longer than I thought it would but in the end Lord Dunbeath couldn't stand the sight of me – and eventually he came out to see what I was about. My intention was to ask for work. I persevered and he has found a need for me.'

'But why, Alexis? Why did you do this?'

'I had to do something, Mona – I cannot live here forever. I need to repay you and Andrew for eating you out of house and home, to say nothing of repaying you for saving my life. You have all been too good to me. I can take your hospitality no longer.'

'Oh, Alexis. You had no need to do this. And to put yourself through such an ordeal!'

She was about to say more but Zweig cut across her. He looked over at James.

'Lord Dunbeath told me he has a boat moored here at Dunbeaton that his father used to reach their lands on the Dark Isles. Do you know it, James?'

'Aye, of course I do. Everyone knows it,' James replied sulkily. 'Nobody has ever dared touch it though.'

'Dunbeath has great need to be in London urgently,' continued Zweig, calmly ignoring James's petulant tone, 'and I have agreed to sail him there. We shall leave at dawn tomorrow. I could see that he was desperate – he has to be there within a week – and so I set a high price for my work. He is rewarding me well and I shall be able to give you both all I owe and more when I return.'

He finished eating and then asked James to show him where the boat lay. He thanked Mona once again and the two men left the cottage and began their descent to the quay, Zweig leading the way and James walking in his threatening, surly manner behind him. Zweig was only too aware of the rancorous mood that he could feel behind him and knew that he would need a different approach for the boy. He might be just as deranged as Dunbeath, Zweig thought to himself, but another tactic was called for this one. This jealousy James had for him, muddled in with the guilt that weighed on him over his brother's death, had to be faced. It was clear to Zweig that the boy was too dangerous to leave as he was.

The two men stopped at a bend in the path and looked down on the quay. Zweig turned to James to ask which of the boats was Dunbeath's but the boy hardly lifted his eyes before he threw out a halfhearted attempt at a wave in the general direction of the harbour.

Zweig decided to adopt a kindly tone.

'You seem out of sorts, James. What ails you?'

The question was too much. James looked away in a bitter fury, unable to articulate his resentment. Zweig came closer and took him by the arm.

'James,' he whispered urgently, 'you must listen. I need your help. You must tell me how you found your way into the castle. It is vital that I go there tonight before I leave.'

This was the breaking point for James. He was sick of the thought of the castle and sick of Zweig's hold over him. He stared back at him with bitterness.

'You ask for more,' he spat out, his fierce hatred finally given voice. 'I wish I had never set eyes on you. I saved your life, my mother feeds you. And yet you still ask for more.'

Zweig had seen such distorted behaviour before. There was only one way to respond. He now fixed James with a granite gaze.

'Yes, I shall ask for more. And yes, James, you will help. We have our bargain, do we not?' All trace of Zweig's co-operative approach had gone and his voice now carried the threat of unlimited menace. He would not be denied.

'We have our bargain,' replied James in a shrill, angry tone, 'but how can I trust you not to break it? You are leaving for London and with you goes your side of our agreement. The English would not be able to hold you if you were no longer here. The telescope is all I have in the world yet you will not give it to me! How would I know where it was if you didn't come back? How can I even be sure you're not planning to take it with you? You must give it to me.'

Zweig looked James squarely in the face, his eyes as black as death.

'Must?' he said, and his voice was now suddenly loud. 'Must? What nonsense is this you're blathering now, James?'

But this was an insult too many for James. With a roar he threw himself at Zweig, frantically thrashing at him with his fists. A blow struck Zweig's shoulder and another landed on his chest. Then the big man stepped smoothly to one side and expertly felled James with a single heavy punch to the side of his face. There was never going to be a contest and as James reeled, shocked by the blow, Zweig slipped behind him and grabbed his arms, forcing him to the ground.

The two were motionless for a time as James's shuddering calmed and his anger subsided. He quietly sobbed in defeat and Zweig knew that the time had come to change his tactics. Giving up his hold, he jumped to his feet and burst out laughing. He extended his hand and pulled James upright, then embraced the weeping boy.

'You're right to be angry James,' he said, still laughing. 'I understand. You must have your security. But so must I. You see, if I give you the telescope, you could easily run off to the English and tell them about me. That's why I had to keep it in the first place. Yet I understand you very clearly that you'd want to know where it is if, for some reason, I fail to come back.

'So, here is my proposal. Let us give it to your mother for

safekeeping. In that way, if I don't manage to return or if you don't hear from me in a month, let's say by the end of May, then she is to give it to you. You can wait that long, can't you James?'

He smiled encouragingly at the boy, very obviously appearing to be solving his problems. Now he moved to close the bargain.

'But, if I do this then you have to meet my wishes as well – you have to show me the way into the castle. There, do you agree?'

James was exhausted and hurt. His breathing was short and ragged but he had been listening hard. After a pause he lifted his eyes from the ground.

'A month. I get the telescope when you return. And Mother will have it in the meantime and she will give it to me if you don't come back. Yes, all right, I agree.'

* * *

Major Sharrocks crept towards where his redcoat spy lay hidden in the dune grass. As the trooper heard him he turned his head and put the telescope down.

'Come on,' whispered Sharrocks, 'the colonel's changed his orders. He says we've got better things to do than this. He wants us back at barracks. What's happening anyway?'

'A fight,' said the soldier. 'That bloke that was staring on the beach just laid out one of the fisherfools.'

'Did he?' said Sharrocks, without much interest. L'Arquen's change of focus had infected him as well. 'Good. Would that these Scots madmen all killed each other. Then we could go home. Come on, we're finished here. The colonel will want to know about this – and he'll want to know why you're late as well if you hang about much longer.'

* * *

Zweig took little time to look over Dunbeath's boat. He checked the sheets for knots and wear, and then pulled the sails out of the locker and examined them carefully for fraying and any small tears that would widen if they hit foul weather. He ran his expert eye over a host of potential problem areas but eventually he straightened.

'She's still trim, James. I've no doubt she will get Lord Dunbeath to London. Help me get this awning off the cabin roof, would you? And then we can go back to the cottage and ask for your mother's help with our agreement.'

James came forward and the two men finished making the boat ready for the coming journey. Finally Zweig gave a satisfied nod to the boy.

'Thank you for your help, James. Now, why don't you go back to the house and I'll meet you there? I shall get the telescope from its hiding place and bring it along presently.'

It was a few minutes later that the three of them were sitting around the cottage table. Zweig had the wooden telescope in his hand, hidden in its oilcloth and he held it up briefly to show James. Then he smiled broadly at Mona.

'Madam, we have a great service that we would like you to do for us. We have something here that we would ask you to keep safe. We'd like you to hide it very carefully from view until I return from London. Would you do that, Mona? It is a simple task but it would mean everything to us both.'

'Why? What is it?'

'Mona. I knew you would ask that and I understand why you should do so. And I'm sorry to say that I'm not able to answer – but can you not trust us with this? Just for a little time? You see, it is a pact between James and myself and ...' he leant forward towards Mona, his huge personality fully trained on her, '... it's important to me that you keep it hidden from us both. But, if anything should happen to me, Mona, if I'm arrested, or do not return a month from now, then please let James have it. But not before. Can you do that for us, madam? I would not ask you to do this if it was not important.'

Mona looked uncomfortable and began to mutter her concerns, but Zweig's smiling certainty made her fall silent.

'Please, do this one last thing for me, Mona,' he said softly, 'I shall return soon and Lord Dunbeath will pay me out and I'll be able to repay you more than handsomely for your kindness towards me. All will be well.'

Mona looked questioningly across at James. The boy nodded.

'Aye', she said when she saw this, 'I'll do as you ask.'

She looked more closely at James's face and saw that a large bruise was emerging on his face.

'You're hurt, James. How did you come by that?'

'I fell on the path,' he replied and turned away from her. Mona glanced over to Zweig but he continued to smile blandly back at her.

'Here, James,' he said, and handed the boy the bundle. James's face brightened at once and he grabbed it from the captain and held it longingly to his chest. He then ran his hand slowly over the cloth as he felt for the jewels. He sat stroking it for a few moments and it was with an evident effort that he then passed it over to his mother.

'There, madam,' said Zweig with the air of a man who had just completed a complex business arrangement, 'that is done. Many thanks to you. Now, do you have any clothes you could let me have for the journey to London? I dare say the east coast winds will make the voyage a wet one.'

Mona stood up and Zweig followed her to a corner where a pile of oiled clothes had been thrown. The pair dropped to their knees to sort through them.

Zweig glanced over to where James was sitting at the table, still brooding, and made sure that he couldn't be seen or heard. He then leant across and whispered fiercely in Mona's ear.

'Whatever you do, madam – do not let James have that

229

bundle. My life depends on it.'

She looked up in alarm and saw that he was utterly serious.

'Please. Do this for me, Mona. Never let him have it. Whatever happens, do not let him open the wrapping. Don't be concerned, no harm will come – I shall return soon and everything will be resolved. But please, please, trust me on this.'

They stared at each other for some seconds before Mona's resistance cracked. She knew only too well her son's fragile state of mind.

'Yes. All right. I promise,' she whispered.

Zweig stood up, his arms full of waterproof gear. He beamed at her with affection and gratitude and then strode back to where James was still sitting at the table.

'I must get some sleep now,' he said to the boy. 'Wake me at midnight will you, James, and we'll sail the boat down to the castle together.'

With that Zweig lay down on the rushes in the corner of the cottage and was immediately asleep for the first time in three days.

* * *

Sophie drew back the curtains in her room, relieved that the need to hide behind them like a prying neighbour had come to an end at last. Immediately she did so she felt another curtain lift from the gloom that had been so affecting her mood. She now stopped with her hand on the heavy fringe of the drape and looked down towards the empty spot where Zweig had been sitting. In an instant she found herself thinking about the two men who were in such a struggle over her, and of their wildly different characters – the one impetuous, difficult, presumptuous and the other so determined and patient. She thought of Zweig again and his incredible vigil. What a fighter he was! But, what had it meant?

Where will all this all end? she thought once more, only too aware of how little power she had to influence its outcome. But wherever matters might lead, she knew that her first aim was still to protect her father. She had to see Dunbeath pay off the debt or to see out the hundred days. As long as Zweig was away in London, she was safe. As for marriage – well, she still had to play for time, whatever that might mean or she might have to promise.

* * *

Zweig was immediately awake when James shook his shoulder at midnight. Mona had filled a sack with food for the journey to London and Zweig picked this up as he left. Together the two men set off towards the quay.

It didn't take long for Zweig to have the boat in seaworthy order. The jacht was about thirty five feet long and gaff rigged, ideal for the journey he thought, a tiller helm and a small cabin below, just large enough for a pair of narrow cots and a table. Zweig had seen similar boats in the Baltic and he had no doubt that she would be like them, sturdily built for coastal waters and quite capable of a hundred or more sea miles on a good day.

He knew there would be no time to be squandered but he was confident he should have Dunbeath in London for his meeting. His anxiety, though, was sleep and he wondered if the angry lord could put his hand to steering a course. Nonetheless, he stuffed some cordage into his bag to hold the tiller amidships if his hopes were not met.

Two hours later Zweig and James had the boat readied and in a further few minutes they had sailed her the few furlongs down to the castle. They anchored about fifty yards from the beach and then lifted the small tender down from its cradle on the cabin roof. They dropped it into the water and Zweig climbed down, set the oars in their rowlocks and rowed the two men to the shore. They dragged the dinghy up onto the sand and then set off to walk to where the colossal boulders were clustered under the castle wall.

Zweig had judged the tide well. It was at its lowest and the rocks showed high above the slopping waves. James looked at them grimly as they approached and shuddered at the memory of a similar night.

He spoke in a low whisper to Zweig.

'The sea's calm. You'll have no trouble getting in there.'

They reached the sea wall and were about to clamber onto the gigantic stone by the entrance gap when James stopped and turned to Zweig. He spoke in an urgent tone – half mumble, half whisper.

'Before we go further, Zweig. Tell me again of our bargain.'

'Very well. If you wish,' replied the captain, softly. 'Your mother has the telescope hidden. If I don't return within a month from this night she will give it to you. But I shall return, James, have no fear on that. Dunbeath will pay me out and give me the boat. Once I'm safely away from the English, your mother will give you the telescope. I also intend you to have twenty pounds from the money I shall give her.'

He extended his hand towards James.

'There, you have my word on that agreement.'

James took his hand and shook it.

'Yes. I agree. Now, I'll show you the way into the castle.'

* * *

Zweig passed easily through the cave and pushed at the flagstone with his shoulder. He pulled himself up into the storeroom and a few minutes later he was padding through the castle's ancient passages, moving with extraordinary stealth for such a colossal man. He carefully climbed a back staircase and soon reached the third floor; then set off down the corridor there. He began to count the doors on the side that gave onto the beach.

This was the door that led to the fifth window, he thought. And here he threw the dice. If he was right then this would be Sophie's bedroom. But if it was Dunbeath's or the fat man's, then his plans were finished.

He noiselessly opened the door and crept towards the bed. As he looked down he silently gave thanks when he saw that it was indeed Sophie, and he stood for a moment contemplating her beautiful profile and listening to her childlike breathing. Then he reached down and put the palm of his hand deftly across her mouth.

She woke immediately and sat up with a start, snatching at the bedclothes. Her eyes opened wide with terror but Zweig ignored her alarm and began to speak to her in German in a low, firm voice.

'I shall take my hand away now, Sophie. And if you desire my death you have only to scream. I have no doubt that Lord Dunbeath would do you the honour of shooting me.'

He slipped his hand away and Sophie shrank back, pulling the blanket towards her. She was greatly shocked. But she had not screamed.

Zweig set down by her bed. He was now on one knee, his head close to hers. His eyes were down as he spoke to her, his voice low, hoarse and almost breaking in its intensity.

'You will know, Sophie, that I have agreed to sail Lord Dunbeath to London. It will be a desperate race to get him there in time and I've no doubt my good lord will make me risk all in the name of his ambition. Much can go against me on this journey and if I don't return I need you to know certain things. But if I should succeed and come back to Scotland...then I wish that you would think on these same things before you see me again.'

He paused as if searching for the right words. Then he started again.

'Sophie. I love you. I have always loved you. And I shall never stop loving you until the moment I die. For three days and as many nights you've seen me outside this castle, telling you of that love. For every second of that hard, hard trial you must have known that I was speaking only to you.'

His head dropped further.

'When I put you in the waves that awful night, with my ship and everything I'd built disappearing beneath me, I felt my heart break in my chest. If you had died, I would have died too, but God brought you here and then he decided that I should live too. Yes, I lived – and now I live as I never did before.

'Sophie, should I come back from London ... I am asking you to return to Königsberg with me. You will have heard of my agreement with Lord Dunbeath and you'll know that even though I was ruined, even from nothing, I have conjured up a boat and the money to start again. You know full well what I can do in life. Think of what we could do together! Think of the excitement, the joys, the plans we could make, the things we would discover. Perhaps the children we would have. And the love we would share.'

Zweig paused, and he seemed to be struggling with a terrible memory. His voice faltered.

'There is something else that I would ask you to think on. There were thirty four men with me when we left our homes in Königsberg and I have now to see their mothers and wives. I must support these women and their families as their menfolk would have done. They died because of me and their lives must carry on. I owe it to them. But Sophie, I need your help to do this.

'Please, Sophie, think on my poor words while I am away. Please agree that you will come away with me when I return. Hear the sound of my heart while I am gone - you have only to listen to the wind in the leaves or the waves on the shore. And when you hear them, you will be hearing my voice too ... I shall be saying to you, again and again and again ... Sophie, I love you,

I love you, I love you.'

Zweig stopped, his eyes were on the floor and he rose quickly to his feet. He turned and walked to the door without a backwards glance.

Sophie looked at his departing back. She hadn't said a word.

Chapter 19

Once he'd closed the door to Sophie's bedroom Zweig walked noiselessly down the staircase to the entrance hall. He opened the front door and stepped out, quietly closing it again behind him. Then he turned and hammered heavily with the huge knocker.

Before long Dunbeath appeared, his arms filled with rolls of charts and diagrams.

'Good morning, my lord. You have everything?'

Dunbeath handed the charts to him and Zweig began to truss them together with a length of twine. The two men worked together for some minutes, packing the presentation, when Zweig looked up to see Sophie coming to the bottom of the stairs in a long nightdress and with a silk shawl about her shoulders.

'And a good morning to you, Miss Kant,' he said as she handed some further charts to the earl. Dunbeath looked these over and then handed them to Zweig, together with a small travelling bag that he'd brought downstairs with him.

'You take very little, my lord,' Zweig said, feeling its weight, 'do you not need clothes for your meeting?'

'Hmm?' muttered Dunbeath, distracted by checking that he had included all the material he'd require for the Board. 'Taking little? I need only enough to get me to my house in London. I have clothes for a hundred of these absurd gatherings once I'm there.'

Zweig picked up Dunbeath's bag and the rolled charts.

'We must make a start sir, there is no time to be lost.'

He turned and headed down towards the shore but Dunbeath held back for a moment.

'Goodbye my dearest,' he said to Sophie, once Zweig was out of earshot. She looked at Dunbeath, his tenderness surprising her. 'I spoke to Mr Hume yesterday,' he continued, 'and he has agreed to stay here at the castle with you while I'm away. If that army officer, L'Arquen, should call again he will be here to deal with him. You have only to stay out of sight. Don't be afraid, my dearest, and have no fear for me either, for I shall do our work justice with the Board. You will see, I shall return with the Prize.'

He took her hands and quickly kissed them, then turned and walked down to the beach to join Zweig. By now James had disappeared back to Dunbeaton and together the two men rowed out to the boat and hauled the tender onto the cabin roof of the jacht. They lashed it down and Zweig made his way back to the cockpit. He looked out to sea.

'There will be a fresh breeze out there when we're clear of the land, my lord. We shall be making good time soon.'

* * *

David Hume came into the great salon just as dawn was breaking. He saw Sophie standing in the huge bow window, looking out at the vastness of the sea and at the speck on the horizon that was all that remained of Dunbeath's rapidly disappearing boat.

'Many apologies for my lateness, Sophie. I intended to rise earlier. Did they get away?'

Sophie continued to look distractedly at the sea's shining surface and the flecks of white that danced on the tips of the waves.

'Yes, they did,' she said in a dull voice, 'but God knows when they will return. Zweig may have had powder with him when he came but he carries another explosive now.'

Hume pulled his dressing robe tighter about himself.

'Ah, you refer to Dunbeath's Urquhain curse, of course. Yes, we have seen something of that these past few days, have we not? I hope he can keep the Rage in his pocket while he is with your ship's captain. The determination he showed out there on the dunes doesn't lead me to think he's a man that would tolerate too much insurrection. And as for the Board, I only hope they give him an attentive reception.'

Sophie turned back to the room and smiled at Hume with an air of resignation.

'I'm sure the work will speak for itself. Let us hope so anyway.'

She was about to walk towards the fire when Hume gave an apologetic cough.

'Forgive me, but I awoke in the night with a strange thought. I am no sailor of course, I have scarcely ever been to sea, but I wondered about our captain's intentions.'

'What do you mean, Mr Hume?'

'Well, as I say, I know little about it, but would you not have thought that he should have left when the tide was at its highest rather than its lowest? Surely the ebbing of a high tide would have taken him out to sea rather than the other way round?'

'How strange,' replied Sophie, now struck by the same thought. 'I must say that your logic would appear to be correct. No, I have no idea why that should have been. Now you'll excuse me please, Mr Hume, I shall dress and breakfast. And then perhaps we might explore the Dilemma a little further. I have been thinking more on Tit for Tat.'

Indeed, how very strange, she thought to herself as she walked from the room. Whatever was Zweig up to with the tide? Perhaps it had something to do with his visit to her? The only thing she could be certain of was that everything he did was for a reason. Quite what, only time would tell.

* * *

For three days Zweig stayed close to the shore as he sailed south, snatching sleep whenever he felt the wind was steady enough for him to lash the tiller. He'd managed to doze fitfully for the occasional hour but the accumulation of lost sleep was being added to the energy he'd spent on the dunes. Together, they were

238

taking their toll.

On the fourth morning, Dunbeath emerged from the cabin. He yawned and asked how they were progressing. He had spent much of his time on board preparing the speech he intended to give to the Board and, as he felt increasingly confident of getting to London in time for the meeting, his manner had become less hostile towards Zweig. Bit by bit he was beginning to fall under the spell of the big man's personality.

'We do well, my lord,' replied Zweig cheerfully, 'this wind is a gift from God. I believe he wants the world to know you have discovered his secrets. That point you can see over there to starboard is Flamborough Head and I have hopes of being in London the day after tomorrow.

'But, I'm afraid I have need of rest. I have stolen some minutes' sleep with the tiller tied but I must have more, I fear. Can you come and steer for an hour or two? I can easily explain how.'

Dunbeath looked doubtful for a second but then became more interested. He couldn't believe it would be hard to hold a tiller and the captain never seemed to do anything more demanding than look ahead and make the occasional adjustment. He now came aft and sat alongside Zweig. The truth was that he was rather fascinated by how the boat worked and he listened hard as the captain took him through where to aim and how to keep the sails filled.

* * *

Sophie sat by the enormous fireplace, her Prisoner's Dilemma calculations laid out beside her on one of the gilt sofas. She was lost, deep in thought, and she now lifted her head and stared into the distance, working through a chain of logic. David Hume sat opposite her on a library chair and watched in silence. He knew her mind well enough by now to pick his moment to comment.

Smiling at the signs of her concentration, he saw a change come over her face as if she'd reached a conclusion. He leant forward.

'What are you imagining now, my dear?'

'These Gesellschaftspiele,' she replied dreamily, 'the power these parlour games have to show us the way.'

'I greatly agree,' laughed Hume, 'but where are your thoughts taking you now?'

'Well,' she replied, 'we were talking before of the success of the Tit for Tat strategy in inducing people to co-operate and then rewarding them for continuing to do so. Its aim was clearly to find people that one could have three point relationships with. However, you'll remember that Tit for Tat also punished defectors by responding to their choice and immediately defecting if this was what they had done.'

'Indeed I do,' said Hume, setting down the book he'd been reading. 'The strategy prospered through its clarity because a defector knew that the other person would follow his choice and do what he did.'

'Quite,' continued Sophie, 'but I now see that the approach contains a great weakness. What if the other person kept defecting? When would the Tit for Tat strategy pull them out of their one point feud? What if the rewards of co-operation became lost in the blindness of their hatred? We see this all about us, do we not - people who cannot forgive and think it would be a weakness to do so? They have no way out of their hostility and as time passes they lose sight of any other way of living. And it's not just individuals either – there are whole groups of people trapped in this way too. I understand that on some of the islands of the Mediterranean Sea, for example, there are families that have been at war with each other for generations.'

'Why look so far afield?' Hume said with a laugh. 'Why, we have clans here in Scotland who have been sworn enemies since time out of mind. They say the Campbells and the MacDonalds will never find a soft word for each other, however long one might wait, let alone consider the idea of co-operation. And Lord Dunbeath's own clan, the Urquhain, are known throughout Scotland for their fierceness. Indeed, Dunbeath's fabled Urquhain Rage is much admired by his people.'

Hume rose to his feet and walked over to the fireplace, humming quietly to himself as he thought about what Sophie had just said.

'You must be quite right, Miss Kant – about Tit for Tat being used as a reason for conflict. How often has one seen an opening triviality between people grow into a war? And always are the words 'well, they started it' used as the motive to punish each other. It has often seemed to me that the only conflict in history that had an indisputable cause was the Trojan War, and that was because it was over a beautiful woman. I cannot think of another with such a clear explanation. And what have all these wars ever produced or gained? Nothing.'

'But, what if one was not a warrior, Mr Hume?' said Sophie, looking up at him. 'As you said some time ago, there is a great difference between a committed defector, completely satisfied with his actions, incapable of seeing the benefits of co-operation – and someone who's made a mistake and knows no way back to the comfort of trust and the great dividends of three point relationships. What if there's an accident or an unthinking error? Followed by a series of recriminations from which there becomes no escape? Tit for Tat will not help because it has no mechanism for people to start afresh.'

She looked down at her notes again.

'I believe the only way around this is to break the discipline of Tit for Tat – *and forgive occasionally*. Not every time, of course, because one's opponents would take advantage of that. But, randomly. My poor workings here suggest that a rough average of once in every three offences gives the best returns. I think of it as Generous Tit for Tat because its big heartedness allows a defector to think again. The world is not rational and mistakes are made – Generous Tit for Tat stops accidents from becoming vindictive cycles, what I believe the Italians call vendettas.'

Hume stood pondering on what Sophie had said. She was continuing to work through her calculations on the sofa when he had a sudden thought.

'Perhaps this is what people mean when they talk about turning the other cheek? To do so constantly – in other words to play Always Co-operate – would allow the other person to take one for granted. But to do so occasionally would give someone who regrets his actions the chance to change his behaviour. Is it possible that Tit for Tat is an eye for an eye and Generous is to turn the other cheek? I am not a believer, Sophie, but do you think that Christians believe their Lord played these parlour games?'

* * *

It was only half an hour since Zweig had asked Dunbeath to take the helm. He had given him the clearest of instructions – but much was going wrong. Dunbeath's attention had wandered away from Zweig's orders for a few minutes and the sails were now backing and filling in the most alarming way. Even to Dunbeath's untutored eye, the boat was sliding fast towards the coastline. In his anxiety to correct the course, he'd compounded the problem and had loosened sheets and forced the boat to run before the wind.

Dunbeath was now on the verge of panic, completely bewildered by his inability to get the boat to do what he wanted and increasingly unable to solve the problem. He stared again at the rapidly looming cliffs and realised he had only one option. He swallowed his pride.

'Zweig! Zweig!' he shouted. 'Quickly man. Or we're finished!'

In an instant Zweig was on deck. He summed up the situation in a glance and pushed the tiller hard over. He clapped

Dunbeath's hand to it.

'Don't move!' he ordered.

The captain slipped like lightening around the jacht, tightening sheets and slackening others. He flew back to take the tiller from Dunbeath and, without a word, pushed it hard over to put the boat about. The sails swung across and filled again. As the boat was carried by the rushing tide a black rock came roaring alongside, missing its beam by a coat of paint.

Almost immediately, Zweig put in a further tack and the boat's head came up. He closed Dunbeath's hand on the tiller again and once more he flashed forward to reset the sails. The boat heeled as it came up closer to the wind but, inch by heart-stopping inch, it pulled away from trouble.

Zweig came aft to take the tiller and only then did he remove his eyes from the sails and look over towards Dunbeath's pinched and anxious face. There was something about the man's expression and the complete collapse of his arrogant confidence that made Zweig instinctively burst out laughing. There was not slightest trace of recrimination in the laugh, but simply the joy of being alive. And then Dunbeath started to laugh too. Tightly at first. But, as the tension left him, more and more, until his head went back and tears ran down his cheeks. Then he began to roar uncontrollably, consumed by the total and joyful laughter of release and the two men stood on the deck, shaking, staring at each other, sharing a hilarity that could only come from having so narrowly avoided death.

A lifetime of suspicion and repressed feelings burst in Dunbeath. He had never in his whole life allowed himself to be as dominated as he had these past few minutes and he had never had anyone be so unthinkingly forgiving towards him when he'd failed. But the captain had not judged him and Dunbeath suddenly felt completely intoxicated with relief, even light-hearted. And safe. It had taken a terrifying crisis to do it, a vision of death, but for the first time in his life he felt open and happy.

And so the two of them sailed on towards London, catching each other's eye and then collapsing into the simple laughter of small boys – as only people who have just escaped death can do.

Dunbeath had only to say: 'did you see that rock?' for them to break down in tears of laughter once more. Yet again, Zweig's extraordinary will and charisma had brought someone swinging from hostility and doubt through a complete reversal of opinion to the warmth of a trusting friendship

Chapter 20

Once the dam had burst there was little to hold back the flood and a friendship between Zweig and Dunbeath, so impossible to imagine only a few days before, now grew by the hour. Zweig spent much of that and the following day showing the earl the rudiments of sailing and it quickly became clear that this was a skill that he took to with interest and enthusiasm. For a man that had known only a deep sense of antagonism towards the ways of the world, the excitement of finding an inanimate object that reacted to his wishes and intelligence and yet worked with ever-changing natural conditions, became a joy to him.

Now the pair barely stopped speaking except when they slept. Having established Dunbeath as a helmsman capable of following simple orders, Zweig had felt able to grab at some much needed rest and before long he was as alert and forward thinking as he'd been before his long vigil.

For his part, Dunbeath found Zweig compelling company. The two men scarcely drew breath as they spent hours discussing a range of navigational matters and, in particular, the various approaches that the German merchants employed in the Baltic. The many ways that Zweig described how the lack of an effective measurement of longitude had limited their wider trading activities was of great interest to Dunbeath. He'd always taken an academic approach to astronomy and the experience of now bringing his deep knowledge of theoretical navigation to the realities of life at sea was hugely exhilarating to him.

The next two days passed quickly for them both and it seemed no time at all before Dunbeath's little craft was working its way up the Thames and mooring by Execution Dock at Wapping. By then the friendship between the men was firmly established, heightened as it was by the importance of Dunbeath's mission, but also by such an extraordinary swing in the earl's opinion of Zweig that it could only be described as the zeal of the convert.

The captain now carefully secured the boat to a trot of grain barges and Dunbeath went below to gather up his charts. Together the two men set off in the direction of The Prospect, the most prominent of the waterside inns that lined the riverbank, and it was only a few minutes later that they were negotiating with the ostler there for a carriage to carry them to the earl's London house.

Within an hour the coachman was pulling up outside a fabulous neo-classical mansion off St. James's Street, nestled in its own courtyard and with a view down to the park. Dunbeath paid off the carriage and knocked hard on the front door. Half a minute later there was still no response and he banged again, louder this time. There was a further wait until the door opened a crack and a disheveled man, unshaven and with his clothing unbuttoned, gave them a sharp and unwelcoming scowl.

'What do you want? What business have you here?'

'Headley, it is me, your master! Let us in and open up the house.'

The butler took a step backwards in horror and began a series of flustered apologies and excuses.

'I'm afraid I hardly recognised you, my lord,' he said, gazing in dismay at Dunbeath's appearance. 'I am more used to seeing you dressed for the city. It's been so long since we've had the pleasure of your company. Let me see, it must be three, or even four years. Perhaps more.'

Dunbeath could not have cared less about the state of the house nor the unreadiness of his servants. He dropped his bag and carried the presentation into a large and lavishly decorated drawing room where he pulled the dustsheet off a sofa.

'Captain, set yourself here. Let me unroll these charts for you now we're able to spread ourselves.'

Within minutes the great mansion was in uproar as the butler roused up the household. Servants appeared from every door,

246

their features strained in shock, pulling on livery and clattering about, opening blinds and pulling back curtains. Martins, the housekeeper, bustled in, confused and tongue-tied, apologising in stammered bursts for the state of the house. But once Dunbeath had settled her with an unconcerned wave of the hand, she embarked on a series of curt orders to the bewildered maids to open windows, light fires and make beds with all the furious efficiency of a staff sergeant under enemy fire.

Dunbeath was completely oblivious to the activity that had erupted around him. Going over to a desk in the window, he pulled a sheaf of paper from a drawer. He set to scrawling a letter and then called out for the butler.

'Headley, have the carriage prepared with all haste. Ask Makepeace to join me here.'

He looked about the room and gestured to an anxious looking footman.

'You, when you're dressed you're to drive with Makepeace down to Greenwich. Find the Royal Observatory – you'll see it on the hill there – and take this letter to Mr James Bradley. He's the Astronomer Royal, they'll all know him. Deliver it to him in person with my compliments and ask him to come back here with you immediately. He will know that it's of the utmost urgency. You're to see that Makepeace is driving with all speed. Go now.'

He passed the letter over to the footman and turned again to his butler.

'Now Headley, my friend Captain Zweig and I shall need hot water for bathtubs. And send for a barber. We must both be at our best tomorrow, close shaved, pressed finery and powered wigs. Have a tailor come immediately. Captain Zweig is a bigger man than I am and if he is to fit into my clothes they will need some adjustment.

'Zweig, if you please. Let me show you these charts and I shall explain to you how I am to win the Prize. I want you to be with me at the meeting if you'd be so kind, should anyone wish for the opinion of the experienced captain that will be running the final sea trials.'

Zweig bowed, murmuring that he was most flattered and more than happy to be used in such a role. And so, for the next two hours, the two men sat with their heads together talking in low voices as Dunbeath rehearsed his presentation yet again.

* * *

On another sofa, five hundred miles further north, Sophie sat in her usual place, surrounded as ever by reams of calculations. She was staring into space, turning over a thought in her head, when David Hume came into the room, whistling lightly as he straightened his coat.

'Helloa, Miss Kant,' he called out as he saw her, 'I know that look. Behind those beautiful eyes I perceive a great machine is at work.'

'Mr Hume!' said Sophie, delightedly. 'Well, yes you are right in the sense that I was indeed thinking. In fact, I was thinking about something you said yesterday. About turning the other cheek. I know you are not a believer but the more I consider it, the more I feel the Lord might have been sitting here with us exploring the Prisoner's Dilemma.'

'In what way, Sophie?'

'Well, we've spoken much of the success of co-operation in long term relationships between people who want to build societies rather than exploit others – what the Dilemma would call three point achievers – people whose instinct is to trust rather than not to. You have called them doves. And your parable of the conflict between the hawks and the doves was most illuminating because it showed how the hawks will quickly run short of doves to kill and have then to meet others like themselves in bloody and exhausting battles.

'Now, imagine that like the hawks and doves of your story, there are whole coalitions of people who think the same way. They assemble to take up the fight against a common enemy. Which of the sides will be the more successful? Those in which people are joined by trust or those that are joined by fear?'

She gestured towards her pages of calculations.

'We have found, have we not, that the numbers tell their own story. Co-operators are the ones who trust each other enough to stay silent, who look for partners to have stable and lengthy co-operative relationships with, and who have found that trust and virtue are the cornerstones of how to win in life. They have found that co-operation wins.

'But, have you not noticed how some men regard people who wish to trust others as 'stupid'? You often hear it. They are astonished that their fellow man doesn't see the world as the competitive, unforgiving place that they do and they think him foolish for not doing so. Not only foolish, but weak. Well, didn't we see just this with Lord Dunbeath when you first played the Dilemma with him?'

'Yes, indeed Sophie, and one sees this constantly being repeated in life,' replied Hume.

'Then think back to the time of the Roman Empire, Mr Hume, particularly about how the Roman government would have behaved in small and unruly provinces like Judea. Their society was wholly structured with rules and laws, hierarchies, competition, suppression. A society in which there was no trust or individual thought. Only laws. Where the word of law was truth. A society of hawks, in other words.

'And suddenly a man was attracting huge crowds and saying that none of this mattered. That only love and trust did. As I say, a man who seemed to understand the great lessons the Dilemma is showing us. He talked of the power of co-operation and the death of defection. And thousands were inspired. His vision saw the end of winners and losers. It was a vision in which everybody, regardless of who they were, could win.

'Can you imagine how terrifying he was to the Romans and to everything they stood for? Their whole authority depended on them being seen as ruthless defectors. No wonder he had to be obliterated.'

* * *

In his study at Craigleven, L'Arquen lounged back in a chair, his feet crossed on the surface of his beautiful desk. A decanter of whisky was close by and he held an empty glass in his hand. It was plain that his poise had slipped. He stared blankly into the distance, his lips tight and a bitter, brooding look in his eye. Fruitless days had been spent scouring the vast openness of the Caithness landscape for rebels, and in his frustration his thoughts had now turned back to that arrogant and obnoxious man, Dunbeath. Perhaps he was the ringleader of this whole thing? Why not? Certainly he was the power around here. And he had so blatantly lied to him about that beautiful girl – of that he was quite certain. Yet again L'Arquen thought about Sophie – the few seconds he'd seen her had been enough for her image to crowd in on him. Not only lied, but the bastard had had the impertinence to shout at him, a colonel in His Majesty's army.

He came to a decision and sat up. He yelled at the closed door.

'Guard! Get Major Sharrocks in here. Now!'

* * *

'I must admit,' continued Sophie, 'that I never understood why the Lord said that the meek would inherit the earth. It seemed so preposterous to me that I often wondered if it wasn't an error of translation. But now I think I understand.

'It's because the strong would naturally think of themselves as winners that they'd always ignore the meek. Their own ambition and greed would lead them to compete with each other rather than bother with people they'd regard as not worthy of their attention or who had nothing that they would want to take. Do they not sound like hawks to you, like defectors? Isn't it because these people have such an unshakable regard for themselves that they place a higher value on their endeavours than the meek do? They think far more highly of themselves.'

Sophie set her papers down alongside her on the sofa and stood up. Hume could see that she was continuing to think through her conclusions.

'But the meek will co-operate,' she continued. 'Haven't you noticed how it's always the same people, often those with the least, who are the most generous? Their instinct is to share, to co-operate and by doing so, to build. The bonds that unite them are stronger than the bonds of fear and suspicion that unite those who rely only on laws and rules – people who carefully weigh and measure each exchange they ever make.

'The proof of the fallibility of laws for me is the existence of lawyers. What are lawyers except guardians of the intricate exchanges that defectors weave? There are no lawyers in Always Co-operate or even with those who would play co-operate until they're led by their Tit for Tat strategy to defect in return. It's because there's no need for them. In fact, I seem to remember that St Paul wrote something about this. Wasn't it that the law brought about wrath? And that where there was no law, there was no violation? Just so, co-operators are the ones who stay silent and get three points not those who distrust and only get one. I had always assumed that by meek the Lord meant oppressed, downtrodden, poor. But, see that he uses none of these words. He says meek – an attitude of mind, not a state of affairs.'

David Hume smiled yet again as she spoke. He adored her more than ever when she was in full flood like this.

'I like that very much, Sophie. Where does this lead you?'

'Well, to a further conclusion, Mr Hume. Isn't it an inescapable observation that tormenters ultimately always lose? It is because in the end nobody wants to deal with them. They take too much, always insisting on having five points, thinking it is their right. In the same way, I believe this is why tyrannies must fail. In fact, the more authoritarian they are, the quicker they will fall. It must be because a society that's built on the assumption of hierarchy and a rigid measurement of exchange – where exchanges are expected by return and in the exact amount of the deed – will always be vulnerable to being eaten away from the inside by any act of sacrifice or altruism. Or, indeed, long term trust. Fear makes for a poor soil and the roots of a lasting society will never thrive in it.

'The meek, however, don't "keep the score." Their faith is in the goodness of other people. Their belief is that that virtue will always, ultimately, be reciprocated. They trust until proven wrong. Some of them may eventually fight back against hawks, like your retaliator doves, but their instinct is always to form continuous, unbroken three point relationships – in spite of the repeated evidence of free riders and other exploiters. If this were not true, how could they ever survive?'

'I think you must be right, Sophie,' muttered Hume, carefully thinking through what she was saying. 'Like you, I couldn't see how the doves could ever win until we imagined a sprinkling of retaliators amongst them taking advantage of the depleted and weakened hawks. To use your picture of the ancient world, didn't the Roman empire collapse to the co-operation message of Christianity, in spite of their laws and hierarchies? It's widely believed that it was the barbarians who led to the fall of Rome but by then the empire had converted. And the barbarians? Of course they converted also in time, their ferocity tamed by the new co-operators. And I think that sometimes a co-operator can appear to lose but still win.'

He looked about himself as if trying to remember something

and then waved over towards where a large tapestry hung on the wall.

'Why, there is the very story I was looking for. King Solomon and the two women. Do you remember the tale? Both of them claimed that a baby was theirs and appealed to the king to decide between them. The king ordered that the child should be cut in half so they could share it. Then the truth emerged. It was the love of the real mother that made her agree to let the lying woman have the baby rather than see it killed. She immediately wanted the baby to survive, even if it meant her losing the child. The wise king knew at once that the woman who chose to get no points was the one who should get five.'

'Mr Hume explains the bible,' said Sophie with a laugh. 'Wherever will the Dilemma take us next!'

David Hume gave her an affectionate smile.

'But Sophie,' he continued after a short pause, 'the most remarkable conclusion that comes through your interrogation of the game is that it's the *same* selfish, self-interested instinct for survival in us that makes us defect in the one-time Prisoner's Dilemma yet leads us to co-operate in long term relationships. Because? Because it is rational to be selfish. Quite simply, it is the way to win. Perhaps we see it everywhere? My friend John Brown, the great physician in Edinburgh that I believe I have mentioned to you before, told me recently that he and his colleagues constantly saw examples of our very particles fighting for supremacy within our bodies. You would have thought that they would all work towards our wellbeing but apparently they do not. In fact, did we not see that with Lord Dunbeath's fever? What was the heat in him except his very particles at war? And Brown astonished me even further by saying that the anatomy schools found examples of children, yet unborn, whose organs had taken nourishment from their sick mothers, even though they were sucking the very life out of them. To the point that the mother died. Yes, you are right to appear surprised, Sophie. I was myself. An unborn child killing its own mother in the struggle to survive. We think it's our minds that make us selfish but it's plainly far deeper than that – our very particles are selfish. All nature is selfish. This is the universal truth – everything, every living thing, is putting itself first.'

Sophie looked sadly away. She thought for a second and then murmured more to herself than to Hume.

'I hope you and your medical friends are wrong. Perhaps the mother's particles were sacrificing themselves so that her child might live?'

* * *

There was a knock on the door and L'Arquen pulled himself together. The decanter and glass had been put out of sight. Major Sharrocks came into the room.

'Ah, good, you're here at last, Sharrocks. I have been thinking about that Dunbeath creature. The liar. He is the kind of Scot that you called the enemy within, the enemy of the Union. You were never more right than when you said that. We chase around looking for invisible highlanders while their clan chiefs sit in their castles, making their plans. And what plans are these? Why, to support a man who thinks he should reign instead of our rightful king. We don't know yet that Dunbeath has sided with the uprising – but I'm quite certain that he's lied to me. I have to conclude, therefore, that it is his intention to support this Bonnie Prince Charlie. I've decided not to wait any longer, Sharrocks. I've decided to crush him before he can crush us. Update me now, what is your latest information on the matter?'

'Well, sir, I withdrew surveillance about a week ago as you ordered but not before one of my men reported that the fellow we saw sitting on the dune had given up his staring at the castle. He was last seen fighting with one of the fishermen and knocking him to the ground.'

'Fighting eh? I wonder what that was about. Still, where there's a fight, you'll generally find resentment in the loser. Apply some pressure there. See the fisherman and ask him what he's got to say. Let me see some action. Action, Sharrocks, action! I'm unhappy with your lack of initiative. Get on with it. Use your imagination, major, and quickly – or you may find me using mine on you.'

Chapter 21

'Mr Smith! Mr Smith!'

The enormous outline of his landlady stood in Adam Smith's doorway, her great bulk blocking out the light as she stood shouting at him. A maid hid behind her, peering at Smith over her mistress's shoulder. For the third time, the woman took a deep breath and drew herself up, the better to bellow.

'Mr Smith! If you do not calm yourself I shall call for the doctor.'

At last Smith seemed to notice that someone was in his room. He stopped his roaming and stared at the floor, shaking slightly as a racehorse might after a spirited sprint.

'What? What is it?'

'What is it, sir? Why it is you, sir! You have marched about the room these past two hours, quaking as if for a fit, shouting your nonsense into the air. Are you not aware of what you do, Mr Smith? Much more of this and I shall have to give you notice. I have other tenants to think on you know. Why sir, are you ill?'

Adam Smith continued to be rooted to the spot. He didn't lift his eyes.

'I am quite well, I thank you. I am simply giving voice to the debates that I conduct in my head. Who else am I to speak to? I am quite able to hold both sides of an argument and I wish to hear them out. So, I am loud. So, no doubt you think me insane. Well, I do not think this makes the debate any the less.'

He began to calm down and now looked up and smiled at the vastness in his doorway.

'Still, I apologise. You are too good to me, madam. I thank you.'

One smile was enough. The landlady melted. She beamed back at him and gently closed the door. Smith remained still for a moment and then seemed to come out of his daze. He smiled again, this time to himself, and leant down to the floor and picked up David Hume's letter from where it had fallen from his fingers.

* * *

Makepeace had found the Observatory surprisingly easily on the hill at Greenwich and was directed into the presence of the Astronomer Royal as soon as his assistant was told on whose errand he had come. James Bradley now tore open Dunbeath's letter and read it twice. He then urgently began to pick up some papers.

'By God, your master has run it close this time,' he said to Makepeace. 'The meeting is tomorrow morning. We never thought he would come. I must see him immediately and decide if he should show the Board his work.'

They went immediately to Dunbeath's carriage and Makepeace soon had his team at a warm canter for the drive back to St James's. Bradley had for some months doubted whether the earl was keeping up with the field in the race to find a solution to the problems of longitude but he was not to be disappointed now and it was only two hours later that he was leaning back in his chair at Urquhain House with a look of blank astonishment on his face.

'Lord Dunbeath, I cannot believe that you have completed the celestial mapping that we started so many years ago. It is hardly credible. I have no words to express my congratulations. We have reached many of the same conclusions in London that you have here, but you have gone so much further in finding practical solutions to the problems that have dogged us. And your work on the Transit of Venus at such a high latitude as the north of Scotland is absolutely critical to the solution.'

'There has been much heartache over the years, Mr Bradley, and many a wrong turn,' replied Dunbeath. 'The fieldwork was the least of it. Of course, it took much time but I was under water in my conclusions for many a long month until I met a German collaborator recently who was the key to completing the work. My collaborator was a woman. Yes, I can see that you're surprised at that information, but her extraordinary insights showed me the way when I was lost. More even than that, she has perfected a method of calculation that will allow the time needed to make a determination of longitude for an experienced navigator come down from four hours to just over two. Let me show you her method.'

It was a further hour before the Astronomer Royal looked up from Dunbeath's explanations and spoke to him again with renewed admiration.

'Well, this is brilliant work, Lord Dunbeath. I feel quite certain that the Board will agree. And unless the king continues to interfere, I would trust that the Prize is won by celestial navigation – by you – when we see the Board tomorrow, and not by that pox-ridden machinery of Mr Harrison's.'

'What!' shouted Dunbeath incredulously, flying off his chair in alarm. 'Has that Yorkshire fraud still not been exposed for the total charlatan that he is? Why, he's just a damned carpenter, nothing more.'

James Bradley looked unhappily down at the carpet.

'I see that news of Mr Harrison's technical developments have not reached you in Scotland, Lord Dunbeath. Harrison is now claiming that he has perfected a clock that he says will prove to be accurate on sea voyages to an almost uncanny degree. Of course, we've done everything in our power at the Observatory to find fault with it and indeed the Board of Longitude is as one with us on this, but I fear ...'

'You fear what?' said Dunbeath fiercely, his colour rising. 'What is it?'

'Well, it is the king. It seems that Mr Harrison appealed to Viscount Rothley for help and through him he was able to gain an audience with His Majesty. God knows what passed between them but it is said that the king believes Mr Harrison has been treated unfairly by us. Can you credit it? Just because he has not liked the tests we have set for him these past fifteen years and has complained and quibbled at every turn. He says we have refused him funding, but why should we use our precious resources – resources that were voted for us by Parliament for celestial navigation – on such an absurd venture as his?'

Dunbeath had jumped to his feet in anger and he now began to stalk around the room, his arms stabbing the air.

'A clock! A clock!' he kept repeating. 'I've worked for twelve years measuring these lunar distances. And other men have slaved over them in other places for even longer than I have. The sacrifices we've made! And now I find a damned clock is to be in the same room as me. And being given consideration by the Board of Longitude!'

Zweig had been sitting quietly, listening to the two men's discussion. He now assessed the situation and saw how easily all could be lost by Dunbeath's temper. He rose from where he was sitting on a sofa and stood in front of the earl's furiously striding figure, forcing him to come to a standstill. He fixed him with an unblinking look.

'Lord Dunbeath,' he said, 'we shall have need of your fervour and energy tomorrow but you are among friends this evening. Let me put a proposal to you. If you are happy to do so you may call on me as a seaman to say that I know of no other nation, and certainly not the German empire, that would ever countenance trusting our fleets to something so prone to break down as a clock.

'The heavens do not break, they do not disappoint or confuse. We fleet owners and captains have been trained to rely on the planets for generations and we would not change our view for a collection of wheels and springs. Anyone who would say differently has not been to sea. If you wish me to, I shall say this to your Board and to any others there may be in the room. No doubt it will be full of landsmen with not a true sailor among them.'

Dunbeath stopped and looked at Zweig with admiration and gratitude.

'Would you? Would you do this for me, Captain Zweig? It would mean a great deal to me and to Mr Bradley if you would give the Board your professional views. Its members would be much influenced by the opinion of a foreign expert. Britain's world trade depends on winning the race for a universal solution and if you put doubt in their minds about the clock it would play strongly on them when they come to make a decision.'

He reached down and took Zweig's hand.

'Yet again, captain, I have reason to thank you.'

* * *

James was working at his nets early the next morning when Major Sharrocks rode up with an escort of three troopers. The officer dismounted and walked over, barking loudly at him with his usual ill-tempered menace.

'A word with you, fisherman. What's your name?'

'James McLeish.'

'Well, Mr McLeish. You may be just the man to help us. I've seen you often with your friend, the one that likes his glaring at the castle. He doesn't seem to be doing it any more. Do you know where he is?'

'Aye,' replied James sulkily, 'I might. But he's no friend of mine. What's it to you, anyway?'

'Never mind what it's got to do with us,' snapped Sharrocks sharply, 'I know he's no friend of yours, McLeish. My men tell me they saw him treating you ill some days ago. So, where is he? Quick man, out with it, or I'll have you into Craigleven and ask you there. No doubt you've heard that Scotsmen go in but do not come out. Would you like that?'

James thought for a moment. Why should he care if the redcoats knew where Zweig was? And why should he run the risk of getting into trouble for lying? Of being tortured by these cruel people, just to spite them because they were English? No, he had no reason for protecting either Zweig or that bastard Dunbeath. In fact, he'd like to see them both in hell.

'He's gone to London. With Lord Dunbeath. His lordship had to be there in haste and they sailed down together.'

But, with instant horror, he saw how appalled Major Sharrocks was to hear this.

'What?' Sharrocks screamed at James. 'Gone to London! By heaven, Colonel L'Arquen will not like to hear this. When did they go?'

'Over a week ago,' said James, his voice wavering as panic rose in him and his chest tightened. He had no idea that Sharrocks would have reacted in this way.

Sharrocks flung himself at his horse. He mounted and jerked its head round, then stared at James with horrible menace.

'I'll want to speak to you further about this. I know you by name now, James McLeish, so don't be foolish and think you can avoid me. Colonel L'Arquen will no doubt want to talk to you himself. And, McLeish, I know my colonel – if he does, I advise you to find your tongue.'

Sharrocks shouted a further order and the troop careered off at a furious gallop. James stood as still as a stone, knocked silent, utterly terrified at what he'd just unleashed on himself. His head spun and a sickness rose in his throat. He was at first paralysed with inaction but quickly became manic in his terror, and he now ran headlong back to the cottage. His mother looked up from her work as he threw the door open and was immediately aware that something had gone badly wrong. She set her sewing down and listened as James stammered out the story of Sharrocks' cross-questioning. Even though he tried to exaggerate the extent of his resistance to Sharrocks, his heart quailed as he saw how horrified his mother was at the news.

'You didn't tell them who Alexis was, did you?' she asked breathlessly when he'd finished. 'Oh James, I know full well your dislike for the man but if you let slip to the English who he is, they would certainly hang him when he gets back from London. They know what was in that ship. And they'll want to know who's been sheltering him! They'll think we're with the uprising. They'll blame us. Oh God, James. What have you done?'

She thought for a few moments. Then she turned back to look fiercely into her son's ash-grey face.

'You have to get away. You can't let them take you to Craigleven. They'll have it all out of you in five minutes if you go in there. If those soldiers come again I'll say you've gone out with the fishing fleet. We could even say that you'd drowned. No, better still, just disappear. Go to Edinburgh and hide yourself there until this rebellion is over. I've no doubt larger matters will be filling people's heads by then. And, who knows, the English may lose the war and be thrown out of Scotland. Yes, we have to hope for that. That's the best thing to do. Disappear. Go to Edinburgh.'

'But I have no money, Mother. I'll starve. They'll find me in a ditch. The only thing of value I have is the package that Zweig left with you for safekeeping. If you give it to me, I'll be able to sell it when I get to Edinburgh.'

A dark look came into Mona's face.

'I can't give it to you, James. You know that I gave my word not to hand it over unless Alexis didn't return. I will not break my bond.'

James was too desperate by now to be put off by what he believed had been half-meant promises.

'You must give it to me,' he shouted, his fear mounting by the second in the face of her reluctance. 'Mother, it's all I have in the world. How am I to survive if I'm not able to sell it? It's the only money I have.'

Mona McLeish looked back at her son with suspicion, her anxiety raised by his evident panic.

'But what is it that matters so much? What's in that bundle anyway, James? Why is it so important?'

James turned away, biting his lip.

'I … I can't say,' he stammered. 'It is between myself and Zweig. It's of great value. It was something Zweig had with him when he swam ashore from the shipwreck. And he promised it to me for saving his life.'

James looked at Mona imploringly.

'Mother!' he wailed finally, his voice breaking with a mixture of fear and desperation. 'I must have that package. If I'm to live I must have it. Mother, I'm your son! Do you put Zweig before me? Do you?'

By now he was sobbing on his knees before her and Mona looked at him for a few seconds.

'Wait here,' she said at last, her lips set in a tight line, and left the cottage.

James was still on his knees when she came back a short while later and handed him the long object wrapped in its oilskin.

* * *

Hume set the book he was reading down on the sofa beside him. It was dull stuff and he knew he'd far rather be talking to Sophie – by a long way the most stimulating woman he had ever met … in his limited experience, he admitted to himself, ruefully. More difficult to admit was the sense of loss he felt when she wasn't in the room with him.

Why, Mr Hume, he thought with sudden pleasure, realising that he was more than a little in love with her. Perhaps there was hope, after all, that he might find a wife for himself one day if he was capable of having these feelings.

He was rather pleased with his conclusion and now

wandered from room to room, looking for Sophie like a bored puppy. He even put his head into the kitchen before he set off with a sigh to haul himself up the long climb to the observatory. If she was nowhere else, he thought, she would be up there.

She was indeed, but as Hume came into the glass sided room he was immediately aware of a change in her mood. He now stood watching her as she went about in a desultory way, tidying papers and moving instruments in a dispirited fashion.

'I was wondering where you were, Sophie. I've become so used to seeing you by the fire with your workings. I hope you're not sickening. Or have you given up on the Dilemma?'

'I must be honest with you, Mr Hume,' she replied with a sigh, 'I have become dejected by where it is taking us. I'm afraid the conclusions are pointing me in directions I do not wish to go. They show me things I do not wish to find.'

Hume took a step towards her, a look of concern on his face.

'I am so sorry to hear that, Sophie. I know from experience how hard the road can feel when we enquire too closely into our natures. But what is it that's bothering you so?'

'Well, it was when we were speaking of King Solomon and the power of a mother's love ... and I heard myself talking about it with all the dispassionate manner of a doctor discussing a patient. That's not as it should be, we're not dissecting a body here, we're not cutting people up to see how they work. We're humans – feelings and hopes as well as flesh and blood. It was the story of the two women that brought me to my senses. One was so evil that she would even see a child killed rather than admit to her selfishness. Yet the other would sacrifice everything, even to agreeing to this wicked woman having her child, rather than see it harmed. Such a great love as this must be the most pure and wonderful thing in the world. But where was the Prisoner's Dilemma in this? Where in the Dilemma is there room for passion and compassion, the great love a mother has for her child or a woman might have for a man? Where is such love in all this mathematics and talk of hawks and doves, of free riders and defectors?'

Sophie came to an abrupt stop and walked to the window. She gazed out of it, clearly upset at her thoughts. Hume was standing quietly and after a brief pause she turned back to face him.

'Are we not doing exactly what St Paul told us not to do?' she continued, tersely. 'Understanding all mysteries and yet lacking charity? Lacking love? Are we not simply the sounding brass and tinkling cymbals that he warned us of?'

Hume sighed and stepped towards her. He took her hands in his.

'Dear Sophie,' he said softly, 'only a heart and mind as great as yours could find yourself in conflict on this. To have the intellect to analyse what you see but also the compassion to be saddened by the fact that you can. Lord Dunbeath is the most fortunate of men that you should have come into his life. But, yes, I do understand your thoughts and the questions you ask. And indeed I have an answer to them although you may not like to hear it.'

Sophie smiled, warmed by Hume's kindness.

'Well, I have come this far, Mr Hume. Perhaps I should stay and hear the worst.'

'Very well,' began Hume, 'I believe the logic we have found is this. We do good – but the Dilemma tells us that we are doing it to get rewards. Although these acts may have a selfish origin we learn that altruism and virtue attract others and lead to trusting relationships. Unlike defectors, co-operative people do not look for *exact* exchange or *immediate* rewards, yet they expect a return at some point nonetheless. And we know that some of these co-operators will not tolerate continued defection – they will either avoid it or sometimes fight back, be a retaliator we called it.

'Visible charity or compassion enhances one's reputation and we applaud it in people. If one lacks for these feelings then the Dilemma shows us that such a person is a rational fool. But, if we are to be applauded, it seems that charity must be seen to come at a price – after all, who do we more admire: the rich man that gives alms that mean nothing to his purse or an act of kindness that involves some effort?'

Hume looked out to sea, picking his words with care.

'So, where then is the 'pure' love that you spoke of?' he continued. 'Love that is not part of the intricate human transactions we have exposed? Why do we think of this love as a mystery described only by the poets and saints? Why don't more of us practice what we admire so much?

'I'm afraid the reason is this. It is because when we commit ourselves to others in such a way that we give ourselves up to them – we lose control. In fact this loss of control is our priceless gift to them, the ultimate sign of love. It is a sign that the person who loves in such a wonderful, completely selfless way, has stopped playing the game. After all, how can one play a game if one ignores the rules? Unconditional love may be the greatest sacrifice we can make to another person but it comes at a great cost, because it leads to one being dangerously revealed and exposed. And, so dangerously vulnerable.'

Hume paused and then seemed to rally as he looked at Sophie's sad face again.

'And here, I fear, is laid bare the greatest of paradoxes, Sophie. We admire the givers in life, the compassionate, the charitable, the great hearts. We are against self-interest. We applaud love. So why are not more of us compassionate, openly unselfish, even altruistic? Sophie, it is because we are afraid of it ruling our lives. There can be no avoiding the fact that this is understandable – because what is obvious is that the more that *other* people show compassion and give love, the better it is for us. And, equally, the more that *we* can practice self-interest, the better it is for us also. That is what the Prisoner's Dilemma shows us. So here is your answer. We may admire such love in others and we may like to benefit from it – but it doesn't suit us to give it ourselves.'

Sophie stood up silently as Hume finished speaking. Then she looked away and a tiny groan came from her.

'I see,' she said. 'I understand what you mean. What a mess. What a tangled mess we make of the precious lives we have.'

* * *

Once he had the bundle in his hand, James ran from the cottage and climbed high onto the dunes. He didn't slow until he had reached a secret spot he knew, far from the cottage and far from where prying eyes might possibly see him. Nevertheless, he looked carefully about himself, making doubly certain that he was alone. Once he was satisfied, he turned his attention to the wrapping and his hands shook as he untied the twine and wrenched the oilcloth off the long bundle in his hand.

For a second he stood stupefied, unable to take in the sight of the wooden fake.

For a further second he stared at it in disbelief. Then he gave a great bellow of anger and fear as he flung it to the ground. Terror at the thought that he must now stay and be interrogated by Sharrocks swept over him like one of the breaking waves on the far shore – and any shred of loyalty he might have had towards Zweig had gone forever.

Chapter 22

'How can you eat that, Zweig?' said Dunbeath with a mixture of exasperation and admiration.

Zweig glanced up but then went back to his breakfast.

'You should do so yourself, my lord,' he replied. 'I dare say you feel yourself too agitated for food, but this mutton is quite excellent.'

He continued to chew as he looked Dunbeath up and down.

'You look the part, I must say, my lord. I would not refuse you the Prize in that finery.'

'You are a new man yourself, captain,' replied Dunbeath, glad to be distracted from his frayed nerves. 'That powered wig has turned you into quite the Englishman. I've no doubt we shall be seeing you at court if we prevail today.'

There were a few final changes that Dunbeath felt he had to make but it was not long before the two men emerged from the great mansion for the short ride to Whitehall. Outside the front entrance an exquisite carriage waited for them, four perfectly matched white horses standing calm yet alert to the coachman's orders.

As they crossed the courtyard towards the carriage in silence, both men carried rolled charts, each lost in his thoughts, each gathering himself for the meeting ahead. Dunbeath climbed stiffly into the coach first, his face tight with determination.

But Zweig had been very aware all morning of the mounting tension in Dunbeath and he knew only too well the dangers of his brittle personality. He now put his foot on the riding plate and dropped the bundle of charts he was holding inside onto the carriage seat.

'One minute, my lord,' he said, 'I need a quick word with your man.'

He climbed up beside Makepeace and whispered to him.

'Who knows what we may find today. Do you carry a

weapon?'

'Indeed I do, sir,' said Makepeace grimly, and showed Zweig a heavy cudgel that he kept under the bench, 'never fear for that.'

Zweig returned to the carriage and Makepeace called to his team. There was a clatter of bridles and harnesses and then, together, they set off for the Admiralty.

* * *

James McLeish had walked the seven miles to Craigleven in less than two hours. Now he presented himself to the sentries manning the roadblock outside the lodges.

'I want to see Major Sharrocks. It's urgent. I have information I wish to give him.'

The guard looked at him sourly, wary of trouble from embittered Scots. However, there was something so blankly insistent about James's manner that made the redcoat put his suspicions to one side and, instead, he called over the other sentry.

'This trooper here will take you to the major,' he said to James, 'I hope what you have to say is worthwhile, my friend, or you shall suffer for wasting his time. And so shall I.'

But it was only half an hour later that Sharrocks was knocking hard on L'Arquen's door and then nudging James forward into the office.

L'Arquen rose from his desk with his usual mock courtesy.

'Major Sharrocks has told me who you are,' he purred. 'He has informed me that you have something to tell us but that you wish me to hear it first. I am most interested and I would be obliged if you would proceed. I understand you told Major Sharrocks that Lord Dunbeath went to London over a week ago – with that ruffian we saw outside the castle. What is their business there?'

James wrung his cap in his hands.

'Ruffian? Someone has misled you there, sir,' he said. 'No,

that man is no ruffian at all; his name is Alexis Zweig and he was the captain of the ship that was bringing gunpowder from Prussia. He survived the explosion when the ship sank.'

Even L'Arquen's studied insouciance slipped as he heard this. But he recovered quickly.

'Indeed, that is most interesting. Yes, most interesting. You are right, I was indeed misinformed. But why have you decided to tell me this now? How do I know that you're telling me the truth? My men reported that you were seen fighting with this man you say is called Zweig. Perhaps you are inventing all this to cause trouble for an innocent person?'

At this, James protested passionately.

'Oh no, sir! I have my reasons to speak about Zweig as I do and I want nothing more than to see him hang. And I have no love for Lord Dunbeath either. I shall tell you everything I know about them.'

'My goodness, Sharrocks,' murmured L'Arquen softly, 'we seem to have found an intelligent Scotsman. At last.'

* * *

The boardroom of the Ripley Building at the Admiralty had long been considered one of the architectural glories among even the most admired of Whitehall's many offices. Under a highly ornate plaster ceiling it was finely panelled in carefully jointed lime wood. At one end was an outsized built-in bookcase whose soaring, curved top held a colossal clock that seemed designed to dictate the tempo of naval business. Opposite this, at the other end of the room, a large pair of double doors had been incorporated into the panelling. These opened onto an adjoining room but were now closed, as for all gatherings of the Board of Longitude.

Along the outside wall, five long windows opened virtually from ceiling to floor and gave out onto the Admiralty's perfectly proportioned courtyard. From these windows light flooded into the large rectangular room. A magnificent mahogany table usually ran down its centre but now, as at all full meetings of the Board, it had been pushed back to be nearer to the fireplace opposite the windows, so that space was made for members of the Board to clearly see the presentations.

Rumours that the meeting would be showing possible candidates for the Longitude Prize had circulated for some time and the day's sitting had attracted considerable interest across a wide section of civil servants and merchants. Thus, while the Committee sat serenely in their places at the table talking idly to each other in a superior manner, they were hemmed in at both ends by excited and gossiping spectators standing shoulder to shoulder and pressing forward from the main body of the crowd that had gathered on the staircase landing.

Lord Dunbeath now stood before the table. Behind him were three easels, loaded with a mass of celestial charts and sample calculations. He had been speaking for over an hour and was bringing his case to a close.

'And so, my lords, gentlemen, the secrets of longitude at sea are laid bare at last. The celestial mapping so necessary for success is now complete and these charts, together with the conversion tables I have set before you, have given us the means to calculate a ship's position ... wherever it may be on the open seas.'

He approached the Board's table and now stood in front of the upturned faces of its silent members.

'When the conditions for the Prize were set down by this Committee many years ago, your honours' criterion of success was to be able to determine a vessel's position within a half degree of longitude. My lords, gentlemen, as a result of my research, this is now possible!'

The pitch in Lord Dunbeath's voice rose higher and he took two steps backwards so he could better address the room at large.

'In conclusion, I believe you can be quite certain that from this day forth, there will be no reason why our ships should ever be lost again. I say to you that what you have seen here are the keys we have been searching for, found at last, that will allow our great nation to use Edinburgh as the universal meridian for all maritime charts – and for our navies to dominate the oceans. With these keys, my lords, gentlemen, we can unlock the race for world trade and secure the safety of the realm, now, and for generations to come.'

He came to a stop. There was a profound silence. Then the Chairman of the Board of Longitude rose to his feet and, without referring to any of his other members, he began to applaud. First one, then two others followed his lead and soon the whole room was clapping loudly. Some of the spectators even called out Dunbeath's name while a few of the more high-spirited among the crowd let out a series of uncouth cheers.

Dunbeath gave a slight bow and the room began to fall quiet again. But in their enthusiasm for Dunbeath's astonishing break-throughs, nobody had noticed that the double doors to the side of the room had been slightly open as he'd been giving his presen-tation. These were now suddenly thrown back and all eyes turned to see that the king and his party had been listening in the next room. A gentleman usher brought his rod down on the wooden floor, once then twice, and the king swept into the boardroom, followed by a small crowd of favoured retainers. Alongside him, smiling broadly with the triumph of being given an invitation to leave Hampton Court for the day, his father's old friend, Prince Friedrich von Suderburg-Brunswick-Luneburg puffed away with the effort of having stood for so long. As always, his preposterous hussars jostled to stay close to their master.

'Many congratulations, Lord Dunbeath!' called out the king, 'I heard your conclusions. You have made a wonderful contribution to solving the problem of longitude with your discoveries and I believe the whole nation has cause to thank you. Who knows, the Prize may very well be won soon.'

He paused, theatrically, and looked around the room with a particularly ingenuous set to his features.

'However, we have yet to hear from Mr Harrison, have we not?'

The Chairman turned an angry scarlet. He was a committed advocate of the lunar distance method and he had hoped to avoid having to give time to John Harrison, a man he considered as little more than a dangerous upstart. But he knew he had to give way to the royal command and he now forced a smile of agreement and waved forward a group of men that had been standing in the far doorway.

In spite of the king's obvious patronage, there was a low murmur of disapproval as Harrison made his way to the front of the room. He ignored the evident ill feeling and had his two assistants set down a large box on the table in front of the Board.

'Your Majesty, my lords, gentlemen,' he said in a strong North Country accent as his men took the cover off the box, 'this is my latest clock. The third that I have made and submitted before this Board for your honours' consideration. I have been working on these marine chronometers for twenty years, but I am pleased to say that they have finally rewarded my efforts in full.

'As your honours commanded, this latest of mine was sent on yet another sea trial. It travelled in His Majesty's warship, Agamemnon, to the island of Jamaica in the West Indies, and has just returned from an arduous journey of fifteen weeks, a journey of the most violent storms and heavy seas and extreme variations in temperature and humidity. When the Agamemnon docked at Deptford this chronometer was taken under the custody of a guard of marines to Greenwich. There it was measured against the land clocks of the Royal Observatory.'

There was a deep silence in the room. All eyes were on

273

Harrison. He turned towards the king.

'Your Majesty, my chronometer was found to have deviated from the best clocks at the Observatory by just one second.'

The room erupted. Some of the crowd clapped and cheered while many of the celestial navigation supporters shouted out with frenzied complaints. But the crowd quickly fell silent again as the king began to speak.

'That is an astonishing piece of timekeeping, Mr Harrison,' he said, 'and I'm sure you have earned our profound admiration for your result.' He paused as he gazed around the room with a trace of ham drama and then continued, 'but you will have to forgive me if I ask how this great achievement of yours can solve the problems of longitude?'

'Well, Your Majesty,' replied Harrison solemnly, with more than a hint of a rehearsed dialogue, 'we are all aware that the earth takes exactly twenty four hours to rotate around the sun.'

He stooped down and picked up a small globe from the Board's table and pointed to the lines of longitude, arranged on its surface like the slices of an orange.

'When, for example, it is noon here in London,' he indicated with his forefinger, 'it will not be noon at Your Majesty's dockyard in Plymouth for a further seven minutes. And, indeed, it will not be noon in Georgetown in the American colony, for another five hours, twenty three minutes and forty five seconds. So, if one knows the exact time in London, the home port, and one knows the time on board the vessel one is travelling in, then it is a simple matter of computing the longitude, once the latitude – where one's ship is on the curve of the globe – has been factored in. Every hour of difference equates to fifteen degrees. Thus, if you are three hours behind the time in London then you are at sea in the Atlantic Ocean some forty five degrees west of here.'

'I understand,' said the king in such a way that there were few in the room that didn't see he was almost speaking in prepared lines, 'and your clock will be set to the time in the home port. But how can one tell accurately what time it is on board?'

'Why, by measuring noon from the height of the sun, Your Majesty,' said Harrison. 'Please allow me to demonstrate with this globe.'

The king's party moved closer to the front of the room and now stood to watch Harrison while a visibly agitated Dunbeath was edged to one side. Harrison threw the globe high into the air and as it reached its apex the upwards movement stopped, paused for a fraction of a second, and then started to descend. Harrison caught it again.

'You saw the globe pause as it reached the top of its flight, Your Majesty? Just as the globe stopped in the air, so the sun reaches the highest point in its arc each day, what we call its zenith, before starting its downward journey again. That is the point when it is noon. And it is easy to measure. Indeed, I believe that even the most callow of midshipmen would be trusted to reckon this point with a sextant within a few months of joining Your Majesty's navy. Or, indeed, any navigator on one of our great trading ships. In fact, I foresee that ships will carry two chronometers in time. One would be at the time in the home port and the other would be altered with the progress of the ship. In this way a vessel would be more independent of the weather and a regular sighting of the sun would become less necessary. In any event, the calculations for longitude are then easily completed and an exact position for the ship can be arrived at within just a few minutes. Not hours, but minutes.'

There was a murmur of approval as John Harrison said this, followed by an expectant hush. It was clear that the king was about to speak and the room fell silent. He appeared to be thinking through what he'd just heard and then turned slightly to address the Committee's table.

'Gentlemen of the Board. As you know, this great nation of ours is famous throughout the world for its many geniuses. Nonetheless, it must be rare to have two together in one room as we do here today. We should celebrate it. But I do not envy you in your decision making. Both of the methods perfected by these gentlemen are wonderful breakthroughs in our understanding of navigation, are they not? And both set our country years ahead of other nations. Since that is so, would it not seem wrong to reward the endeavours and brilliance of one of these great men and condemn the other to public failure?'

There was a murmur of approval in the room. The king held up a hand in a faintly apologetic manner.

'Of course, I would not wish to interfere, gentlemen, but if I could be permitted an opinion on how this may be resolved, might not you members of the Board consider that the Prize could be … shared?'

Dunbeath could take no more. He had been struggling to contain his rage during Harrison's performance but, king or no king, this suggestion made him lose all control.

'Shared!' he shouted as all eyes in the room turned on him. 'Shared? The perfection of the heavens shared with this coxcomb craft … this, this box of tricks. A mere mass of metal?'

'Lord Dunbeath, I beg you,' the king murmured serenely, 'do not distress yourself in this way. I have told you already of my admiration for your achievements. But just as there is greatness in both solutions, so there are deficiencies. You, yourself, will acknowledge that no planetary readings are possible when there is heavy cloud. That could last for many days, particularly in some intemperate regions.'

All pretence at an amateur's ignorance had been dropped. The king continued smoothly on.

'Nor is it possible to take daylight readings for six days in every month when the moon is so close to the sun that it disappears. I also understand you to have said that it can take over two hours to compute one's position with the lunar distance method – even with your great advances. In two hours a ship could be on the rocks.

'Set against this, the marine clock, Mr Harrison's so called chronometer, is quicker to use and, as he says, can be largely independent of the weather. But it is fragile and vulnerable and must be subject to doubt. So, surely the two systems should be taken on voyages together? To support one another? I merely suggest to the experts here in this room that there are strengths and weaknesses in both methods. And so I posed my question, Lord Dunbeath, simply for the Board's consideration – and I ask it again – might we not try to avoid confrontation and schism on this point? Would it not be possible to co-operate?'

But of all the words the king could utter, such an echo of the co-operation games that had so maddened Dunbeath in Scotland now made him throw self-restraint to the winds.

The Urquhain Rage descended.

'Co-operate? Co-operate!' he shouted, advancing on the king. And then, with a roar, he lifted his arm.

In an instant, Zweig had him by the wrist – but not before the prince's hussars had moved with almost incredible speed to draw their sabres. The small crowd around the men gave a collective gasp and quickly parted. Everyone froze. But, the king seemed to be the only man in the room to remain completely unperturbed and he now lifted his hand to stop any violence.

'Please, gentlemen,' he said placidly, 'there is no need for arms. Calm yourself, Lord Dunbeath. I shall withdraw and leave the Board to its deliberations.'

He turned to the hussars.

'Sheath your swords, gentlemen, I beg you.'

The king moved to go. Then, almost as if a thought had just occurred to him, he turned back and spoke in a low murmur into Dunbeath's ear.

'My lord, I hear unhappy reports from Scotland,' he whispered. 'Of an uprising against me. I wonder that you are here at all. Should you not be raising a militia to fight this invader when he lands? Hmm? This … Bonnie Prince Charlie?'

He made as if to finally leave but then seemed to have a further thought. Once more, he turned back and again he muttered softly to Dunbeath.

'Or, perhaps you agree with his plan?'

With this the king and his retinue moved towards the door and everyone in the long room bowed, except Dunbeath.

* * *

Outside the porticoed entrance to the Admiralty the king's carriage stood waiting, a footman poised to open the door and drop the step.

The king emerged into the courtyard and calmly made his way to the coach. The door was smartly swung wide for him and he had his hand on the carriage's side when he suddenly hesitated and turned to the old prince, still wheezing along beside him.

'Did you see that man, prince?' he murmured serenely in German. 'He raised his arm to me. He made to strike the King of England. Remarkable, wouldn't you say? I wonder that nothing can be done to stop such a madman from threatening the crown again. Can you imagine what would have happened to his like in the old country, eh?'

With that he climbed into the carriage and the prince creaked his whale body downwards to a semblance of a bow.

The coach pulled away and the prince walked back to where Dumm and Kopf were lounging by the front door, reddened with the pleasure of action like a pair of fighting cocks. The prince was quite sure of what the king had said: he knew a hinted order when he heard one, and he now spoke loudly to his little army in the obscure slang they always used, its strange army vocabulary mixed in with their extraordinary local Hanoverian dialect. As ever, they were confident in their secret language.

'You both saw the intended assault on His Majesty,' the prince barked, crazed with self-importance. 'We cannot let this pass. This Dunbeath and his like must be taught a lesson they will never forget.'

Zweig had followed the royal party down the stairs with the intention of seeing what the aftermath of Dunbeath's madness was likely to bring. He had buried himself as best he could in the knot of people by the door but the prince had made no effort to drop his voice, so confident was he that nobody would be able to understand what he was saying.

Zweig broke away and hurried back to the Board's meeting room. He saw Lord Dunbeath talking to the Astronomer Royal.

'My lord,' he said urgently, 'you must come with me immediately. There is not a moment to lose.'

Dunbeath began to protest but Zweig took him firmly by the arm and repeated the one word warning – 'immediately!' Dunbeath nodded a farewell to Bradley and together the two men hurried through the far door and ran down a back staircase. On the ground floor they came to a long corridor and Zweig moved quickly down it, looking into the rooms to either side. Eventually he found one he evidently liked. They ducked into a small, unlocked office whose windows gave out onto the courtyard and Zweig held open the door and virtually pulled Dunbeath inside.

'Wait here, my lord,' he said urgently, 'your life is in great danger. Do not stir until I come for you.'

He walked quickly over to the sash window and opened it. With a quick movement he removed his hat and pulled a long ostrich feather from the brim and placed it on the window sill. Then he closed the window again.

Zweig left the room and locked the door from the outside. He put the key in his pocket and walked coolly back to the front entrance and left through it, wandering casually away from the waiting guards. He found Makepeace with the carriage amongst a group of other drivers and took him to one side and told him briefly about the dangers to his master.

'Drive your team along the wall there and stop at the window that I have marked with an ostrich feather. Wait for us there. I shall go back for his lordship and we shall join you presently. And, Makepeace, have that cudgel of yours to hand. I might have use of it.'

Zweig then strolled slowly back through the gaggle at the front door and found the corridor again. He carefully checked that he hadn't been seen or followed and then quickly unlocked the door, locking it again once he was inside. As he did so the carriage drew up outside and Zweig moved like lightening to open the window.

'Out of here, my lord. Makepeace has the carriage waiting!'

Dunbeath needed no second prompting. He scrambled through the window and jumped to the ground. He opened the carriage door and was about to climb into it when, with the worst of timing, Dumm and Kopf were returning from their fruitless search for the earl. They now glanced down to see his hurrying figure disappearing into the coach.

With a cry they hurtled up the side of the courtyard just as Zweig was jumping down from the window ledge. The two hussars were almost on him when Zweig yelled urgently to the coachman.

'Go, Makepeace! Quickly man, drive on. And throw down the stick!'

In one swift move Makepeace had the team moving and had leant under the seat for the cudgel. Zweig caught it and immediately swung at the leading hussar. The prince's soldiers were on him by now, their sabres flashing, any suggestion of foppishness long gone. But Zweig had seen a hundred fights in untold ports and many of them had involved him. He swung the heavy weapon above his head with a roar and his immense strength and evident experience of hand to hand fighting made the hussars shrink momentarily back. That was enough for Zweig. He lunged forward and with half a dozen lightening blows he had their swords knocked from their hands and the arm of one broken and the collarbone of the other.

Zweig was not interested in victory but only in escape and after a few more carefully aimed swings he raced after the departing coach and leapt onto the step while he grabbed a handhold with his free arm. He shouted to Makepeace.

'Drive on! Drive on!'

The carriage swept through the low wall that formed a boundary to the Admiralty courtyard and out into Whitehall. Behind them the prince watched the coach's lurching body and wildly turning wheels and then looked towards where his broken bodyguards were struggling to their feet. In a voice thick with anger, he shouted into the face of one of the king's aides, still standing by the door.

'Get General Mallender! Tell him, find where Lord Dunbeath house. We make visit. I finish him!'

* * *

Once the carriage had rounded the corner and started up The Mall, Makepeace reined in the horses and Zweig climbed inside. The big man's blood was up and he laughed loudly when he saw Dunbeath's downcast look.

'By heaven, my lord, cheer yourself! It was great good fortune that I should have known the army dialect those toy soldiers were using, wasn't it? I used to provision their garrison. I learnt their nonsense so that I could do business with them. We used to call it "Armee Rede". I didn't like it at all when I heard them say they were planning on arresting you for attempting to strike the king.'

'Attempting? I would have done so if it hadn't been for you, captain,' said Dunbeath mournfully, 'you saved me from myself. I've no doubt those fancy butchers of his fat friend would have happily run me through. Well, we are where we are. But, what do we do now?'

'Well, they will certainly be sending men to your house even as we speak,' replied Zweig. 'I would suggest that we do not return there but go directly to the boat and get back to Scotland as fast as we can. They won't know how we travelled here and the river will be the last place they'll think of looking.'

'Yes, you must be right. There's no point in staying here. But, what of you, Zweig?' Dunbeath said, with unexpected concern, 'I have put you in harm's way. Why do you not make your way back to Königsberg from here? Nobody knows your name. They won't be chasing you in London, they'll be looking for me. I've no doubt you can pick up a vessel if you ask around the port and I have your money with me already.'

Zweig laughed. Leaving Sophie behind was the last thing he wanted – he knew full well he had to return to Scotland. Even as he smiled at Dunbeath he saw yet another opportunity to bind himself ever closer to the man. And to win an even deeper trust.

'And allow you to put yourself on the rocks again at Warleigh Point? No, my lord, I believe our bargain included a return journey.'

Dunbeath looked at him carefully.

'Captain,' he said quietly, 'I dare say I would be able to find a man in Wapping, or even two, to help me sail back. Perhaps Makepeace has some knowledge of boats. You have no need to come with me. You have found yourself caught up in my affairs and my madness, and I would think no less of you if you left me now.'

'Enough of this,' laughed Zweig. He snatched off his wig and put his head out of the window. 'Makepeace, not St James's,' he shouted. 'Take us instead to Wapping with all speed. I believe we may yet catch the tide if we hurry.'

Zweig came back inside the carriage and it wasn't long before his enormous good humour had spread to Dunbeath. Yet again they had escaped death, and yet again they celebrated it with the hilarity that can only come from such close shaves. By the time they arrived at Wapping, Makepeace had wondered more than once quite what could be causing the pair of them to be shrieking with laughter so much.

The coachman quickly found where the jacht was moored and his master and Zweig clambered over the barges to get on board. They pulled off their court dress and Dunbeath went back to where Makepeace stood with the horses.

'Do you know how to sail a boat by any chance?'

'Why yes, my lord. I was brought up on the river. My father delivered grain from Essex. I am the first of my family to have dry feet.'

'Excellent. Would you consider coming back to Scotland with us? I shall see you well rewarded for it if you would agree.'

'With pleasure, my lord. It will make a welcome change of air for me.'

'Excellent again, Makepeace. Then I suggest that you leave the carriage at one of the inns here and collect it when you return. I shall give you the funds to come back by road.'

But, half an hour later, Makepeace was trying yet another inn on the waterside. Two had said they had no space to store the coach. Now he was hearing the same news from a third.

'With great sorrow I must refuse you, driver. There is no room in my stable at all.'

'Can you not lodge it with a neighbour of yours?' asked Makepeace.

'I doubt it very much, sir. We all have much custom at this time of year. But perhaps my boy could return it to your own mews?'

Fatally, Makepeace thought this was a good plan.

'Yes, if you're willing and the lad is able to handle the team. There's money for you both if you can. The address is Urquhain House in St James's. If he goes to the park there he'll find it easily enough. Let him know that he can do me a favour while he's at it. My name is Hugh Makepeace and I'd be grateful if he could see my wife and tell her that I'm sailing up to The Castle of Beath with his lordship and I'll be back in three or four week's time.'

Makepeace left the carriage with the innkeeper and within the hour the tide had turned and the three men were sailing down the Thames. By now their wigs and coats had been consigned to the tiny cabin and the drama of their fight and escape had them all in high spirits. Together they worked the sheets and sails as they tacked down the river, each of them pleased for their own reasons to be leaving London and heading for the open sea.

* * *

The stable boy was, indeed, a capable driver and within a couple of hours he was turning off Pall Mall and swinging the beautiful carriage and its team of horses into the forecourt of Urquhain House.

He was about to jump down and rouse out a servant when from all sides a troop of guards hurled themselves at the coach, wrenching open its doors and climbing on its roof.

'Where's Lord Dunbeath?' screamed a uniformed officer.

''oo d'yer mean?'

'You know! Lord Dunbeath. This is his carriage. Where is he? And the other man he had with him?'

'I don't know what yer about,' said the boy once more, 'but the three men that was in the coach sailed off in a boat. I was just paid to bring the man's carriage back 'ere. I was told to tell the coachman's missus that they've all gone up to Scotland and that she's not to expect him back for a month.'

Chapter 23

A low mist hung over the ghostly outline of St James's Palace. The sprawling Tudor buildings sank into the blankness of the watery atmosphere and only the ancient cloisters were dimly visible, picked out by the thin light of their hanging lanterns. Through the still air the cobbles rang with the heavy boots of sentries as they marched endlessly back and forth through the gloom. Although it had earlier been a beautiful spring day, the rain that afternoon had made the brickwork sodden and the damp still hung heavy as a group of army officers in red frock-coats hurried to keep their appointment.

Before long they had gathered in a small room off Friary Court, pine panelled and with a large turkish carpet on the floor. The door opened and they immediately stopped their discussions and stood to attention. General Mallender entered with the old Prince von Suderburg-Brunswick-Luneburg snuffling along behind him, the thunder in his face still unable to disguise the self-satisfaction that shone from him at being at the centre of affairs. Mallender asked the men to settle themselves.

'Well gentlemen, you will have heard about the attempted assault on His Majesty earlier today and you'll know that we are looking for the Earl of Dunbeath to answer for it. We now learn that he has sailed off, apparently to his stronghold in Scotland. As you know the current situation in that country is giving us cause for concern and we have reason to believe that the clan chiefs will be gathering soon to decide whether to support Charles Edward Stuart in an uprising against King George.

'It's vital that we stamp out such talk and Lord Dunbeath's behaviour today gives us an excellent opportunity to make an example of our intentions. We want something to let the clan leaders think on. They need to be in no doubt that we shall not stand for any Scottish chief thinking that he can show disrespect to the English king!'

There was a murmur of agreement in the room and Mallender looked out at his officers' determined expressions.

'By great good fortune, we have a troop of light dragoons, Harrington's Horse, garrisoned near to Dunbeath's castle. It is commanded by Colonel George L'Arquen. Some of you may know him. I suggest, gentlemen, that you have an arrest warrant drawn up which will be signed by the prince here and sent up to Scotland to have the colonel bring Dunbeath back to London.

'And, Captain Meynell,' Mallender continued, turning to the duty officer who was taking the minutes, 'you might make the warrant plain to Colonel L'Arquen that we would shed few tears if Dunbeath was to be killed while resisting arrest.'

Mallender began to pick up his papers, clearly bring the meeting to an end. Then he looked into the room again.

'Frankly, gentlemen, I can think of few of our number who would carry out this order with the enthusiasm of George L'Arquen.'

The officers rose to their feet, laughing. L'Arquen's reputation was obviously well known to them.

* * *

Two days had passed since James McLeish had told L'Arquen about Dunbeath's flight to London. And for two days the colonel had hardly slept. He still couldn't believe that he'd let the man slip between his fingers and he poured himself another glass of whisky and, yet again, he brooded over his strategy.

He had to guess that the Board of Longitude meeting was the cause of Dunbeath going, he concluded. Dunbeath had said his life's work was at stake and he'd certainly looked as if he was speaking the truth. There was no faking the letter from the Board, either. But what was he doing with that man Zweig if he wasn't involved with the rebellion? He must be. He was probably seeing the other clan chiefs even now. And he'd lied to him. Of that he was certain – he'd lied about the girl. Maid indeed! God, she was beautiful though.

He shouted to his guard to find Sharrocks and five minutes later he was looking at the major from under half closed eyelids.

'How many men do you have keeping Dunbeath's castle under surveillance now?'

'I put two of them back, sir. One on the dunes and one on the headland where he can watch for the boat. As well as observe the far side of the castle.'

L'Arquen looked at him bitterly.

'Tell them to keep their damned eyes open. And Sharrocks, if you ever withdraw surveillance again I shall break you to the ranks. I should never have allowed you to do it before.'

* * *

Hume stood in front of the fire warming himself as a slight chill seemed to have come with the new day. He looked over as Sophie came up from the kitchen with firewood in her arms.

'Why, Mr Hume. Good morning,' she greeted him.

'Good morning to you too, Miss Kant.'

'I was thinking of you just now,' Sophie said as she put the logs by the grate, 'these sticks made me think of something my brother liked to say and I thought to share it with you. Have I ever told you about my brother?'

'Yes, you have mentioned his work in moral philosophy at the university in Königsberg,' replied Hume. 'Why, what was it that made you think of him?'

'He used to have a little saying. Let me see, the German is *Aus so krummen Holze, als woraus der Mensch gemacht ist, kann nichts ganz Gerades gezimmert werden*, and I suppose you would say it in English as "out of the crooked ..." I'm not sure what 'Holze' translates as. It is a collection of Zweige. Holy Mary, Zweig again. I mean branches.'

'Timber?'

'Yes, that would be it. Timber. So, "out of the crooked timber of humanity, no straight thing can ever be made."'

'A depressing observation, Miss Kant. Still, I dare say your work on the Prisoner's Dilemma has led you towards his views.'

'Well, my brother is still very young and is yet to record his thinking in a published text. And I must confess that we find much of what he has to say unformed and esoteric. But I believe that in time his thoughts will be less mysterious, and easier to follow.'

Sophie shook some stray bark off her arm and into the grate.

'I raise him,' she continued, 'because he has been developing an idea that I think may be of use to us in thinking about the meanings that arise as we explore the Dilemma. His central belief was that one should always act on principles that are capable of being turned into a universal law of nature. He believed our actions should always be judged as if they are the result of a commandment of reason, what he calls a 'categorical imperative'. The idea is that if you act on principles that you can will to be universal law, you are acting on law that you – with the help of your reason – have given to yourself. My brother thinks that all duty and obligations should derive from this, applying reason in this way.

'In short, he would have us constantly doing everything in our power to promote good in human beings. To simplify somewhat, he thinks that the question we should always ask ourselves is: 'what if everyone did this?' And, if we ask ourselves this question, and only act if we believe that everyone should act as *we* do, then it will promote the best of actions in us.'

'I can see why you've been thinking of him,' replied Hume, 'aren't these almost the exact words we've used ourselves when we've been discussing the way the Dilemma directs us? What if everyone behaved like a free rider? Or indeed, what if everyone simply practiced Always Co-operate?'

'Well, I keep thinking of what the point of these games is,' continued Sophie, 'and it is surely that they show us a simplified version of the world. They are trying to show an unchanging prescription for life and I wonder if, like my brother's thinking, they do not lead to a view of ethical behaviour that can be universalised. Is that not what so many of the ancients were pointing us towards? To make every act achieve the response that you seek from others – and seek for yourself? This sounds very like a continuous three point relationship to me.'

'Ah, the idea of reciprocity, yet again,' said Hume. 'But the Dilemma has shown us how hard it is to maintain a controlled exchange when there are only two people playing. How much harder is it with three or more, let alone to distill this into a universal law? And although one can say that the larger the group the more must be the benefits of co-operation, there's also no doubt that the obstacles that stand in its way become ever greater.

'Tit for Tat doesn't work in this complex structure. It only works between individuals. But Tit for Tat begins to behave like Always Co-operate once people have shown themselves to be trustworthy. The opposite must also be true: free riders – people who defect and don't reciprocate – must be excluded. And they have to be excluded literally as well, otherwise their behaviour will rapidly spread at the expense of more productive citizens.'

Hume looked away in thought.

'Perhaps,' he continued, 'what we have here are the beginnings of something we might call morality. If this truth is to be acknowledged by society, though, there must be a mechanism to punish not just defectors but also people who are failing to punish defectors. There must, in my view, be some way of imposing social ostracism to deal with this but I'm not sure what it is.'

Sophie was looking thoughtfully towards the great bow window as Hume said this. Her gaze was blank with concentration and, after a few moments, she murmured back to him.

'Perhaps the punishment is simply not to be one of the winners in life?'

Hume said nothing. He knew Sophie well enough by now to know that she would be working through a chain of logic. She continued to look dreamily into the distance as she began to speak again.

'You see, while there are obvious benefits from winning there's also a reward for co-operators if they *lose* – because they are able to sleep at night. Perhaps being a co-operator actually makes you *feel* better? In German we would call this *ethisches Gefuhl* – I think you would speak of sympathetic feelings, Mr Hume. Why, isn't this exactly the sympathy that you said your friend, Adam Smith, believed we had to apply to mitigate market forces? And that we had to create institutions to apply and govern it?'

Her gaze sharpened as she warmed to her thought process and she now turned to look directly at Hume.

'Yes, that must be it – co-operators just feel better. They're content that they've done the right thing. If they win then they've met someone they like and trust. And, if they've lost? Well, they still know they've behaved well and they sleep easy because they don't have guilty consciences.'

She left the fireplace and began to walk slowly around the persian carpet between the gilt sofas, still deep in thought.

'But, much more importantly than that, they think it is how they will get to heaven. Just as we bargain with each other, so, do we not also bargain with God? Perhaps we know no other way to relate to the idea of God than this? What else are all those offerings, prayers, good works and sacrifices if they're not the way that people bargain with God? And to what end? Well, to co-operate. Because people believe that God wants them to co-operate. What is the urge to do good, to co-operate, than the ultimate shadow of the future – their wish to get to what they believe to be heaven?'

Hume felt for his cuff as he looked at her with fascination. He thought for a moment.

'But, the opposite might also be true, Sophie,' he said. 'Perhaps defectors have no sense of guilt? They just view co-operators as stupid. They think of them as people who deserve to be beaten. In fact, how often do you hear these people say 'there's only one life' as if that gives them permission to behave badly, to defect? As you know, I have no belief in God, no place for him in my thinking. Although I may admire the faith I see in others, I believe instead in our natural benevolence. Still, the more I think on it, the more I see that these defectors are often the people who seem to think little of God or believe him to be only a comfort to the weak. They think of life as having a finite length and, in that sense, they view it all as a one-time Prisoner's Dilemma. No wonder they snatch at every advantage they can. How different that is to how people view life in the cultures and religions of the East. One reads often about the belief there in reincarnation. That must be the ultimate shadow of the future, mustn't it? To think that you're going to live all over again – and be rewarded for living well. As if there was some kind of celestial ladder to be climbed. It's hardly surprising that these people have elevated co-operation into a religious tenet. I believe some of them call this belief 'karma' do they not?'

'I have heard these tales myself, Mr Hume. I think it is indeed called karma,' said Sophie. 'For myself, I believe all this distills down to one great conclusion – that there is only one story in life and one philosophy. And that is to believe in the power of love. Is that not what co-operation is? Is it not the belief in other people's good nature, in which the shadow of the future leads us to a shared vision? A vision based on trust, on forgiveness, on openness and on creation?'

Sophie looked intently at Hume, her mind very obviously clear now.

'This seems so universally true,' she continued. 'When one looks at people who are completely foreign to one – you mentioned the people of the East, for example – the same deep currents seem to be flowing in all cultures: love, family, ritual, loyalty, friendship. For all the superficial differences between people, wherever they live, whatever their religions, surely that is why even deeply strange cultures are understandable to us at the more profound levels of motives and social habits.'

'I have reached very many of the same conclusions myself, Sophie,' replied Hume. 'Perhaps our moral sentiments have evolved like everything else? Why shouldn't we have evolved our instincts for survival by assessing who we can work with in society? It's becoming increasingly plain to me that what we are constantly doing in our lives is making rational choices that benefit our wellbeing. These choices are problem solving mechanisms, they are the way of settling the Prisoner's Dilemma, and they decide between short term expediency and longer term rewards. In favour of the latter.'

Sophie nodded.

'You may wonder what I mean by evolve,' Hume went on. 'I mean for our minds to have developed to give us the knowledge to know instinctively, as you put it, Sophie, 'in the blink of an eye', who we trust and who we don't. More than that we are instinctively weighing up the history of our exchanges with each other and constantly looking at the bill, the cost to us. But, you might ask, how can such a complicated process work?'

Hume was sitting on one of the great gilt sofas and he leant over to a table next to him and picked up a small box. Without any warning he threw it in a loop towards Sophie's right hand.

'Catch!' he called out. Without thinking, Sophie shot out her arm and easily caught it in mid air.

'Now, observe what you've just done,' Hume continued with a smile. 'Can we truly appreciate your achievement? You have judged in a fraction of a second the velocity of that box, its trajectory and its direction. And your eyes have linked to your brain and this has co-ordinated a thousand muscles and other tissues. It's astonishing. It would take you a year or more of your mathematics to try and understand the mechanics of what you've just achieved.

'Yet you did all that instinctively, in less time than it takes to blink. And all for something as trivial as catching a box. Think, from that, how much more attuned we must be to survival and to finding people that will help us survive. I believe the thought processes of reason are like the box catching. They are so deeply ingrained in our minds that the trust and co-operation instinct is in our very natures. I don't think the Prisoner's Dilemma is to be discovered any more than other things that are vital for life. Like air or water. I think how we deal with the Dilemma is part of the person we are, it is who we are. Is this not remarkable?'

David Hume raised his arms upwards as he made the point and beamed in pleasure.

'So, there we are,' he said as he let them drop. 'Now, Sophie, all this profundity has exhausted me. I think a breath of sea breeze is called for. Will you join me in a walk?'

'No, I thank you, I'll be needed here to help Annie prepare dinner. I shall see you later.'

* * *

Seventy miles to the north of London, and not long before the traveller reached the great cathedral city of Peterborough, the Cambridgeshire village of Stilton slumbered peacefully under its ancient roof stones, the walls of its cottages and houses gleaming a dull orange grey in the dying rays of the beautiful spring day.

Of all the famous coaching stops on the Great North Road the Bell Inn there was renowned for its hospitality and today, as so often, laughter and raised voices flowed out of its open windows and into the cobbled courtyard.

Sitting by the open door as the last of the sun threw a million motes about the taproom a group of redcoated soldiers basked in its glow, gossiping and laughing with their foaming pots on the table in front of them, never left still for long.

Through the door a figure in a grey uniform came blinking into the sudden gloom. He saw the soldiers but sat at an adjoining table, calling for a servant as he did so.

'Pease pudding and watered milk, if you'd be so kind. And make all haste, would you?'

One of the soldiers pulled a face as he heard the order and called across to the stranger.

'Where are you from, mate?' He pointed at a large embroidered silver greyhound on the newcomer's arm. 'What's the insignia? Never seen that before. Won't you have some ale with us?'

'Thank you, but no,' replied the man briskly. 'There can be no friendship or jollity when we have our duty. You don't know the sign of the greyhound, my friend? I am a King's Messenger. Speed is all, nothing is allowed to slow us or stand in our way.'

'Where are you bound for?'

'Scotland. Right up in the far north of the place. Sore arse time, it's going to take me days. I think we'll all be going there soon if this Bonnie Prince Charlie joker carries on much more. They're getting ready for war in London.'

'So we've heard. What's your errand?'

'An arrest warrant for one of the nobs up there. Poor sod, my guv'nor told me it looked more like a death warrant to him.'

* * *

Makepeace was at the tiller of the jacht as the little craft beat northwards in the fresh westerly that came over its beam. Zweig looked once more at the set of the sails.

'A fine course, Mr Makepeace,' he called out. He turned to

Dunbeath and laughed lightly. 'Thank God for Mr Makepeace, I believe we have a helmsman that will allow me some sleep.'

Dunbeath laughed in reply and Zweig went below.

* * *

L'Arquen took another pull of his whisky and then brought the crystal rummer down hard on the surface of his desk with a snort of anger. He looked around his study sourly. What was he doing here? Hundreds of miles from anywhere he wanted to be and anyone he'd want to speak to. No rebels found and now this damned Dunbeath business. That bastard, lying so openly.

The more that L'Arquen brooded on the matter the more that questions arose in his mind. Why had Zweig been staring at the castle? He was obviously demanding attention, that much was clear, but attention about what? Had Zweig been bringing the arms and powder for Dunbeath? And then it had blown up and Dunbeath was refusing to pay him? That made sense. The one thing he could be sure of was that he wasn't chasing the girl … Dunbeath would never have said that if it had been true.

L'Arquen suddenly sat up.

Of course, the girl. What was he doing, waiting for Dunbeath to reappear when the girl was there? She would know what was going on. Why didn't he pay her a visit and give her the chance to tell him what all this was about? And, if she didn't? Then he'd see how she liked that Williams animal. That would be worth seeing. Dunbeath wouldn't like it but to hell with him.

He jumped up from his chair, boiling with anger and the lust for revenge.

He pulled open the door the door of his study. The guard looked at him nervously.

'You, go and bring Major Sharrocks here. No, don't. Find him and tell him to make the troop ready. We ride in five minutes. Good God, why do I have to do everything myself?'

Chapter 24

L'Arquen set the troop a fierce pace and the seven miles from Craigleven to the great Urquhain stronghold passed quickly by. The men had ridden in complete silence, each one of them aware of the tension between their officers. As they hurtled over the castle's land bridge they saw with mute apprehension how L'Arquen brought them to a skidding halt at the front entrance and jumped down from his horse, bristling with anger and intent. He banged furiously on the door and when, a minute later, it was opened by Annie, the short wait had been enough to infuriate him still further. He barged past her slight figure and glowered around the hall. Sharrocks followed closely behind.

The colonel glared into Annie's face.

'Where is Mr Hume?' he shouted.

'He's walking on the dunes, your honour.'

'And where is your niece?' growled L'Arquen with heavy sarcasm.

'I don't know who you mean, sir.'

L'Arquen pulled a pistol violently from its leather case and pointed it at the old woman's forehead. He was now almost screaming.

'The girl! You know who I mean. Find her and bring her here immediately or she'll be looking for a new aunt.'

There was a soft creak from the staircase and L'Arquen looked up to see Sophie calmly walking down towards him. She came to a stop close to the bottom and stood gazing down on the two officers without the slightest sign of fear. L'Arquen was now quite rigid, his gaze fixed on her, the pistol still locked on the housekeeper's head. Without taking his eyes from Sophie, his manner changed in an instant from fury to menace.

'Take the old bag out onto the dunes, Sharrocks, and see what she knows. Don't come back here until I call for you. And, if you see Hume returning, you are to detain him. I wish for some time

296

with this young lady to see what she knows of domestic duties.'

Sophie turned and walked with slow and silent dignity back up the staircase. She reached the top and made for the door to the great salon. L'Arquen strode after her, his heavy, purposeful stride echoing on the wooden floor.

'Now,' he said, once they were in the room, 'what is your name?'

Sophie looked steadily into L'Arquen's flushed face. She was quite composed and her voice carried no tremor of anxiety.

'What do you want here? Lord Dunbeath is away on vital business. He will not be pleased to hear how you have treated his housekeeper.'

'Ah, not a maid and certainly not from Inverness. Yes, I know Dunbeath's away. He's in London with Captain Alexis Zweig. You seem surprised that I should know these things. Yes, Zweig – the man Lord Dubeath told me was just a ruffian chasing after you! Believe me, I shall settle the score with him for this when he returns'.

He stared balefully at Sophie, his head tilted back in his arrogance.

'Tell me,' he muttered, 'what is that accent of yours? Let me think, I have spent time at Court and I believe I know a German inflexion when I hear it. Now, why would a German girl be here and why would Lord Dunbeath have lied to me about where you came from?'

As he said these last few words, the truth suddenly came to him.

'The shipwreck! Of course. You must have come from Germany with that Zweig fellow. My God, how many others of you are alive? I was told you'd all died but I see I've been lied to again. And why exactly would Dunbeath wish to mislead me about you both? Is he leading this uprising? Was Zweig bringing him the powder?'

As he said this he began staring at Sophie with a renewed

intensity. His voice trailed off and he took a step towards her.

'You're in great danger here,' he said in an unnaturally thick tone. 'I could have you hanged for arming our enemies you know. I have only to call my men and you'd be swinging in the wind at the next assizes. You will have need of a friend to escape this. Someone who can explain your presence here away. I could be that friend. Yes, your only hope is for my protection.'

He had taken two more steps forward and was now so close to her that Sophie could see only too plainly what his protection would involve.

L'Arquen paused. His breathing was heavy and coming in rasping bursts, his chest rising and falling at an unnatural pace. Then he lost all restraint. A hand shot out and grabbed Sophie's hair. He bent her head back, all the time making strange noises at the back of his throat. His glazed eyes fastened on her shirt and his free hand pulled at the fastening of the leatherwork he wore across his chest and waist. It fell to the floor with a crash. He now moved his hand to her collar. He put his fingers down the open neck of her clothing and Sophie could see his eyes narrow as he gathered himself to tear her clothes open. But still she refused to plead. Still she refused to scream. She knew there was nobody in the castle to hear her. L'Arquen tensed as he began to pull.

Suddenly, there was a sharp knock on the door and the sound of a throat being cleared.

'Ahem!'

L'Arquen swung round and Sophie looked over his shoulder. In the doorway a tall, thin young man with a pronounced nose was standing in a dusty travelling coat, open at the front. He was staring at the bottom corner of a tapestry.

'Mr Adam Smith, ma'am,' he said brightly, 'at your service. Forgive my intrusion – the front door was open.'

With a furious snort, L'Arquen dropped his hold on Sophie and picked up his belt. He strode to the door, pausing as he passed to stare at the young man with an enraged, vindictive look.

Adam Smith simply beamed his beatific smile back at him.

* * *

As L'Arquen emerged from the castle, still bristling in his anger, David Hume was returning from his walk. Hume was about to hail him with a polite word of greeting when L'Arquen turned his maddened features on him.

'Mr Hume,' he spat out bitterly, 'God knows why you are allowing yourself to stay here. With this Dunbeath traitor. I wish you to let me know the instant he returns from London. I shall be leaving men at this entrance and you are to inform them if you see or hear of anything.'

Hume looked at him in surprise but thought better than to say anything. L'Arquen stalked away, past his silent and rigid troopers, and hurled himself at his horse. The animal could feel the tension in the man and instantly reacted to his rough handling. It reared and L'Arquen slashed at its flank with his whip as the poor beast became the depository of his humiliation. He looked up and saw Sharrocks.

'Station two men here, major,' he bawled at him, 'outside this entrance. They are to report to you the minute that Dunbeath returns.'

Sharrocks began to organise his troop as L'Arquen spurred his horse and rode violently off alone towards Craigleven. Hume stared after him, still bewildered by the events that had clearly been taking place while he'd been on the dunes. He went inside the castle and climbed the stairs, his pace quickening as he heard the sound of a conversation carrying to him from the great salon. One of the speakers was Sophie but the other was a male voice that he thought he vaguely remembered. He pushed open the door with interest and anticipation.

Inside, Sophie and Adam Smith were sitting next to each

other on a sofa, talking together like old friends. Hume looked at them with astonishment.

'Mr Smith! Why, you are the last person I was expecting to find here! By all that's wonderful, it's certainly good to see you. But why did you come?'

'Well, I had to,' said Smith, giving Hume the great honour of looking directly at him, 'your letters describing the implications of the Prisoner's Dilemma excited me too greatly. I'm sure my landlady would agree. She became irked by my discussions with myself and threatened me with notice. But I couldn't stay in Edinburgh, anyway, when such remarkable things were being talked about here. I had to hear more for myself. Miss Kant has kindly been telling me something of the conclusions you've been coming to and I must say I'm even more pleased that I've made the trip.'

'And I am most pleased that he did so, too,' added Sophie with feeling. Hume noticed now that she seemed pale and drawn. 'He arrived in the nick of time. That man L'Arquen was about to treat me most ill. And since Mr Smith saw him at his mischief I have no doubt that he will be bent on revenge against us all. There's more, I'm afraid. The colonel seemed to know everything about Alexis Zweig and he's convinced that Lord Dunbeath has sided with the rebels. How can we get a message to them before they return? We have to tell them to stay away.'

'I passed L'Arquen as I came in just now,' said Hume, 'and he's stationing men to report to him when the boat gets back.' He turned to speak to Smith. 'I believe I told you in Edinburgh that Dunbeath was a zealot in Scotland's cause. I fear that this Colonel L'Arquen will draw the same conclusion and will find some reason to arrest him when he returns from London. Yes, you're right Sophie. We have to find a way of telling them of the danger they're in.'

Sophie had been deep in thought, gazing towards the far end of the room while Hume had been talking. Now she came out of her reverie.

'Ah, I've just thought of something. Perhaps there is a way.'

* * *

Zweig and Dunbeath sat in a contented silence as the little jacht made good progress along the Lincolnshire coast. Makepeace had gone below to sleep and Zweig took advantage of his absence. He looked over at Dunbeath.

'So, what are your plans now, my lord?' he asked.

'I was just having those same thoughts myself, captain. I was in two minds about what to do before we left Scotland but I'm quite decided now. My country's future is in the balance and I fear that this is no longer the time to be looking at the stars. I wanted to win the Longitude Prize but that was not to be. Now I must think of the clan and of Scotland. The Stuarts were great supporters of the Urquhain and I've decided that I shall side for Prince Charles Edward and gather my people together for the coming war. L'Arquen and his kind would like to wipe us out entirely but we shall see it differently. In any event, I rather feel the events in London may have seen me burn my bridges somewhat with the English.'

Zweig gave a loud laugh.

'I think you may have put some of my high explosive under them, my lord.'

Dunbeath looked at Zweig and gave a boyish giggle. Then his mood turned serious once again.

'But, what about you, captain? Why don't you stay? We shall have need of good men and I would reward you handsomely if you fought alongside us.'

'No,' replied Zweig softly, slowly shaking his head, 'I believe I must see many a wife and mother before I do anything else. And tell them of the deaths of their loved ones. They need to be told. And, they will be in sore need of money.'

Dunbeath looked at him with admiration.

'Well said! In that case I shall commission you to bring us guns and powder once you have returned to Königsberg. It's plain that you know where to get them and I believe we shall soon be using a great amount of both if I guess correctly at how the English will respond to Prince Charles Edward's challenge. Will you take the task on?'

'Aye, willingly,' said Zweig. ' But I fear I must ask for funds to buy such a cargo. When you meet with the other clan chiefs, Lord Macdougall will tell you where I had agreed to land their powder before. Tell them all that I shall be back with new supplies before the autumn. And this time,' he laughed, 'I shall have your navigation to bring me to the right bay.

'But, my lord,' he continued after a carefully weighted pause, 'we must speak of Miss Kant. What shall I tell her father when I return?'

'Tell him, please,' replied Dunbeath, 'that his debt to you is discharged and that he is not to be anxious for money ever again. But, tell him also that I desire to marry his daughter. When this war is over we shall visit him and he will know her by a new name – the Countess of Dunbeath. Will you do that for me?'

'Why, indeed willingly,' said Zweig. He swallowed hard, determined not to show the slightest sign of surprise or reluctance. Marriage! Marriage, he thought to himself again, and drove his nails hard into the palm of his hand to keep his manner cool. Well, he'd been right that she'd made an impression on the earl but that had obviously grown since Dunbeath had said she was under his protection. Marriage! He knew now that the stakes had been raised far higher than he'd imagined.

But he said nothing. Yet again, he would wait. Why should he play his hand before the game had really started? Instead, he looked away and turned his attention back to the balance of the boat.

And together they sailed on for Scotland.

* * *

L'Arquen brought the glass up to his lips and drank heavily, brooding on what he should do, asking himself once more why he didn't just go and bring the girl in. And let Williams loose on her for an hour or two.

Why didn't this bloody war start? How much easier things would be if only it did. There wouldn't be any of this tiptoeing about then. By God, he'd have her hands in those contraptions of Williams before she could blink if he only knew where they all stood. His lips tightened as he thought bitterly about the way she'd looked at him. There'd be no more of that if he had her in here. And who the hell had been that skinny fellow? Another damned Scots plotter come to see Dunbeath?

He put his head in his hands.

What could he do but keep watching? The McLeish boy hadn't been much good about who the girl was. He'd like to find out though. The moment Dunbeath came back he'd round up the lot of them. That would keep Williams happy. That would solve the whole thing.

His head throbbed and he reached for the decanter again.

Chapter 25

Once the troop had returned to barracks, David Hume saw that even Sophie's great spirit was severely wounded by L'Arquen's attack on her. He now attempted to settle her stretched anxieties.

'I don't believe you should be too concerned by his threats, my dear,' he said. 'He may have his suspicions but he has no evidence against you. And, even if he should think further about arresting you, he would soon find out from me that he was trifling with the intended wife of the richest aristocrat in Scotland.'

Adam Smith had joined them in the salon and he now nodded his agreement.

'And the colonel might not think it would help his prospects if I was to let his superiors know of his attempt on your honour. He would have to reckon with me before I would deny that.'

Hume smiled inwardly at Smith's boyish show of loyalty and turned back to Sophie.

'No, Miss Kant, I don't think we shall hear more from the man until Lord Dunbeath returns with Captain Zweig. Now, more importantly, you were going to tell me of your plan to warn them of L'Arquen's presence.'

* * *

Later that afternoon, Sophie and Hume sat happily with Adam Smith by the fire, listening to him as he spoke about their findings on the Prisoner's Dilemma.

'The most unavoidable conclusion from your games,' Smith was saying to them, 'seems to me to be also the most shocking. It is that altruism, goodness, generosity, kindness – all the qualities that we hold most dear – can now be seen more clearly as investments in the expectation of a later reward.'

He saw David Hume lift his head.

'I know, Mr Hume, I know – you will think me too sweeping in my choice of words. Very well, it is the actions that are investments, not the sentiments. And I shall also agree with you, before you wish me to, that many of these sentiments are not done knowingly. They are more to be gathered together under what you would refer to as 'benevolence'. But allow me, please, to continue with my point. Knowingly or unknowingly, the people behaving in this way want their investment to be returned.

'What the Dilemma seems to have told you is that the key factor is the timescale. The defector is looking for a short-term gain. The co-operator is looking further out, beyond the immediate choices or exchanges that have to be made. Sophie has told me that you called this process 'the shadow of the future' and it must be people's ability to make this vision of paramount importance that's driving their co-operative strategies. Or should I say *instincts* rather than strategies because you say that the one has almost become the other as we humans have developed.'

Adam Smith thought for a couple of seconds as he stared wildly about himself.

'These strategies show themselves,' he continued, 'because we never know when we shall meet the people we are playing with again. And, because of that, we must constantly be weighing up a present advantage against possible future gains or losses.'

'Quite so,' said Hume, delighted to have the younger man taking part in their discussions. 'The underlying conclusion of the Prisoner's Dilemma is that we are all, endlessly, looking for partners that can be trusted. It is a fact of life. In a world of defectors, Tit for Tat works at its best once a co-operator finds another co-operator. Are these not your thoughts too, Sophie?'

Sophie had been frowning slightly but she now looked up.

'I would go further than that,' she said. 'I think our ability to identify people who are real co-operators, not just opportunists that might just be pretending to be them, is a huge advantage.

Honesty really is the best policy in finding partners; people who will help you survive. It seems obvious to me now that the most powerful reason to be trustworthy in society is to get other co-operators to play with you! To build a reputation, spoken or believed.'

As she said this, Hume looked steadily at Adam Smith.

'This is what we spoke of in Edinburgh, is it not? However little we may like it, we have to recognise that we are good for a reason. And that reason is the wish to succeed and rise above our fellow man. If you agree with this then you have to agree that altruism and compassion are just selfishness given new clothes. It is appalling to contemplate but look at it we must. It is the key to understanding our natures. If you are kindly to someone because it makes you feel better, or gets you a reward, then your compassion is selfish, not selfless. Yet for all that I believe it is the act itself that matters, and not the motive.'

'Ah, here is an argument that I have heard many times,' said Smith quickly. 'If we are selfless only because it leads to gains for ourselves, should the motive concern us? Does it matter if a man saves a drowning companion because he wants the glory rather than to do good? That it is the deed that counts, not his reason for it? How often have I attended as Professor Hutcheson and his colleagues in Glasgow argued about whether benevolence that was due to vanity or self-interest was still benevolence. That a man may do a good deed, even if he should do it out of pride or self regard? You must be right, Hume – that altruism and virtue are showing themselves to be just selfishness by another name; a subtle and clever expression of it, to be sure, but nonetheless practiced unknowingly for that end.'

'That still leaves us, Mr Smith,' continued Hume, 'with the question of why people are ever truly, deeply, perhaps even secretly, altruistic. Sophie's view is that it springs from the urge in them to feel better. I agree, that may be so for many of us. On the other hand, it may simply be that some people do things in

306

life to a greater excess than his fellows. Some are more intelligent, others can run faster.

'Perhaps what we are seeing in them is just the instinct for virtue as a survival strategy exaggerated in some people more than in others? After all, do not some of us speak too much or laugh too heartily? Why not give too much as well?'

Hume looked away, pleased with his conclusion, and then lumbered to his feet.

'Now, Mr Smith,' he puffed, 'perhaps I can tempt you to fill your Edinburgh lungs with some of this wonderful sea air? There are superb views to be had from the headland. Will you walk with me out there?'

* * *

Zweig was at the helm while Dunbeath munched on an apple he'd found at the bottom of the bag of food that Annie had put out for him. There had been a silence for some time with just the sound of the boat slicing through the choppy water for company. Makepeace continued to snore in the cabin below.

Zweig glanced over towards Dunbeath. He had been judging the right moment to bring up the subject.

'You mentioned something interesting to me that day on the dunes when we first met,' he said gently. 'This was before we learnt something of our natures and found that we could trust each other. You said we were in '... another damned Prisoner's Dilemma' your words were to me. What did you mean by that?'

Dunbeath gave a short laugh.

'Ah, the Dilemma. I had quite forgotten about it. How long ago that all seems. Well, if you're interested, let me explain.'

And Dunbeath began to outline his great game and the different views that the Castle of Beath had heard so hotly debated.

* * *

The market town of Northallerton lay comfortably in the Vale of Mobray, east of the great stretch of the Pennines and to the west of the open moorland of North Yorkshire. To the weary rider it had always made a welcome sight, prosperous and busy.

For many years the army base there controlled the road to Scotland and sharp eyes were now wide open, alert to the warlike noises coming down from the north.

A soldier in a grey uniform led his horse wearily towards the warmth of the blacksmith's fire, directed inside by one of the sentries that had stopped him on the road.

'Hey,' the guard called out to the farrier, 'King's Messenger needs assistance here. Carrying an urgent letter from Prince von Brunswick-Something or Somesuch. He'll leave you this horse for shoeing. Needs a fresh one quickly though.

'Poor bugger's ridden all the way up from London and he's still got hundreds of miles to go.'

* * *

Smith and Hume were about to set off for their walk. Sophie stood at the door with them and, as she waved them on their way, she looked down the drive to where two of the Craigleven redcoats were standing guard. She wandered down to where they stood, watching her in an embarrassed silence.

'Good day to you, men. You seem in need of warm soup.'

The soldiers looked about themselves, terrified that Sharrocks, or even worse, L'Arquen, was about to see them talking to her. They saw nothing and both of them nodded gratefully. A few minutes later Sophie emerged again with a good lunch on a tray.

They fell on the vegetable broth and bread with a ravening hunger. Now they slowed their manic eating with a large hunk of cheese each and a flagon of spring water.

'You are too good to us, ma'am. We are not used to such kindness,' said one.

'I am sorry for your trouble,' said the other. 'His lordship must be in terrible trouble if our colonel is after him. I fear he is not a man to cross, ma'am. His reputation goes before him.'

* * *

Dunbeath was coming to the end of his description of the many discussions and conclusions on the Prisoner's Dilemma that Hume and Sophie had been having before he had left for London.

'Sophie was very convincing in her analysis that co-operation wins in life,' he said. 'She laid much merit on this Tit for Tat instinct and its odd child, a subsidiary strategy that she referred to as Generous. David Hume found it fitted well with many of his own thoughts and they spent hours together filling each other's heads with the idea that any good there may be in us has a rational basis. I did not like to argue with her too greatly. You and I are men of the world, Zweig, and we know only too well the evil that lurks in us all. Sophie has such a kind and caring nature that I could not bring myself to argue that her views on the world were just so many mathematical theories.'

'I heard from others that she was a promising mathematician, my lord' replied Zweig. 'That was before we left Königsberg.'

'There is no doubt of that, captain. She will be of great benefit to me in my researches. Once this war is won.'

Zweig said nothing in reply but just looked ahead into the wind. Then he turned to Dunbeath.

'I wonder about your game, my lord. Perhaps it's possible that too much digging can spoil a garden? I should not like to think that the gift of trust and the way we deal with each other are so many scribbles on a piece of paper. And where is the beauty of love? Where was that in Sophie's view of the world?'

Chapter 26

Hume and Smith had walked some two miles along the coast. They were comfortable in each other's company, largely silent because the noise of the wind had limited their conversation. Now they turned back for the castle as the breeze dropped.

'You were quite right in your opinion of Miss Kant,' said Smith. 'I do not believe I have ever met a more sinuous, inventive mind.'

'Yes, she is extraordinary, isn't she?' replied Hume. 'I have told her about your ideas, of course, and we have spoken much about how your pin makers and their specialisations fit into the results that the Dilemma points us to. It seems to me that there is a great deal of similarity in the two views. They both show us that social benefits can derive from what could be regarded as individual selfishness. That what we see as progress in society stems from self-interest and from that into benevolence. As she has said often, it is hard to distinguish between these in our developed state, so firmly are the principles of co-operation set in the very elements of our instincts.'

'Quite so,' replied Smith, looking into the sky, 'although I am troubled by her description of the impact of what she called free riders. As I understand it she explains them almost as a constant reminder to society of what a defector looks like – and therefore an example of what trusting people should avoid and organise against. But one has to ask what happens when free riders cease to be peripheral in society and become so numerous that even the most co-operative of people have to behave in the same fashion to protect their interests and even sometimes their very survival.'

'How very interesting, Mr Smith, can you please explain what you mean a little further?'

'Well let me give you an example,' continued Adam Smith, gazing out at the grey surface of the sea, 'I have been reading much recently about the arguments for enclosing common land.

I find this fascinating because these commons seem to be almost societies in miniature. Why do I say that? Well, because there are often no laws at all to govern their use and instead the people that put their animals out on them have evolved intricate systems and mutual understandings that give them each a fair return without the guidance of an authority. This shouldn't work in theory but clearly it does in practice. Is this not what the Greeks might have called a democracy? Those who wish to enclose the commons see it differently. They speak of peasants as being unable to control their greed, and of how the more rapacious of them would easily take more than their rightful share. The argument runs that if a man were to graze more cattle on the common than was considered to be his right, then his neighbours would respond by grazing more themselves out of understandable self-protection.

'Indeed, you might say that it would be a foolish man who sat idly by while his neighbour took so much of the available pasture that it was to his own detriment. The logical outcome of this is that he would be bound to respond. He, too, would put out more cattle, the rest of the commoners would also respond until – of course, you can see where I am going with this argument – the land collapses. It becomes overgrazed and can't recover. And then everyone in society suffers. Selfishness has led to the downfall of the whole community. Indeed, I have heard this phenomenon described as the 'Tragedy of the Commons'.

'I'm sure you can see the reasoning: when individuals act independently of each other and rationally consult their own self-interest then they will ultimately deplete a limited resource, even when it is clearly not in their interest to do so. In fact, one can imagine that after a certain point where the depletion is advanced, people will behave in an increasingly selfish manner to snatch at whatever is left. They'd be fools not to.'

'How intriguing,' said Hume when Smith finally brought his gaze back from the sea and had begun once more to see where his feet were landing. 'I must say that in that case it's hard to escape the conclusion that where an end is in sight – a finite resource is a good example – then people's behaviour would be viewed by society as a series of *one-time* Prisoner's Dilemmas. Just like Lord Dunbeath's original game. And, like that, defection would be the only conceivable option. The benefits of co-operation would have broken down. The strategy no longer works.'

There was a silence while Smith was evidently thinking this through.

'In fact, I think the same mechanism works everywhere. Even the educated classes fall victim – the very people who would look to govern the peasants and commoners. Didn't we see exactly the same deranged behaviour twenty years or so ago with what was called The South Sea Bubble? Wasn't that caused because there were a limited number of shares available and a kind of madness overcame people to acquire them – whatever the price?'

He paused and stared at his feet again.

'I would say there could be another way of looking at this,' he said at last. 'I remember you telling me of the early games with Dunbeath and of how you were close to returning to Edinburgh. Perhaps there is an equivalent in society? Where a whole section of co-operators – or at least people who would think of themselves as co-operators – simply leaves the others to what they regard as their errors, and remove themselves.'

'Do you have an example of what you mean?' replied Hume.

'Well, do you recall the Pilgrim Fathers?' continued Adam Smith. 'Instead of continuing their conflict with a society they disagreed with, they left and set up afresh in the American colony. How appropriate that they should have called it the New World!'

'How good it is to have you here, Smith,' Hume smiled when he heard this. 'You have set your finger on a sore I have been avoiding. And it is this ... how does society control itself while the Dilemma's internal forces are working themselves through? If you recall, the immortal Thomas Hobbes faced up to this in that great work of his, *Leviathan*. His view was that man's selfish nature needed laws to stop him from descending into evil. That he needed the guiding hand of kings or religion or legal restraint to stop him from destroying himself. Do you remember the famous words he used to describe what would happen if this didn't happen? "No arts. Continual fear and danger of violent death. And the life of man, solitary, poor, nasty, brutish and short."'

Hume shook his head, smiling to himself at the power of the words.

'But can we say that he was wrong?' he continued. 'Is the Dilemma telling us that all man needs to do is to trust? That the Dilemma's natural forces will prevail? Can we really believe that when defectors occur they will ultimately fail because, just as the hawks thrived for a time but then declined because they had to end up meeting each other, their very nature leads to their mutual destruction?'

Smith nodded in agreement.

'Yes, I think something like this must be happening,' he said. 'You told me how Miss Kant's theory was that the early Christians undermined the very Hobbesian nature of the Roman empire. But it took centuries. In just the same way I imagine that the underlying success of co-operation will always win. However, it takes a very long time. In the meantime, there is much repression, unfairness, tyranny and death. Oppressive regimes may fail but they do so only at a huge price to the people in that society. And also in giving people the accepted wisdom that man is essentially bad.

'I must say that your work on the Dilemma has made me completely revise my outlook on the nature of society in general. I had thought at first that individuals had enough common interest in the future to make them combine to create a society that excluded people they thought were destructive.'

Adam Smith had come to a stop on the path and he now turned to Hume.

'But when I heard from you about the findings from the Prisoner's Dilemma,' he continued, 'I thought that what was really going on was not that people were protecting society in this way but that society itself was the result of individuals striving in their own self-interests. Society, if you like, was a by-product of an efficient market.

'However, I must confess that since I have arrived here I have thought again. I now see that the underlying principle of the Dilemma is the search for the right partners, people that one can trust. Once people have found these new partners they are then able to precipitate out of a society of hawks leaving these so-called selfish rationalists to their fate. They avoid them. In other words, rather than have retaliator doves, the doves simply leave the hawks to their own fate and go off to form a new society.

'Perhaps the virtuous are virtuous for no other reason than that it enables them to join forces with others who are virtuous – to their mutual benefit. Because they have defined themselves in that way and are convinced that it suits them to get together. They have stopped being individuals and have become a group!'

Hume stroked the embroidery on his coat sleeve and laughed as a great wave of satisfaction swept through him.

'Mr Smith! I've rarely heard anything so elegant!'

They walked on until they reached the headland, each of them deep in their own thoughts. As they looked out to sea Hume turned once again to Adam Smith.

'Well, you've certainly given me a way through the tangle I was in such difficulties with. Then light my way, please, through one last problem. Let us take one of these societies you describe as having broken away. Precipitated out as you called it. A society of doves. Very well, according to you, everyone in it is trusting each other and indulging in constant three point relationships.

My question is this – does such a society not stultify? Good lord, doesn't this utopia of theirs suffer from a lack of challenge? How would anything ever change if there were no unreasonable or ambitious men to make it do so? Wouldn't it decline in ambition if everyone was co-operative? Just as actions have reactions I rather think that it must be inevitable that this general goodness should come under pressure from time to time. After all, do people ever behave better or become more inventive than when they are in danger? Or are having their lives threatened?'

'Hmm,' murmured Smith, the challenge Hume had put making him stare madly about himself. 'I would like to ponder on that. There must be much in what you say.'

* * *

Zweig was at the helm with Makepeace when Dunbeath came up from sleeping below. The boat was creaming through the waves and Dunbeath looked forward with the wind in his face.

He turned to look at Zweig, who smiled back at him.

Dunbeath looked towards the horizon again, his eyes squinting and his face gleaming. He felt completely secure with Zweig. He was quite sure of where he was going. He felt strange. He felt happy.

Chapter 27

It was early evening and L'Arquen walked briskly through Craigleven's stable block, his speed disguising the slight lurch in his step. As he passed by them, shirt-sleeved troopers stiffened to attention and stopped grooming their horses, only too aware of their colonel's black mood.

At the far end of the building, Major Sharrocks stood speaking to one of his men. As he strode up to question him, L'Arquen's voice could be easily heard by the whole troop.

'Any progress, major?'

'No sir,' replied Sharrocks smartly, 'still no sign of them. But I'm sure we shall sight their boat soon. We have two guards at the castle's entrance and a further man on the dunes.'

L'Arquen looked at him sourly, as if he'd just received a confession of personal failure.

'Harken, Sharrocks,' he said in a low voice that nonetheless carried to the others. To a man they froze. 'Keep looking, keep looking. Report to me immediately you see something.'

* * *

The King's Messenger rode on. He had cut his sleep down to four hours a night but he still felt the journey was never going to end.

He was now in central Scotland and ahead of him was yet another roadblock, the guards at it calling on him to halt. He pointed to his silver greyhound insignia and shouted down at them.

'King's Messenger with urgent orders for the 17th Dragoons in Caithness. From Prince von Brunswick-Luneburg! Let me pass. How far to Perth?'

The man swung the barrier upwards and called back.

'Twelve miles!'

The messenger galloped on.

* * *

Sophie, Hume and Adam Smith were finishing a simple dinner of lamb stew, the dining room lit by lanterns and candlelight. An echo of another dinner in Edinburgh, Hume thought to himself. He listened to Smith as he spoke to Sophie in the chair opposite him, all the time gazing at the far end of the table.

'Hume and I were discussing something on our walk this afternoon, Miss Kant. We spoke about whether society is not the better for being threatened by the occasional defector. His view was that a society of co-operators, constant three pointers, however trusting and supportive it might be, would become complacent and dulled over time. He wondered whether there wasn't a natural desire in our natures, of which we are quite unaware, that needs the threat of defectors to keep society's edge sharp and the dream of liberty and fairness alive.'

'Yes, Mr Hume and I have touched on much the same topic, ourselves,' replied Sophie. 'Do you have any thoughts on the matter?'

'I have, indeed, been thinking on it. If you'll permit me to propose them, I believe I do have some views.'

Adam Smith sat back in his chair and now stared at one of the ceiling bosses.

'I would suggest that there are two great potential threats that must be constant reminders of the need for vigilance, however settled or co-operative a society may appear.

'The first is the madman. The person for whom neither losing nor winning are important. This kind of man is deadly to others because he rejects the concept of a repeated Prisoner's Dilemma. For his own reasons, perhaps a warped background, perhaps bitter experiences – or possibly he simply has too much power or security and thinks he has no need to care about the reactions of other people – whatever his motive is, he views every choice and exchange as a one-time game. These people are the tramplers in life. For whatever reason, they are completely unafraid of, or unable to see, what you have called the 'shadow of the future.''

Sophie nodded.

'I quite agree,' she replied with a light laugh. 'They are impossible to deal with. We may have had some experience of that here in these past few weeks. And what do you see as the other threat?'

'Let me ask you something before I answer that,' said Adam Smith. 'Let us imagine that you and I are playing the Dilemma. We have agreed to play a game of a hundred turns. This is unusual because we've decided on a game with a finite limit. It has a clear end in other words. Early in the game, of course, we find that we can trust each other. But has the Dilemma also not shown us that instead of being truly good we are being good for a reason? That we are trying to lure the other person into being co-operative back? And perhaps lure is a good word because what we are really doing is appearing to be co-operative while, actually, we are waiting for the opportunity to make a quick killing at the other's expense?'

'Really, Mr Smith!' said Sophie, 'you are beginning to sound like Lord Dunbeath.'

'Am I? Well think on this. We are on the hundredth turn. This is your last opportunity to make a choice. What will you play now? Let me answer for you because it is difficult to ever imagine you being devious or disloyal. But you *would* be, Miss Kant. You would be no different to anyone else. You would *have* to defect. You'd take five points because I would then have no opportunity left to respond, to punish you. You'd be foolish not to. The game would be over.

'But I'd know that you would do this! And so I'd defect on the ninety ninth turn in anticipation of it. Ha! Then again, you'd be bound to know that I would do this so you would inevitably defect before this – on the ninety eighth turn. And so we go back. When would we ever co-operate under this logic? I think of it as

318

a backward induction paradox and it is, I think, where the parlour games we have been playing depart from people's behaviour in real life. There *are* ends in life. People choose to bring things to a close and they frequently defect when they do so. How often have we seen this in friendships? The closer that people have been, the greater the bitterness is when one lets the other down. Am I not right?'

'It's difficult to argue with your logic,' broke in Hume as Sophie dropped her head, deep in thought about what Smith had just said. 'But when do we ever play in life in the knowledge that we have a finite number of turns?'

'Quite,' replied Smith with all the steeliness of a hunter closing in on his prey. 'That is the exact point I was about to make. Let us return to who is the most dangerous player. Is he not the person who knows that only *he* is playing a finite game when everyone else thinks that they are repeating forever? He is the ultimate betrayer. Unknown to the other players, indeed to society as a whole, he is planning on grabbing five points because only he knows that the game is coming to an end. While all the good, trusting, three-point wishing people think it is continuing, he has lured them into looking away, but only so he can stab them in the back.'

Sophie seemed to come out of a daydream as Adam Smith reached the end of his argument.

'Yes, I see your point,' she now said slowly. 'He is a super free rider, isn't he? He doesn't defect knowing that he's going to continue to live in that society. He knows he won't be. He doesn't mind dealing it a mortal blow because he knows he won't have to deal with the people ever again. Yes, he is indeed dangerous. Perhaps this is why we hate betrayal so much? And perhaps this accounts for why society reserves its greatest contempt and most severe punishments for traitors?'

* * *

Evening was falling as Zweig looked closely at the coast. He studied the shape of the cliffs as they snaked into the distance and then referred back to some rudimentary charts that he'd found in a forward locker on the boat.

'I believe that is Calghoustie Head,' he said to Dunbeath, pointing to a spit of land. 'With this wind on our beam there is every chance we shall see the castle tonight.'

They sailed on, with Zweig piling on yet more canvas as the thought of journey's end made the men urge the little craft forward. The wind freshened and moonlight lit their path. At about two the following morning they rounded a headland and the enormous fortress came into view in the distance.

'There it is, my lord, The Castle of Beath,' said Zweig. 'You must be pleased to be back.'

'Yes, I am indeed' replied Dunbeath, and he squinted into the breeze to look at it. He stood studying its outline for some seconds but stiffened as something caught his eye and he became quite still, concentrating his gaze forward.

'What's that hanging down from the observatory?' he murmured. 'Pass me that glass, Zweig, if you'd be so kind.'

He took the telescope that Zweig handed him and focused it. The enlarged image swam into view. It showed a huge white cloth, suspended from the battlements of the Grey Tower.

'It looks like they've hung a bed sheet up there, captain,' said Dunbeath, his eye still to the glass. 'It must be a white flag – does that mean they've surrendered in some way? Here, look for yourself.'

Zweig took the telescope and with the practiced art of a mariner he focused on the castle for a moment. He adjusted the setting and then set it down.

'No, my lord, I don't believe it is a white flag. I think it's what you first said it was. It is indeed a bed sheet. You speak excellent German, as you know, but perhaps your knowledge of the language has been shaped mainly by your scientific interests. It could be that you do not know some of our more domestic terms. The German word for bed sheet is spelt *Laken* but we pronounce it...'

'L'Arquen!' said Dunbeath, grimly.

'Yes, my lord, Sophie would assume that we'd understand the sheet's meaning. I'm afraid she's warning us that the colonel is aware of our trip and I've therefore no doubt that the English are at the castle. If L'Arquen knows where you've been then he'll know that I'm with you too. And, therefore, we have to assume that he'll know who I am – and that, I fear, would put you in great danger for consorting with me. He'd be bound to conclude that I was bringing the powder and munitions for you.'

Dunbeath was rapidly becoming agitated at the memory of L'Arquen. And with Zweig's logic. His temper began to rise.

'My God, captain, if the English know all this then they'll know by now that Sophie must have arrived with you ... if they have so much as touched her! I dread to think if that monster L'Arquen has questioned her. What are we to do, Zweig? Their spies will be watching out for our arrival. We must continue up the coast and then walk back and hope we can evade their sentries.'

'No, my lord. I have another suggestion,' replied Zweig. 'Why do we not go into the castle from the sea without the redcoats seeing us? By great good fortune the tide should be at its lowest in an hour or so and we can then enter under cover of darkness – by a hidden cave that I'm aware of.'

Zweig briefly told Dunbeath about the long forgotten escape route.

'We can take the boat's tender down to the rocks before dawn without being seen,' he continued. 'I suggest we keep the jacht well away from the coast and then row in while the night is still dark. But where can Makepeace take the boat when we leave it, my lord?'

Dunbeath thought for a moment and then turned to the

coachman.

'Stand well out from the coast, Makepeace. Be sure not to be seen. Then sail the boat around that promontory you can see up there, that's Dunbeaton Head, and anchor it near a shallow beach you'll see about three miles further on. You'll be able to get in close to the shore and it's a safe anchorage. But if we're taking the tender you'll have to stay on the boat until I can have you picked up. I'll send my housekeeper down to that small village at the end of the beach there and she'll get one of the fishermen to bring a rowing boat round the headland for you later.'

They unlashed the dinghy from its housing on the cabin roof and slid it gently into the sea. Dunbeath and Zweig climbed in and Makepeace waved them off as the captain rowed quietly towards the castle in the dark, pulling with long powerful strokes.

'We shall land at low tide, my lord,' Zweig whispered. 'That is the only point at which one can enter by this escape route. I shall stay at the castle while we complete our business and then I'll leave on the next low tide this afternoon and row back to where Makepeace will have anchored the boat. You're quite sure that I'll be able to see it when I round the headland?'

Dunbeath nodded.

'Yes, yes quite sure. It's a wide, open bay and you'll see it clearly.'

Half an hour later Zweig brought the little craft skillfully alongside the largest of the great boulders under the castle wall. He put his arm out to steady Dunbeath as the earl clambered up onto it. Then he jumped out himself, holding the boat's painter.

'I'll put a long line on her. The tide will rise before I leave this afternoon and she'll need some slack. Now, my lord, let me show you how to go here. You see that gap between the rocks? When I touch your arm, you are to jump down and run through that entrance into a cave. Go to the back of it as fast as you can and climb up on the ledge you'll find there. There will be no time to be wasted between the waves, and take care of your footing, the cave will be wet and dark and we have no light with us.'

Dunbeath dropped down and Zweig heard his feet slopping on the sodden sand of the cave floor. Then he called out that he was on the ledge and Zweig jumped down himself. It was only a few seconds before he was up and taking the lead on the stone steps. He reached the flagstone and pushed it upwards, holding it open for Dunbeath as they emerged into the storeroom.

'Good God!' said Dunbeath, 'I've lived in this castle all my life and I had no idea of this. Not even rumours. How did you know about it, Zweig?'

Zweig smiled in the darkness.

'You know how fishermen do talk,' he said, and Dunbeath knew very well not to question him further.

Once they were safely in the castle there was little need for quiet and before long the sound of their voices brought the others from their beds and they gathered in the great salon, still dressed in their night clothes. Adam Smith was introduced to an amazed Dunbeath and, before long, Annie had breakfast on the table, everyone eating in the highest of spirits, hugely elated that the men had got into the castle without L'Arquen's sentries seeing them.

'The bed sheet was a brilliant conception, my dearest one,' said Dunbeath, beaming with pride at Sophie, 'Captain Zweig spotted it immediately for what it was.'

Sophie laughed and gave an ironic bow towards Zweig.

But while she may have smiled as she ate, she was incredulous too. The last time she had seen the two men they had been sworn enemies, only brought together by a desperate need to co-operate. And now they were the best of friends! How did Zweig do it? Had he drugged him?

Dunbeath held his arms out to Sophie and then blew her a kiss. She smiled back at him, astonished at such a show of affection. Yet another mystery, she thought. He was a man transformed. What alchemy did Zweig possess?

She leant forward as Dunbeath moved to nuzzle her tenderly on the cheek.

'I have thought of little but you,' he said, quite unconcerned at who should hear him. 'I began to wish that I was not in London.'

'But you were, my lord,' Sophie beamed at him, 'for all our futures. How did your meeting with the Board of Longitude progress? Did they accept our findings? And the Prize?'

Dunbeath laughed, easily and without any of his old rancour.

'It was a great success,' he replied, 'I tried to kill the King of England and Captain Zweig saved my life. Do not look so downcast, my sweet. I am quite decided in my own mind that it was for the best. The Board did not award the Prize and I have lived to fight another day. We shall finish this war now and then I shall win the Prize with another king. I am delayed, that is all.'

Chapter 28

James McLeish had slept little since he'd discovered Zweig's deception with the wooden telescope. Dark thoughts raged constantly in him, pulling him in every direction, all of them bound up in hatred. The muscles in his face seemed to have developed a life of their own. Worst of all, his own mother had taken to asking him a barrage of questions, suspicious that the English soldiers hadn't returned to interrogate him further.

'I decided not to sell Zweig's gift to me,' he'd lied. 'I shall bluff it out if the redcoats want to speak with me again. I am not going to run away. Not now, not ever.' She had seemed mollified for a while, even heartened by this sudden show of courage. But her newfound respect was wearing thin as she saw the tension that increasingly showed in everything he did. However, just as she wondered about her son, so he was thinking about her, too and he saw how she was now looking at him, questioning and incredulous.

If she were ever to discover that he'd been to Craigleven, he thought for the thousandth time, she would give him a harder life than even that colonel was capable of. Still, he was sure he'd done the right thing. Why should he suffer for those bastards, Alexis Zweig and the earl? He was quite clear in his own mind: he'd made his bed, now he must lie in it.

Unable to sleep yet again, he had left the cottage early and was working on his nets as the first thin strips of dawn began to show in the east and the blackness of the night was losing its fight with the first faint streaks of the coming day. He glanced up towards the horizon. Then he looked again, his eye caught by a faint speck in the distance, a small boat, far out and hardly visible, beating up to pass the headland. His keen fisherman's eye was rarely misled – and he was quite sure that the boat he'd seen was Dunbeath's jacht.

He dropped his net and got quickly to his feet. He had thrown in his lot with the English and they would want to know about this. He climbed the dunes to see where the boat was going and then turned and set off for Craigleven with the glazed expression of a man with the clearest of purposes, a man obsessed with revenge.

* * *

Dunbeath cradled the glass of whisky his old housekeeper had handed him.

'I'm going to get some sleep now, but you're to wake me in a couple of hours, Annie. We arrived here by rowing boat and the London coachman, Makepeace, has taken my father's jacht around Dunbeaton Head and he'll have anchored it in the bay beyond it. Go into Dunbeaton to get provisions for our luncheon rather than Wick, will you, and find a fisherman there that can take a boat round the headland to pick him up. Zweig and I took the tender so Makepeace has no way of getting ashore. Quiet and secret now, Annie. We don't want the English to know anything of this. We cannot have L'Arquen know that we're back.'

* * *

The thin light from the tollhouse for the Meikle Ferry at Portnacoulter shone in the distance.

The King's Messenger rode on. Wet and cold, his glorious uniform splattered with mud, he gritted his teeth once more.

The final miles were always the worst, he knew, trying to cheer himself and rise above the constant pain in his neck. Craigleven was said to be some miles south of Wick, so this had to be the last day. His map was clear that once he'd crossed the Firth of Dornoch here, the rest was easier.

The ferryman asked about his insignia and they spoke for a time about his ride.

'From London! How much further do you have?'

'It is dawn now. Tomorrow's will see me there.' He was practically speaking to himself. 'I shall sleep this evening and cover the rest at night. Many thanks for the crossing.'

'God speed!'

He rode on.

* * *

The trooper found Major Sharrocks in Craigleven's library, writing up yet another report for L'Arquen on the latest futile search for rebels. Sharrocks glanced up as the man knocked on the door.

'That fisherman wants to see you again, sir. He's outside. Shall I send him in?'

Sharrocks breathed a sigh of relief. This had to be action.

'Yes, good. You've done well, trooper.'

A few seconds later Sharrocks summed James up with a glance as he came into the room. Hell's teeth but he looked ready for death, he thought. He knew this type well – nervous as a weasel. The kind that would do anything to save his skin and could never be trusted in a fight – bluster and show before it but no bottom when the banging started. He looked at him again and saw the stress that was plain in every twitch of his features. He understood the reasons for it – Sharrocks wouldn't have wagered on the boy's chances of staying alive if the Jacobites ever discovered that he was helping them.

But the major showed none of this as he stood to welcome him.

'Good morning to you, Mr McLeish,' he called out brightly, 'you must have set out early this morning. What do your sharp eyes show you now? The men I have at the castle have told me nothing.'

'Lord Dunbeath's boat. I saw it just as dawn was rising. Far out – trying to get up the coast without being seen. It's here now. I walked up the headland and she's anchored about three miles north of Dunbeaton.'

Major Sharrocks leapt immediately to his feet, calling for the trooper.

'Find McLeish here a horse. Rouse out two of the men. Quickly now. I want to leave at once.'

A horse was found and half an hour later James was leading the little group up a path, high on the dunes, well out of sight of the village. In a further five minutes they were looking down on Dunbeath's boat, her sails dropped, as it rocked gently at anchor about fifty yards from the shore.

'How do we get out to it, McLeish?' Sharrocks was now frantic for action.

'There's a rowing boat at the end of the bay. The lightkeeper uses it to get to the beacon. I'll go for that.'

James brought the boat close to the shore and Sharrocks could hardly contain his aggression and he ran out to it through the shallow water and hurled himself in.

'Row! Come on man. Pull!' James McLeish stretched his arms out at the oars and the little craft shot forward towards Dunbeath's jacht. Sharrocks looked ahead and his eyes narrowed as he saw Makepeace come on deck and give them a friendly wave. Then his lips tightened and he reached for the pistol at his belt. As the tender came closer, he stood up in the boat, pointing it at the coachman's head.

'Don't move. Stay where you are,' he shouted.

James climbed on board, tying the dinghy to the rail.

Sharrocks clambered up after him.

'Right, you, where's Zweig?' he screamed. 'Where's the earl?'

'Just myself here, soldier,' replied Makepeace with a shrug.

Sharrocks handed James the pistol.

'Shoot him if he moves,' he bellowed, and went below to the tiny cabin. As he reached the bottom of the short steps he immediately saw the court finery and wigs on the bunks and he flung them on the floor, roaring with rage. Then he searched the minute space for any sign of Dunbeath or Zweig and found a tool chest. He manically rummaged through it, snatching up an axe. Almost beside himself with fury, he came back on deck and advanced on Makepeace.

'Where are they?' he screamed at the coachman's blank expression. Makepeace shrugged once more and Sharrocks seemed to lose control. With a maddened roar he brought the axe down, narrowly missing the coachman but destroying the tiller. Makepeace at last made to stop him but Sharrocks lifted the axe once more, murder written on his face, and he took a step backwards. By now the major was almost deranged with anger, motivated no doubt by the thought that L'Arquen would blame him for letting Dunbeath and Zweig escape. He continued with his berserk swinging, rampaging through the boat, bringing the axe down on the compass, the cleats and winches, slicing sheets and slashing through halyards.

Eventually, he came to a stop, exhausted. The boat was smashed beyond repair. 'McLeish,' he panted, 'get the anchor up.'

Makepeace was bundled at pistol point into the rowing boat and as James rowed the three of them back to the shore, Dunbeath's wrecked boat began a new journey, drifting helplessly out to sea.

Chapter 29

'And then the fat prince stood there, shouting his head off to his toy soldiers. Charge! Kilt them! Kilt them! Goodness, how he was wobbling, Sophie,' laughed Dunbeath, 'he looked as if he'd just left the jelly mould. By the way, Zweig, what regiment had those two ever been near?'

Zweig grinned in reply and the stories ran on. Breakfast had been over some time before and now the two men had their friends in thrall as Dunbeath reeled off a catalogue of their adventures. Hume and Sophie gazed on, amazed at the change that had taken place in the earl. Amused, energetic and generous with his praise for Zweig, the catastrophic trip had invigorated him in a way they would never have thought possible – even if he'd won a dozen prizes. Yet again, Sophie stole a look at the miracle worker. She'd heard their stories but she still didn't understand how Zweig had done it, how Dunbeath's trust had been won. But won it most certainly was.

Eventually, a lull came in the conversation and Dunbeath called Zweig to his side.

'Perhaps we might have a quiet word together?' he murmured and then turned to the others. 'Would you excuse me if I took the captain away for a minute?'

The two men walked over to the window alcove and began to speak in low voices.

'How do you see your next steps, captain?'

'Your jacht should have me back in Königsberg in two or three weeks,' said Zweig, urgent and serious now. 'It will take me a further two to find the arms and gunpowder and arrange a ship and crew to bring them back. All being well, I believe I shall see you and your men at Lord Macdougall's landing place in two months time. I shall get word to you through his contacts.'

'Excellent,' replied Dunbeath. 'Our friends here must know nothing of this – we have to protect them should anything go amiss. We'll keep them amused for now and they'll be unlikely to suspect anything. You will be setting sail after we've dined and I intend to leave here myself by the escape route at dawn tomorrow. I'll have no trouble in getting to Inverness, I know of many that will see that I get there safely. I'll be able to rendezvous with some of the clan chiefs once I'm in the city and then I'll get word out to my own people. Now, are you ready to set off later ? I think the tide should be at its lowest at around four o'clock this afternoon and you can leave by the cave then. I have your money ready in gold.'

Zweig nodded.

'Good. All is well,' he said.

'Before you go, captain, there is one last service that you could do for me.'

'Of course, just name it.'

'I would be greatly in your debt if you would speak to Sophie about what she wishes you to tell her father.'

'Yes, willingly, my lord. Let me call her over now.'

Zweig wandered over to where Sophie was standing with Hume and Smith by the fire.

'Sophie, might we speak? Gentlemen, with your leave.' She looked up in surprise as he gestured towards the bow window. They strolled over to the alcove and Zweig looked calmly out towards the open sea.

'Lord Dunbeath tells me you are to be married,' he said quietly in German. Like a great fisherman, he would do nothing to spook his prey. 'I wish you joy,' he continued, smiling. 'I shall see your father when I get to Königsberg and tell him that the debt has been repaid and that you will be staying here in Scotland.'

'Yes,' replied Sophie, in a completely neutral tone, 'please tell him that. And send my love to my mother. Tell them I am content here and that I look forward to seeing them again when his lordship's war is over.'

Zweig smiled again but chose to say nothing. There was an odd silence. Then Sophie put her head closer to his. She spoke quietly.

'Did you really save Lord Dunbeath's life?'

'I don't think he intended to die,' replied Zweig with a crooked grin. He looked over to where Dunbeath stood talking to David Hume by the fire. 'He becomes hot, does he not? But, yes, I saved the life of the man you would choose to marry rather than me.'

Sophie gaze moved to the window and she looked out at the ocean.

'Yes, he becomes hot.'

They both laughed, easily and without pretence. There was another, far more comfortable silence. Then Zweig turned to her.

'You have made your choice between the two of us, Sophie, and I have no doubt you feel you have chosen wisely. With Dunbeath there will be wealth and titles, servants and certainty. With me it would have been nothing but desperate stakes, wild ventures and awful risks. No certainty at all, only insecurity. We would never have had a quiet moment or even been sure of the clothes on our backs – always rising and falling, winning and losing. Exciting some might say. But a settled, comfortable life? No.'

Sophie stared out of the window. She didn't move and there was another silence.

Then Zweig played his final card.

'Lord Dunbeath told me of the Prisoner's Dilemma. When we were journeying back from London in the boat.'

Sophie immediately brought her attention back to him.

'Did he? What did you make of it?' she asked quickly.

'I found it interesting. Then I thought of how we might have been, Sophie. There was no dilemma for me.'

'What do you mean?'

Zweig looked intently at her. His eyes were clear. He was never more serious. All pretence had gone. There was no strategy.

There were to be no more games.

'You must know that I would stay silent. You must know that I would only think of us together and not of myself. There would be no future for me if you were not there. And if you should decide to defect and confess then I should *still* stay silent – I would happily hang for you in a thousand lives before I ever betrayed you. I would go to my death with a smile on my face knowing that you would be going free.'

He spoke quietly and his eyes never left hers.

'I have told you this many times ... I love you. I showed you my heart in the days when I was on the dunes. And I told you again when I came to your room before I left for London and cried my bitter tears. Sophie, I would care nothing of dying. You could make your own choice in the Dilemma but I would be content to be hanged if it meant your freedom. You would know that my love for you could never die.'

Sophie looked steadily back at him. Then she rose to her feet and was about to walk to the fire when she turned back.

'I know who you are,' she said, quietly. 'You are a madman.'

* * *

Sharrocks called for the duty officer when he returned to Craigleven.

'Where is Colonel L'Arquen?'

'He's out hunting highlanders, sir. I believe he is due to return shortly.'

'In which case take this prisoner and hold him until he gets back.'

He turned to Makepeace, still bound tightly at the wrists.

'Mr Makepeace. I'm quite sure you know little of what you are caught up in. But in the name of everything that you hold dear, I give you one last chance – will you not tell me where Lord Dunbeath and the other man are?'

Makepeace's face was a mask. He had been in Dunbeath's service for many years and he knew only loyalty to the Urquhain. He would stubbornly protect his master.

Sharrocks put his head closer to Makepeace and spoke quietly to him in an almost caring tone.

'We shall put you in a cell now but I urge you to think again about your silence, my friend. My colonel is a devil for getting people to co-operate with him.'

Makepeace jutted his chin. But there was no disguising the anxiety that showed on his face.

* * *

Dunbeath went to the door that led to the kitchens and shouted for his housekeeper. She appeared a few moments later, smoothing her apron.

'There you are Annie, he said, 'have you been to Dunbeaton yet?'

'No, my lord. Not yet.' She wiped her hands as she spoke. 'I was going soon to get food for our dinner. I'll talk to Gordon McKay about Makepeace then.'

'Good, good,' said Dunbeath. 'There will be many for luncheon I fear. And fetch up the finest wines from the cellars. We are celebrating are we not? The Urquhain are preparing to rise and we shall soon have the king over the water returned to us at last. Captain Zweig will be leaving when the tide is at its lowest at around four o'clock, so let us eat at two.'

Annie nodded and hurried away.

* * *

Makepeace heard Major Sharrocks coming as his heels rang down the stone corridor. The cell door opened.

'The colonel has returned. He wishes to see you.'

The guard led off but as Makepeace passed him Sharrocks touched his arm.

'Please, remember that the Scots are our enemies, Mr Makepeace. The truth now, or he will be hard on you.'

But far from being hard on him, L'Arquen was friendliness itself when they were shown into his office. Drinks were offered and then the colonel asked Makepeace in a friendly and conversational tone to tell the story of the trip back from London.

'There's very little to tell, sir. His lordship left his meeting at the Admiralty and I drove him back to his boat and helped him sail up here.'

'And the German gentleman?' said L'Arquen, pleasantly. 'Did he accompany you?'

Makepeace fatally hesitated for a second.

'German gentleman? Oh, you'll be referring to his lordship's sailing master? Yes, he came with us.'

'I see. And you threw them over the side on your way back did you? Major Sharrocks tells me that they were not on board when he took you off. Apparently you had no rowing boat with you. Had they used it to row ashore earlier?'

'Yes sir,' replied Makepeace, 'they took the tender when we anchored.'

'A great shame,' murmured L'Arquen looking down sadly at the floor. Then after a pause he shook his head. 'Yes, it is a shame indeed that you do not see fit to tell me the truth.'

'But I am, sir,' blustered Makepeace.

L'Arquen shook his head with a show of deep sorrow at finding yet another example of human frailty.

'It won't do, Mr Makepeace. No, I'm afraid it just won't do at all. You see, the problem for you is that when the boat was spotted sailing around the headland it had no tender with it. And you were the only person that my major found on deck when you'd anchored. Now, let me ask you again. When did Lord Dunbeath and Captain Zweig get off?'

335

Makepeace looked bewildered for a moment but then became sullen.

'I don't know. I don't know round here.'

He closed his mouth with a studied finality.

'You disappoint me, Mr Makepeace,' said L'Arquen politely. 'Now, Major Sharrocks is going to take you back to your room and a gentleman called Trooper Williams will visit you later to ask you again about your trip. If you do think you have anything else to tell me I should be delighted to hear it when you feel ready.'

* * *

James pushed open the door of the cottage. He immediately sensed the chill in the atmosphere. Mona was sitting on a low chair by the hearth. She didn't look up when he came in, but continued to stare silently into the smoking peat.

'Mother?' said James, and a slight questioning note came into his voice.

'You were seen, James,' his mother murmured in a dead voice. 'You were seen with the redcoats.'

James's mind raced.

'Aye. Well, I was just showing them where the old beacon is. There's no harm in that is there?'

Mona had risen to her feet. Now she stood, looking James in the face.

'You've betrayed them, James, haven't you? You've betrayed Alexis and you've betrayed the earl. You've betrayed your country. And you've betrayed me.'

'Mother, please! Listen, you must listen. It was Zweig that betrayed me! He lied to me. He stole the telescope. Mother! Please!'

Mona turned to stare at the smouldering turf.

'Leave, James,' she said in a whisper, 'I have no sons now.'

Chapter 30

Annie and Sophie had worked a miracle and a luncheon to stay in the memory was being served in the dining room. Much of Dunbeath's fine old Bordeaux wine was flowing, and laughter and storytelling filled the ancient room with noise and warmth. In each of the different people that sat around the table there seemed to be a mood of change and fresh starts – Zweig was returning to Königsberg, Dunbeath to join the uprising, Sophie to be starting a new life as a married woman and the two philosophers going back to Edinburgh with the excitement of their many discussions and discoveries.

Dunbeath looked down the table, hardly able to believe the changes that had taken place over the past few months. More than anything, he felt able to admit, the changes to himself.

He now gazed down to where Adam Smith was speaking to Sophie in an unintelligible rattle. What did he make of all this he wondered? Even though he'd only met him that day, Dunbeath felt a great attraction towards the strange, unworldly young man, and he now called out to him as the party began to fall quiet.

'So, Mr Smith, my friend David Hume tells me that you feel my little game may have contributed to your thinking.'

'Yes, indeed, my lord,' replied Smith, his eyes glued to the fireplace. 'Yes, I think the Prisoner's Dilemma has taken us all on a journey.'

'And where do you think it has taken you?'

Smith's gaze began its customary careering sprint before it settled on the sideboard.

'Well, my lord, I believe it has shown us how trust is the calling card of co-operation and how co-operation is the key to a constructive society.'

'Ah, I see Sophie has been bewitching you as well, Mr Smith,' replied Dunbeath. 'You should know that I am still a sceptic of this thinking. I'm afraid I have spent far too long in this world not to know that however much the Dilemma may want us to have these three point relationships, the temptation to take five is never far from the surface in all men.'

Well, I don't believe I would argue with you too greatly on that, Lord Dunbeath. No more would I argue that a butcher might knowingly sell you bad beef. He might and you might pay for it, but you would not buy from him again. His stock would be damaged in your eyes. In just the same way, it seems to me that Miss Kant's free riders are damaging their reputations and their futures in society because they are seen as a threat to its stability.'

'And where is this leading you?' said Dunbeath to a now silent table.

'It is leading me without deviation, sir, to the belief that all society is a market,' replied Smith, 'and that it is an error to imagine that society is one thing and commerce is another. Tit for Tat is without doubt a building block in our understanding of this. But I also feel that even this insight is too crude, too simplistic, to be the whole story.

'I'm increasingly certain that what is going on is that we are selling ourselves to each other, just as much as we might sell our services, our goods or our specialisations. Just as a trader might lay out his wares for sale, so we are laying out our characters and talents – and our *trustworthiness* – for others to look at. We do this in what we say, in how we behave, in how we look … we are endlessly writing advertisements for ourselves. These bill posters of ours are appealing in everything we do for the co-operation of others.'

Smith leant forward and took a deep pull of his wine as he stared into space, clearly thinking through what he was going to say next. The others waited in silence, intrigued.

'And, why are we doing this?' he continued. 'Well, to survive, first and foremost, by finding people who will help us do so. That is the lesson of life. But once we think we've done that? Then our aim is to win – to win against each other. And, to achieve this, we will employ every artifice, every trick and every instinct we're able to call on.

'This much I think is plain. But I still do not find it enough to explain our strivings. You see, the Dilemma would have us all looking for long-term, co-operative, three point relationships. A society of doves trustingly building a New Jerusalem. But we do not see this. That is why you don't agree with Sophie's conclusions – you don't see it either. So, why aren't we happy with three points? What is it that makes us want more? Why do we strive so much and why do we fight so hard to progress? Why are we not content to enjoy our survival, but want to win against each other – and to be *seen* to win?' Adam Smith was unaware that all eyes were upon him. He had now become dreamy, rolling bread under his fingers and staring into the far distance.

'And then I realised why. I suddenly saw that we are trying to do more than survive in this life – we are trying to survive in future lives as well. As Mr Hume once said to me: 'none of our ancestors died celibate'. Each of us is proof of an unbroken success as our ancestors passed on their lines. And we are doing the same. Seeing the future and plotting, plotting, plotting to have our lines continue.'

Dunbeath had had enough of this.

'Now Mr Smith, I believe you go too far. Think again, I beg you.'

'Too far?' said Smith, suddenly looking at Dunbeath. 'Do I? Then I apologise. But answer me then the question that I put to myself, my lord – why did man ever hunt large animals? Why would a man have risked his life trying to kill a great elk or a mammoth when he could kill a rabbit or a fowl more easily? The answer cannot be for the meat because no man or even his family could have eaten a dead mammoth before the meat was spoiled. A guinea fowl or a brace of duck or two would have been far easier to find and far less dangerous to hunt. So, why would a man put himself through the uncertainty and danger of hunting large and dangerous animals when he could have trapped smaller ones more easily?

'There was not only the risk of the chase. There was the waste as well. A man would never have been able to carry a dead mammoth, let alone have made use of it all himself where it was killed. So, he'd have had to allow other people to take some. He'd have to have tolerated their theft. Why would he do that? Why would he appear to have a social conscience or be interested in helping other people? And then I realised why. The answer, I believe, is that just as we trade our specialisations in life so the mammoth hunter was trading an unmovable and perishable commodity, a transient success, for a reward he could carry around with him at all times – *his reputation*. The community's gratitude and goodwill for his generosity, people's respect for his courage and so on. That was his reward.

'This hunter was helping society just as rich men, not unlike your forebears, might build a beacon to warn passing vessels of rocks in a bay. It was erected at your ancestor's expense yet its light benefits everybody. But it also shines out with the boast of the Urquhain's social standing. These sorts of actions lead men to be admired, storing up a bank of goodwill to be exchanged later for other services and rewards.'

Adam Smith came to a stop and seemed to come out of his reverie. He looked up and down the table as if judging whether to go on. Then he stared at the ceiling.

'But, much more than this,' he continued, 'these kind of acts make men attractive to women. These actions are for show. They are the peacock's plumage. Men do such things so that women will think well of them – and will want to have their offspring. These men are saying to the world ... see, look how strong I am, observe my courage and skills, see how I provide, see how *I win*, see what my line will inherit! Yes, my lord, the more you look at my chain of logic ... the more you see a bed at its end.'

There was a collective gasp from the others and Dunbeath was on his feet in an instant.

'Mr Smith. Now, you *do* go too far.'

'I am surprised at you, my lord,' replied Smith without the slightest sign of fear or of backing down, 'you of all people should know that scientists have to think these dangerous thoughts. In your own field, did not the great Galileo suffer for his discoveries? And is there anyone now, in this enlightened age, who would say that he was wrong?

'No, I believe I am right. My parable holds. Killing the mammoth was difficult. It took tenacity and cunning and valour and ability. Admirable qualities to set on a bill poster, advertising yourself and your character. These qualities bring prestige and admiration. And in doing so, they bring an invitation to the bedroom. Women look at them and wish their children to have these same qualities and more. However, we forget something here at our peril. Yes, men may do these things to attract women but I rather imagine they do them also to attract other men too. Because they know that they so often control the choices of women. How dangerous would allowing a daughter to marry who she liked be to an ambitious father? So, I believe the urge to achieve these public displays of attractiveness is the key principle. That's why they were worth the increased hunting risk and why, for example, your own ancestors were so keen to reach the top of the heap.'

Dunbeath stared at Adam Smith as he talked, his mouth a tight line; but he said nothing.

'What better way could there be of getting society's attention,' Smith continued, 'of telling other people that one is of privileged and successful stock, than to carry round a huge billboard that says so – an advertisement. Like a great name, a title. In your family's case, an earldom. It proclaims, 'I am a leader amongst men,' your bill poster says so. It spells out your success, your status, your specialisation – it spells out what you're selling.

'To be recognised publicly is nothing less than where the logic of the Prisoner's Dilemma would lead us. It is the end result of a mechanism that allows a person to say 'here I am, a proud and successful co-operator. I am trustworthy – yet I am *rewarded*. Look at me. See how attractive I am. Have my children. Let the line continue!'

Nobody at the table moved. Smith looked through the window, out to the open sea, smiling his beautiful smile. There was a long silence while everyone waited for the Urquhain Rage to descend.

But the blackness was broken by Zweig. With a huge laugh he threw up his hands.

'Mr Smith. I wish you'd told my sister about this. If she'd known, she might not have married that idiot farmer of hers!'

Dunbeath and David Hume roared. Even Adam Smith's face creased into a wide grin. The crisis passed.

'Let me ask you this, Captain Zweig,' continued Dunbeath as the laughter died, his humour now restored. 'You have seen much of the world - do you not agree with me that it is the ugly force of greed that makes us what we are? Self-interest leads to more self-interest in my view. Not Mr Smith and Sophie's belief that it leads to goodness in us.'

'Well I am just a foolish sailor,' replied Zweig, 'but I must agree with you that greed can be so powerful that it can even overcome caution, even our fears. Let me show you something. Do you have a gold guinea, my lord?'

Dunbeath fished in his pocket and passed a guinea to Zweig. He held it up for the table to see.

'Let me auction this for you. Let us see who will give you the most for it. The only condition of the game is that the under-bidder, the next losing bid, also has to pay you as the seller.'

Adam Smith brought his gaze down from the ceiling.

'I'll bid you a penny.'

'And I'll bid you tuppence,' said Hume. 'So, Mr Smith, you

owe Lord Dunbeath a penny. And you have nothing to show for it.'

The auction continued, each new bid being met by shrieks of laughter as the price went up and up and the under-bidder's exposure grew. Eventually greed gave way to fear as the bids came closer to a pound. The party's hilarity was partly a reaction to Smith's shocking theory and partly a sign of end-of-an-era high spirits. And when David Hume offered more than the face value of the guinea, just so Adam Smith was committed to paying the losing amount, it seemed the funniest thing that anybody had ever seen. The wine flowed and the little group's flushed, laughing faces as they glowed in the candlelight, showed how close their friendship had become through the trials of recent events.

Eventually, Dunbeath glanced through the window and saw the first signs of gathering dusk.

'I'm sorry that the party must end,' he said, 'but it approaches four and the tide will soon be at its lowest. Zweig, you must leave now if you're to get out through the escape route. Let us go down to the cave to see you off. Sophie, perhaps you'd like to come with us to take your leave of the captain and give him any messages you may have for your family?'

Zweig rose and warmly shook the others by the hand. There were many good wishes for the future and David Hume gave Zweig's arm an admiring squeeze.

'Goodbye, captain. I shall never forget your days on the dunes. I learnt much from watching you there.'

Zweig went to the hall to retrieve his wet weather jacket and then joined Dunbeath and Sophie in the storeroom. Once they were there the earl leant down and lifted the corner of the flagstone. It came away and he put his hand into the hole and pulled up the large stone.

'Now, captain,' he said, 'let me do this before we go through the cave.'

He went to a shelf in the room where he had left two huge leather pouches and handed them to Zweig.

'Here is the gold, the very finest. This bag is for Herr Kant – the debt repaid. And this other one is for as much powder, arms and ammunition as you can buy with it.'

Zweig took the heavy sacks from him and Dunbeath then walked over to where a large piece of material was hanging from a hook. It was a cloak of black grogram lined with white silk and he handed it to Zweig with a smile.

'And here is my father's old boat cloak for your journey. Something for you to remember the Urquhain by before we meet again. I fear it will become colder as you head for Königsberg. You will need it.'

Zweig smiled in gratitude, touched by the gesture. He shook Dunbeath by the hand.

'Thank you, my lord,' he said, 'I shall see you again soon. Where we agreed.'

Dunbeath nodded.

'You must go now,' he muttered. 'We'll help you with the boat.' He took one of the bags back from the captain and stepped into the hole. Sophie and Zweig carefully followed him down the wet stone steps to the cave and together they gathered on the ledge at the back.

'I'll go first,' said Dunbeath, 'and get the boat in the water. I'll shout when I'm on the boulder and then you follow next, Sophie.'

Dunbeath ran through the cave towards the light at the opening. There was none of the urgency of previous sprints as the sea was flat and limpid, with the slightest of swells slopping water gently against the rocks. The oiliness of the surface and the clammy atmosphere were odd, not unlike the calm before the great storm of the Swarzsturmvogel's sinking.

As Dunbeath reached the mouth of the cave he clambered up the handholds on the side of the giant boulder, manhandling the gold after him. But no sooner had he climbed out of sight than

Sophie turned in the half darkness of the cave and looked searchingly into Zweig's face.

'And, so you go.' She spoke quietly. 'But, listen. Tell me quickly. Tell me again of your choice in the Dilemma.'

'You do not need me to say it, Sophie.' Zweig held her by the shoulders. 'I would stay silent. You know that I would always stay silent. Why would I mind if I died as long as you went free?'

At the other end of the cave Dunbeath leant down towards the gap. He shouted in a hoarse whisper for them to come. After a few seconds there was the sound of running feet and Sophie came through the gap. Dunbeath put his arm down and pulled her up.

There was more splashing and Zweig appeared. He swung the gold bag up to Dunbeath and then pulled himself easily up the rock. The three now stood together on the boulder.

Dunbeath had the tender in the water with the bow pointing away.

'You have no time to lose, captain. You'll have read the weather better than me – there's a bad storm coming and you'll need to be in the jacht before it hits. Let's hurry now. Hold the stern here, would you Sophie? I'll undo the rope.'

Zweig climbed into the boat and settled himself at the oars. Dunbeath passed him the gold and the captain stored it carefully in the bow. Sophie was on her haunches, holding the back panel while Dunbeath untied the painter from where it had been coiled around a sharp rock. He threw it down into the boat.

Sophie rose to her feet. She looked intently at Zweig and for the shortest of seconds their eyes met. She gave an almost imperceptible nod of her head. He looked away, busy with putting the oars backwards for the first stroke.

And then she stepped into the stern.

Zweig pulled twice and the rowing boat was instantly ten feet from the shore. Dunbeath stared at it and then at Sophie, sitting now, gazing back at him. His face was twisted in bafflement, quite unable take in what he was seeing.

'What are you doing, Sophie?' he said in an odd voice. 'You have got in the boat. You are not going, you know.'

But her anguished face told him everything. She was in agony – but she had made her decision.

'No, Sophie,' mumbled Dunbeath, looking at her as she rocked on the swell, his face a ghastly mix of pain and disbelief.

'No, you cannot go.' There was a pause. 'You cannot,' he whispered. 'I love you. I need you here.'

She continued to look back, her sorrow for him clear, her face crumpled in distress.

The little craft bobbed in the flat calm. Then Zweig dropped the oars and rose to his feet, the Urquhain cloak hanging down over his enormous frame. He bowed deeply to Dunbeath.

'My lord, I wish you farewell.'

'No, no!' said Dunbeath with growing realisation and panic, his face collapsing in pain. Then, like a stricken pilgrim, he slowly dropped to his knees, his hands held out in front of him. His voice cracked as he looked pleadingly at the only two people he had ever loved.

'No, Sophie! No, Alexis! Don't leave me here. Don't leave me. Take me with you. Please!'

Slowly Zweig dipped the oars in the water. The distance doubled in a stroke and then doubled again. Dunbeath let out one last tortured cry. He had only one thing left to offer.

'No! Please, don't go! Take me with you! I'll co-operate. Please, I'll agree. Don't defect. Please, don't defect!'

Chapter 31

Dunbeath lay where he'd collapsed on the boulder, no longer looking out to the open sea and the faint outline of the rowing boat as it disappeared slowly into the distance. But, at last, an unconscious survival instinct told him he had to get to his feet and he dropped down to the gap and stumbled, weeping, through the cave. Somehow he climbed the steps and made his way to the salon.

Smith and Hume rose immediately from their seats by the fire. One glance at Dunbeath's wild eyes and frantic look was enough for them to know that some terrible disaster had struck.

'She's gone, Hume! She went with Zweig! Oh God, she's chosen to be with Zweig. What am I to do, Hume? What am I to do?'

He fell to the ground in front of them, broken and sobbing as the two men exchanged a glance before they ran over to comfort him.

Outside, the wind was freshening and the afternoon dusk was fast turning to gloom. In the distance came a loud crack of thunder.

* * *

Major Sharrocks knocked and came smartly into L'Arquen's office.

'You sent for me, sir?'

L'Arquen rose from behind his desk, dropping the letter opener he had in his hand and peeling off his gloves. He glanced briefly towards his major.

'I'm going to retire now, Sharrocks. Wake me when he breaks.'

* * *

Hume and Smith had somehow managed to get Dunbeath onto a sofa, and he now sat there, curled over and shattered beyond any pretence of dignity. Hume had an arm around his shoulder to keep him upright and a glass of whisky ready for his lips. They looked up as the door opened and Annie stumbled into the room, her eyes red with weeping. She seemed to have aged twenty years and had clearly reverted to the oblivion she'd so often sought from drink in the past.

'Master!' she cried with a wild gasp. 'Terrible news. Gordon McKay has come just now from Dunbeaton. They have looked everywhere for your lordship's boat but they cannae find it! They've been searching these past four hours. I fear there's no sign of your man, Makepeace either.'

'What!' shouted Dunbeath, jumping up, suddenly energised by the appalling news. 'It must be there. I told Makepeace to anchor it in the bay. It can't be gone!'

Another enormous clap of thunder cracked overhead, far louder than before, as the storm broke beyond Dunbeaton's headland with a terrifying savagery.

'My God. Look at this weather! Look at this weather! Where is the boat? What will they do if it isn't there? I must go and search for them.'

The earl looked wildly from Hume to Smith and then ran out of the room. They heard him as he took the tower steps, two at a time, hurtling manically up to his observatory.

David Hume looked over to where Smith sat staring towards the bow window, deep in thought.

'Mr Smith. You may as well retire to your room. I shall stay up with Lord Dunbeath. I fear I have seen these signs before, many years ago when we were students. I'm afraid the shock of Sophie leaving may have pulled the trigger for another collapse.'

But Adam Smith seemed not to have heard him and instead looked over with a feverish glint in his eye. Hume glanced up and Smith quickly turned his gaze back towards the window.

'Isn't this of the greatest interest?' he said quickly, plainly very excited. 'We have been playing these games, speaking all the time of our interpretations of them – and here, laid out for us to see, is the clearest example of the Dilemma in action we could ever imagine.'

'Please, Mr Smith, please' replied Hume quickly. 'I beg you, sir. Not now.'

'Do you not see, Mr Hume?' Smith carried breathlessly on, ignoring Hume's plea. 'Miss Kant has done exactly as I predicted. She has chosen one man over the other. No doubt she sees in Zweig some greater qualities she wishes for her children! How very interesting this is.

'And, as to the game itself, do you not also see that the captain was working to bring it to an end all the time? He knew that he was creating that rare thing: a finite event. We spoke of life as having ends that the theory did not, and here is just such a case. As for Sophie, well, did she not see the hundredth turn as she looked at Zweig's boat? That trust and co-operation counted for nothing when her life had come to such a choice? She was finally faced with a one-time Prisoner's Dilemma. There was no future in her thinking. There was no further need for reciprocity. We know what to expect at such a time … she could only defect.'

'Mr Smith,' repeated Hume in a broken voice. 'I beg you once more. This can all wait until we are back in Edinburgh.'

Adam Smith took no notice. His face was flushed and he continued hectically on, the words tumbling out.

'The only thing I don't understand is why Lord Dunbeath should be showing such concern for them. Didn't we agree that there would be no hatred like the one we reserve for people who betray us? For the traitors in life?'

He looked over at last to where David Hume was sitting, silent now, bent, his shoulders drooping.

'Why, Mr Hume,' Smith said in his rapid rattle, an uncomprehending half smile on his face, 'is the smoke from the fire bothering you? Your eyes are watering.'

Hume just looked ahead.

'Please, Mr Smith, go to your room now. You are very young, sir. Yes, you are very young.'

* * *

David Hume stayed with Dunbeath throughout the night. At first he tried to speak to him, to ease his mind with conversation. But Dunbeath seemed not to notice. He ignored his old friend and paced backwards and forwards by the windows, muttering occasionally to himself and frantically scanning the surface of the sea with the Domenico Salva, over and over again, first with hope and then with mounting despair, the sky constantly lit by huge sheets of lightening as the storm raged above them.

Eventually Hume dozed in his chair, but Dunbeath searched manically on, focusing and refocusing the eyepiece of the telescope. Again and again he swung it across the wildness of the open sea as mountainous waves rolled in from the blackness of the distant horizon and piled onto the shore.

As he did so, his confused anxiety seemed to mutate into a deranged blankness, and from there to a deep, bleak sadness. Images of Sophie and Zweig came pouring out before him – Sophie smiling at him as she sat by his bed, Zweig laughing at Warleigh Point, Sophie convulsed with her giggles and dimples at the guinea auction, Zweig bellowing with laughter in the carriage after he'd beaten off the hussars, Sophie smiling. Sophie always smiling, smiling, smiling.

* * *

James McLeish pushed further back into the sandy crook of a dune. The storm raged unabated about him and, as the lightening lit up the bay, he could see the great breakers as they pounded the shoreline, and sheets of slashing rain rolling in towards the beach and drowning his little shelter.

He had done as best he could the evening before, fixing an old fishing net over the natural curve of the dune and holding it up with two straight sticks. Then he'd packed grass and sand to form a roof. But this had all been useless against such a storm and he was now drenched and frozen. No sleep had been possible and he stared ahead, his lips moving and his face tight with hatred.

* * *

It was about three in the morning when Major Sharrocks made his way quickly up the main staircase and then down a long corridor towards L'Arquen's bedroom. Inside, the colonel breathed lightly, sleeping peacefully in Viscount Duncansby's fabulous state bed. But at Sharrocks' sharp knock he was immediately awake. He pulled on a gown and went to the door.

'Yes?'

'Makepeace would like to see you, sir.'

They made their way downstairs as the first streaks of dawn came through the large windows of Craigleven's great state-rooms. L'Arquen pushed open the door of his office and saw Makepeace slumped in the chair opposite his desk, a hand buried beneath his coat front.

'Mr Makepeace,' he said, brightly, 'how good to see you again. I understand you have spent some time with Trooper Williams. Good, good. Now, perhaps I can ask you once more, do you have any idea where Lord Dunbeath and Captain Zweig might be?'

Makepeace could hardly speak for his pain.

'They got off,' he mumbled. 'There was a sheet hanging from the castle. The German said it meant you were there.'

L'Arquen's face twitched at the memory of some past slight.

'They rowed to the castle. There's a cave there. It's a way into the castle.'

'What!' screamed L'Arquen. 'You mean Dunbeath and Zweig have been in the castle all this time? Why didn't you tell me this before you treacherous bastard?' He ran towards the chair in his fury and kicked Makepeace in the side. 'Call yourself an Englishman? I shall finish with those two and then come back for you. Have no doubt on that matter.'

He swung round on Major Sharrocks.

'Harken, Sharrocks. Get the troop together. Now we'll settle the score.'

It didn't take Sharrocks long to issue his commands and a few minutes later his men were dressed and standing by their horses in the yard, ready for the order to leave. They looked up as they heard L'Arquen clattering down the stairs and a moment later he emerged to join them, swinging his riding crop, his face set marble hard with the desire for revenge. He strode across the cobbled surface of the stable yard and stepped onto a stone riding block where a man stood, shaking slightly as he held his horse. L'Arquen mounted and lifted the crop to signal the off when, from around the side of the stable block, the sound of galloping hooves and raised voices made him hesitate.

He lowered his arm again as a mounted rider swept into the courtyard and came to a halt in front of him, ragged and mud stained.

'Colonel L'Arquen?' the man asked, breathing hard. 'I am a King's Messenger, sir. I have an urgent order for you from the Prince von Suderburg-Brunswick-Luneburg in London.'

L'Arquen tore open the order and read it. A huge smile broke over his face. He read it again and then threw his head back, bellowing in a triumphant, vicious laugh. For half a minute or more he laughed again and again as his men watched him in silence, only too aware that they were not to join in his merriment.

'Splendid! Splendid!' he called out eventually. 'Read this,

Sharrocks.'

He turned to the messenger.

'You have arrived at the exact moment. Well done indeed my fine fellow. You have brought me the best news you could. Guard, find some food for this man.' Then, almost to himself he muttered, '… if you wait an hour or so you can have some of Lord Dunbeath's cooked goose.'

He lifted his whip again and the troop moved out with L'Arquen at its head, still chuckling loudly at his orders.

Chapter 32

It was now dawn and as the storm blew itself out, a fine, early summer's day broke gently over the length of the bay. A pale light shone on the surface of the sea and it began to calm itself from the wild lunacy of the previous night and into a foamy, apologetic saneness.

But there was no calmness in Dunbeath. For the thousandth time, he swung his beautiful telescope across the open waves and then downwards towards the shoreline. He now carefully worked his way along every foot of the great sandy crescent.

Towards the Dunbeaton end of the beach a large boulder lay embedded in the shore, close to the water's edge. It was the enormous stone that the villagers had used to secure the line from the Schwarzsturmvogel all those months ago. It towered in front of the long line of dunes and as Dunbeath inched the telescope's image along its base he stopped abruptly as he saw a tiny fragment of cloth flapping from behind it in the breeze. It was black. He focused again for a closer view. The wind swung round and the cloth turned over, flicked by a sudden gust. The other side was white.

With a strangled cry Dunbeath dropped the telescope and hurled out of the door, flinging himself down the great tower's spiral staircase.

* * *

The troop galloped on. Two miles had passed and L'Arquen urged his horse on, his face set with anger and determination.

* * *

Dunbeath threw open the castle's front door and ran outside onto the entrance area. He turned frantically to the right to where a flight of stone steps took him down to the lower level and so out onto the beach.

L'Arquen's two sentries, still huddled under the canvas cover they'd used to escape the worst of the storm, jumped to their feet as they saw him. They now stood in confused indecision as Dunbeath began to sprint towards the beach.

'That's him, isn't it?' said one urgently. 'That's the earl. I'm sure of it. I've seen him through the telescope when I've been on watch. What's he doin' here? How did he get past us? Quick, you'd better ride back to Craigleven and tell them that he's somehow got into the castle. Tell them he's gone down to the shore. I'll see where he's going, but I'm going to stay here and watch out unless the German's here as well.'

The other trooper sprinted to his horse and leapt on it, galloping down the land bridge and out onto the Wick turnpike.

He'd ridden about three miles when he saw the troop approaching fast towards him.

'Colonel L'Arquen, sir!' he shouted, swinging his horse round to ride alongside his commanding officer, 'Lord Dunbeath was in the castle all the time! He's just come out and he's running along the beach. Trooper Kingsley is watching out for the German in case his lordship's trying to distract us away from the castle.'

L'Arquen gave no answer. He ignored the man and rode on, staring blankly ahead, spurring his horse forward.

* * *

Dunbeath had reached the boulder. As he rounded it he saw the boat cloak flat on the wet sand, stretched out by the receding tide. Then he saw Zweig's head as he lay on his front, his face to one side, his eyes open. Dunbeath stared at him, hardly able to make sense of what he was seeing. For long seconds he studied Zweig's huge frame and then the calm and accepting features on his unlined face. He saw only peace there. Gone was the man's unquenchable determination, gone the great will to win. Instead, there was only a placid smoothness and he knew in that second that the captain had looked on death with the same certainty that he'd looked on life.

Dunbeath reached a shaking hand down to close the staring eyes. He moved the cloak slightly to wrap it more tightly around Zweig's body, an absurd wish sweeping over him to keep his friend warm against the chill of the early morning. He pulled at the cloak, and then, from the edge of the cloth, he saw a curl. A dark curl.

Frenzied now, he levered the great body over onto its back. Then he saw Sophie, her arms wrapped around Zweig's waist and her face on his chest, her wet hair streaming away, dragged there by the furious pull of the surf.

Dunbeath stared again, his eyes moving wildly from one body to another. He looked at Sophie once more and mumbled to her, calling her name, seeing her but seeing her somehow different, fascinated by a look on her face that he'd never seen before. She was smiling but with a beautiful, unaffected radiance, completely at peace. She was in the arms of the man she loved and with whom she had happily died.

Dunbeath bent over them, utterly absorbed in the picture before him, transfixed by the scene rather than grief stricken, scrutinizing it minutely, taking in what he was seeing and trying desperately to understand it.

How strange are the ways of the mind. From nowhere came words he must have seen on a gravestone somewhere, buried until now but flung forward in his shock.

'Modest as morn, as midday bright,

Gentle as evening, cool as night.'

Gentle as evening, he thought again, staring, broken-heartedly at her beautiful smile.

Suddenly his head dropped forward as if he'd been violently struck from behind. His mouth drew back in his pain and he twisted to see what could have hit him with such a sickening weight.

He straightened and turned. Next to him, quite still and making no attempt to retreat, stood James McLeish. An ancient, fish-gutting knife was in his hand. Dunbeath stared at him, confused.

Who was this man?

He looked with amazement at the knife that dangled from James's fingers. It was so old and ruined that whole sections of the blade had rusted away.

Even in those terrible moments, Dunbeath's mind was turning.

He'd been stabbed with that. That had to be his blood on the blade. Was he finished? Could a second's work with that thing have ended him? Could it really have cancelled out the centuries of gain, the Urquhain wealth, his great learning, the Dunbeath earls? Had this man done for them?

James stood in front of him. Now he was moving from foot to foot. The muscles in his face worked incessantly. His features passed manically from defiant to fearful, apologetic to loathing, his face twisting and contorting as a mass of half completed thoughts flashed through his deranged mind.

Was he trying to say something? Dunbeath wondered, looking at him closely with a strange, detached coolness. But who was he?

Finally James's agitation came to a climax. He flung the knife sideways into the surf and then stared at Dunbeath's bent figure. Now he was openly hostile, challenging the earl to respond.

There was something about the gesture that took Dunbeath back to another time and he suddenly remembered a moonlit night, many months ago, in his observatory. Yes, it came back to him now - this was the person that had pulled his brother off the parapet.

Dunbeath was pleased. It all made sense; the boy was

completing the circle. He swayed as he peered more closely at his rabid twitching. He remembered him well now. He looked at him with interest, quite calmly and without anger. His vision was blurring, but he knew what he wanted to do.

He smiled and spoke in a tone of the softest resignation.

'Thank you.'

Then Dunbeath turned and dropped to his knees. With a final, agonising effort he lifted himself to gaze down at Sophie Kant and Alexis Zweig for the last time. Now he could at last do what he had never been able to do in life. Now they could be together. He fell forward, his arms outstretched. And they lay together, entwined, united finally in the love they all, in their different ways, had wished for.

This was how L'Arquen found them a minute later. The troop slowed and he gazed down from his horse with distaste at the three bodies. He saw that damned earl; good, he was dead. That had saved him a lot of trouble. And the German captain, too. God knows what was going on there. Then he looked at Sophie. What a waste that was. Had he ever seen a more beautiful woman?

His mouth tightened and he turned his horse's head. High above, a screech of gulls wheeled, screaming in the morning air. The surf pounded on the shore. L'Arquen was about to ride off when he turned to his major.

'Sharrocks, bring McLeish in for questioning. I'd be interested in finding out what all this was about.'

He made to go but then turned back with a further thought.

'And have the men go to the village and find some shovels. Get them busy on this.'

He gave a slight grunt and spurred his horse back up the beach.

Chapter 33

The thin sunlight continued to falter and flicker over the coast all that day but by the late afternoon even this half-hearted effort was losing its struggle with the dark clouds that piled up out to sea, waiting their turn to sweep in with yet more rain. A deep gloom now began to settle over Dunbeaton Bay.

David Hume stood where he'd been for so long at the observatory window. For some minutes he'd been watching the troop of dragoons as it travelled slowly along the turnpike in the distance, but with mounting dismay he'd seen that it now wheeled right and was turning down towards the land bridge and the castle. At its head he could just make out L'Arquen, languid and unhurried, a lazy arrogance showing in every curve and mannerism of the way he rode. Even his horse seemed to be deliberately slowing its pace, dawdling as if it regarded the road as its natural possession.

Before long a loud knock at the front entrance echoed around the great hall and Hume gave a deep sigh and stirred himself at last to descend the tower stairs. Eventually he reached the door and pulled hard on the huge brass handle. The failing light fell into the hall and he saw L'Arquen in profile, framed by the open door, gazing sideways down to the long crescent of the beach, pointedly pretending to be unaware of Hume's presence.

'Colonel L'Arquen,' said Hume, tensely. 'Yes?'

L'Arquen dropped his head and turned slowly to face Hume.

'Ah, Mr Hume. There are. No housekeeper, eh? Answering the door yourself, I see. What have you done with the old biddy?' He looked balefully at Hume's waistcoat as it stretched over his stomach and drawled again at him. 'Eaten her, eh?'

Hume sighed once more and L'Arquen pushed past him uninvited and walked up the staircase towards the salon. Hume lumbered along behind him, wheezing at the effort, and followed the colonel into the room. He was waved towards one of the sofas.

'Sit yourself there, my good sir,' L'Arquen ordered brusquely, setting down a leather attaché case on a table. 'So. We must discuss how matters progress now.'

He looked coldly down at Hume for some seconds without speaking. Then he moved to stand with his back to the dead fire.

'Not much cheer here, eh, Mr Hume? Not much here and not much in what we found down there on the beach either.'

Hume said nothing, only too aware that the colonel would have an order of business.

'Well, sir,' L'Arquen said at last. 'You will know that Lord Dunbeath is dead. I've no doubt that the old bat will have told you that. Yes, we found him dead with two others – and we found a sad little tale behind it all too. But I imagine you are already aware of most of it.'

L'Arquen looked at Hume as if gauging what response he was getting and then continued smoothly on.

'Lord Dunbeath was a traitor to the crown, Mr Hume. We know that now. Some months ago it seems he made contact with representatives of Prince Charles Edward Stuart and agreed to bring the Clan Urquhain in for this so-called Pretender, the absurd Bonnie Prince Charlie. Some of Dunbeath's people then travelled to Königsberg in Eastern Prussia where they commissioned a Captain Alexis Zweig to bring gunpowder and arms to supply their needs. It appears this Zweig missed his landfall when he reached Scotland and his ship blew up after it foundered in a severe gale back in early March. I think you know much of the rest. Zweig somehow survived the wrecking and kept low in the village where he was sheltered by a family called McLeish. Zweig used their son – a self-confessed Jacobite sympathiser – to approach Lord Dunbeath about payment for the lost cargo. This man, James McLeish, was sent away by Dunbeath who refused to countenance paying for what he considered to be a failed delivery. You probably know that these Urquhain are famous for their hard bargaining.

'Zweig became incensed at this and forced the earl to deal with him by sitting out on the dunes, gambling that Dunbeath wouldn't let him risk attracting our attention. There was a German doxy with the captain when he arrived ...' L'Arquen's face tightened as a sudden fury took hold but he quickly got on top of himself, '... do you remember Lord Dunbeath telling me she was a maid from Inverness, Mr Hume? I seem to recall you said nothing to disabuse me of that twaddle. Anyway, she was here in the castle with you all and she must have mediated when Dunbeath needed to get to London for a meeting he had to attend. Some kind of agreement was arrived at for Zweig to sail him there and, when the two of them returned, this Zweig rowed off yesterday with the girl. But the boat they'd been given was smashed in the storm last night.

'The girl was dead when Lord Dunbeath discovered them on the shore this morning. She had drowned but Zweig was still very much alive. He accused the earl of sending them to their deaths and a struggle broke out between the men. Zweig was much the stronger man and it didn't take him long to have Dunbeath by the throat and to throttle him to death.'

David Hume looked incredulously at the languorous figure that stood before him with his eyelids drooping, reeling off such unashamed lies.

'Good God, L'Arquen! What fantasy is this that you're weaving?'

L'Arquen stopped him with a waft of his hand.

'But, I haven't finished, my dear sir. I beg you, please let me go on. I told you that this fisherman, the McLeish boy, supported Dunbeath's Jacobite madness and he'd made his way out onto the beach when he saw the men fighting. He witnessed his leader being done to death by the German and he hurled himself on the man and stabbed him through the heart. Zweig died immediately.

Hume jumped to his feet, the force of his anger overcoming his great weight.

'This is all a falsehood, L'Arquen, and you know it! Dunbeath was no traitor. And he had a great friendship for Zweig and the girl. Who has invented this deranged nonsense?'

There was a long silence while the colonel looked coolly at Hume.

'You seem to know a lot about it all, Mr Hume, if I may say so. You may be somewhat rash to be admitting too much in my view. But let me set that aside for a minute and tell you how we arrived at all this. You see, my troop was on the beach as this little drama was playing itself out and McLeish was taken back with us to Craigleven to tell us what had occurred. He readily admitted to one of my troopers, a man called Williams, that he had joined the rebels and that Lord Dunbeath was the leader of the Caithness uprising. He then told us about how he had avenged his master's death.'

Hume took a step forward, his florid features a lurid red, twisted in disbelief.

'Where is the evidence for this? Let me see the bodies at once. And I wish to speak to this James McLeish. I shall not let this calumny about Lord Dunbeath be accepted, L'Arquen.'

'Sadly, Mr McLeish took it upon himself to try and run off after his discussions with Trooper Williams. I'm afraid that he was shot by my men while he was attempting to escape. As to the earl and the other bodies, they were buried on my orders. This is as it should be. My authority allows it. You would require an Act of Parliament to have them disinterred now.'

The two men stood staring at each other. A faint smile flickered over L'Arquen's lips. The truth was beginning to dawn on Hume.

'What is to become of Lord Dunbeath's property and fortune, colonel? I believe he was the last of his line.'

'He was a proven traitor, Mr Hume. I'd be obliged if you would remember that. His lands and houses, along with everything he owned, will all now pass to the crown. As you know, it is the way. The law is quite clear about treachery of this kind and hands down the maximum punishment for it. The possessions of those who betray their country are always immediately forfeited.'

'I see. And you, colonel? No doubt your snout will also be in the trough?'

L'Arquen gazed at Hume, quite untouched by the insult, his eyes saturated with power.

'I do believe there is a mechanism for such things, Mr Hume. Possibly a minor pourboire will reach me. Such matters as this would rank as a military prize. But I dare say it won't amount to more than twenty percent of the whole estate. Perhaps a house or two as well, given by a grateful government of course, for stamping out such a dangerous rebellion.'

An overwhelming urge to vomit swept over David Hume. He felt his face burn.

'I shall fight you, L'Arquen. I shall fight you every minute of every day. This is nothing but theft. You have no evidence that Lord Dunbeath was a traitor. And I know that he was not. I shall bring a case against you for this fraudulence of yours. I shall drag you through the courts and everyone will see you for the liar that you are.'

'No evidence, my dear sir?' murmured L'Arquen. 'Of course I have evidence.'

He moved to pick up the attaché case and took some pages out from it.

'Why, here is Mr McLeish's evidence written out in full. Here is his mark under the statement together with the signatures of two witnesses. He made the confession before his unfortunate attempt to escape.'

For the first time since he had arrived L'Arquen now smiled

broadly.

'But there's more than that.'

He laughed as he pulled out some further sheets of paper from his valise.

'Yes, much more, Mr Hume. In fact, what I have here is your own testimony, clear as daylight and ready for your signature. I rather think that this would carry the day.'

'What! What are you talking about now, L'Arquen?'

'Really, Mr Hume. For an intelligent man you can be remarkably stupid at times. Tell me first, though, where is your young friend, Mr Adam Smith?'

'He is well beyond you, L'Arquen,' Hume spat back. 'I sent him away this morning. He will be miles from here by now.'

'No. No, I fear you are wrong there, sir. You see, we picked him up on the road many hours ago. He is with us at Craigleven. In fact, he is with Trooper Williams even as we speak. He is my prisoner, you see, rather as you are here if I should but care to choose it.' He paused as if to think. 'He is very young, isn't he? And I've no doubt he displays much promise. Do you think he will be sitting there silently while my man speaks to him? And not implicating you in with this nest of traitors and Jacobites we've found here? Or, indeed, will you be silent yourself and continue to maintain your own innocence? And refuse to implicate him? Can you really trust him to say the same thing as you? After all, Mr Hume, what were you both doing at the castle in the first place – it looks bad doesn't it? But I would hate to see either of you hanged for treason. And so I only hope that your young friend will be signing his evidence soon ...'

L'Arquen paused for effect.

'... and not trying to escape.'

There was another pause while David Hume stared back. But he was quiet now and L'Arquen languidly smiled again.

'Very good, Mr Hume. Let us complete our business then. You are to sign this statement without delay. A trap will be coming for you in an hour together with an escort of my men to take you to Wick. You will be reunited with Mr Smith there and you will both take the dawn stagecoach for Edinburgh. Here is your letter of safe passage to show at the checkpoints on the way. And here are five guineas for your expenses on the journey.'

Hume continued to wait, knowing that there would be more.

'You must be aware of how much I esteem you, Mr Hume. That *Treatise* of yours was of the first rank. For that reason I don't believe that you should be misunderstood or mistreated when it becomes known that you gave evidence against Lord Dunbeath. Now, permit me to suggest a proposal that may solve matters. I have a cousin, General James St Clair, and he has been ordered by the Secretary of State to lead a military expedition against the French in Quebec. He is in need of a secretary and I believe you could be just the man for the role. I have taken the liberty of preparing a letter of introduction for you to give to him in London and I'm quite sure it will suffice when you meet him there. I would not return to Scotland for some time if I was you.'

L'Arquen walked over to the table in the alcove and picked up a quill and an inkwell. He brought them back to the fireplace.

'Now, Mr Hume. You have not yet signed. Come along there, please don't try my patience. The earl is dead. You should be looking after yourself now.'

David Hume sighed and looked past where L'Arquen was standing and out through the great curved window to the sea beyond. He was quite calm now. There was nothing else the man could do to threaten him.

'Do you know the truth of why I came here, Colonel L'Arquen?' he said quietly. 'Lord Dunbeath had invited me to Caithness to play a game he'd created – he thought to convince me about how the powerful succeed but instead it showed how virtue wins in life. I didn't come here for politics or rebellion and nor did Adam Smith. You know that. We came here to experiment with Dunbeath's game. He called it the Prisoner's

Dilemma and it explained how co-operation has evolved in us humans to be the cornerstone of a healthy society. We played it often and discovered how the tramplers in life, people like yourself, will always ultimately lose. We called you hawks, you know. You would probably tell me that you would be pleased to be called that.'

'How very revealing,' replied L'Arquen smoothly, in a tone of blank disinterest, 'I must confess that I do not feel as if I have been a loser. Quite the reverse, I rather feel as if I have won.' He picked up the quill and handed it to Hume. 'No doubt you'll be telling me next that this co-operation of yours disagrees with the conclusions of Thomas Hobbes. And that his idea of a social contract is wrong. You know, Mr Hume, you and Smith are exactly the kind of frail creatures – dreamers and ninnies – who most need my kind of authority to guarantee your freedom. You are among the most feeble in life. Without strong leaders like myself to organise and protect you, you people wouldn't last a month on your own. You're all as useless as children.'

'No, colonel,' said Hume, and his voice had quite recovered its strength. 'Your type will always lose in the end. You may win now but be pleased with your victory while it lasts. You will always be seen for what you are, a defector, a selfish snatcher, unlovely and unloved, a man to be avoided.'

Hume leant forward and signed his name with a flourish.

'There. That's over. Please go now, Colonel L'Arquen. We have nothing left to say to each other.'

L'Arquen smiled again as he leant down to put Hume's statement in his case.

'Actually, I do have one last question for you, Mr Hume.'

Hume groaned silently and his heavy shoulders sagged.

'Yes, what is it?'

'I dare say the army will be in Edinburgh before too long. When we've crushed this pathetic uprising of yours. I've no doubt we shall have to spend time there putting in some proper leadership for Scotland ... and I'd be obliged if you'd give me the name of your tailor. I have much admired his work and I notice that you do too, always stroking that embroidered stuff at your wrist.'

Hume stared at the colonel. There was a long silence. No words came to him.

'No?' said L'Arquen eventually, a smirk flickering across his face. 'No matter, Mr Hume. I imagine I shall be able to struggle on with that fellow of mine in Jermyn Street.'

He picked up his hat from where he'd left it by the fireplace and laughed for a final time.

'Enjoy Quebec, Mr Hume,' he said. 'Enjoy Quebec.'

Acknowledgements

At the heart of this book are the bones of a short story by Sir Arthur Conan Doyle called 'The Man from Archangel'. I always thought it was a wonderful tale and, in my enormous gratitude to the Master for using its outline, I have retained the names of the pair in his narrative, Alexis and Sophie.

The pieces on navigation were influenced by Dava Sobel's book, *Longitude*, the story of John Harrison's long fight to have his marine chronometers recognised as the inventive masterpieces they were and to win the Longitude Prize. The story is one of terrible injustice and deceit as the celestial navigation establishment conspired to make it impossible for him to win.

Perhaps perversely, I have chosen to make Dunbeath represent that entrenched scientific position.

Interestingly, as in the story here, it was indeed the intervention of a king, the very English George III though rather than his father, the more Germanic George II, who insisted that Harrison's genius should be rewarded.

The central idea in this book, of course, is the conceit that the characters in the story have invented game theory, two hundred years before it was actually formalised. As I understand it, many of the theory's conclusions that are in the book were indeed expounded by David Hume in his *Treatise* and elsewhere, but they were arrived at without the kind of mathematical basis that's imagined here. And, as for Adam Smith's views, it was true that he was at his most uncertain when he tried to offset his insights into how markets work with what he called a need in humans for 'sympathy' towards one another. However, any story that relies as heavily on game theory as this one does cannot fail to acknowledge its debt to John von Neumann, the brilliant polymath whose original ideas were first published in 1944 in *The Theory of Games and Economic Behaviour*.

It was two colleagues of von Neumann's at the RAND

Corporation some years later who came up with the idea for the Prisoner's Dilemma while working on irrationality analysis. It's formed the centerpiece for game theory ever since and large scale, computer-driven competitions were, and still are, run to find the optimal point scoring solutions. It was as a result of these events that one of the leading participants in the field, Anatol Rapoport, originated Tit for Tat and Generous.

While many of game theory's major concepts such as zero sum games, hawks and doves, free riders, tragedy of the commons, the dollar auction and so on are quite well known, I have tried to reduce the concepts behind them into a chain of logic to fit with, and hopefully illustrate, the story. Any errors are entirely mine in those places where I felt the unfolding of the tale was more important than getting the theory or the philosophy wholly accurate. I hope so anyway.

I'm indebted to a number of books that I raided for guidance. In particular, *The Evolution of Co-operation* by Robert Axelrod, *The Logic of Life* by Tim Harford, *The Selfish Gene* by Richard Dawkins, *A Beautiful Mind* by Sylvia Nasar (a biography and later Oscar winning movie about John Nash, an economist who won the Nobel Prize for his work on game theory and whose Nash Equilibrium Dunbeath says is 'like many a marriage') and *The Prisoner's Dilemma* by William Poundstone. This last is not only a biography of John von Neumann but also a social history of game theory and more specifically the role that the RAND Corporation put it to during the Cold War and the nuclear arms race.

But, more than any other, I must acknowledge my debt to Matt Ridley whose brilliant book *The Origins of Virtue* had me staring out of the window when I first read it fifteen or so years ago and which forms the basis of many of the arguments in this story.

Wilson Mizner once said that if you borrow from one author it's plagiarism but if you borrow from lots it's research … so, if in the course of my research I have lifted a thought or phrase from any of these books in too amateurish a manner then I can only apologise and hope that imitation is indeed regarded by their authors as the sincerest form of flattery.

I'm also grateful to a number of other writers and their books including *Game Theory at Work* by James Miller, *The Compleat Strategist* by JD Williams, *Game Theory: A Nontechnical Introduction* by Morton D Davis and *Game Theory* by Ken Binmore.

As to the book itself, I'm hugely indebted to the many people who read it at various stages and whose advice and help were so important to me. I'd particularly like to thank Stephen Durbridge, who saw the story in an earlier form and who was tremendously encouraging about it and suggested that I turn it into a novel; and William Boyd, who so generously gave up his time to read an early draft and then offered me enormously helpful counsel and direction on the writing. I'd also like to thank Susanne Burri of the LSE for her suggestions on the philosophy, Luke Meynell for his advice on the army in Scotland and Stuart Carnegie for his help with the Baltic, tides, winds and sailing. Many people read the book and I'm particularly grateful for the views and advice I received from Patsy Pollock, Christopher and Carola Chataway, Don Boyd, Charles Sturridge, Paul and Marie Kingsley, Geoff and Dawn Culmer, Ros Levin, Don Grant, my daughter Lucy Davenport and her husband Dominic, my niece and nephew, Charlotte and Simon D'Arcy and my sons, Kerin and William. My agent, Piers Russell-Cobb and Tariq Goddard of Zero Books each gave me huge encouragement and help and I'm enormously grateful to them both. Last, of course, I'd like to thank Gillie, my wife, for her insights when she read the manuscript and for all her love and support during the long writing of this book.